John James Audubon, Lucy Green Bakewell Audubon

The life of John James Audubon, the Naturalist

John James Audubon, Lucy Green Bakewell Audubon

The life of John James Audubon, the Naturalist

ISBN/EAN: 9783337024383

Printed in Europe, USA, Canada, Australia, Japan

Cover: Foto ©Raphael Reischuk / pixelio.de

More available books at **www.hansebooks.com**

THE

LIFE

OF

JOHN JAMES AUDUBON,

THE NATURALIST.

EDITED BY HIS WIDOW.

WITH AN INTRODUCTION BY JAS. GRANT WILSON.

NEW YORK:
G. P. PUTNAM & SON.
1869.

THE TROW & SMITH
BOOK MANUFACTURING COMPANY
46, 48, 50 Greene Street, N. Y.

INTRODUCTION.

In the summer of 1867, the widow of John James Audubon, completed with the aid of a friend, a memoir of the great naturalist, and soon after received overtures from a London publishing house for her work. Accepting their proposition for its publication in England, Mrs. Audubon forwarded the MSS., consisting in good part of extracts from her husband's journals and episodes, as he termed his delightful reminiscences of adventure in various parts of the New World. The London publisher placed these MSS. in the hands of Mr. Robert Buchanan, who prepared from them a single volume containing about one fifth of the original manuscript.

The following pages are substantially the recently published work, reproduced with some additions, and the omission of several objectionable passages inserted by the London editor. Should Mrs. Audubon hereafter receive her manuscript, containing sufficient material for four volumes of printed matter, and including many charming episodes "born from his traveling thigh," as Ben Jonson quaintly expressed it, the American public may confidently look forward to other volumes, uniform with this one, of the Naturalist's writings.

I do not deem it necessary to say aught in commendation of the labors of the loving and gentle wife in preparing the following admirable memoir of her grand and large-hearted husband, —

> "That cheerful one, who knoweth all
> The songs of all the winged choristers,
> And in one sequence of melodious sound,
> Pours out their music."

Her delightful volume will better speak for itself. Nor do I deem it requisite to dwell at length on the works of

Audubon, pronounced by Baron Cuvier to be "the most splendid monuments which art has erected in honor of ornithology."

He was an admirable specimen of the Hero as a man of science. To quote an eloquent writer: " For sixty years or more he followed, with more than religious devotion, a beautiful and elevated pursuit, enlarging its boundaries by his discoveries, and illustrating its objects by his art. In all climates and in all weathers ; scorched by burning suns, drenched by piercing rains, frozen by the fiercest colds ; now diving fearlessly into the densest forest, now wandering alone over the most savage regions ; in perils, in difficulties, and in doubts ; with no companion to cheer his way, far from the smiles and applause of society ; listening only to the sweet music of birds, or to the sweeter music of his own thoughts, he faithfully kept his path. The records of man's life contain few nobler examples of strength of purpose and indefatigable energy. Led on solely by his pure, lofty, kindling enthusiasm, no thirst for wealth, no desire of distinction, no restless ambition of eccentric character, could have induced him to undergo as many sacrifices, or sustained him under so many trials. Higher principles and worthier motives alone enabled him to meet such discouragements and accomplish such miracles of achievement. He has enlarged and enriched the domains of a pleasing and useful science ; he has revealed to us the existence of many species of birds before unknown ; he has given us more accurate information of the forms and habits of those that were known ; he has corrected the blunders of his predecessors ; and he has imparted to the study of natural history the grace and fascination of romance."

Of the man himself, Christopher North said, after speaking lovingly and appreciatively of him, " He is the greatest Artist in his own walk, that ever lived." The love of his vocation, after innumerable trials, successes and disappointments gave the lie to the *Quo fit Mæcenas* of Horace, and was to the end of his long life most intense. Neither his friends, Sir Walter Scott, or John Wilson, notably happy as they were in their home relations occupied a place in the domestic circle of husband and father, with a more beautiful display of kind, ennobling, and generous devotion, than John James Audubon ; and nothing in his whole character stands out in a purer and more honorable light, than his discharge of all the duties of home. In private life his virtues endeared him to a large circle of devoted admirers ; his sprightly conversation, with a slight French accent ; his soft and gentle voice ; his frank and fine face, " aye gat him friends in ilka place." With those whose privilege it was to know the Naturalist, so full of fine enthusiasm and intelligence ; with so much simplicity of character, frankness and genius, he will continue to live in their memories, though " with the buried gone ; " while to the artistic, literary, and scientific world, he has left an imperishable name that is not in the keeping of history alone. Long after the bronze statue of the naturalist that we hope soon to see erected in the Central Park, shall have been wasted and worn beyond recognition, by the winds and rains of Heaven ; while the towering and snow-covered peak of the Rocky Mountains known as Mount Audubon, shall rear its lofty head among the clouds ; while the little wren chirps about our homes, and the robin and reed-bird sing in the green meadows ; while the melody of the mocking-bird is heard in the cypress swamps of Louisiana, or the shrill scream of the eagle on the frozen shores of the Northern seas, the name of John James Audubon, the gifted Artist, the ardent lover of Nature, and the admirable writer, will live in the hearts of his grateful countrymen.

In the preface to the London edition of this work, I find the following just and generous words :—

" Audubon was a man of genius, with the courage of a lion and the simplicity of a child. One scarcely knows which to admire most—the mighty determination which enabled him to carry out his great work in the face of difficulties so huge, or the gentle and guileless sweetness with which he throughout shared his thoughts and aspirations with his wife and children. He was more like a child at the mother's knee, than a husband at the hearth—so free was the prattle, so thorough the confidence. Mrs. Audubon appears to have been a wife in every respect worthy of such a man : willing to sacrifice her personal comfort at any moment for the furtherance of his great schemes ; ever ready with kiss and counsel when such were most needed ; never failing for a moment in her faith that Audubon was destined to be one of the great workers of the earth.

"The man's heart was restless ; otherwise he would never have achieved so much. He must wander, he must vagabondize, he must acquire ; he was never quite easy at the hearth. His love for Nature was passionate indeed, pursuing in all regions, burning in him to the last. Among the most touching things in the diary, are the brief exclamations of joy when something in the strange city—a flock of wild ducks overhead in London, a gathering of pigeons on the trees of Paris—reminds him of the wild life of wood and plain. He was boy-like to the last, glorying most when out of doors.

"Of the work Audubon has done, nothing need be said in praise here. Even were I competent to discuss his merits as an ornithologist and ornithological painter, I should be silent, for the world has already settled those merits in full. I may trust myself, however, to say one word in praise of Audubon as a descriptive writer. Some of his reminiscences of adventure, some of which are published in this book, seem to me to be quite as good, in vividness of presentment and careful coloring, as anything I have ever read."

J. G. W.

51 St. Mark's Place, .
    New York, April, 1869.

CONTENTS.

x   *Contents.*

LIFE OF AUDUBON.

CHAPTER I.

Audubon's Ancestry — His Childhood — First Visit to America — The Bakewell Family — Aspirations — Youthful Recollections — A Marvellous Escape.

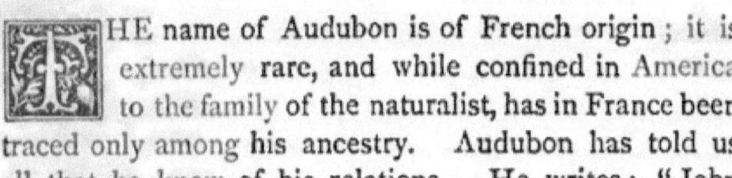HE name of Audubon is of French origin ; it is extremely rare, and while confined in America to the family of the naturalist, has in France been traced only among his ancestry. Audubon has told us all that he knew of his relations. He writes : " John Audubon my grandfather was born at the small village of Sable d'Olonne, in La Vendée, with a small harbor, forty-five miles south from Nantes. He was a poor fisher-man with a numerous family, twenty-one of whom grew to maturity. There was but one boy besides my father, he being the twentieth born, and the only one of the numerous family who lived to a considerable age. In subsequent years, when I visited Sable d'Olonne, the old inhabitants told me that they had seen the whole of this family, including both parents, at church several times on Sunday."

The father of the naturalist appears to have caught at an early age the restless spirit of his times, and *his* father, who saw in it the only hope the youth had of obtaining distinction, encouraged his love of adventure. He himself says of his start in life : " When I was twelve years of age my father provided me with a shirt, a dress of warm clothing, his blessing, and a cane, and sent me out to seek my fortune."

The youth went to Nantes, and falling in with the captain of a vessel bound on a fishing voyage to the coast of America, he shipped on board as a boy before the mast. He continued at sea, and by the age of seventeen was rated as an able-bodied seaman.   At twenty-one he commanded a vessel, and at twenty-five he was owner and captain of a small craft.   Purchasing other vessels, the enterprising adventurer sailed with his little fleet to the West Indies.   He reached St. Domingo, and there fortune dawned upon him.   After a few more voyages he purchased a small estate.   The prosperity of St. Domingo, already French, so influenced the mariner's interests, that in ten years he realized a considerable fortune.   Obtaining an appointment from the Governor of St. Domingo, he returned to France, and in his official capacity became intimate with influential men connected with the government of the First Empire.   Through their good offices he obtained an appointment in the Imperial navy and the command of a small vessel of war.   A warm sympathy with the changes wrought by the revolution, and an idolatrous worship of Napoleon, must have contributed greatly to his success.

While resident in France he purchased a beautiful estate on the Loire, nine miles from Nantes ;—there, after a life of remarkable vicissitude, the old sailor died, in 1818, at the great age of ninety-five, regretted, as he deserved to be, on account of his simplicity of manners and perfect sense of honesty.   Our Audubon has described his father as a man of good proportions, measuring five feet ten inches in height, having a hardy constitution and the agility of a wild cat.   His manners, it is asserted, were most polished, and his natural gifts improved by self-education.   He had a warm and even violent temper, described as rising at times into "the blast of a hurricane," but readily appeased.   While residing in the West Indies, he frequently visited North America, and with some foresight made purchases of land in the French colony of Louisiana, in Virginia, and Pennsylvania. In one of his American visits he met and married in Louisiana a lady of Spanish extraction, named Anne Moynette, whose beauty and wealth may have made her equally attractive. A family of three sons and one daughter blessed this union, and the subject of this biographical sketch was the youngest of the sons. A few years after his birth Madame Audubon accompanied her husband to the estate of Aux Cayes in the island of St. Domingo, and there miserably perished during the memorable rising of the negro population.

The black revolt so endangered the property of the foreigners resident in St. Domingo, that the plate and money belonging to the Audubon family had to be carried away to New Orleans by the more faithful of their servants. Returning to France with his family, the elder Audubon again married, left his young son, the future naturalist, under charge of his second wife, and returned to the United States, in the employment of the French government, as an officer in the Imperial navy. While there he became attached to the army under Lafayette. Moving hither and thither under various changes, he seldom or never communicated with his boy ; but meanwhile the property which remained to him in St. Domingo was greatly augmenting in value. During a visit paid to Pennsylvania, the restless Frenchman purchased the farm of Millgrove on the Perkiomen Creek, near the Schuylkill Falls. Finally, after a life of restless adventure, he returned to France and filled a post in the marine ; and after spending some portion of his years at Rochefort, retired to his estate on the Loire. This estate was left by Commodore Audubon to his son John James, who conveyed it to his sister without even visiting the domain he so generously willed away.

The naturalist was born on his father's plantation, near New Orleans, Louisiana, May 4th, 1780, and his earliest recollections are associated with lying among the flowers of that fertile land, sheltered by the orange trees, and watching the movements of the mocking-bird, "the king of song," dear to him in after life from many associations. He has remarked that his earliest impressions of nature were exceedingly vivid; the beauties of natural scenery stirred "a frenzy" in his blood, and at the earliest age the bent of his future studies was indicated by many characteristic traits. He left Louisiana while but a child, and went to St. Domingo, where he resided for a short period, previous to his departure for France, where his education was to be commenced.

His earliest recollections of his life in France extend to his home in the central district of the city of Nantes, and a fact he remembered well was being attended by two colored servants sent home from India by his father. He speaks of his life in Nantes as joyous in the extreme. His step-mother, being without any children of her own, humored the child in every whim, and indulged him in every luxury. The future naturalist, who in the recesses of American forests was to live on roots and fruits, and even scantier fare, was indulged with a "carte blanche" on all the confectionery shops in the village where his summer months were passed, and he speaks of the kindness of his stepmother as overwhelming. His father had less weakness, and ordered the boy to attend to his education. The elder Audubon had known too many changes of fortune to believe in the fickle goddess; and notwithstanding his wife's tears and entreaties, determining to educate his son thoroughly, as the safest inheritance he could leave him, he sent the young gentleman straightway to school. Audubon laments that education

in France was but miserably attended to during the
years that succeeded the great political convulsions.
Military education had usurped all the care of the First
Empire, and the wants of the civil population were but
sparingly heeded. His father, from natural predilections,
was desirous that the boy should become a sailor, a cadet
in the French navy, or an engineer ; and with these views
before him, he decided on the course of study his son
should follow. Mathematics, drawing, geography, fencing
and music were among the branches of education pre-
scribed ; it being evident that a complex course of
instruction was not among the misapprehensions the old
sailor's professional prejudices had nurtured. Audubon
had, for music-master, an adept who taught him to play
adroitly upon the violin, flute, flageolet, and guitar. For
drawing-master, he had David, the chief inventor and
worshipper of the abominations which smothered the
aspirations of French artists during the revolutionary
generation. Nevertheless it was to David that Audubon
owed his earliest lessons in tracing objects of natural
history. Audubon was, moreover, a proficient in dancing,
—an accomplishment which in after years he had more
opportunities of practising among bears than among men.

Influenced by the military fever of his time, he
dreamed in his schooldays of being a soldier ; but
happily for natural science his adventurous spirit found
another outlet. Fortunately his instruction was under
the practical guidance of his mother, and large scope was
allowed him for indulging in nest-hunting propensities.
Supplied with a haversack of provisions, he made
frequent excursions into the country, and usually returned
loaded with objects of natural history, birds' nests, birds'
eggs, specimens of moss, curious stones, and other objects
attractive to his eye.

When the old sailor returned from sea he was

astonished at the large collection his boy had made, paid him some compliments on his good taste, and asked what progress he had made in his other studies. No satisfactory reply being given, he retired without reproach, but, evidently mortified at the idleness of the young naturalist, seemed to turn his attention towards his daughter, whose musical attainments had been successfully cultivated. On the day following the disclosure father and son started for Rochefort, where the elder held some appointment. The journey occupied four days, and the pair did not exchange one unnecessary word during the journey. Reaching his official residence, the father explained that he himself would superintend his son's education ; gave the boy liberty for one day to survey the ships of war and the fortifications, and warned him that on the morrow a severe course of study should be commenced. And commence it did accordingly.

More than a year was spent in the close study of mathematics ; though whenever opportunity occurred the severer study was neglected for rambles after objects of natural history, and the collection of more specimens. At Nantes, Audubon actually began to draw sketches of French birds,—a work he continued with such assiduity that he completed two hundred specimens.

His father was desirous that he should join the armies of Napoleon, and win fame by following the French eagles. Warfare, however, had ceased to be a passion of the youth, and he was sent out to America to superintend his father's property. He has recorded in affecting language his regret at leaving behind him the country where he had spent his boyhood, the friends upon whose affections he relied, the associations that had been endeared to him. While the breeze wafted along the great ship, hours were spent in deep sorrow or melancholy musings.

On landing at New York he caught the yellow fever, by walking to the bank in Greenwich Street to cash his letters of credit. Captain John Smith, whose name is gratefully recorded, took compassion on the young emigrant, removed him to Morristown, and placed him under the care of two Quaker ladies at a boarding-house, and to the kindness of these ladies he doubtless owed his life. His father's agent, Mr. Fisher, of Philadelphia, knowing his condition, went with his carriage to his lodging, and drove the invalid to his villa, situated at some distance from the city on the road to Trenton. Mr. Fisher was a Quaker, and a strict formalist in religious matters ; did not approve of hunting, and even objected to music. To the adventurous and romantic youth this home was little livelier than a prison, and he gladly escaped from it. Mr. Fisher, at his request, put him in possession of his father's property of Mill Grove, on the Perkiomen Creek ; and from the rental paid by the tenant, a Quaker named William Thomas, the youth found himself supplied with all the funds he needed.

At Mill Grove young Audubon found "a blessed spot." In the regularity of the fences, the straight and military exactness of the avenues, Audubon saw his father's taste, nay, his very handiwork. The mill attached to the property was to him a daily source of enjoyment, and he was delighted with the repose of the quiet milldam where the pewees were accustomed to build. "Hunting, fishing, and drawing occupied my every moment," he writes ; adding, " cares I knew not, and cared nothing for them."

In simple and unaffected language he relates his introduction to his wife, the daughter of William Bakewell, an English gentleman who had purchased the adjoining property. Mr. Bakewell lived at Fatland Ford, within sight of Mill Grove, but Audubon had avoided the

family, as English, and objectionable to one who had been
nurtured with a hatred towards " perfidious Albion." The
very name of Englishman was odious to him, he tells us;
and even after his neighbor had called upon him, he was
uncivil enough to postpone his advances in return. Mrs.
Thomas, the tenant's wife at Mill Grove, with a woman's
desire to see what the issue might be, urged her young master to visit the Bakewell family; but the more he was
urged the more hardened his heart appeared to be against
the stranger.

The winter's frosts had set in. Audubon was following some grouse down the creek, when suddenly he came
upon Mr. Bakewell, who at once dissipated the Frenchman's prejudices by the discovery of kindred tastes.
Audubon writes : " I was struck with the kind politeness
of his manners, and found him a most expert marksman,
and entered into conversation. I admired the beauty of
his well-trained dogs, and finally promised to call upon
him and his family. Well do I recollect the morning, and
may it please God may I never forget it, when, for the first
time I entered the Bakewell household. It happened
that Mr. Bakewell was from home. I was shown into a
parlour, where only one young lady was snugly seated at
work, with her back turned towards the fire. She rose on
my entrance, offered me a seat, and assured me of the
gratification her father would feel on his return, which,
she added with a smile, would be in a few minutes, as she
would send a servant after him. Other ruddy cheeks
made their appearance, but like spirits gay, vanished from
my sight. Talking and working, the young lady who
remained made the time pass pleasantly enough, and to
me especially so. It was she, my dear Lucy Bakewell,
who afterwards became my wife and the mother of my
children."

Mr. Bakewell speedily returned, and Lucy attended to

the lunch provided before leaving on a shooting expedition. "Lucy rose from her seat a second time, and her form, to which I had before paid little attention, seemed radiant with beauty, and my heart and eyes followed her every step. The repast being over, guns and dogs were provided, and as we left I was pleased to believe that Lucy looked upon me as a not very strange animal. Bowing to her, I felt, I knew not why, that I was at least not indifferent to her."

The acquaintance so pleasantly begun rapidly matured. Audubon and Bakewell were often companions in their shooting excursions, and finally the whole Bakewell family were invited to Mill Grove.

The Bakewell's are descendants of the Peverils, great land owners of the northern part of Derbyshire, known as the Peak of Derbyshire, and rendered historical by Sir Walter Scott's novel of "Peveril of the Peak." Miss Peveril married one of the retainers of the Court of William the Norman, by name Count Bassquelle, which name was corrupted into Basskiel, afterwards into Bakewell. From some of the descendants of this marriage the town of Bakewell was founded; some members removed to Dishley, Leicestershire, one of whom was the grazier and improver of the breed of sheep, another was well known as a geologist.

The property of Audubon was separated from Bakewell's plantation by a road leading from Norristown to Pawling's Landing, now Pawling's Bridge, or about a quarter of a mile apart; and the result of the friendly relationship established between the two households gave rise to a series of mutual signals, chalked on a board and hung out of the window. The friendship deepened. Lucy Bakewell taught English to Audubon, and received drawing lessons in return. Of course no one failed to predict the result; but as a love affair is chiefly interesting to those immediately concerned, we pass on to other matters.

At Mill Grove Audubon pored over his idea of a great work on American Ornithology, until the thought took some shape in his fervid mind. The work he had prepared for himself to do was an 'Ornithological Biography,' including an account of the habits and a description of the birds of America; that work which in its completed form Cuvier pronounced to be "The most gigantic biblical enterprise ever undertaken by a single individual." However, it was only after his drawings and his descriptions accumulated upon him that Audubon decided to give the collection the form of a scientific work.

Audubon speaks of his life at Mill Grove as being in every way agreeable. He had ample means for all his wants, was gay, extravagant, and fond of dress. He rather naïvely writes in his journal, "I had no vices; but was thoughtless, pensive, loving, fond of shooting, fishing, and riding, and had a passion for raising all sorts of fowls, which sources of interest and amusement fully occupied my time. It was one of my fancies to be ridiculously fond of dress; to hunt in black satin breeches, wear pumps when shooting, and dress in the finest ruffled shirts I could obtain from France." He was also fond of dancing, and music, and skating, and attended all the balls and skating parties in the neighborhood. Regarding his mode of life, Audubon gives some hints useful to those who desire to strengthen their constitution by an abstemious diet. He says :—" I ate no butcher's meat, lived chiefly on fruits, vegetables, and fish, and never drank a glass of spirits or wine until my wedding day. To this I attribute my continual good health, endurance, and an iron constitution. So strong was the habit, that I disliked going to dinner parties, where people were expected to indulge in eating and drinking, and where often there was

not a single dish to my taste. I cared nothing for sumptuous entertainments. Pies, puddings, eggs, and milk or
cream was the food I liked best; and many a time
was the dairy of Mrs. Thomas, the tenant's wife of Mill
Grove, robbed of the cream intended to make butter for
the Philadelphia market. All this while I was fair and
rosy, strong as any one of my age and sex could be, and
as active and agile as a buck. And why, have I often
thought, should I not have kept to this delicious mode of
living?"

Note here a curious incident in connection with his
love of skating and his proficiency as a marksman. Having been skating down the Perkiomen Creek, he met Miss
Bakewell's young brother William, and wagered that he
would put a shot through his cap when tossed into the air,
while Audubon was passing full speed. The experiment
was made, and the cap riddled. A still more striking
incident is thus related. "Having engaged in a duck-
shooting expedition up the Perkiomen Creek with young
Bakewell and some other friends, it was found that the ice
was full of dangerous air-holes. On our upward journey
it was easy to avoid accident, but the return trip was attended with an event which had nearly closed my career.
Indeed, my escape was one of the inconceivable miracles
that occasionally rescues a doomed man from his fate.
The trip was extended too far, and night and darkness
had set in long before we reached home. I led the party
through the dusk with a white handkerchief made fast to
a stick, and we proceeded like a flock of geese going to
their feeding ground. Watching for air-holes, I generally
avoided them; but increasing our speed, I suddenly
plunged into one, was carried for some distance by the
stream under the ice, and stunned and choking I was
forced up through another air-hole farther down the stream.
I clutched hold of the ice and arrested my downward

progress, until my companions arrived to help me. My
wet clothes had to be changed. One lent me a shirt,
another a coat, and so apparelled I resumed my homeward journey. Unable to reach Mill Grove, I was taken
to Mr. Bakewell's house chilled and bruised. It was
three months before I recovered, notwithstanding the
advice of able physicians called in from Philadelphia."

The quiet life young Audubon led at Mill Grove was
interrupted by an incident in his life which might have
proved serious to one owning less energy and hardihood
than he possessed. A "partner, tutor, and monitor,"
one Da Costa, sent from France by the elder Audubon
to prosecute the lead mine enterprise at Mill Grove, began to assume an authority over young Audubon which
the latter considered unwarranted. An attempt was made
to limit his finances, and Da Costa, unfortunately for
himself, went further, and objected to the proposed union
with Lucy Bakewell, as being an unequal match. Audubon resented such interference, and demanded money
from Da Costa to carry him to France. The French
adventurer suggested a voyage to India, but finally agreed
to give Audubon a letter of credit upon an agent named
Kanman, in New York. With characteristic earnestness
Audubon walked straight off to New York, where he arrived in three days, notwithstanding the severity of a
midwinter journey. The day following his arrival he called upon Mr. Kanman, who frankly told him he had no
money to give him, and further disclosed Da Costa's
treachery by hinting that Audubon should be seized and
shipped for China. Furious at his treatment, Audubon
procured money from a friend, and engaged a passage on
board the brig Hope, of New Bedford, bound for Nantes.
He left New York, and after considerable delays, surprised his parents in their quiet country home

CHAPTER II.

EXPLAINING to his father the scandalous conduct of Da Costa, young Audubon prevailed so far that the traitor was removed from the position which he had been placed in with such hasty confidence. He had also to request his father's approval of his marriage with Miss Lucy Bakewell, and the father promised to decide as soon as he had an answer to a letter he had written to Mr. Bakewell in Pennsylvania. Settled in the paternal house for a year, the naturalist gratified in every fashion his wandering instincts. He roamed everywhere in the neighborhood of his home, shooting, fishing, and collecting specimens of natural history. He also continued his careful drawings of natural history specimens, and stuffed and prepared many birds and animals—an art which he had carefully acquired in America. In one year two hundred drawings of European birds had been completed, —a fact which displays marvellous industry, if it does not necessarily imply a sound artistic representation of the birds drawn. At this period the tremendous convulsions of the French empire had culminated in colossal preparations for a conflict with Russia. The conscription

threatened every man capable of bearing arms, and Audubon appeared to believe that he stood in some danger of being enrolled in the general levy. His two brothers were already serving in the armies of Napoleon as officers, and it was decided that their junior should voluntarily join the navy. After passing what he called "a superficial examination" for an appointment as midshipman, he was ordered to report at Rochefort. Entering upon his duties in the French marine, he was destined to make at least one short cruise in the service of France. Before entering the service he had made the acquaintance of a young man named Ferdinand Rosier, to whom he had made some proposal of going to America. On the return of the vessel in which he acted, it was proposed that he and Rosier should leave for America as partners, under a nine years' engagement. The elder Audubon obtained leave of absence for his son ; and after passports were provided, the two emigrants left France at a period when thousands would have been glad of liberty to follow their footsteps.

About two weeks after leaving France, a vessel gave chase to the French vessel, passed her by to windward, fired a shot across her bows, and continued the chase until the captain of the outward bound was forced to heave his ship to, and submit to be boarded by a boat. The enemy proved to be the English privateer, Rattlesnake, the captain of which was sadly vexed to find that his prey was an American vessel, carrying proper papers, and flying the stars and stripes. Unable to detain the vessel, the privateer's crew determined at least to rob the passengers. "They took pigs and sheep," writes Audubon, "and carried away two of our best sailors, in spite of the remonstrances of the captain, and of a member of the United States Congress, who was a passenger on board, and was accompanied by an amiable daughter. The

Rattlesnake kept us under her lee, and almost within pistol-shot for a day and a night, ransacking the ship for money, of which we had a great deal in the run under the ballast, which they partially removed, but did not go deep enough to reach the treasure. The gold belonging to Rosier and myself I put away in a woolen stocking under the ship's cable in the bows of the ship, where it remained safe until the privateers had departed. Arriving within thirty miles of Sandy Hook, a fishing-smack was spoken, which reported that two British frigates lay off the entrance, and had fired on an American ship ; that they were impressing American seamen, and that, in fact, they were even more dangerous to meet than the pirates who sailed under "a letter of marque." The captain, warned of one danger, ran into another. He took his vessel through Long Island Sound, and ran it upon a spit in a gale. But finally floated it off, and reached New York in safety.

From the introductory address in the first volume of Audubon's 'Ornithological Biography,' published at Edinburgh, in 1834, many passages may be cited as an exposition of the high aspirations which stimulated the young naturalist to his task. These passages may be divided into scientific and artistic. Belonging to the first category are constant references to that thirst for accurate and complete knowledge regarding wild animals, and especially birds, their habits, forms, nests, eggs, progeny, places of breeding, and all that concerned them. But, after all, Audubon was not at heart a man of science. He gathered much, and speculated little, and was more a backwoodsman than a philosopher. In his rough great way he did good service, but his great physical energy, not his mental resources, was the secret of his success.

His crude artistic instincts inspired him with the desire to represent, by the aid of pencil, crayon, or paint, the form, plumage, attitude, and characteristic marks of his feathered favourites. In working towards this end, he labored to produce life-like pictures, and frequently with wonderful success. Strongly impressed with the difficulties of representing in any perfect degree the living image of the birds he drew, he labored arduously at what we may call forcible photographs in colours, his first aim being fidelity, and his next, artistic beauty. How much chagrin his failures cost him may be gleaned from the lamentations he makes over his unsuccessful efforts in the introductory address referred to above. Regarding the means he adopted to secure a faultless representation of the animals he desired to transcribe, he writes :—" Patiently and with industry did I apply myself to study, for although I felt the impossibility of giving life to my productions, I did not abandon the idea of representing nature. Many plans were successively adopted, many masters guided my hand. At the age of seventeen, when I returned from France, whither I had gone to receive the rudiments of my education, my drawings had assumed a form. David had guided my hand in tracing objects of large size : eyes and noses belonging to giants and heads of horses, represented in ancient sculpture, were my models. These, although fit subjects for men intent on pursuing the higher branches of art, were immediately laid aside by me. I returned to the woods of the n w world with fresh ardour, and commenced a collection of drawings, which I henceforth continued, and which is now publishing under the title of ‘ The Birds of America.’ "

To resume the narrative of Audubon’s journey back to Mill Grove. Da Costa was dismissed from his situation, and Audubon remained his own master. Mr. William Bakewell, the brother of Lucy, has recorded some interesting particulars of a visit to Mill Grove at this period. He says :—" Audubon took me to his house,

where he and his companion Rosier resided, with Mrs.
Thomas for an attendant. On entering his room, I was
astonished and delighted to find that it was turned into a
museum. The walls were festooned with all sorts of
birds' eggs, carefully blown out and strung on a thread.
The chimney-piece was covered with stuffed squirrels,
racoons, and opossums ; and the shelves around were
likewise crowded with specimens, among which were
fishes, frogs, snakes, lizards, and other reptiles. Besides
these stuffed varieties, many paintings were arrayed upon
the walls, chiefly of birds. He had great skill in stuffing
and preserving animals of all sorts. He had also a trick
of training dogs with great perfection, of which art his
famous dog Zephyr was a wonderful example. He was
an admirable marksman, an expert swimmer, a clever
rider, possessed great activity, prodigious strength, and
was notable for the elegance of his figure and the beauty
of his features, and he aided nature by a careful attendance to his dress. Besides other accomplishments, he
was musical, a good fencer, danced well, had some acquaintance with legerdemain tricks, worked in hair, and
could plait willow-baskets." He adds further, that
Audubon once swam across the Schuylkill river with
him on his back,—no contemptible feat for a young ath-
lete.

The naturalist was evidently a nonpareil in the eyes
of his neighbors, and of those who were intimate enough
to know his manifold tastes. But love began to interfere
a little with the gratification of these Bohemian instincts.
On expressing his desire of uniting himself to Miss
Bakewell, Audubon was advised by Mr. Bakewell to obtain some knowledge of commercial pursuits before getting married. With this intention, Audubon started for
New York, entered the counting-house of Mr. Benjamin
Bakewell, and made rapid progress in his education by

losing some hundreds of pounds by a bad speculation in
indigo.

The leading work done by the imprisoned naturalist
was, as usual, wandering in search of birds and natural
curiosities. While so engaged he made the acquaintance
of Dr. Samuel Mitchel, one of the leading medical men
in New York city, and distinguished as an ethnologist.
Dr. Mitchel was one of the founders of the Lyceum of
Natural History, and of the 'Medical Repository,' which
was the first scientific journal started in the United States.
Audubon prepared many specimens for this gentleman,
which he believed were finally deposited in the New York
Museum. After a season of probation, during which Mr.
Bakewell became convinced of the impossibility of tutor-
ing Audubon into mercantile habits, the naturalist gladly
returned to Mill Grove. Rosier, who had likewise been
recommended to attempt commerce, lost a considerable
sum in an unfortunate speculation, and eventually returned to Mill Grove with his friend.

Audubon remarks that at this period it took him but
a few minutes, walking smartly, to pass from one end of
New York to another, so sparse was the population at
the date of his residence. He adds, in reference to his
absent habits and unsuitability for business, that he at
one time posted without sealing it a letter containing
8000 dollars. His natural history pursuits in New York
occasioned a disagreeable flavor from his rooms, occasioned by drying birds' skins ; and was productive of so
much annoyance to his neighbours, that they forwarded a
message to him through a constable, insisting on his abat-
ing the *nuisance.* An excellent.pen and ink sketch of
his own appearance at this time has been left by Audubon. He says : " I measured five feet ten and a half
inches, was of a fair mien, and quite a handsome figure ;
large, dark, and rather sunken eyes, light-coloured eye-

brows, aquiline nose, and a fine set of teeth ; hair, fine
texture and luxuriant, divided and passing down behind
each ear in luxuriant ringlets as far as the shoulders."
There appears excellent reason to believe that Audubon
quite appreciated his youthful graces, and, with the *naï-
veté* of a simple nature, was not ashamed to record them.

After returning to Mill Grove, Audubon and his friend
Rosier planned an expedition towards the west, at that
time a wild region thinly populated by a very strange
people.

The journey of Audubon and Rosier to Kentucky had
for its purpose the discovery of some outlet for the
naturalist's energies, in the shape of a settled investment,
which would permit of his marriage to Miss Bakewell.
In Louisville Audubon determined to remain, and with
this purpose in view he sold his plantation of Mill Grove,
invested his capital in goods, and prepared to start for
the west. His arrangements being complete, he was
married to Miss Bakewell on the 8th of April, 1808, in
her father's residence at Fatland Ford. Journeying by
Pittsburg the wedded pair reached Louisville with their
goods in safety. From Pittsburg they sailed down the
Ohio in a flat-bottomed float called an ark, and which
proved to be an exceedingly tedious and primitive mode
of travelling. This river voyage occupied twelve days,
and must have given the naturalist wonderful opportunities of making observations. At Louisville he commenced trade under favorable auspices, but the hunting
of birds continued to be the ruling passion. His life at
this period, in the company of his young wife, appears to
have been extremely happy, and he writes that he had
really reason " to care for nothing." The country around
Louisville was settled by planters who were fond of hunting, and among whom he found a ready welcome. The
shooting and drawing of birds was continued. His

friend Rosier, less fond of rural sports, stuck to the counter, and, as Audubon phrases it, "grew rich, and that was all he cared for." Audubon's pursuits appear to have severed him from the business, which was left to Rosier's management. Finally the war of 1812 imperilled the prosperity of the partners, and what goods remained on hand were shipped to Hendersonville, Kentucky, where Rosier remained for some years longer, before going further westward in search of the fortune he coveted. Writing of the kindness shown him by his friends at Louisville, Audubon relates that when he was absent on business, or "away on expeditions," his wife was invited to stay at General Clark's, and was taken care of till he returned.

It was at Louisville that Audubon made the acquaintance of Wilson, the American ornithologist. Wilson, a Scottish weaver, had been driven from Paisley through his sympathies with the political agitators of that notable Scottish town ; and finding a refuge in the United States, had turned his attention to ornithology. From the pages of Audubon's 'Ornithological Biography' it may be interesting to reproduce an account of the meeting between the two naturalists. "One fair morning," writes Audubon, "I was surprised by the sudden entrance into our counting-room at Louisville of Mr. Alexander Wilson, the celebrated author of the 'American Ornithology,' of whose existence I had never until that moment been apprised. This happened in March, 1810. How well do I remember him, as he then walked up to me ! His long, rather hooked nose, the keenness of his eyes, and his prominent cheekbones, stamped his countenance with a peculiar character. His dress, too, was of a kind not usually seen in that part of the country ; a short coat, trousers, and a waistcoat of gray cloth. His stature was not above the middle size. He had two volumes under his arm, and as he approached the table at which I was working, I thought I discovered something like astonish ment in his countenance. He, however, immediately proceeded to disclose the object of his visit, which was to procure subscriptions for his work. He opened his books, explained the nature of his occupations, and requested my patronage. I felt surprised and gratified at the sight of his volumes, turned over a few of the plates, and had already taken a pen to write my name in his favor, when my partner rather abruptly said to me, in French, 'My dear Audubon, what induces you to subscribe to this work? Your drawings are certainly far better; and again, you must know as much of the habits of American birds as this gentleman.' Whether Mr. Wilson under stood French or not, or if the suddenness with which I paused, disappointed him, I cannot tell; but I clearly perceived that he was not pleased. Vanity and the encomiums of my friend prevented me from subscribing. Mr. Wilson asked me if I had many drawings of birds. I rose, took down a large portfolio, laid it on the table, and showed him,—as I would show you, kind reader, or any other person fond of such subjects,—the whole of the contents, with the same patience with which he had shown me his own engravings. His surprise appeared great, as he told me he never had the most distant idea that any other individual than himself had been engaged in forming such a collection. He asked me if it was my intention to publish, and when I answered in the negative, his surprise seemed to increase. And, truly, such was not my intention; for, until long after, when I met the Prince of Musignano in Philadelphia, I had not the least idea of presenting the fruits of my labors to the world. Mr. Wilson now examined my drawings with care, asked if I should have any objections to lending him a few during his stay, to which I replied that I had

none. He then bade me good-morning, not, however,
until I had made an arrangement to explore the woods
in the vicinity along with him, and had promised to
procure for him some birds, of which I had drawings in
my collection, but which he had never seen. It happened
that he lodged in the same house with us, but his retired
habits, I thought, exhibited either a strong feeling of
discontent or a decided melancholy. The Scotch airs
which he played sweetly on his flute made me melancholy
too, and I felt for him. I presented him to my wife and
friends, and seeing that he was all enthusiasm, exerted
myself as much as was in my power to procure for him
the specimens which he wanted. We hunted together,
and obtained birds which he had never before seen ; but,
reader, I did not subscribe to his work, for, even at that
time, my collection was greater than his. Thinking that
perhaps he might be pleased to publish the results of my
researches, I offered them to him, merely on condition
that what I had drawn, or might afterwards draw and send
to him, should be mentioned in his work as coming from
my pencil. I at the same time offered to open a corres-
pondence with him, which I thought might prove beneficial
to us both. He made no reply to either proposal, and
before many days had elapsed, left Louisville, on his way
to New Orleans, little knowing how much his talents were
appreciated in our little town, at least by myself and my
friends.

"Some time elapsed, during which I never heard of
him, or his work. At length, having occasion to go to
Philadelphia, I, immediately after my arrival there,
inquired for him, and paid him a visit. He was then
drawing a white-headed eagle. He received me with
civility, and took me to the exhibition rooms of Rembrandt Peale, the artist, who had then portrayed Napoleon
crossing the Alps. Mr. Wilson spoke not of birds or

drawings. Feeling, as I was forced to do, that my company was not agreeable, I parted from him; and after that I never saw him again. But judge of my astonishment some time after, when on reading the thirty-ninth page of the ninth volume of ' American Ornithology,' I found in it the following paragraph :—

"'*March* 23, 1810.—I bade adieu to Louisville, to which place I had four letters of recommendation, and was taught to expect much of everything there; but neither received one act of civility from those to whom I was recommended, one subscriber, nor one new bird; though I delivered my letters, ransacked the woods repeatedly, and visited all the characters likely to subscribe. Science or literature has not one friend in this place.'"

CHAPTER III.

AT Louisville it was discovered that business was suffering from over-competition, and no further time was to be lost in transferring the stock to Hendersonville. Before leaving Louisville to take up his residence at Hendersonville, farther down the Ohio river, Audubon took his wife and young son back to her father's house at Fatland Ford, where they resided for a year.

Audubon and his partner Rosier arranged their migration with the remaining stock, and entered upon their voyage of one hundred and twenty miles down the Ohio to Hendersonville. Arriving at this place, they found the neighborhood thinly inhabited, and the demand for goods almost limited to the coarsest materials. The merchants were driven to live upon the produce of their guns and fishing-rods.

The clerk employed for the firm had even to assist in supplying the table, and while he did so Rosier attended to the business. The profits on any business done was enormous, but the sales were so trifling that another change was determined on. It was proposed that the stock in hand should be removed to St. Geneviève, a settlement on the Mississippi river, and until it was ascertained how the enterprise would prosper, Mrs.

Audubon should be left at Hendersonville, with the family of Dr. Rankin, who resided in the immediate neighborhood. Of the adventurous voyage to St. Geneviève, Audubon gives this graphic account :—

" Putting our goods, which consisted of three hundred barrels of whiskey, sundry drygoods, and powder, on board a keel-boat, my partner, my clerk, and self departed in a severe snow-storm. The boat was new, staunch, and well trimmed, and had a cabin in her bow. A long steering oar, made of the trunk of a slender tree, about sixty feet in length, and shaped at its outer extremity like the fin of a dolphin, helped to steer the boat, while the four oars from the bow impelled her along, when going with the current, about five miles an hour.

" The storm we set out in continued, and soon covered the ground with a wintry sheet. Our first night on board was dismal indeed, but the dawn brought us opposite the mouth of the Cumberland River. It was evident that the severe cold had frozen all the neighboring lakes and lagoons, because thousands of wild water-fowl were flying to the river, and settling themselves on its borders. We permitted our boat to drift past, and amused ourselves by firing into flocks of birds.

" The third day we entered Cash Creek, a very small stream, but having deep water and a good harbour. Here I met Count De Munn, who was also in a boat like ours, and bound also for St. Geneviève. Here we learned that the Mississippi was covered with floating ice of a thickness dangerous to the safety of our craft, and indeed that it was impossible to ascend the river against it.

" The creek was full of water, was crowded with wild birds, and was plentifully supplied with fish. The large sycamores, and the bare branches of the trees that fringed the creek, were favorite resorts of paroquets, which came at night to roost in their hollow trunks. An agreeable circumstance was an encampment of about fifty families of Shawnee Indians, attracted to the spot by the mast of the forest, which brought together herds of deer, and many bears and racoons.

"Mr. Rosier, whose only desire was to reach the destination and resume trade, was seized with melancholy at the prospect occasioned by the delay. He brooded in silence over a mishap which had given me great occasion for rejoicing."

A narrative of Audubon's stay at Cash Creek, and perilous journey up the Mississippi, is picturesquely given in his journal, and from which the following is extracted :—

"The second morning after our arrival at Cash Creek, while I was straining my eyes to discover whether it was fairly day dawn or no, I heard a movement in the Indian camp, and discovered that a canoe, with half a dozen squaws and as many hunters, was about leaving for Tennessee. I had heard that there was a large lake opposite to us, where immense flocks of swans resorted every morning, and asking permission to join them, I seated myself on my haunches in the canoe, well provided with ammunition and a bottle of whiskey, and in a few minutes the paddles were at work, swiftly propelling us to the opposite shore. I was not much surprised to see the boat paddled by the squaws, but I was quite so to see the hunters stretch themselves out and go to sleep. On landing, the squaws took charge of the canoe, secured it, and went in search of nuts, while we gentlemen hunters made the best of our way through thick and thin to the lake. Its muddy shores were overgrown with a close growth of cotton trees, too large to be pushed aside, and too thick to pass through except by squeezing yourself at every few steps; and to add to the difficulty, every few rods we came to small nasty lagoons, which one must jump, leap, or swim, and this not without peril of broken limbs or drowning.

" But when the lake burst on our view there were the swans by hundreds, and white as rich cream, either dipping their black bills in the water, or stretching out one leg on its surface, or gently floating along. According to the Indian mode of hunting, we had divided, and approached the lagoon from different sides. The moment our vedette was seen, it seemed as if thousands of large, fat, and heavy swans were startled, and as they made away from him they drew towards the ambush of death ; for the trees had hunters behind them, whose touch of the trigger would carry destruction among them. As the first party fired, the game rose and flew within easy distance of the party on the opposite side, when they again fired, and I saw the water covered with birds floating with their backs downwards, and their heads sunk in the water, and their legs kicking in the air. When the sport was over we counted more than fifty of these beautiful birds, whose skins were intended for the ladies in Europe. There were plenty of geese and ducks, but no one condescended to give them a shot. A conch was sounded, and after a while the squaws came dragging the canoe, and collecting the dead game, which was taken to the river's edge, fastened to the canoe, and before dusk we were again landed at our camping ground. I had heard of sportsmen in England who walked a whole day, and after firing a pound of powder returned in great glee, bringing one partridge ; and I could not help wondering what they would think of the spoil we were bearing from Swan Lake.

" The fires were soon lighted, and a soup of pecan nuts and bear fat made and eaten. The hunters stretched themselves with their feet close to the camp-fires, intended to burn all night. The squaws then began to skin the birds, and I retired, **very** well satisfied with my Christmas **sport.**

"When **I** awoke in the morning and made my rounds through **the** camp, I found a squaw **had been** delivered of beautiful twins during the **night, and I saw** the same squaw at work tanning deer-skins. She had cut two vines at the roots of opposite **trees, and** made a cradle of bark, in which the new-born ones **were** wafted to and fro with a push of **her** hand, while from time to time she gave them the breast, and was apparently as unconcerned **as** if the event had not taken place.

"**An** Indian camp on a hunting expedition is by **no** means a place of idleness, and although the men do little more than hunt, they perform their task with an industry which borders on enthusiasm. I was invited by three hunters to a bear hunt. A tall, robust, well-shaped fellow assured me that we should have some sport **that** day, for he had discovered **the haunt of one of** large size, and he wanted **to** meet **him face to face; and** we four started to see how he would fulfill his boast. **About** half a mile from the camp he **said he perceived his tracks,** though I could see nothing; **and we rambled** on through the cane brake until we came to an immense decayed **log,** in which he swore the bear was. I saw his eye sparkle with joy, **his rusty** blanket was thrown off his shoulders, his brawny arms swelled with blood, as he **drew his** scalping-knife from his belt with a flourish which showed that fighting was his delight. He told me to mount a small sapling, because a bear cannot climb one, while it can go up a large tree with the nimbleness of a squirrel. The two **other** Indians seated themselves at the entrance, and the hero **went in** boldly. **All was** silent for a few moments, when he came out and **said the bear** was dead, and **I** might come down. The Indians cut a long vine, went into the hollow tree, fastened it to the animal, and with their united force dragged it out. I really thought that this was an exploit. Since then I have seen many Indian exploits, which proved to me their heroism.

" In Europe or America the white hunter would have taken his game home and talked about it for weeks, but these simple people only took off the animal's skin, hung the flesh in quarters on the trees, and continued their hunt. Unable to follow them, I returned to the camp, accompanied by one Indian, who broke the twigs of the bushes we passed, and sent back two squaws on the track, who brought the flesh and skin of the bear to the camp.

" At length the nuts were nearly all gathered, and the game grew scarce, and the hunters remained most of the day in camp; and they soon made up their packs, broke up their abodes, put all on board their canoes, and paddled off down the Mississippi for the little prairie on the Arkansas.

" Their example made a stir among the whites, and my impatient partner begged me to cross the bend and see if the ice was yet too solid for us to ascend the river. Accordingly, accompanied by two of the crew, I made my way to the Mississippi. The weather was milder, and the ice so sunk as to be scarcely perceptible, and I pushed up the shore to a point opposite Cape Girardeau. We hailed the people on the opposite bank, and a robust yellow man came across, named Loume. He stated that he was a son of the Spanish governor of Louisiana, and a good pilot on the river, and would take our boat up provided we had four good hands, as he had six. A bargain was soon struck; their canoe hauled into the woods, some blazes struck on the trees, and all started for Cash Creek.

" The night was spent in making tugs of hides and

shaving oars, and at daylight we left the Creek, glad to
be afloat once more in broader water. Going down the
stream to the mouth of the Ohio was fine sport ; indeed,
my partner considered the worst of the journey over,
but, alas! when we turned the point, and met the mighty
rush of the Mississippi, running three miles an hour, and
bringing shoals of ice to further impede our progress, he
looked on despairingly. The patron ordered the lines
ashore, and it became the duty of every man ' to haul the
cordella,' which was a rope fastened to the bow of the
boat ; and one man being left on board to steer, the others, laying the rope over their shoulders, slowly warped
the heavy boat and cargo against the current. We made
seven miles that day up the famous river. But while I
was tugging with my back at the cordella, I kept my eyes
fixed on the forests or the ground, looking for birds and
curious shells. At night we camped on the shores. Here
we made fires, cooked supper, and setting one sentinel,
the rest went to bed and slept like men who had done
one good day's work. I slept myself as unconcerned as
if I had been in my own father's house.

"The next day I was up early, and roused my partner two hours before sunrise, and we began to move the
boat at about one mile an hour against the current. We
had a sail on board, but the wind was ahead, and we
made ten miles that day. We made our fires, and I lay
down to sleep again in my buffalo robes. Two more days
of similar toil followed, when the weather became severe,
and our patron ordered us to go into winter quarters, in
the great bend of the Tawapatee Bottom.

"The sorrows of my partner at this dismal event were
too great to be described. Wrapped in his blanket, like
a squirrel in winter quarters with his tail about his nose,
he slept and dreamed away his time, being seldom seen
except at meals.

"There was not a white man's cabin within twenty miles, and that over a river we could not cross. We cut down trees and made a winter camp. But a new field was opened to me, and I rambled through the deep forests, and soon became acquainted with the Indian trails and the lakes in the neighborhood.

"The Indians have the instinct or sagacity to discover an encampment of white men almost as quickly as vultures sight the carcass of a dead animal ; and I was not long in meeting strolling natives in the woods. They gradually accumulated, and before a week had passed great numbers of these unfortunate beings were around us, chiefly Osages and Shawnees. The former were well-formed, athletic, and robust men, of a noble aspect, and kept aloof from the others. They hunted nothing but large game, and the few elks and buffaloes that remained in the country. The latter had been more in contact with the whites, were much inferior, and killed opossum and wild turkeys for a subsistence. The Osages being a new race to me, I went often to their camp, to study their character and habits ; but found much difficulty in becoming acquainted with them. They spoke no French, and only a few words of English, and their general demeanor proved them to be a nobler race. They were delighted to see me draw, and when I made a tolerable likeness of one of them with red chalk, they cried out with astonishment, and laughed excessively. They stood the cold much better than the Shawnees, and were much more expert with bows and arrows.

"The bones we threw around our camp attracted many wolves, and afforded us much sport in hunting them. Here I passed six weeks pleasantly, investigating the habits of wild deer, bears, cougars, racoons, and turkeys, and many other animals, and I drew more or less by the side of our great camp-fire every day ; and no one can have an idea of what a good fire is who has never seen a camp-fire in the woods of America. Imagine four or five ash-trees, three feet in diameter and sixty feet long, cut and piled up, with all their limbs and branches, ten feet high, and then a fire kindled on the top with brush and dry leaves ; and then under the smoke the party lies down and goes to sleep.

" Here our bread gave out ; and after using the breast of wild turkeys for bread, and bear's grease for butter, and eating opossum and bear's meat until our stomachs revolted, it was decided that a Kentuckian named Pope, our clerk, and a good woodsman, should go with me to the nearest settlement and try and bring some Indian meal. On the way we saw a herd of deer, and turned aside to shoot one ; and having done so, and marked the place, we continued our journey. We walked until dusk, and no river appeared. Just then I noticed an Indian trail, which we supposed led to the river ; and after following it a short distance, entered the camp we had left in the morning. My partner, finding that we had no wheaten loaves in our hands, and no bags of meal on our backs, said we were boobies ; the boatmen laughed, the Indians joined the chorus, and we ate some cold racoon, and stumbled into our buffalo robes, and were soon enjoying our sleep.

" The next day we tried it again, going directly across the bend, suffering neither the flocks of turkeys nor the droves of deer we saw to turn us aside until we had Cape Girardeau in full sight an hour before the setting of the sun. The ice was running swiftly in the river, and we hailed in vain, for no small boat dare put out. An old abandoned log-house stood on our bank, and we took lodgings there for the night ; we made a little fire, ate a little dried bear's meat we had brought, and slept comfortably.

"What a different life from the one I am leading now; and that night I wrote in my journal exactly as I do now; and I recollect well that I gathered more information that evening respecting the roasting of prairie-hens than I had ever done before or since. Daylight returned fair and frosty, the trees covered with snow and icicles, shining like jewels as the sun rose on them; and the wild turkeys seemed so dazzled by their brilliancy, that they allowed us to pass under them without flying.

"After a time we saw a canoe picking its way through the running ice. Through the messenger who came in the boat, we obtained after waiting nearly all day, a barrel of flour, several bags of Indian meal, and a few loaves of bread. Having rolled the flour to a safe place, slung the meal in a tree, and thrust our gun barrels through the loaves of bread, we started for our camp, and reached it not long after midnight. Four men were sent the next morning with axes to make a sledge, and drag the provisions over the snow to the camp.

"The river, which had been constantly slowly rising, now began to fall, and prepared new troubles for us; for as the water fell the ice clung to the shore, and we were forced to keep the boat afloat to unload the cargo. This, with the help of all the Indian men and women, took two days. We then cut large trees, and fastened them to the shore above the boat, so as to secure it from the ice which was accumulating, and to save the boat from being cut by it. We were now indeed in winter quarters, and we made the best of it. The Indians made baskets of cane, Mr. Pope played on the violin, I accompanied with the flute, the men danced to the tunes, and the squaws looked on and laughed, and the hunters smoked their pipes with such serenity as only Indians can, and I never regretted one day spent there.

"While our time went pleasantly enough, a sudden

and startling catastrophe threatened us without warning. The ice began to break, and our boat was in instant danger of being cut to pieces by the ice-floes, or swamped by their pressure. Roused from our sleep, we rushed down pell-mell to the bank, as if attacked by savages, and discovered the ice was breaking up rapidly. It split with reports like those of heavy artillery; and as the water had suddenly risen from an overflow of the Ohio, the two streams seemed to rush against each other with violence, in consequence of which the congealed mass was broken into large fragments, some of which rose nearly erect here and there, and again fell with thundering crash, as the wounded whale, when in the agonies of death, springs up with furious force, and again plunges into the foaming waters. To our surprise, the weather, which in the evening had been calm and frosty, had become wet and blowy. The water gushed from the fissures formed in the ice, and the prospect was extremely dismal. When day dawned, a spectacle strange and fearful presented itself: the whole mass of water was violently agitated; its covering was broken into small fragments, and although not a foot of space was without ice, not a step could the most daring have ventured to make upon it. Our boat was in imminent danger, for the trees which had been placed to guard it from the ice were cut or broken into pieces, and were thrust against her. It was impossible to move her; but our pilot ordered every man to bring down great bunches of cane, which were lashed along her sides; and before these were destroyed by the ice, she was afloat, and riding above it. While we were gazing on the scene, a tremendous crash was heard, which seemed to have taken place about a mile below, when suddenly the great dam of ice gave way. The current of the Mississippi had forced its way against that of the Ohio; and in less than four hours we witnessed the complete breaking up of the ice.

" During that winter the ice was so thick, the patron said we might venture to start. The cargo was soon on board, and the camp given up to the Indians, after bidding mutual adieus, as when brothers part. The navigation was now of the most dangerous kind ; the boat was pushed by long poles on the ice, and against the bottom when it could be touched, and we moved extremely slowly. The ice was higher than our heads, and I frequently thought that if a sudden thaw should take place we should be in great peril ; but fortunately all this was escaped, and we reached safely the famous cape.

" But the village was small, and no market for us, and we determined to push up to St. Geneviève, and once more were in motion between the ice. We arrived in a few days at the grand tower, where an immense rock in the stream makes the navigation dangerous. Here we used our cordellas, and with great difficulty and peril passed it safely. It was near this famous tower of granite that I first saw the great eagle that I have named after our good and great General Washington. The weather continued favorable, and we arrived in safety at St. Geneviève, and found a favorable market. Our whiskey was especially welcome, and what we had paid twenty-five cents a gallon for, brought us two dollars. St. Geneviève was then an old French town, twenty miles below St. Louis, not so large, as dirty, and I was not half so pleased with the time spent there as with that spent in the Tawapatee Bottom. Here I met with the Frenchman who accompanied Lewis and Clark to the Rocky Mountains. They had just returned, and I was delighted to learn from them many particulars of their interesting journey."

CHAPTER IV.

AUDUBON soon discovered that Geneviève was no pleasant place to live in. Its population were mostly low-bred French Canadians, for whose company, notwithstanding certain national sympathies, he had no liking. He wearied to be back at Hendersonville beside his young wife. Rosier got married at Geneviève, and to him Audubon sold his interest in the business. The naturalist purchased a horse, bade adieu to his partner, to the society of Geneviève, and started homeward across the country. During this journey Audubon met with a terrible adventure, and made a miraculous escape from impending death. This episode in Audubon's life is related by him in the following words :—

"On my return from the upper Mississippi, I found myself obliged to cross one of the wild prairies, which, in that portion of the United States, vary the appearance of the country. The weather was fine, all around me was as fresh and blooming as if it had just issued from the bosom of nature. My knapsack, my gun, and my dog were all I had for baggage and company. But, although well moccasined, I moved slowly along, attracted by the brilliancy of the flowers, and the gambols of the fawns around their dams, to all appearance as thoughtless of danger as I felt myself.

· "My march was of long duration. I saw the sun sinking beneath the horizon long before I could perceive any appearance of woodlands, and nothing in the shape of man had I met with that day. The track which I followed was only an old Indian trail, and as darkness overshadowed the prairie, I felt some desire to reach at least a copse, in which I might lie down to rest. The night-hawks were skimming over and around me, attracted by the buzzing wings of the beetles which form their food, and the distant howling of the wolves gave me some hope that I should soon arrive at the skirts of some woodland.

"I did so, and almost at the same instant a fire-light attracting my eye, I moved towards it, full of confidence that it proceeded from the camp of some wandering Indians. I was mistaken. I discovered by its glare that it was from the hearth of a small log cabin, and that a tall figure passed and repassed between it and me, as if busily engaged in household arrangements.

"I reached the spot, and presenting myself at the door, asked the tall figure, which proved to be a woman, if I might take shelter under her roof for the night? Her voice was gruff, and her dress negligently thrown about her. She answered in the affirmative. I walked in, took a wooden stool, and quietly seated myself by the fire. The next object that attracted my notice was a finely formed young Indian, resting his head between his hands, with his elbows on his knees. A long bow rested against the log wall near him, while a quantity of arrows and two or three racoon skins lay at his feet. He moved not; he apparently breathed not. Accustomed to the habits of the Indians, and knowing that they pay little attention to the approach of civilized strangers, I addressed him in French, a language not unfrequently partially known to the people of that neighbourhood. He raised his head, pointed to one of his eyes with his finger, and gave me a significant glance with the other; his face was covered with blood.

" The fact was, that an hour before this, as he was in the act of discharging an arrow at a racoon in the top of a tree, the arrow had split upon the cord, and sprung back with such violence into his right eye as to destroy it for ever.

" Feeling hungry, I inquired what sort of fare I might expect. Such a thing as a bed was not to be seen, but many large untanned buffalo hides lay piled in a corner. I drew a time-piece from my pocket, and told the woman that it was late, and that I was fatigued. She espied my watch, the richness of which seemed to operate on her feelings with electric quickness. She told me there was plenty of venison and jerked buffalo meat, and that on removing the ashes I should find a cake. But my watch had struck her fancy, and her curiosity had to be grati-fied by an immediate sight of it. I took off the gold chain which secured it around my neck, and presented it to her. She was all ecstasy, spoke of its beauty, asked me its value, and put the chain round her brawny neck, saying how happy the possession of such a watch would make her. Thoughtless, and, as I fancied myself, in so retired a spot, secure, I paid little attention to her talk or her movements. I helped my dog to a good supper of venison, and was not long in satisfying the demands of my own appetite.

" The Indian rose from his seat as if in extreme suffering. He passed and repassed me several times, and once pinched me on the side so violently, that the pain nearly brought forth an exclamation of anger. I looked at him, his eye met mine, but his look was so forbidding, that it struck a chill into the more nervous part of my system. He again seated himself, drew his butcher-knife from its greasy scabbard, examined its edge, as I would do that of a razor suspected dull, replaced it, and again taking his tomahawk from his back, filled the pipe of it with tobacco, and sent me expressive glances whenever our hostess chanced to have her back towards us.

"Never until that moment had my senses been awakened to the danger which I now suspected to be about me. I returned glance for glance to my companion, and rested well assured that, whatever enemies I might have, he was not of their number.

"I asked the woman for my watch, wound it up, and under the pretence of wishing to see how the weather might probably be on the morrow, took up my gun, and walked out of the cabin. I slipped a ball into each barrel, scraped the edges of my flints, renewed the primings, and returning to the hut, gave a favorable account of my observations. I took a few bear-skins, made a pallet of them, and calling my faithful dog to my side, lay down, with my gun close to my body, and in a few minutes was to all appearance fast asleep.

"A short time had elapsed when some voices were heard, and from the corner of my eyes I saw two athletic youths making their entrance, bearing a dead stag on a pole. They disposed of their burden, and asking for whiskey, helped themselves freely to it. Observing me and the wounded Indian, they asked who I was, and why the devil that rascal (meaning the Indian, who, they knew, understood not a word of English) was in the house? The mother, for so she proved to be, bade them speak less loudly, made mention of my watch, and took them to a corner, where a conversation took place, the purport of which it required little shrewdness in me to guess. I tapped my dog gently, he moved his tail, and with indescribable pleasure I saw his fine eyes alternately fixed on me and raised towards the trio in the corner. I felt that he perceived danger in my situation. The Indian exchanged the last glance with me.

" The lads had eaten and drunk themselves into such condition that I already looked upon them as *hors de combat ;* and the frequent visits of the whiskey bottle to the ugly mouth of their dam, I hoped would soon reduce her to a like state. Judge of my astonishment when I saw that incarnate fiend take a large carving-knife, and go to the grindstone to whet its edge. I saw her pour the water on the turning machine, and watched her working away with the dangerous instrument, until the cold sweat covered every part of my body, in despite of my determination to defend myself to the last. Her task finished, she walked to her reeling sons, and said, ' There, that'll soon settle him ! Boys, kill yon ——, and then for the watch ! '

" I turned, cocked my gun-locks silently, touched my faithful companion, and lay ready to start up and shoot the first who might attempt my life. The moment was fast approaching, and that night might have been my last in this world, had not Providence made provision for my rescue. All was ready. The infernal hag was advancing slowly, probably contemplating the best way of despatching me whilst her sons should be engaged with the Indian. I was several times on the eve of rising, and shooting her on the spot, but she was not to be punished thus. The door was suddenly opened, and there entered two stout travellers, each with a long rifle on his shoulder. I bounced up on my feet, and making them most heartily welcome, told them how well it was for me that they should have arrived at that moment. The tale was told in a minute. The drunken sons were secured, and the woman, in spite of her defence and vociferations, shared the same fate. The Indian fairly danced with joy, and gave us to understand that, as he could not sleep for pain, he would watch over us. You may suppose we slept much less than we talked. The two strangers gave me an account of their once having been themselves in a similar situation. Day came fair and rosy, and with it the punishment of our captives.

" They were quite sobered. Their feet were unbound, but their arms were still securely tied. We marched them into the woods off the road, and having used them as Regulators were wont to use such delinquents, we set fire to the cabin, gave all the skins and implements to the young Indian warrior, and proceeded, well pleased, towards the settlements."

At the period at which this incident occurred " Regulator Law " was the high tribunal in the Western States. A savage and outcast population fringed the settled territories, and among these the most dastardly crimes were current. " Regulator Law " was administered by a body of American citizens, and was akin to a Vigilance Committee in its self-assumed functions. The punishment of felons, who could defy or were likely to escape the law of the land, was the special duty of the Regulators, and the name acquired a terrible significance in the western wilds. Audubon relates that a notorious freebooter, named Mason, frequented Wolf's Island in the Mississippi, and with a gang of marauders played pirate with impunity in that river. He stripped the laden barges of all the valuables, stole horses, and proved himself to be beyond the reach of the law. A party of Regulators descended the river, but failed to find him. Finally, he was shot through the ready wit of one man. This Regulator met the ruffian in the forest, and,

unsuspected, turned after him and dogged his steps.
Mason retired to a quiet dell, hobbled his horse to prevent it escaping, and crept into a hollow tree. The
Regulator went off for assistance to the nearest place,
and returning with armed men, the plunderer was shot
down, and his severed head was stuck on a pole hard by,
to deter others from following the same life. The punishment adjudged by these Regulators was mercifully
apportioned to the crimes of the evil-doers ; but Audubon
relates a rather severe sentence passed upon one who was
neither thief nor murderer.

"The culprit," says Audubon, "was taken to a place
where nettles were known to grow in great abundance,
completely stripped, and so lashed with them, that
although not materially hurt, he took it as a hint not to
be neglected, left the country, and was never again heard
of by any of the party concerned."

In November, 1812, soon after his father's return to
Hendersonville, Audubon's second son, John Woodhouse,
was born. John Woodhouse and his only brother, Victor,
were destined to become companions of their father in
his hunting expeditions, and were afterwards able to
assist materially in collecting and drawing birds for the
great work.

A few weeks after Audubon's return to Hendersonville, the western section of the state of Kentucky and the banks of the Mississippi suffered from a
very severe shock of earthquake. In the month of
November, the Naturalist was riding along on horseback,
when he heard what he imagined to be the distant
rumbling of a violent tornado. "On which," says he, "I
spurred my steed, with a wish to gallop as fast as possible
to the place of shelter. But it would not do ; the animal
knew better than I what was forthcoming, and instead of
going faster, so nearly stopped, that I remarked he placed

one foot after another on the ground with as much pre-
caution as if walking on a smooth sheet of ice. I thought
he had suddenly foundered, and, speaking to him, was on
the point of dismounting and leading him, when he all of
a sudden fell a groaning piteously, hung his head, spread
out his four legs, as if to save himself from falling, and
stood stock still, continuing to groan. I thought my
horse was about to die, and would have sprung from his
back had a minute more elapsed; but at that instant all
the shrubs and trees began to move from their very roots,
the ground rose and fell in successive furrows, like the
ruffled waters of a lake, and I became bewildered in my
ideas, as I too plainly discovered that all this awful
commotion in nature was the result of an earthquake. ·

"I had never witnessed anything of the kind before,
although like every other person, I knew of earthquakes
by description. But what is description compared with
reality? Who can tell of the sensations which I experienced when I found myself rocking, as it were, upon my
horse, and with him moved to and fro like a child in a
cradle, with the most imminent danger around me? The
fearful convulsion, however, lasted only a few minutes,
and the heavens again brightened as quickly as they had
become obscured; my horse brought his feet to the
natural position, raised his head, and galloped off as if
loose and frolicking without a rider.

"I was not, however, without great apprehension
respecting my family, from which I was many miles
distant, fearful that where they were the shock might have
caused greater havoc than that I had witnessed. I gave
the bridle to my steed, and was glad to see him appear as
anxious to get home as myself. The pace at which he
galloped accomplished this sooner than I had expected,
and I found, with much pleasure, that hardly any greater
harm had taken place than the apprehension excited for

my own safety. Shock succeeded shock almost every
day or night for several weeks, diminishing however, so
gradually, as to dwindle away into mere vibrations of the
earth. Strange to say, I for one became so accustomed
to the feeling, as rather to enjoy the fears manifested by
others. I never can forget the effects of one of the
slighter shocks which took place when I was at a friend's
house, where I had gone to enjoy the merriment that in
our western country attends a wedding. The ceremony
being performed, supper over, and the fiddles tuned,
dancing became the order of the moment. This was
merrily followed up to a late hour, when the party retired
to rest. We were in what is called, with great propriety,
a log-house ; one of large dimensions, and solidly constructed. The owner was a physician, and in one corner
were not only his lancets, tourniquets, amputating knives,
and other sanguinary apparatus, but all the drugs which
he employed for the relief of his patients, arranged in jars
and phials of different sizes. These had some days
before made a narrow escape from destruction, but had
been fortunately preserved by closing the doors of the
cases in which they were contained.

"As I have said, we had all retired to rest. Morning
was fast approaching, when the rumbling noise that pre-
cedes the earthquake began so loudly as to awaken the
whole party and drive them out of bed in the greatest
consternation. The scene which ensued was humorous
in the extreme. Fear knows no restraint. Every person, old and young, filled with alarm at the creaking
of the log-house, and apprehending instant destruction,
rushed wildly out to the grass enclosure fronting the
building. The full moon was slowly descending from
her throne, covered at times by clouds that rolled heavily
along, as if to conceal from her view the scenes of terror
which prevailed on earth below.

"On the grass-plot we all met, in such condition as rendered it next to impossible to discriminate any of the party, all huddled together in a state of almost perfect nudity. The earth waved like a field of corn before the breeze; the birds left their perches, and flew about not knowing whither; and the doctor, recollecting the danger of his gallipots, ran to his office, to prevent their dancing off the shelves to the floor. Never for a moment did he think of closing the doors, but, spreading his arms, jumped about the front of the cases, pushing back here and there the falling jars, but with so little success, that before the shock was over he had lost nearly all he possessed.

"The shock at length ceased, and the frightened females, now sensible of their dishabille, fled to their several apartments. The earthquakes produced more serious consequences in other places. Near New Madrid, and for some distance on the Mississippi, the earth was rent asunder in several places, one or two islands sunk forever, and the inhabitants who escaped fled in dismay towards the eastern shores."

While resident at Hendersonville, Audubon entered upon a new adventure with his brother-in-law to carry on business at New Orleans, under the firm of "Audubon & Co." In this speculation he embarked all the fortune at his disposal; but instead of attending to his interests he remained hunting in Kentucky, and soon afterwards was informed that all his money had been swept away in business misadventures.

At this juncture the father of Audubon died; but from some unfortunate cause he did not receive legal notice for more than a year. On becoming acquainted with the fact he travelled to Philadelphia to obtain funds, but was unsuccessful. His father had left him his property in France of La Gibitère, and seventeen thousand dollars which had been deposited with a merchant in Richmond, Virginia. Audubon, however, took no steps to obtain possession of his estate in France, and in after years, when his sons had grown up, sent one of them to France, for the purpose of legally transferring the property to his own sister Rosa. The merchant who held possession of the seventeen thousand dollars would not deliver them up until Audubon proved himself to be the son of Commodore Audubon. Before this could be done the merchant died insolvent, and the legatee never recovered a dollar of his money. Returning from Philadelphia to Hendersonville, the unfortunate Audubon cheerfully endeavored to provide for the future, about which he felt considerable anxiety. Gathering a few hundred dollars, he purchased some goods in Louisville, and returned to business in Hendersonville. In his journey he met with General Toledo, who was raising volunteers to go to South America, and who offered him a colonel's commission in the adventure. Audubon, however, preferred remaining at home. The business prospered; he purchased land and a log cabin, with a family of negroes thereto, and seemed to be comfortably settled.

The prosperous career of Audubon was prematurely closed by the arrival of a former partner, who joined him, and whose presence seemed to herald disaster. This partner advised him to erect a steam mill at Hendersonville, a place which was totally unfitted for any such speculation. An Englishman, named Thomas Pease, joined in partnership, and having lost his money in an absurd project, separated from Audubon on no pleasant terms. In order to carry on the mill with renewed vigor, other partners were added; and in connection with it Mr. Apperson was established at Shawnee Town, Mr. Benjamin Harrison at Vincennes in Indiana, and Nathaniel Pope, an old clerk of Audubon's, on the Mississippi river. All of these parties failed in supporting the concern at Hendersonville, which was only continued through the desperate measure of taking in still more partners. Finally, the mill went down, after ruining all concerned. The naturalist speaks with bitterness of the "infernal mill," and in an equally fierce strain of a steamer purchased by the concern, and afterwards sold to a party down the Mississippi, who cheated the sellers out of most of the purchase money. From this date his difficulties appeared to increase daily; bills fell due, and unmeasured vexations assailed him. He handed over all he possessed, and left Hendersonville with his sick wife, his gun, his dog, and his drawings,—but without feeling really depressed at his prospects. The family reached Louisville, where they were kindly received by a relative, and Audubon had time to think over some scheme for raising support for his family. Possessed of considerable skill as an artist in crayons, he conceived the project of starting as a portrait draughtsman. As he started at very low prices, his skill soon became known, and in a few weeks he had as much work as he could do. His family were settled with him, and his business spread so far into Kentucky, that affluence was again enjoyed by the wanderer. Audubon succeeded so well in portraying the features of the dead, that a clergyman's child was exhumed in order that the artist might have an opportunity of taking a portrait of the corpse.

In illustration of his reputation as a crayon drawer, Audubon relates that a settler came for him in the middle of the night from a considerable distance, to have the portrait of his mother taken while she was on the eve of death. Audubon went with the farmer in his wagon, and with the aid of a candle made a satisfactory sketch. This success brought other successes, and the portrait painter seemed to have got a new start in life. Shortly after-

3*

wards he received an invitation to become a curator of the museum at Cincinnati, and for the preparation of birds received a liberal remuneration. In conjunction with this situation he opened a drawing school in the same city, and obtained from this employment additional emolument sufficient to support his family comfortably. His teaching succeeded well until several of his pupils started on their own account. The work at the museum having been finished, Audubon fell back upon his portrait painting and such resources as his genius could command. Applying for assistance to an old friend whom he had aided and assisted into business, the ungrateful wretch declared he would do nothing for his benefactor, and further added that he would not even recommend one who had such *wandering habits.* On more occasions than this his genius for discovery was made an argument against him.

CHAPTER V.

Rambles in Kentucky—Migrations into the Wilds of Kentucky—Rifle Shooting—Driving Nails with Bullets—Daniel Boone "Barking Squirrels"—Festivities on Beargrass Creek—Wild Scenes in the Woods—Hunting the Racoon—Visit from the Eccentric Naturalist, Rafinesque—Daniel Boone, the Famous Hunter.

DURING his residence in Kentucky, Audubon spent all his leisure time in rambles through the wilds in search of natural history specimens. A variety of amusing incidents occurred in these travels, and the wanderer has given several of these in a full and connected form. His ready gun supplied abundant fare to his homely table. Wild turkeys, deer, and bears supplied constant wants, after a fashion that suited the hunter well. While resident there, a flat-boat reached the shore, containing ten or twelve stout fellows with their wives, and declaring themselves to be "Yankees," asked for work as wood cutters. Audubon, thinking that the boat contained wheat, held parley with the occupants, and finding that they were "likely" fellows, proposed to engage them to cut down a government lot of one thousand two hundred acres of fine timber he had purchased. The wood cutters made fast their craft to the bank, started a camp on shore, and, with their wives, managed to cook their meals out of the game supplied by the forest. Audubon and his miller visited the camp in the morning, was rather pleased with the appearance of the fellows, and engaged the gang. Commencing work, they soon

showed their excellent training, felling the trees after the
fashion of experienced woodmen. The daily and weekly
allowance of wood contracted for was safely delivered,
and Audubon had reason to feel much contentment with
his servants. The miller was satisfied ; and the master,
to prove his appreciation of the valuable services, sent
various presents of game and provisions to the strangers.
Finding they had neglected to forward their usual supply
one day, Audubon went off to their camp, found that
the "Yankees" had gone off bodily, had taken his
draught oxen with them, and had harried the place of
all that could be lifted. He and his miller hunted down
the river for the fugitives, but they had got a start and
were not to be caught. Finding an escape into the
Mississippi, the runaways voyaged out of reach of their
victim, and a rare accident alone placed one of them
within Audubon's power. While on board a Mississippi
steamer, Audubon saw a hunter leave the shore in a
canoe and reach the steamer. No sooner had the passenger reached the deck, than he recognized in him one
of his plunderers ; but the woodcutter, fearing an arrest,
leaped into the stream and swam towards the shore.
Entering a canebrake, he was lost to sight, and the
naturalist was never gratified by either hearing of, or
seeing any one of the fellows again.

In referring to Kentuckian sports, Audubon remarks
that that State was a sort of promised land for all sorts of
wandering adventurers from the Eastern states. Families
cast loose from their homesteads beyond the mountains,
wandered westward with their wagons, servants, cattle,
and household gods. Bivouacking by some spring, in
a glade of the primeval forest, near some well known
"salt lick," where game would be plentiful, these Western representatives of the patriarchs moved on towards
new resting-places, from which the red man, not without

serious danger, had been driven. When a voyage by water was meditated as the easiest means of transporting the family and the baggage, a group of emigrants would build an ark on some creek of the upper waters of the Ohio, and in a craft forty or fifty feet long drift down the stream, carrying upon the roof the bodies of carts and wagons, upon the sides the wheels of the same.

Within these floating mansions the wayfarers lived, not without fear of impending dangers. To show a light through the loopholes within range of a redskin's rifle was certain death to the inmate; and night and day, while these arks drifted under umbrageous forests, their occupants were busy considering how their lives might be most dearly sold. Audubon notices curious practices connected with testing the skill of marksmen, not uncommon in his own time in Virginia. "At stated times, those desiring a trial of skill would be assembled," writes the naturalist, "and betting a trifling sum, put up a target, in the centre of which a common-sized nail is hammered for about two-thirds of its length. The marksmen make choice of what they consider a proper distance, which may be forty paces. Each man cleans the interior of his barrel, which is called *wiping* it, places a ball in the palm of his hand, pouring as much powder from his horn upon it as will cover it. This quantity is supposed to be sufficient for any distance within a hundred yards. A shot which comes very close to the nail is considered that of an indifferent marksman; the bending of the nail is, of course, somewhat better; but nothing less than hitting it right on the head is satisfactory. One out of three shots generally hits the nail, and should the shooters amount to half-a-dozen, two nails are frequently needed before each can have a shot. Those who drive the nail have a further trial amongst themselves, and the two best shots out of these generally settle the affair; when all the sportsmen adjourn to some house, and spend an hour or two in friendly intercourse, appointing, before they part, a day for another trial."

While at the town of Frankfort, Audubon had an opportunity of seeing the celebrated Daniel Boone "barking squirrels," or, in less technical phrase, driving them out of their hiding-places by firing into the bark of the tree immediately beside the position they crouch into. Audubon went out with Boone to see the sport, and writes:—

"We walked out together, and followed the rocky margins of the Kentucky river until we reached a piece of flat land thickly covered with black walnuts, oaks, and hickories. As the mast was a good one that year, squirrels were seen gamboling on every tree around us. My companion, a stout, hale, and athletic man, dressed in a homespun hunting shirt, bare-legged and moccasined, carried a long and heavy rifle, which, as he was loading it, he said had proved efficient in all his former undertakings, and which he hoped would not fail on this occasion, as he felt proud to show me his skill. The gun was wiped, the powder measured, the ball patched with six-hundred thread linen, and the charge sent home with a hickory rod. We moved not a step from the place, for the squirrels were so numerous that it was unnecessary to go after them. Boone pointed to one of these animals which had observed us, and was crouched on a branch about fifty paces distant, and bade me mark well the spot where the ball should hit. He raised his piece gradually, until the bead (that being the name given by the Kentuckians to the sight) of the barrel was brought to a line with the spot which he intended to hit, and fired.

" I was astounded to find that the ball had hit the piece of the bark immediately beneath the squirrel, and shivered it to splinters ; the concussion produced by which had killed the animal, and sent it whirling through the air, as if it had been blown up.

"The snuffing of a candle with a ball I first had an opportunity of seeing near the banks of Green River, not far from a large pigeon roost, to which I had previously made a visit. I heard many reports of guns during the early part of a dark night, and knowing them to be those of rifles, I went towards the spot to ascertain the cause. On reaching the place, I was welcomed by a dozen of tall, stout men, who told me they were exercising for the purpose of enabling them to shoot under night at the reflected light from the eye of a deer or wolf by torch-light.

"At a distance of fifty paces stood a lighted candle, barely distinguishable in the darkness. One man was placed within a few yards of it, to watch the effects of the shots, as well as to light the candle, should it chance to go out, or to repair it, should the shot cut it across. Each marksman shot in his turn. Some never hit either the snuff or the candle. One of them, who was particularly expert, was very fortunate, and snuffed the candle three times out of seven, whilst all the other shots either put out the candle, or cut it immediately under the light."

During his residence in Kentucky, Audubon had frequent opportunities of joining in the great American festival of the 4th July. The particular occasion he describes as a "Kentucky Barbecue," and instances a very delightful jubilee held on the Beargrass Creek, at which all the settlers, with their wives and families, assisted. The festival was held in a forest glade by the river's side : the company arrived in their wagons, bringing provisions of every kind, such fruits as the country afforded, wine, and "Old Monongahela " whiskey. When the company had assembled, an immense cannon, built of wood hooped with iron, and lighted by a train, was fired, after which orations were made by various oracles. The good things provided were then largely enjoyed, after which dancing was indulged in with an enthusiasm suitable to such an occasion. Music was provided by various amateurs, and the fun was only closed by a ride home in the starlight.

"A maple sugar camp" was always a pleasant refuge to Audubon while wandering in the woods. He describes the wild appearance these camps presented when suddenly reached in the darkness, afar in the woodland solitudes, and only heralded by the snarling of curs and the howlings of the sugar-makers.

Huge log fires, over which the sugar caldrons were boiled, gave the appearance of a witch incantation to a spectacle in which picturesquely-dressed Indians, rough backwoodsmen, and their strangely-dressed wives and children took part. Raised on a few stones placed around the fires, the sugar kettles were constantly tended by the women, while the men "bled" the sugar maple trees, stuck into the wounds they made, cane pipes, which drained the juice, and collected the maple sap into vessels made by splitting up a "yellow poplar" into juice troughs. Ten gallons of sap are required to make one pound of fine-grained sugar, which in some instances is equal to the finest make of candy. Such sugar sold in Kentucky, in the time of Audubon, for as much as a dozen cents in scarce seasons.

Racoon hunting was a pastime much enjoyed by Audubon, and he has left plentiful records of his enjoyment of the sport. He describes the hunter's visit to a homestead, and the preparations for a racoon hunt. The cost of ammunition was so considerable in the west, while the naturalist roved about, that the axe was reckoned a cheaper implement than the rifle to secure the prey. From the naturalist's journal the following description is given, in-spired by the writer's own peculiar enthusiasm. The cabin is made comfortable by a huge pile of logs laid across the fire; the sweet potatoes are roasted in the ashes; and when all is ready the hunters begin their work.

"The hunter has taken an axe from the wood pile, and returning, assures us that the night is clear, and that we shall have rare sport. He blows through his rifle, to ascertain that it is clear, examines his flint, and thrusts a feather into the touchhole. To a leathern bag swung at his side is attached a powder-horn; his sheathed knife is there also; below hangs a narrow strip of homespun linen. He takes from his bag a bullet, pulls with his teeth the wooden stopper from his powder-horn, lays the ball on one hand, and with the other pours the powder upon it, until it is just overtopped. Raising the horn to his mouth, he again closes it with the stopper, and re-stores it to its place. He introduces the powder into the tube, springs the box of his gun, greases the 'patch' over some melted tallow, or damps it, then places it on the honeycombed muzzle of his piece. The bullet is placed on the patch over the bore, and pressed with the handle of the knife, which now trims the edges of the linen. The elastic hickory rod, held with both hands, smoothly pushes the ball to its bed; once, twice, thrice has it re-bounded. The rifle leaps as it were into the hunter's arms, the feather is drawn from the touchhole, the powder fills the pan, which is closed. 'Now I am ready,' cries the woodsman. A servant lights a torch, and off we march to the woods. 'Follow me close, for the ground is covered with logs, and the grape-vines hang every-where across. Toby, hold up the light, man, or we'll never see the gullies. Trail your gun, sir, as General Clark used to say—not so, but this way—that's it. Now then, no danger you see ; no fear of snakes, poor things ! They are stiff enough, I'll be bound. The dogs have treed one. Toby, you old fool, why don't you turn to the right ?—not so much. There, go ahead and give us a light. What's that ? who's there ? Ah ! you young rascals ! you've played us a trick, have you ? It's all well enough, but now, just keep behind or I'll——' In fact, the boys with eyes good enough to see in the dark, although not quite so well as an owl, had cut directly across to the dogs, which had surprised a racoon on the ground, and bayed it, until the lads knocked it on the head. 'Seek him, boys !" cries the hunter. The dogs, putting their noses to the ground, pushed off at a good rate. 'Master, they're making for the creek,' says old To-by. On towards it therefore we push. What woods, to be sure ! We are now in a low flat covered with beech trees.

"The racoon was discovered swimming in a pool. The glare of the lighted torch was doubtless distressing to him ; his coat was ruffled, and his rounded tail seemed thrice its ordinary size; his eyes shone like emeralds ; with foaming jaws he watched the dogs, ready to seize each by the snout if it came within reach. They kept him busy for some minutes ; the water became thick with mud ; his coat now hung dripping, and his draggled tail lay floating on the surface. His guttural growlings, in place of intimidating his assailants, excited them the more, and they very unceremoniously closed upon him. One seized him by the rump and tugged, but was soon forced to let go ; another stuck to his side, but soon taking a better-directed bite of his muzzle, the coon's fate was sealed. He was knocked on the head, and Toby re-marks, 'That's another half dollar's worth,' as he handles the thick fur of the prey. The dogs are again found look-ing up into a tree and barking furiously. The hunters employ their axes, and send the chips about.

" The tree began to crack, and slowly leaning to one side, the heavy mass swung rustling through the air, and fell to the earth with a crash. It was not one coon that was surprised here, but three, one of which, more crafty than the rest, leaped from the top while the tree was staggering. The other two stuck to the hollow of a branch, from which they were soon driven by one of the dogs. Tyke and Lion having nosed the cunning old one, scampered after him. He is brought to bay, and a rifle bullet is sent through his head. The other two are secured after a desperate conflict, and the hunters with their bags full, return to the cabin."

While resident in Kentucky, Audubon was visited by the eccentric naturalist, Rafinesque, whose manner of life, dress, and oddities of conduct appear to have greatly amused even one so little attentive to formalities as the ornithologist. The stranger reached the banks of the Ohio in a boat, and carrying on his back a bundle of plants which resembled dried clover. He accidentally addressed Audubon, and asked where the naturalist lived. Audubon introduced himself, and was handed a letter of introduction by the stranger, in which the writer begged to recommend " an odd fish," which might not have been described in published treatises. Audubon innocently asked where the odd fish was, which led to a pleasant explanation and a complete understanding between the two naturalists.

" I presented my learned guest to my family," writes Audubon, "and was ordering a servant to go to the boat for my friend's luggage, when he told me he had none but what he brought on his back. He then loosened the pack of weeds which had first drawn my attention. The naturalist pulled off his shoes, and while engaged in drawing his stockings down to hide the holes in his heels, he explained that his apparel had suffered from his journey."

This eccentric's habits were neither tidy nor cleanly. He would hardly perform needful ablutions, and refused a change of clean clothing, suggested as being more comfortable. "His attire," remarks Audubon, "struck me as exceedingly remarkable. A long loose coat of yellow nankeen, much the worse for the many rubs it had got in its time, and stained all over with the juice of plants, hung loosely about him like a sack. A waistcoat of the same, with enormous pockets, and buttoned up to the chin, reached below over a pair of tight pantaloons, the lower part of which were buttoned down to the ankles. His beard was as long as I have known my own to be during some of my peregrinations, and his lank black hair hung loosely over his shoulders. His forehead was so broad and prominent that any tyro in phrenology would instantly have pronounced it the residence of a mind of strong powers. His words impressed an assurance of rigid truth, and as he directed the conversation to the study of the natural sciences, I listened to him with great delight. He requested to see my drawings, anxious to see the plants I had introduced besides the birds I had drawn. Finding a strange plant among my drawings, he denied its authenticity ; but on my assuring him that it grew in the neighborhood, he insisted on going off instantly to see it.

"When I pointed it out the naturalist lost all command over his feelings, and behaved like a maniac in expressing his delight. He plucked the plants one after another, danced, hugged me in his arms, and exultingly told me he had got, not merely a new species, but a new genus.

"He immediately took notes of all the needful particulars of the plant in a note-book, which he carried wrapt in a waterproof covering. After a day's pursuit of natural history studies, the stranger was accommodated with a bed-room. We had all retired to rest ; every person I imagined was in deep slumber save myself, when of a sudden I heard a great uproar in the naturalist's room. I got up, reached the place in a few moments, and opened the door ; when, to my astonishment, I saw my guest running naked, holding the handle of my favorite violin, the body of which he had battered to pieces against the walls in attempting to kill the bats which had entered by the open window, probably attracted by the insects flying around his candle. I stood amazed, but he continued jumping and running round and round, until he was fairly exhausted, when he begged me to procure one of the animals for him, as he felt convinced they belonged to a 'new species.' Although I was convinced of the contrary, I took up the bow of my demolished Cremona, and administering a smart tap to each of the bats as it came up, soon got specimens enough. The war ended, I again bade him good-night, but could not help observing the state of the room. It was strewed with plants, which had been previously arranged with care.

"He saw my regret for the havoc that had been created, but added that he would soon put his plants to rights—after he had secured his new specimens of bats.

Rafinesque had great anxiety to be shown a cane-brake, plenty of which were to be found in the neighborhood. The cane-brake is composed of a dense growth of canes, measuring twenty or thirty feet in height, and packed so closely that a man's body requires to be forced between the shafts of the canes. An undergrowth of plants and trailing climbers further prevents progression, which has to be accelerated by pushing the back between the canes. Game of all sorts frequent the cane-brakes, in which travelling is rendered disagreeably exciting by the presence of bears, panthers, snakes, and serpents. The cane-brakes are sometimes set fire to, and the water collected

in the separate joints explodes like a shell. The constant fusilade occasioned by such explosions in the midst
of a conflagration has occasioned the flight of parties not
conversant with the cause, and who believed that the Indians were advancing with volleys of musketry. I had
determined that my companion should view a cane-brake
in all its perfection, and leading him several miles in a
direct course, came upon as fine a sample as existed in
that part of the country. We entered, and for some time
proceeded without much difficulty, as I led the way, and
cut down the canes which were most likely to incommode
him. The difficulties gradually increased, so that we
were presently obliged to turn our backs and push our
way through. After a while we chanced to come upon
the top of a fallen tree, which so obstructed our passage,
that we were on the eve of going round, instead of thrusting ourselves through amongst the branches ; when from
its bed, in the centre of the tangled mass, forth rushed a
bear with such force, that my friend became terror struck,
and in his haste to escape made a desperate attempt to
run, but fell amongst the canes in such a way that he was
completely jammed. I could not refrain from laughing
at the ridiculous exhibition he made, but my gaiety however was not very pleasing to the discomfited naturalist.
A thunder-storm with a deluge of rain completed our experience of the cane-brake, and my friend begged to be
taken out. This could only be accomplished by crawl-
ing in a serpentine manner out of the jungle, from which
the eccentric naturalist was delighted to escape, perfectly
overcome with fatigue and fear. The eccentric was more
than gratified with the exploit, and soon after left my
abode without explanation or farewell. A letter of
thanks, however, showed that he had enjoyed the hospitality, and was not wanting in gratitude."

In his Kentucky rambles Audubon had more than

one opportunity of seeing and hunting with the famous
Colonel Boone, the Kentucky hunter, and hero of a mul-
titude of desperate adventures. On a particular occasion
Boone spent a night under Audubon's roof, and related
some of his adventures, among others, the following. On
a hunting expedition in which Boone was engaged, the
wanderer was afraid of Indians, and he consequently
damped out his fire before falling asleep. He had not
lain long before strong hands were laid upon him, and he
was dragged off to the Indian camp. Avoiding every
semblance of fear, Boone neither spoke nor resisted.
The Indians ransacked his pockets, found his whisky
flask, and commenced to drink from it. While so engaged a shot was fired, and the male savages went off in
pursuit, while the squaws were left to watch the prisoner.
Rolling himself towards the fire, Boone burnt the fasten-
ings which bound him, sprang to his feet, and after hacking three notches in an ash tree, afterwards known as
"Boone's Ash," fled from the neighborhood. In years
after, an engineer in Kentucky made the ash a point for a
survey. A lawsuit arose out of a boundary question, and
the only chance of closing it was by identifying " Boone's
Ash." The hunter was sent for, and after some searching he pointed out the tree, in which the notches were
detected after the bark had been peeled away. Boone's
extraordinary stature and colossal strength struck Audubon as remarkable among a remarkable race ; and the
dreaded foe of the red man was notable for an honesty
and courage that could not be questioned.

CHAPTER VI.

ON the 12th of October, 1820, Audubon left Cincinnati in company with Captain Cumming, an American engineer who had been appointed to make a survey of the Mississippi river, and after fourteen days of drifting down the Ohio, the flat-boat which contained the scientific "expedition" reached the Mississippi river. The naturalist had failed to receive the money due to him at Cincinnati, and vexed and discouraged, he determined even without means to seek a new field for employment.

From a letter addressed to the Governor of Arkansas at this date, it is evident that Audubon had determined on a lengthened excursion in the pursuit of ornithological specimens, including the States of Mississippi, Alabama, and Florida, afterwards retracing his steps to New Orleans up the Red River, down the Arkansas, and homeward to his wife. He had received letters of recommendation from General, afterwards President Harrison, and from Henry Clay, and good prospects seemed to dawn. He had determined in any case to complete one hundred drawings of birds before returning to Cincinnati, and he fulfilled this resolve.

"On a clear frosty morning in December," writes Audubon in his journal, "I arrived at Natchez, and found the levee lined with various sorts of boats full of western produce. The crowd was immense, and the market appeared to be a sort of fair. Scrambling up to the cliffs on which the city is built, I found flocks of vultures flying along the ground with outspread wings in the pursuit of food. Large pines and superb magnolias crowned the bluff, and their evergreen foliage showed with magnificent effect. I was delighted with the spectacle of white-headed eagles pursuing fishing-hawks, and surveyed the river scenery sparkling in bright sunlight with a new pleasure. Far away across the stream the shores were lost in the primitive forests, and a mysterious unknown seemed to lie beyond me. I was impressed with the pretty houses of the upper town, built of painted brick or wood ; and to complete my feeling of enjoyment, my relative, Mr. Berthoud, gave me letters from my wife and sons, received by the weekly mail which then brought letters to Natchez from all parts of the Union. The town owned three thousand inhabitants ; was composed of an upper town and a lower town, the latter chiefly built up of beached flat-boats, converted into cabins by a rascally and nondescript population. The planters' houses in the upper town were models of luxury and comfort, but the church architecture prevalent rather detracted from the beauty of the place. I found the mocking-bird in abundance, and the pewee fly-catcher at home in its winter quarters. The old Spanish fort was still visible in ruins, and a rumor reached me that many houses had been buried in the river by a slip of the bank. At Natchez, I was amazed to see a white-headed eagle attack a vulture, knock it down, and gorge itself upon a dead horse. M. Garnier, who kept the largest hotel in the place, befriended me in many ways, and I also formed an acquaintance with M. Charles Carré, the son of a French nobleman of the old régime. From Carré I

had a history of Natchez, as he had lived to witness the
career of that town under the Spaniards, French, and
Americans."

In connection with his residence in Natchez he tells
a significant story. A companion of his, voyaging, having worn his shoes down, had no money to get them repaired or to purchase new ones. The naturalist was
likewise without the means ; but Audubon called upon a
shoemaker, explained that his friend was in want of shoes,
had no money to pay for them, but that if he chose he
should have the portrait of himself and his wife in return
for two pairs of boots. The shoemaker was satisfied with
the proposal, and the portraits were sketched in a couple
of hours, after which the naturalist and his friend bade
the shoemaker good-bye, each being fitted with new boots.
After some stay in Natchez, Audubon left for New Orleans with his friend Berthoud, in a keel-boat belonging
to the latter, but which was taken in tow of the steamer.
Not long after leaving, Audubon discovered that one of
his portfolios, containing some drawings of birds he prized
highly, was missing. Full of chagrin, he could only
recollect that he had brought it to the wharf and had
placed it in the hands of a servant, who had evidently
forgotten to put it on board the keel-boat. How to recover it was a serious consideration. Letters were instantly despatched to M. Garnier, M. Carré, and friends
of Berthoud, to use their utmost endeavors to recover the
lost portfolio. After towing as far as Bayou Sara, the
steamer threw off the keel-boat, and with the aid of the
current and the oars Audubon continued his course to
Baton Rouge, on the way to New Orleans. Large flocks
of beautiful ducks were passed in various eddies, and the
naturalist was amused by groups of negroes catching
catfish in the river or scooping out shrimps with their
nets.

"Nearing New Orleans, the country became perfectly level, and from the embankments or levees we could see the great river winding on for miles. The planters' houses became more visible against groves of dark cypresses covered with hanging vine plants, and odorous winds blew perfumes of the orange flowers across the stream down which the boat so lazily drifted. Landing on the banks, I made my way to the swamps, and shot several beautiful boat-tailed grakles and a whole covey of partridges. Thousands of swallows in their winter home flew about us, and the cat-birds mewed in answer to their chatterings. Doves echoed soft notes through the woods, and the cardinal grosbeak sat on the top branches of the magnolia, saluting us by elevating his glowing crest. On the 6th of January, and when nearing New Orleans, a sharp frost was felt which left some traces of ice, but at the same time we had green peas, artichokes, and other summer esculents on shore fresh from the garden."

On arriving at New Orleans, Audubon was relieved to find that the lost portfolio had been found, and was located safely in the office of the 'Mississippi Republican' newspaper. He however found no work to do, and had to live for some days in the boat he came with. The money he had, not much, was stolen from him, and he had not even as much as would pay a lodging he took in advance. Amid all his difficulties he still kept wandering to the woods, got additions made to his specimens, and filled his portfolio with new drawings. Meeting an Italian painter, Audubon explained his anxiety to have work. The Italian introduced him to the director of the theatre, who offered the naturalist one hundred dollars per month to draw for him, but a fixed engagement could not be entered upon.

On the 13th of January he called upon Jarvis the painter, who objected to his manner of painting birds.

He suggested that he might assist the artist in filling-in backgrounds, and was requested to come back.

"I went back again," writes the naturalist, "but found Mr. Jarvis had no use for me : he appeared in fact to fear my rivalry. Meeting a friend, I was taken to the counting-house of Mr. Pamar, where I was asked what I would take the portraits of three children for. I answered, One ·hundred dollars ; but various delays occurred which prevented me from entering upon this engagement. I wished for the money to send home to my wife and children.

"*January* 14. Visited the levees, and found them crowded with promenaders of every hue and nation. The day was Sunday, and amusements were much indulged in. Various quadroon balls held in the evening. Do not see any good-looking or handsome women ; all have a citron hue. Time passed sadly in seeking ineffectually for employment. I was fortunate in making a hit with the portrait of a well-known citizen of New Orleans. I showed it to the public ; it made a favorable impression, and I obtained several patrons. A few orders for portraits relieved my necessities, and continuing my work of painting birds, the time passed more pleasantly.

"*February* 5. Spent my time running after orders for portraits, and also in vain endeavors to obtain a sight of Alexander Wilson's 'Ornithology,' but was unsuccessful in seeing the book, which is very high priced. Obtained some new birds and made copies.

"*March* 12. Of late have been unable to make many entries in my journal. Near our lodgings, on the south angle of a neighboring chimney-top, a mocking bird regularly resorts, and pleases us with the sweetest notes from the rising of the moon until about midnight, and every morning from about eight o'clock until eleven, when he flies away to the Convent gardens to feed. I have noticed that bird, always in the same spot and same position, and have been particularly pleased at hearing him imitate the watchman's cry of ' All's well!' which comes from the fort, about three squares distant ; and so well has he sometimes mocked it that I should have been deceived if he had not repeated it too often, sometimes several times in ten minutes.

" *March* 21. Read in the papers this morning that the treaty between Spain and the United States is concluded, and that a clause provides that an expedition is to leave Natchitoches next year to survey the boundary line of the ceded territory. I determined to try for an appointment as draughtsman and naturalist. I wrote to President Monroe, and was quite pleased at the prospect before me. I walked out in the afternoon of the day on which I formed the project, and saw nothing but hundreds of new birds in imagination within range of my gun. I have been struck with the paucity of birds in the neighborhood of New Orleans during a season I had expected to meet with them. Many species of warblers, thrushes, &c., which were numerous during the winter, have migrated eastward towards Florida, leaving swallows and a few water-birds almost the sole representatives of the feathered race.

" *March* 31. My time has been engrossed thinking over and making plans about the Pacific expedition. I called on Mr. Vanderlyn, the historical painter, with my portfolio, to show him some of my drawings and ask him for a recommendation. He said they were handsomely done, and was pleased with the coloring and positions of the birds drawn. He was however a rude-mannered man, treated me as a mendicant, and ordered me to lay down my portfolio in the lobby. I felt inclined to walk off without farther comment, but the thought of further-ing my prospects in connection with the expedition in-

duced me to submit. In half an hour he returned with
an officer, and with an air more becoming asked me into
his private room. Yet I could see in his expression that
feeling of selfish confidence which always impairs in some
degree the worth of the greatest man who has it. The
perspiration ran down my face as I showed him my
drawings and laid them on the floor. An officer who was
with the artist, looking at the drawings, said with an oath
that they were handsome. Vanderlyn made a like re-
mark, and I felt comforted. Although he failed in painting women himself, he spoke disparagingly of my own
portraits ; said they were too hard and too strongly
drawn. He sat down and wrote his note while I was
thinking of my journey to the Pacific, and I cared not a
picayune for his objections to my portraits so that my
prospects of going with the expedition were furthered.
Vanderlyn gave me a very complimentary note, in which
he said that he never had seen anything superior to my
drawings in any country, and for which kindness I was
very thankful. His friend, the officer, followed me to the
door, asked the price of my portraits, and very courte-
ously asked me to paint his likeness."

Audubon's fortunes in New Orleans varied exceedingly. From the sorest penury and deepest distress he
was suddenly raised by the happy spirit he possessed and
the untiring energy of his character. One day he was
going about seeking for a patron to obtain a few dollars
by drawing a portrait ; the next he was dining with Governor Robertson of Louisiana, who gave him a letter of
recommendation to President Monroe in connection with
the expedition to Mexico. He had determined to go to
Shipping Port, Kentucky, but his departure was hindered
by an engagement from a few pupils. He writes in his
diary :—

" *June* 16. Left New Orleans in the steamer Columbus, Captain John D'Hart, for Shipping Port, Kentucky. Been greatly oppressed while at work lately, and greatly tormented by mosquitoes, which prevented my sleeping at night. Much disappointed by one patron at New Orleans, who affected great interest in me, but would not pay one hundred dollars he owed."

It happened however that Audubon was not to return to his family as soon as he expected. The voyage to Shipping Port was cut short by the acceptance of a situation in the family of Mrs. Perrie, who owned a plantation at Bayou Sara, in Louisiana. The duties accepted by Audubon were apparently simple enough. He was to teach Mrs. Perrie's daughter drawing during the summer months, at sixty dollars per month. His lessons would absorb one half of the day, and with a young friend, Mason, he was to have the rest of his time free for hunting. Board and lodging were provided for the two friends, and Mrs. Perrie's aim appears to have been to provide an opportunity for Audubon to carry on his pursuits under the guise of an employment which would be congenial, and not interfere with his work.

" We arrived at the landing at the mouth of the bayou on a hot sultry day, bid adieu to our fellow-passengers, climbed the hill at St. Francisville, and rested a few minutes at the house of Mr. Swift. Dinner was nearly ready, and we were invited to partake, but I had no heart for it. I wished myself on board the Columbus ; I wished for my beloved Lucy and my dear boys. I felt that I should be awkward at the table ; and a good opportunity having offered me to go to Mr. Perrie's, we walked slowly on, guided by some of the servants, who had been sent, when the family heard of our coming, to bring our luggage, which they found light.

" The aspect of the country was entirely new to me, and distracted my mind from those objects which are the occupation of my life. The rich magnolias covered with fragrant blossoms, the holly, the beech, the tall yellow poplar, the hilly ground, and even the red clay, all excited my admiration. Such an entire change in the face of nature in so short a time seems almost supernatural ; and surrounded once more by numberless warblers and thrushes, I enjoyed the scene. The five miles we walked appeared short, and we arrived and met Mr. Perrie at his house. Anxious to know him, I examined his features by Lavater's directions. We were received kindly.

"*August* 11. We were awakened last night by a servant requesting me to accompany Mrs. Perrie to the house of a dying neighbor about a mile distant. We went, but arrived too late, for the man was dead, and I had the pleasure of keeping his body company the remainder of the night. On such occasions time flies very slowly, so much so, that it looked as if it stood still, like the hawk that poises in the air over his prey. The poor man had drunk himself into an everlasting sleep. I made a good sketch of his head, and left the house, while the ladies were engaged in preparing the funeral dinner.

"*August* 12. Left this morning to visit a beautiful lake, six miles distant, where we are told there are many beautiful birds. The path led through a grove of rich magnolia woods. On the way we saw a rich-colored spider at work rolling up a horsefly he had caught in his web. He spirted a stream of fluid from his mouth, at the same time rolling the fly in it, until he looked like the cocoon of a silkworm ; and having finished his work, returned to the centre of his nest. This is no doubt the way he puts up his food when he is not hungry, and provides for the future.

"*August* 25. Finished drawing a very fine specimen of a rattlesnake, which measured five feet and seven inches, weighed six and a quarter pounds, and had ten rattles.

Anxious to give it a position most interesting to a naturalist, I put it in that which the reptile commonly takes when on the point of striking madly with its fangs. I had examined many before, and especially the position of the fangs along the superior jawbones, but had never seen one showing the whole exposed at the same time; and having before this supposed that it was probable that those lying enclosed below the upper one, in most specimens, were to replace the upper one, which I thought might drop periodically as the animal changed its skin and rattles. However, on dissection of these from the ligament by which they were attached to the jawbones, I found them strongly and I think permanently fixed there as follows. Two superior, or next to the upper lip (I speak of one side of the jaws only), were well connected at their bases and running parallel their whole length, with apertures on the upper and lower sides of their bases to receive the poison connectedly, and the discharging one a short distance from the sharp point on the inner part of the fangs. The next two fangs, about a quarter of an inch below, connected and received in the same manner but with only one base aperture on the lower side of each, and the one at the point which issues the poison to the wound. The fifth, rather smaller, is also about a quarter of an inch below. The scales of the belly, to the under part of the mouth, numbered one hundred and seventy, and twenty-two from the vent to the tail. The heat of the weather was so great that I could devote only sixteen hours to the drawing.

"*October* 20. Left Bayou Sara in the Ramapo, with a medley of passengers, and arrived safely in New Orleans. My long, flowing hair, and loose yellow nankeen dress, and the unfortunate cut of my features, attracted much attention, and made me desire to be dressed like other people as soon as possible. My

4*

friends the Pamars received me kindly and raised my spirits; they looked on me as a son returned from a long and dangerous voyage, and children and servants as well as the parents were all glad to see me.

"*October* 25. Rented a house in Dauphine street at seventeen dollars per month, and determined to bring my family to New Orleans. Since I left Cincinnati, October 12, 1820, I have finished sixty-two drawings of birds and plants, three quadrupeds, two snakes, fifty portraits of all sorts, and have subsisted by my humble talents, not having had a dollar when I started. I sent a draft to my wife, and began life in New Orleans with forty-two dollars, health, and much anxiety to pursue my plan of collecting all the birds of America."

Audubon speaks with boyish gayety of the comfort which a new suit of clothes gave him. He called on Mrs. Clay with his drawings, but got no work—no pupils. He determined to make a public exhibition of his ornithological drawings.

Under date November 10, he remarks: "Mr. Basterop called on me, and wished me to join him in painting a panorama of the city; but my birds, my beloved birds of America, occupy all my time, and nearly all my thoughts, and I do not wish to see any other perspective than the last specimen of these drawings."

Audubon relates many instances of squatter life on the great American rivers. The features of this peculiar life struck him with a picturesque force that makes his descriptions of the constant emigrations from the East, and the settlement of the wanderers in the West, very interesting indeed. In a detailed account he describes how the settlers in Virginia became impoverished through the reckless system of husbandry pursued, and how, after suffering penury, they determined to emigrate to more fertile lands. He thus graphically narrates the patriarchal wanderings of the wearied wayfarers.

" I think I see them harnessing their horses, and attaching them to their wagons, which are already fitted with bedding, provisions, and the younger children; while on their outside are fastened spinning-wheels and looms, a bucket filled with tar and tallow swings betwixt the hind wheels. Several axes are secured to the bolster, and the feeding-trough of the horses contains pots, kettles, and pans. The servant now becomes a driver, riding the near saddled horse, the wife is mounted on another, the worthy husband shoulders his gun, and his sons, clad in plain, substantial homespun, drive the cattle ahead, and lead the procession, followed by the hounds and other dogs. Their day's journey is short and not agreeable. The cattle, stubborn or wild, frequently leave the road for the woods, giving the travellers much trouble; the harness of the horses here and there gives way, and immediate repair is needed. A basket which has accidentally dropped must be gone after, for nothing that they have can be spared. The roads are bad, and now and then all hands are called to push on the wagon, or prevent it from upsetting. Yet by sunset they have proceeded perhaps twenty miles. Fatigued, all assemble round the fire, which has been lighted; supper is prepared, and a camp being run up, there they pass the night. Days and weeks pass before they gain the end of their journey. They have crossed both the Carolinas, Georgia, and Alabama. They have been travelling from the beginning of May to that of September, and with heavy hearts they traverse the neighborhood of the Mississippi. But now arrived on the banks of the broad stream, they gaze in amazement on the dark deep woods around them. Boats of various kinds they see gliding downwards with the current, while others slowly ascend against it. A few inquiries are made at the nearest dwelling, and assisted by the inhabitants with their boats and canoes, they at once cross the river, and select their place of habitation. The exhalations arising from the swamps and morasses around them have a powerful effect on these new settlers, but all are intent on preparing for the winter. A small patch of ground is cleared by the axe and fire, a temporary cabin is erected ; to each of the cattle is attached a bell before it is let loose into the neighboring canebrake, and the horses remain about the house, where they find sufficient food at that season. The first trading boat that stops at their landing enables them to provide themselves with some flour, fish-hooks, and ammunition, as well as other commodities. The looms are mounted, the spinning-wheels soon furnish some yarn, and in a few weeks the family throw off their ragged clothes, and array them-selves in suits adapted to the climate.

" The father and sons meanwhile have sown turnips and other vegetables ; and from some Kentucky flat-boat a supply of live poultry has been purchased. October tinges the leaves of the forest ; the morning dews are heavy ; the days hot and the nights chill, and the unac-climatised family in a few days are attacked with ague. The lingering disease almost prostrates their whole facul-ties. Fortunately the unhealthy season soon passes over, and the hoar-frosts make their appearance. Gradually each individual recovers strength. The largest ash trees are felled, their trunks are cut, split, and corded in front of the building ; a large fire is lighted at night on the edge of the water, and soon a steamer calls to purchase the wood, and thus add to their comforts during the winter. This first fruit of their industry imparts new courage to them ; their exertions multiply, and when spring returns the place has a cheerful look. Venison, bear's flesh, and turkeys, ducks and geese, with now and then some fish, have served to keep up their strength, and now their enlarged field is planted with corn, potatoes, and pumpkins. Their stock of cattle, too, has augmented: the steamer which now stops there, as if by preference, buys a calf or pig, together with their wood. Their store of provisions is renewed, and brighter rays of hope enliven their spirits.

"'The sons discover a swamp covered with excellent timber, and as they have seen many great rafts of saw-logs, bound for the saw-mills of New Orleans, floating past their dwelling, they resolve to try the success of a little enterprise. A few cross-saws are purchased, and some broad-wheeled 'carry-logs' are made by themselves. Log after log is hauled to the bank of the river, and in a short time their first raft is made on the shore, and loaded with cordwood. When the next freshet sets it afloat it is secured by long grape vines or cables, until, the proper time being arrived, the husband and sons embark on it and float down the mighty stream. After encountering many difficulties, they arrive in safety at New Orleans, where they dispose of their stock, the money obtained for which may be said to be all profit; supply themselves with such articles as may add to their convenience or comfort, and with light hearts procure a passage on the upper deck of a steamer at a very cheap rate, on account of the benefit of their labors in taking in wood or otherwise. Every successive year has increased their savings. They now possess a large stock of horses, cows, and hogs, with abundance of provisions, and domestic comforts of every kind. The daughters have been married to the sons of neighboring squatters, and have gained sisters to themselves by the marriage of their brothers."

He introduces, among other episodes of natural history, an account of the habits of the opossum—"the dissimulator." The walk of this animal he describes as an amble like that of a young foal or a Newfoundland dog. Its movements are rather slow—it travels across the snow-covered ground about as fast as a man could walk—snuffing at every step for traces of the prey it searches after. Entering some cranny, it pulls out a squirrel it has killed, and climbing a tree, secretes itself among the thick branches to eat its repast. Exhausted by hunger in the early spring, the opossum will eat young frogs, and the green growth of nettles and other succulent plants. Unscared by the watchful crows the farmer has killed, the pest creeps into the hen-house, eats the chickens, robs the hen of the eggs she is sitting upon, and commits its devastations with address and adroitness. Prowling about after sunset, it avoids all sorts of precautions, and defies the farmer's guns and curs alike. In the woods it eats the eggs of the wild turkey, and ravenously devours the grapes of the grapevine. When attacked, it rolls itself up like a ball, submits to be kicked and maltreated without moving, feigns death, lies on the ground with shut eyes, and cheats its assailants into the belief that it has been destroyed. When its assailant has gone, life seemingly suddenly returns, and regaining its feet, it scampers off to the wilds.

"Once while descending the Mississippi in a sluggish flat-bottomed boat, expressly for the purpose of studying those objects of nature more nearly connected with my favorite pursuits, I chanced to meet with two well-grown opossums, and brought them alive to the 'ark.' The poor things were placed on the roof or deck, and were immediately assailed by the crew, when, following their natural instinct, they lay as if quite dead. An experiment was suggested, and both were thrown overboard. On striking the water, and for a few moments after, neither evinced the least disposition to move; but finding their situation desperate, they began to swim towards our uncouth rudder, which was formed of a long slender tree, extending from the middle of the boat thirty feet beyond the stern. They both got upon it, were taken up, and afterwards let loose in their native woods.

"In the year 1829, I was in a portion of Lower Louisiana, where the opossum abounds at all seasons, and having been asked by the President and Secretary of the Zoological Gardens and Society of London to forward live animals of this species to them, I offered a price a little above the common, and soon found myself plentifully supplied, twenty-five having been brought to me. I found them extremely voracious, and not less cowardly. They were put into a large box, with a great quantity of food, and conveyed to a steamer bound to New Orleans. Two days afterwards I went to the city to see about sending them off to Europe ; but to my surprise I found that the old males had destroyed the younger ones, and eaten off their heads, and that only sixteen remained alive. A separate box was purchased for each, and the cannibals were safely forwarded to their destination."

CHAPTER VII.

Wife and Sons arrive at New Orleans — Difficulties of Obtaining
a Livelihood — Recollections of an Eccentric — A Bird-fancier
and an Artist — Rifle Practice in a Studio — Audubon's Ar-
rival at Natchez — Attack of Fever — Raffle of a Drawing,
and Results — Audubon studies Oil Painting — The Naturalist
lets loose his Pet Birds — Visit to Bayou Sara — A Den of
Gamblers — Leaves for Louisville with his son Victor — Wan-
derings through the Wilds — Residence at Louisville — An Ad-
venture in the Woods — Floods of the Mississippi — The Waste
of Waters — The Flooded Forest — Slaughter of Game.

ECEMBER 8. My wife and family arrived to-
day by steamer. We dined with our friend Mr.
Pamar, and met my old friend Mr. Rosier in the
evening. We reached our lodging, and all felt happy and
comforted at the reunion, after fourteen months of separation."

For the first two months of 1822, the records of Audubon's life are sparse and imperfect, on account of his
inability to purchase a book to write his journal in! The
one at last obtained was made of thin, poor paper, and
the records entered are rather in keeping with his financial difficulties. It took all his means at this time to
supply his family with the necessaries of life, and in order
to obtain money to educate the children, his wife undertook the duties of a situation, in which she had charge of
and educated the offspring of a Mr. Brand.

"*March* 7. Spring is advancing, with many pleasant
associations, but my bodily health suffers from depres-
sion. I have resolved to leave for Natchez, but grieve to

leave my family. My money is scarce, and I find great difficulty in collecting what is owing to me.

"*March* 16. Paid all my bills in New Orleans, and having put my baggage on board of the steamer Eclat, obtained a passage to Natchez in the steamer, in return for a crayon portrait of the captain and his wife.

"*March* 19. Opened a chest with two hundred of my bird portraits in it, and found them sorely damaged by the breaking of a bottle containing a quantity of gunpowder. I had several portraits to draw during the passage.

"*March* 24. One of the passengers accused Alexander Wilson, the ornithologist, of intemperate habits, but I had the satisfaction of defending his character from aspersion. I had hope of success in Natchez, and soon expected to be followed by my wife and family. My wife in the meantime remained at New Orleans, in the family of Mr. Brand."

In closing his recollections of New Orleans, Audubon relates an amusing history of a painter, whose eccentricities fascinated the naturalist. The genius was first observed by the naturalist on the Levee at New Orleans, and his odd costume and appearance are thus described:

"His head was covered by a straw hat, the brim of which might cope with those worn by the fair sex in 1830; his neck was exposed to the weather; the broad frill of a shirt, then fashionable, flopped about his breast, whilst an extraordinary collar, carefully arranged, fell over the top of his coat. The latter was of a light-green color, harmonizing well with a pair of flowing yellow nankeen trousers and a pink waistcoat, from the bosom of which, amidst a large bunch of the splendid flowers of the magnolia, protruded part of a young alligator, which seemed more anxious to glide through the muddy waters of a swamp than to spend its life swinging to and fro amongst

folds of the finest lawn. The gentleman held in one
hand a cage full of richly-plumed nonpareils, whilst in the
other he sported a silk umbrella, on which I could plainly read 'Stolen from I,' these words being painted in
large white characters. He walked as if conscious of
his own importance; that is, with a good deal of pom-
posity, singing, 'My love is but a lassie yet;' and that
with such thorough imitation of the Scotch emphasis, that
had not his physiognomy suggested another parentage, I
should have believed him to be a genuine Scot. A narrower acquaintance proved him to be a Yankee; and
anxious to make his acquaintance, I desired to see his
birds. He retorted, 'What the devil did I know about
birds?' I explained to him that I was a naturalist,
whereupon he requested me to examine his birds. I did
so with some interest, and was preparing to leave, when
he bade me come to his lodgings and see the remainder
of his collection. This I willingly did, and was struck
with amazement at the appearance of his studio. Several
cages were hung about the walls, containing specimens of
birds, all of which I examined at my leisure. On a large
easel before me stood an unfinished portrait, other pictures hung about, and in the room were two young pupils; and at a glance I discovered that the eccentric
stranger was, like myself, a naturalist and an artist. The
artist, as modest as he was odd, showed me how he laid
on the paint on his pictures, asked after my own pursuits,
and showed a friendly spirit which enchanted me. With
a ramrod for a rest, he prosecuted his work vigorously,
and afterwards asked me to examine a percussion lock
on his gun, a novelty to me at the time. He snapped
some caps, and on my remarking that he would frighten
his birds, he exclaimed, 'Devil take the birds, there are
more of them in the market.' He then loaded his gun,
and wishing to show me that he was a marksman, fired

at one of the pins on his easel. This he smashed to pieces, and afterward put a rifle bullet exactly through the hole into which the pin fitted."

The voyage up the Mississippi to Natchez appears to have been without any circumstance of importance. Under date March 24th, 1822, the naturalist records the fact that he had arrived at Natchez. "I went ashore to see after work—called on Mr. Quigley, who received me cordially. I had prospects of an engagement with Mr. Quaglass, a Portuguese gentleman, who wished me to give lessons in drawing and music and French to his daughter, thirteen years of age. I was received at his house, and received a welcome from his wife. Mr. Quaglass arrived at home in the evening, and his appearance was by no means prepossessing. His small gray eyes and corrugated brows did not afford me an opportunity of passing a favorable judgment. My time has been mostly engaged in hunting, drawing, and attending to my charge. I constantly regret the separation from my family."

Ere long he got an appointment to teach drawing in the college at Washington, nine miles from Natchez. He sent for his sons, and put them to school at Washington, but was depressed in spirits because his work interfered with his ornithological pursuits.

"*July* 8. Constant exposure in the tropical climate, and the fatigue of my journeys to and from Washington, brought on fever and a renewal of a certain kind doctor's attendance, who not only would accept of no remuneration, but actually insisted on my taking his purse to pay for the expenses connected with the education of my sons. Shortly afterwards I made an engagement with Mr. Brevost to teach drawing in an academy just opened in Natchez by that gentleman. But while work flowed upon me, the hope of my completing my book upon the birds of America became less clear ; and full of despair, I feared my hopes of becoming known to Europe as a naturalist were destined to be blasted. I wrote to my wife to join me at Natchez, and there was hopes of it being accomplished.

"*July* 23. My friend, Joseph Mason, left me to-day, and we experienced great pain at parting. I gave him paper and chalks to work his way with, and the double-barrelled gun I had killed most of my birds with, and which I had purchased at Philadelphia in 1805. I also began to copy the 'Death of Montgomery,' from a print. My drawing was highly praised by my friends at Natchez, and Dr. Provan, like a good genius, insisted it should be raffled. I valued it at three hundred dollars, and Dr. Provan sold all the tickets but one, at ten dollars each. He then put my name down for that, saying he hoped it would be the winning one. The raffle took place in my absence, and when I returned, my friend the doctor came and brought me three hundred dollars and the picture, beautifully framed, saying, 'Your number has drawn it, and the subscribers are all agreed that no one is more deserving of it than yourself.' "

"*September* 1. My wife writes to me that the child she was in charge of is dead, and that consequently she had determined to come on to Natchez. I received her with great pleasure at the landing, and immediately got a house hired, in which we might resume housekeeping. In the mean time my wife engaged with a clergyman named Davis, in a situation similar to that which she had held in New Orleans. I was much pleased with the conduct of Mr. Quaglass, whose kindness of heart very much belied his coarse exterior.

"*October* 27. I met a gentleman from Mexico, who proposed to me to go to Mexico and establish a paper-mill in that country. He proposed to supply the funds if I took care of the mill. At Natchez I met Mr. Murray, formerly of Charleston, and Mr. Blackburn, formerly of Cincinnati. They had both suffered heavy reverses of fortune, and appeared to me to be in distress. Their change of fortune was sufficient to reconcile me to my own vexations.

"*November* 3. While engaged in sketching a view of Natchez, an English gentleman named Leacock was introduced to me as a naturalist. He called and spent the evening with me, and examined my drawings, and advised me to visit England and take them with me. But when he said I should probably have to spend several years to perfect them, and to make myself known, I closed my drawings and turned my mind from the thought. My wife, finding it difficult to get her salary for teaching, has resolved to relinquish her situation."

In December there arrived at Natchez a portrait-painter, from whom Audubon received his first lessons in the use of oil colors, and who was in return instructed by the naturalist in chalk drawing. Mrs. Audubon was desirous that her husband should go to Europe, and obtain complete instruction in the use of oil; and with this aim in view she entered into an engagement with a Mrs. Percy to educate her children, along with her own and a limited number of pupils. Mrs. Percy lived at Bayou Sara, and thither Mrs. Audubon removed, while her husband remained at Natchez, painting with his friend Stein, the artist whose instructions in oil painting had been so valuable. After enjoying all the patronage to be expected at Natchez, Audubon and his friend Stein resolved to start on an expedition as perambulating portrait-painters; and purchasing a wagon, prepared for a long expedition through the Southern States.

"I had finally determined to break through all bonds, and pursue my ornithological pursuits. My best friends solemnly regarded me as a madman, and my wife and family alone gave me encouragement. My wife determined that my genius should prevail, and that my final success as an ornithologist should be triumphant.

"*March*, 1823. My preparations for leaving Natchez almost complete.

"*May* 1. Left Mr. Percy's on a visit to Jackson, Mississippi, which I found to be a mean place, a rendezvous for gamblers and vagabonds. Disgusted with the place and the people, I left it and returned to my wife. I agreed to remain with the Percys throughout the summer, and teach the young ladies music and drawing. I continued to exercise myself in painting with oil, and greatly improved myself. I undertook to paint the portraits of my wife's pupils, but found their complexions difficult to transfer to canvas. On account of some misunderstanding, I left the Percy's and returned to Natchez, but did not know what course to follow. I thought of going to Philadelphia, and again thought of going to Louisville and once more entering upon mercantile pursuits, but had no money to move anywhere."

During a visit to a plantation near Natchez, both he and his son Victor were attacked with fever, and Mrs. Audubon hastened to nurse both of them.

"*September* 8. I was asked to go and recruit my health at the Percys, and I went to Bayou Sara. I sent on my drawings to Philadelphia, and resolved to visit that city and obtain employment as a teacher.

"*September* 30. Sold a note for services in Natchez, and with proceeds took steamer to New Orleans.

"*October* 3. Left New Orleans for Kentucky, where I intended to leave my son Victor with my wife's relations, and proceed on my travels. I left Bayou Sara with my son Victor on board the steamer Magnet, bound for the Ohio, and was kindly treated by Captain McKnight,

the commander. After a pleasant voyage we arrived at
the beautiful village of Trinity, but found the water too
low for further navigation. I had resolved to push on my
journey, if Victor was strong enough to undertake the exertion. Two other passengers desired to accompany us,
and after I had left my luggage to the care of the tavern-
keeper, our party crossed Cash Creek, at which I had before spent a pleasant time, and pushed across the country. Victor, who was scarcely fourteen, was a lively boy,
and had no fear of failing. Cleaving our way, Indian-file
fashion, through the cane brakes—through the burnt
forest—through the brushwood-clad banks of the river,
and along the pebbly shore, we reached, after twelve
miles' walking, the village of America. After refreshing
ourselves we covered another seven miles, and reached a
cabin, where we were well received by a squatter family.

"After a bath in the Ohio, my son and myself joined
the rest, and we enjoyed an excellent supper, and a capital sleep in such beds as could be provided. We rose at
break of day and left our kind host and hostess, who
would receive no pecuniary reward. At seven miles
further we found an excellent breakfast at a house owned
by a very lazy fellow, whose beautiful wife appeared to be
superior to her station, and who conducted the household
affairs in a very agreeable manner. We left a dollar
with one of the children, and pursued our way along the
beach of the Ohio. After proceeding some distance, my
son Victor broke down, but after a rest he suddenly revived at the sight of a wild turkey, and resumed his journey in good spirits. We reached Belgrade and continued
our journey. Towards sunset we reached the shores of
the river, opposite the mouth of the Cumberland. On a
hill, the property of Major B., we found a house and a
solitary woman, wretchedly poor, but very kind. She assured us that if we could not cross the river, she would

give us food and shelter for the night, but said that as the moon was up, she could get us put over when her skiff came back. Hungry and fatigued, we lay down on the brown grass, waiting either a scanty meal, or the skiff that was to convey us across the river. I had already grated the corn for our supper, run down the chickens, and made a fire, when a cry of ' Boat coming !' roused us all. We crossed the river Ohio, and I again found myself in Kentucky, the native state of my two sons. We then pursued our onward journey, but my son suffered sorely from lameness. As we trudged along, nothing remarkable occurred excepting that we saw a fine black wolf, quite tame and gentle, the owner of which had refused a hundred dollars for it. Mr. Rose, who was an engineer, and a man of taste, played on the flageolet to lighten our journey. At an orchard we filled our pockets with October peaches, and when we came to Trade Water river we found it low ; the acorns were already drifted on its shallows, and the ducks were running about picking them up. Passing a flat bottom, we saw a large buffalo lick.

"We reached Highland Lick, where we stumbled on a cabin, the door of which we thrust open, overturning a chair that had been put behind it. On a dirty bed lay a man, a table, with a journal, or perhaps ledger, before him, a small cask in the corner near him, a brass pistol on a nail over his head, and a long Spanish dagger by his side. He arose and asked what we wanted ? ' The way to a better place, the road to Sugg's.' ' Follow the road, and you will get to his house in about five miles.' Separating from our companions, who were unable to proceed at the same pace, we reached Green River, were ferried across, and shortly afterwards reached Louisville."

"On the 25th October, 1822," writes Audubon, " I entered Louisville with thirteen dollars in my pocket.

My son Victor I managed to get into the counting-house of a friend, and I engaged to paint the interior of a steamer. I was advised to make a painting of the falls of the Ohio, and commenced the work.

" *November* 9. Busy at work, when the weather permitted, and resolved to paint one hundred views of American scenery. I shall not be surprised to find myself seated at the foot of Niagara."

While painting he mainly resided at Shipping Port, a little village near Louisville. In his journey between Green River and Louisville, he took conveyance in a cart, the owner agreeing to drive the distance. In doing so, the driver missed his route, and in a storm went far off the way. The horses instinctively led the way to a log hut, inhabited by a newly-married pair, who did their utmost to show befitting hospitality. In the midst of a hurricane the host rode off to his father's, some miles distant, for a keg of cider ; the wife baked bread and roasted fowls, and finally determined to sleep on the floor, so that the strangers might have the comfort of a bed.

Of such hospitality Audubon speaks highly, and seems to lament its decadence among residents in the more civilized states of the Union. Some notes upon the effects of the floods which swell American rivers into inland seas are also contained in the journal of his residence at Louisville. Writing of the devastation created by overflows of the Mississippi, he remarks :—

" The river rises until its banks are flooded and the levees overflown. It then sweeps inland, over swamps, prairie, and forest, until the country is a turbid ocean, checkered by masses and strips of the forest, through which the flood rolls lazily down cypress-shadowed glades under the gloomy pines, and into unexplored recesses, where the trailing vine and umbrageous foliage dim the light of the noonday sun. In islets left amid the

5

waste, deer in thousands are driven; and the squatter,
with his gun and canoe, finds on these refuges the game
which he slaughters remorselessly for the skins or feathers that will sell. Floating on a raft made fast by a vine
rope to some stout trees, the farmer and his family preserve their lives, while the stream bears away their habitation, their cut wood, their stores of grain, their stock,
and all their household goods. From creeks of the forest
other rafts float, laden with produce for New Orleans, and
guided by adventurous boatmen who have but vague
knowledge of their devious way, and to whom the navigation of an inland river is not less hazardous than a voyage on a stormy sea would be.

"I have floated on the Mississippi and Ohio when
thus swollen, and have in different places visited the submerged lands of the interior, propelling a light canoe by
the aid of a paddle. In this manner I have traversed
immense portions of the country overflowed by the waters
of these rivers, and particularly whilst floating over the
Mississippi bottom lands I have been struck with awe at
the sight. Little or no current is met with, unless when
the canoe passes over the bed of a bayou. All is silent
and melancholy, unless when the mournful bleating of
the hemmed in deer reaches your ear, or the dismal
scream of an eagle or a heron is heard, or the foul bird
rises, disturbed by your approach, from the carcass on
which it was allaying its craving appetite. Bears, cougars, lynxes, and all other quadrupeds that can ascend
the trees, are observed crouched among their top branches; hungry in the midst of abundance, although they see
floating around them the animals on which they usually
prey. They dare not venture to swim to them. Fatigued by the exertions which they have made in reaching dry land, they will there stand the hunter's fire, as if
to die by a ball were better than to perish amid the waste

of waters. On occasions like this, all these animals are shot by hundreds.

"Opposite the city of Natchez, which stands on a bluff bank of considerable elevation, the extent of inundated land is immense, the greater portion of the tract lying between the Mississippi and the Red River, which is more than thirty miles, being under water."

CHAPTER VIII.

Audubon reaches Philadelphia — Introduction to Sully the Painter — Introduction to the Prince of Conino — A Gigantic Engraver — Meetings with Rosier and Joseph Mason — Visit to Mill Grove and Fatland — A noble Gift — Audubon leaves Philadelphia — Arrival at New York — Meeting with Joseph Bonaparte — Leaves New York, and arrives at Albany — Visit to Niagara — A Voyage down the Ohio to the South — Arrival at Cincinnati — Voyage to Bayou Sara — Meeting Mrs. Audubon — Turns Dancing-master.

AUDUBON reached Philadelphia on April 5, 1824. The journey to that city was undertaken as a desperate venture to obtain help to complete his ornithological work, and he was soon satisfied that the venture would be successful.

"I purchased a new suit of clothes, and dressed myself with extreme neatness; after which I called upon Dr. Mease, an old friend. I was received with kindness, and was introduced to a gentleman named Earle, who exhibited my drawings. I was also introduced to several artists, who paid me pleasant attentions, and I also obtained entrance to the Philadelphia Athenæum and Philosophical Library. I was fortunate in obtaining an introduction to the portrait-painter, Sully, a man after my own heart, and who showed me great kindnesses. He was a beautiful singer, and an artist whose hints and advice were of great service to me. I afterwards saw Sully in London, where he was painting a portrait of the Queen of England, and had an opportunity of returning his kindnesses.

"*April* 10. I was introduced to the Prince Canino, son of Lucien, and nephew of Napoleon Buonaparte, who examined my birds, and was complimentary in his praises. He was at the time engaged on a volume of American birds, which was soon to be published; but this did not prevent him from admiring another naturalist's work.

"*April* 12. Met the prince at Dr. Mease's, and he expressed a wish to examine my drawings more particularly. I found him very gentlemanly. He called in his carriage, took me to Peale, the artist, who was drawing specimens of birds for his work; but from want of knowledge of the habits of birds in a wild state, he represented them as if seated for a portrait, instead of with their own lively animated ways when seeking their natural food or pleasure. Other notable persons called to see my drawings, and encouraged me with their remarks. The Prince of Canino introduced me to the Academy of Arts and Sciences, and pronounced my birds superb, and worthy of a pupil of David. I formed the acquaintance of Le Sueur, the zoologist and artist, who was greatly delighted with my drawings.

"*April* 14. After breakfast met the prince, who called with me on Mr. Lawson, the engraver of Mr. Wilson's plates. This gentleman's figure nearly reached the roof, his face was sympathetically long, and his tongue was so long that we obtained no opportunity of speaking in his company. Lawson said my drawings were too soft, too much like oil paintings, and objected to engrave them. Mr. Fairman we found to be an engraver better able to appreciate my drawings, but he strongly advised me to go to England, to have them engraved in a superior manner.

"*April* 15. I obtained a room, and commenced work in earnest. Prince Canino engaged me to superintend his drawings intended for publication, but my terms being much dearer than Alexander Wilson's, I was asked to discontinue this work. I had now determined to go to Europe with my ' treasures,' since I was assured nothing so fine in the way of ornithological representations existed. I worked incessantly to complete my series of drawings. On inquiry, I found Sully and Le Sueur made a poor living by their brush. I had some pupils offered at a dollar per lesson ; but I found the citizens unwilling to pay for art, although they affected to patronize it. I exhibited my drawings for a week, but found the show did not pay, and so determined to remove myself. I was introduced to Mr. Ensel of Boston, an entomologist, then engaged upon a work on American spiders. Those interested in Wilson's book on the American birds advised me not to publish, and not only cold water, but ice, was poured upon my undertaking. Had a visit from my old partner Rosier, who was still thirsting for money.

" *May* 30. My dear friend Joseph Mason paid me a delightful visit to-day. Showed all my drawings to Titian Peel, who in return refused to let me see a new bird in his possession. This little incident filled me with grief at the narrow spirit of humanity, and makes me wish for the solitude of the woods.

" *June* 12. Giving lessons in drawing at thirty dollars per month. A visit from Rembrandt Peale, who liked my drawings, and asked me to his studio, where I saw his portrait of General Washington, but preferred the style of Sully. Had a visit from Mr. McMurtrie, the naturalist, whose study of shells has made him famous. He advised me to take my drawings to England. I labor assiduously at oil painting. I have now been twenty five years pursuing my ornithological studies. Prince Canino often visited me and admired my drawings. He advised me to go to France. The French consul was still warmer in his sympathies, and kind in his encouraging assurances.

" *June* 26. Anxious to carry out my project of a visit to Europe—anxious to see my wife before leaving—anxious to see my old quarters of Mill Grove—anxious to get more instruction from my kind master, Sully; and altogether unable to settle what course would be the most preferable. I was rejoiced at the progress I made in oil painting, and was overwhelmed with the goodness of Sully, who would receive no recompense for his instructions, and gave me all the possible encouragement which his affectionate heart could dictate.

" *July* 12. Visited by Mr. Gilpin, who thirty-three years ago discovered the lead ore at Mill Grove. Called on Dr. Harlan, an amiable physician and naturalist, and a member of the Academy of Arts and Sciences. Gave him some of my drawings, and he promised me letters to the Royal Academy of France, and afterwards nominated me for membership to the Academy in Philadelphia. He was one of the best men I have met with in the city, and the very best among the naturalists."

This was the beginning of a warm friendship between these two good men, which increased with time, and lasted until the doctor died. At the same time Audubon formed a friendship with Edward Harris, a young ornithologist of refinement, wealth, and education, who outlived Audubon, and extended prompt relief to his wife during her distress after her husband's death. When the naturalist was about to leave Philadelphia, Harris purchased some of his drawings, and on being offered his picture of the Falls of the Ohio, at a sacrifice, declined the purchase, but as he was saying good-bye, squeezed a hundred-dollar bill into his friend's hand, saying, " Mr. Audubon, accept this from me ; men like you ought not to want for money."

" I could only express my gratitude by insisting on his receiving the drawings of all my French birds, which ·

he did, and I was relieved. This is the second instance of disinterested generosity I have met with in my life, the good Dr. Provan of Natchez being the other. And now I have in hand one hundred and thirty dollars to begin my journey of three thousand miles. Before this I have always thought I could work my way through the world by my industry; but I see that I shall have to leave here, as Wilson often did, without a cent in my pocket.

" *July* 26. Reuben Haines, a generous friend, invited me to visit Mill Grove in his carriage, and I was impatient until the day came. His wife, a beautiful woman, and her daughter, accompanied us. On the way my heart swelled with many thoughts of what my life had been there, of the scenes I had passed through since, and of my condition now. As we entered the avenue leading to Mill Grove, every step brought to my mind the memory of past years, and I was bewildered by the recollections until we reached the door of the house, which had once been the residence of my father as well as myself. The cordial welcome of Mr. Wetherill, the owner, was extremely agreeable. After resting a few moments, I abruptly took my hat and ran wildly towards the woods, to the grotto where I first heard from my wife the acknowledgment that she was not indifferent to me. It had been torn down, and some stones carted away; but raising my eyes towards heaven, I repeated the promise we had mutually made. We dined at Mill Grove, and as I entered the parlor I stood motionless for a moment on the spot where my wife and myself were for ever joined. Everybody was kind to me, and invited me to come to the Grove whenever I visited Pennsylvania, and I returned full of delight. Gave Mr. Haines my portrait, drawn by myself, on condition that he should have it copied in case of my death before making another, and send it to my wife.

" *July* 31. Engaged in preparations for leaving Philadelphia, where I received many letters of introduction. Among them are the following :—

"' GILBERT STUART, ESQ.,

"' DEAR SIR,

"' It is hardly necessary for Mr. Audubon to take credentials for an introduction to you ; the inspection of one of his drawings of birds will be sufficient recommendation to your notice. Yet an acquaintance with him of several months enables me to speak of him as a man, and I would consent to forfeit all claims to discernment of character if he does not merit your esteem.

" ' Sincerely your friend,
"' THOMAS SULLY.'"

"' WASHINGTON ALSTON, ESQ.,

"' DEAR SIR,

"' Mr. Audubon will call on you with this, and will be pleased to show you specimens of his drawings in ornithology. He is engaged in preparing a work on this subject for publication, which for copiousness and talent bids fair in my estimation to surpass all that has yet been done, at least in this country. I have great esteem for the character of Mr. Audubon, and am pleased to make him known to you, though I should hesitate to give a letter of introduction to you in favor of an ordinary person, knowing that your time is precious ; but in the present instance I run no risk of intrusion. I shall always remember you with affectionate regard.

" ' Sincerely your friend,
"' THOMAS SULLY.'"

A letter of similar import was given by Mr. Sully to Colonel Trumbull.

" *August* 1, 1824. I left Philadelphia for New York yesterday at five o'clock, in good health, free from debt

5*

and free from anxiety about the future. On arriving at New York a cart took our luggage to our lodgings, and about one hundred passengers perched about us, as I have seen chimney-swallows perched on a roof before their morning flight. I felt happy and comfortable in the city, and sauntered about admiring its beautiful streets and landings. I found most of the parties to whom I carried letters of introduction absent, and I already began to regret leaving Philadelphia so hurriedly. I began to consider whether I should visit Albany or Boston, in the hope of improving my financial position.

"*August* 2. Met Joseph Buonaparte, and his two daughters, and his nephew, Charles, Prince of Canino. Visited the museum at New York, and found the specimens of stuffed birds set up in unnatural and constrained attitudes. This appears to be the universal practice, and the world owes to me the adoption of the plan of drawing from animated nature. Wilson is the only one who has in any tolerable degree adopted my plan.

"*August* 3. Called on Vanderlyn, and was kindly received by him. Examined his pictures with pleasure, and saw the medal given him by Napoleon, but was not impressed with the idea that he was a great painter.

"*August* 4. Called on Dr. Mitchell with my letters of introduction, who gave me a kind letter to his friend Dr. Barnes, explaining that I wished to show my drawings to the members of the Lyceum, and become a member of that institution.

"*August* 9. I have been making inquiries regarding the publication of my drawings in New York; but find that there is little prospect of the undertaking being favorably received. I have reason to suspect that unfriendly communications have been sent to the publishers from Philadelphia, by parties interested in Wilson's

volume, and who have represented that my drawings have
not been wholly done by myself. Full of despair, I look
to Europe as my only hope. With my friend Dr. De Kay
I visited the Lyceum, and my portfolio was examined by
the members of the institute, among whom I felt awkward
and uncomfortable. After living among such people I
feel clouded and depressed; remember that I have done
nothing, and fear I may die unknown. I feel I am strange
to all but the birds of America. In a few days I shall be
in the woods and quite forgotten.

"*August* 10. My spirits low, and I long for the
woods again; but the prospect of becoming known
prompts me to remain another day. Met the artist Vanderlyn, who asked me to give him a sitting for a portrait
of General Jackson, since my figure considerably resembled that of the General, more than any he had ever
seen. I likewise sketched my landlady and child, and
filled my time.

"*August* 15. Sailed up the Hudson for Albany with
three hundred and seventy-five passengers, twenty-three
of whom were composed of a delegation of Indians from
six tribes, who were returning to the West from Washington. Arrived at Albany, but found both De Witt Clinton
and Dr. Beck absent. Money getting scarce, I abandoned
the idea of visiting Boston, but determined to see Niagara.
Engaged a passage at seven dollars on a canal-boat for
Rochester, distant two hundred and sixty-eight miles.
No incident happened to me worth recording, only that
the passengers were doubtful whether or not I was a
government officer, commissioner, or spy. I obtained
some new birds by the way, and in six days I arrived at
Rochester.

"*Rochester, August* 22. Five years ago there were
but few buildings here, and the population is now five
thousand; the banks of the river are lined with mills

and factories. The beautiful falls of the Genesee river,
about eighty feet high and four times as broad, I have
visited, and have made a slight sketch of them. One and
a half miles below is another fall of the same height, but
the water is much more broken in its descent.

"*August* 24. Took passage for Buffalo, arrived safely,
and passed a sleepless night, as most of my nights have
been since I began my wanderings. Left next morning
for the Falls of Niagara; the country is poor, the soil
stiff white clay, and the people are lank and sallow.
Arrived at the hotel, found but few visitors, recorded my
name, and wrote under it, 'who, like Wilson, will ramble,
but never, like that great man, die under the lash of a
bookseller.'

"All trembling I reached the Falls of Niagara, and oh,
what a scene! my blood shudders still, although I am not
a coward, at the grandeur of the Creator's power; and I
gazed motionless on this new display of the irresistible
force of one of His elements. The falls, the rainbow,
the rapids, and the surroundings all unite to strike the
senses with awe; they defy description with pen or pencil; and a view satisfied me that Niagara never had been
and never will be painted. I moved towards the rapids,
over which there is a bridge to Goat island, that I would
like to have crossed, to look on the water which was
rushing with indescribable swiftness below, but was
deterred from the low state of my funds. Walking along
the edge of the stream for a few hundred yards, the full
effect of the whole grand rush of the water was before
me. The color of the water was a verdigris green, and
contrasted remarkably with the falling torrent. The mist
of the spray mounted to the clouds, while the roaring
below sounded like constant heavy thunder, making me
think at times that the earth was shaking also.

"From this point I could see three-quarters of a mile

down the river, which appeared quite calm. I descended a flight of about seventy steps, and walked and crouched on my hams along a rugged, slippery path to the edge of the river, where a man and skiff are always waiting to take visitors to the opposite shore. I approached as near the falling water as I could, without losing sight of the objects behind me. In a few moments my clothes were wet. I retired a few hundred yards to admire two beautiful rainbows, which seemed to surround me, and also looked as if spanning obliquely from the American to the Canadian shore. Visitors can walk under the falling sheet of water, and see through it, while at their feet are thousands of eels lying side by side, trying vainly to ascend the torrent.

" I afterwards strolled through the village to find some bread and milk, and ate a good dinner for twelve cents. Went to bed at night thinking of Franklin eating his roll in the streets of Philadelphia, of Goldsmith travelling by the help of his musical powers, and of other great men who had worked their way through hardships and difficulties to fame, and fell asleep, hoping, by persevering industry, to make a name for myself among my countrymen.

" *Buffalo, August* 25. This village was utterly destroyed by fire in the war of eighteen hundred and twelve, but now has about two hundred houses, a bank, and daily mail. It is now filled with Indians, who have come here to receive their annuity from the government. The chief Red Jacket is a noble-looking man ; another, called the Devil's Ramrod, has a savage look. Took a deck-passage on board a schooner bound to Erie, Pennsylvania ; fare, one dollar and fifty cents, to furnish my own bed and provisions ; my buffalo-robe and blanket served for the former. The captain invited me to sleep in the cabin, but I declined, as I never encroach where I

have no right.   The sky was serene, and I threw myself
on the deck contemplating the unfathomable immensity
above me, and contrasting the comforts which only ten
days before I was enjoying with my present condition.
Even the sailors, ignorant of my name, look on me as a
poor devil not able to pay for a cabin passage.

"In our voyage we had safely run the distance to
Presque Isle Harbor, but could not pass the bar on
account of a violent gale.   The anchor was dropped,
and we remained on board during the night.   How long
we might have remained at anchor I cannot tell, had not
Captain Judd, of the United States Navy, then probably
commandant at Presque Isle, sent a gig with six men to
our relief.   It was on the 29th of August, 1824, and
never shall I forget that morning.   My drawings were
put into the boat with the greatest care.   We shifted into
it, and seated ourselves according to direction.   Our
brave fellows pulled hard, and every moment brought us
nearer to the American shore ; I leaped upon it with
elated heart.   My drawings were safely landed, and for
any thing else I cared little at the moment.   After a
humble meal of bread and milk, a companion and myself
settled to proceed upon our journey.   Our luggage was
rather heavy, so we hired a cart to take it to Meadville,
for which we offered five dollars.   This sum was accepted,
and we set off.

"The country through which we passed might have
proved favorable to our pursuits, had it not rained nearly
the whole day.   At night we alighted, and put up at a
house belonging to our conductor's father.   It was Sunday night.   The good folks had not yet returned from a
distant church, the grandmother of our driver being the
only individual about the premises.   We found her a
cheerful dame, who bestirred herself actively, got up a
blazing fire to dry our wet clothes, and put bread and

milk on the table. We asked for a place in which to rest, and were shown into a room in which were several beds. My companion and myself were soon in bed and asleep; but our slumbers were broken by a light, which we found to be carried by three young damsels, who, having observed where we lay, blew it out and got into a bed opposite ours. As we had not spoken, the girls supposed we were sound asleep, and we heard them say how delighted they would be to have their portraits taken as well as their grandmother, whose likeness I had promised to draw. Day dawned, and as we were dressing we discovered the girls had dressed in silence and left us before we had awakened. No sooner had I offered to draw the portraits of the girls than they disappeared, and soon returned in their Sunday clothes. The black chalk was at work in a few minutes, to their great delight; and while the flavor of the breakfast reached my sensitive nose, I worked with redoubled ardor. The sketches were soon finished, and the breakfast over. I played a few airs on my flageolet while our guide was putting the horses to the cart, and by ten o'clock we were once more on the road to Meadville.

"The country was covered with heavy timber, principally evergreens; the pines and cucumber trees, loaded with brilliant fruits, and the spruce, throwing a shade over the land, in good keeping with the picture. The lateness of the crops alone struck us as unpleasant. At length we came in sight of French Creek, and soon after we reached Meadville. Here we paid the five dollars promised to our conductor, who instantly faced about, and applying the whip to his nags, bade us adieu.

"We had now only one dollar and fifty cents. No time was to be lost. We put our luggage and ourselves under the roof of a tavern-keeper, known by the name of J. F. Smith, at the sign of the 'Travellers' Rest,' and

soon after took a walk to survey the little village that
was to be laid under contribution for our support. Putting my portfolio under my arm, and a few good credentials in my pocket, I walked up the main street, looking
to the right and left, examining the different *heads* which
occurred, until I fixed my eyes on a gentleman in a store
who looked as if he might want a sketch. I begged him
to allow me to sit down. This granted, I remained perfectly silent, and he soon asked me what was in that
'portfolio.' The words sounded well, and without waiting another instant I opened it to his view. He was a
Hollander, who complimented me on the execution of the
drawings of birds and flowers in my portfolio. Showing
him a sketch of the best friend I have in the world at
present, I asked him if he would like one in the same
style of himself. He not only answered in the affirmative, but assured me that he would exert himself in procuring as many more customers as he could. I thanked
him, and returned to the 'Travellers' Rest' with a hope
that to-morrow might prove propitious. Supper was
ready, and we began our meal. I was looked on as a
missionary priest, on account of my hair, which in those
days flowed loosely on my shoulders. I was asked to
say grace, which I did with a fervent spirit. Next morning I visited the merchant, and succeeded in making a
sketch of him that pleased him highly. While working
at him the room became crowded with the village aris-
tocracy. Some laughed, while others expressed their
wonder, but my work went on. My sitter invited me to
spend the evening with him, which I did, and joined him
in some music on the flute and violin. I returned to my
companion with great pleasure; and you may judge how
much that pleasure was increased when I found that he
also had made two sketches. Having written a page or
two of our journals, we retired to rest. With our pockets

replenished we soon afterwards left for Pittsburg, where we arrived in safety.

"*September* 7. I was more politely received than on former occasions at Pittsburg, which I found was due to the reception I had met with in Philadelphia, and some rumors of which had reached the West.

"*October* 9. Spent one month at Pittsburg scouring the country for birds, and continuing my drawings. Made the acquaintance of the Rev. John H. Hopkins. Found him an amiable man, and attended some of his ministrations. I met a Mr. Baldwin, who volunteered to subscribe for my book of birds—the three hundredth name given to me. In the course of my intimacy with the Rev. Mr. Hopkins I was brought to think more than I usually did of religious matters; but I confess I never think of churches without feeling sick at heart at the sham and show of some of their professors. To repay evils with kindness is the religion I was taught to practise, and this will for ever be my rule.

"*October* 24. For some days I have been meditating on purchasing a skiff and going down the Ohio and Mississippi in it, as I had done years before. I purchased a boat, and filling it with provisions, bade my friends adieu, and started in company with an artist, a doctor, and an Irishman. I hauled up the boat at night and slept in it.

"*October* 29. Reached Wheeling after suffering much from wet and rain. The artist and doctor were disgusted with boating, and left. The Irishman was tired of his bargain. My finances were very low. I tried to sell some lithographs of General Lafayette, but did not succeed. I sold my skiff, and took passage in a keel-boat to Cincinnati, with a lot of passengers, army officers, and others. I arrived at Cincinnati, visited my old house, and met many old friends in that city.

"While at Cincinnati I was beset by claims for the payment of articles which years before had been ordered for the Museum, but from which I got no benefit. Without money or the means of making it, I applied to Messrs. Keating and Bell for the loan of fifteen dollars, but had not the courage to do so until I had walked past their house several times, unable to make up my mind how to ask the favor. I got the loan cheerfully, and took a deck-passage to Louisville. I was allowed to take my meals in the cabin, and at night slept among some shavings I managed to scrape together. The spirit of contentment which I now feel is strange, it borders on the sublime ; and, enthusiast or lunatic, as some of my relatives will have me, I am glad to possess such a spirit.

"*Louisville, November* 20. Took lodgings at the house of a person to whom I had given lessons, and hastened to Shippingport to see my son Victor. Received a letter from General Jackson, with an introduction to the Governor of Florida. I discover that my friends think only of my apparel, and those upon whom I have conferred acts of kindness prefer to remind me of my errors. I decide to go down the Mississippi to my old home of Bayou Sara, and there open a school, with the profits of which to complete my ornithological studies. Engage a passage for eight dollars.

"I arrived at Bayou Sara with rent and wasted clothes and uncut hair, and altogether looking like the Wandering Jew.

"The steamer which brought me was on her way to New Orleans, and I was put ashore in a small boat about midnight, and left to grope my way on a dark, rainy, and sultry night to the village, about one mile distant. That awful scourge the yellow fever prevailed, and was taking off the citizens with greater rapidity than had ever before been known. When I arrived, the desolation was so great that one large hotel was deserted, and I walked in, finding the doors all open, and the furniture in the house, but not a living person. The inmates had all gone to the pine woods. I walked to the post-office, roused the postmaster, and learned to my joy that my wife and son were well at Mrs. Percy's. He had no accommodation for me, but recommended me to a tavern where I might find a bed. The atmosphere was calm, heavy, and suffocating, and it seemed to me as if I were breathing death while hunting for this tavern; finding it, the landlord told me he had not a spare bed, but mentioned a German at the end of the village who might take me in; I walked over there, and was kindly received. The German was a man of cultivation and taste, and a lover of natural science, and had collected a variety of interesting objects. He gave me some refreshment, and offered me a horse to ride to Mrs. Percy's. The horse was soon at the door, and with many thanks I bade him adieu. My anxiety to reach my beloved wife and child was so great that I resolved to make a straight course through the woods, which I thought I knew thoroughly, and hardly caring where I should cross the bayou. In less than two hours I reached its shores, but the horse refused to enter the water, and snorting suddenly, turned and made off through the woods, as if desirous of crossing at some other place, and when he reached the shore again walked in, and crossed me safely to the other side. The sky was overcast, and the mosquitoes plentiful; but I thought I recognized the spot where I had watched the habits of a wild cat, or a deer, as the clouds broke away, and the stars now and then peeped through to help me make my way through the gloomy forests. But in this I was mistaken, for when day dawned I found myself in woods which were unknown to me. However, I chanced to meet a black man, who told me where I was, and that I had passed Mrs. Percy's plantation two miles. Turning my horse's head, and putting spurs to him, a brisk gallop soon brought me to the house. It was early, but I found my beloved wife up and engaged in giving a lesson to her pupils, and, holding and kissing her, I was once more happy, and all my toils and trials were forgotten.

" *December* 1. After a few days' rest I began to think of the future, and to look about to see what I could do to hasten the publication of my drawings. My wife was receiving a large income,—nearly three thousand dollars a year,—from her industry and talents, which she generously offered me to help forward their publication ; and I resolved on a new effort to increase the amount by my own energy and labor. Numerous pupils desired lessons in music, French, and drawing. From Woodville I received a special invitation to teach dancing, and a class of sixty was soon organized. I went to begin my duties, dressed myself at the hotel, and with my fiddle under my arm entered the ball-room. I found my music highly appreciated, and immediately commenced proceedings.

" I placed all the gentlemen in a line reaching across the hall, thinking to give the young ladies time to compose themselves and get ready when they were called. How I toiled before I could get one graceful step or motion ! I broke my bow and nearly my violin in my excitement and impatience ! The gentlemen were soon fatigued. The ladies were next placed in the same order and made to walk the steps ; and then came the trial for both parties to proceed at the same time, while I pushed one here and another there, and was all the while singing myself, to assist their movements. Many of the parents were present, and were delighted. After this first lesson was over I was requested to *dance to my own music*, which

I did until the whole room came down in thunders of applause, in clapping of hands and shouting, which put an end to my first lesson and to an amusing comedy. Lessons in fencing followed to the young gentlemen, and I went to bed extremely fatigued.

"The dancing speculation fetched two thousand dollars; and with this capital and my wife's savings I was now able to foresee a successful issue to my great ornithological work."

The remainder of Audubon's residence at Bayou Sara was taken up with preparations for his intended voyage to England,—where he expected to find the fame given to all heroes so tardily in their own countries.

CHAPTER IX.

PRIL 26*th*, 1826. I left my wife and son at Bayou Sara for New Orleans on my way to England, and engaged a passage to Liverpool on board the ship Delos. The vessel did not sail as soon as expected, and I was necessarily delayed at New Orleans. I obtained several letters of introduction from persons in New Orleans to friends in England, and one from Governor Johnson of Louisiana with the seal of the State on it, which saved me the trouble of getting a passport.

" On the 19th of May the steam-tug Hercules towed the Delos out to sea, and with light winds we pursued our voyage. The time was pleasantly spent shooting birds and catching dolphins and sharks, from which I made frequent sketches.

" *May* 27. Had Mother Carey's chickens following us, and desired to get one of the beautiful birds as they swept past, pattering the water with their feet, and returning after long ranges for scraps of oil and fat floated astern. I dropped one with my gun, and the captain kindly ordered a boat to be lowered to recover the shot bird. I examined the bird and found it to be a female.

" *May* 31. Saw a small vessel making towards us; she was a suspicious-looking craft, and our crew had pardonable fears she might prove to be a pirate. A young fat alligator I had with me died to-day, from being placed in salt instead of fresh water—the former being poisonous to the animal.

"Much troubled with anxious thoughts about the purport and expectations of my voyage to England. I had obtained many favorable letters of introduction to friends in England, which I believed would prove of material assistance, and among these was the following :—

" 'New Orleans, May 16, 1826.

" ' Dear Sir,

" ' I have ventured to put in the hands of Mr. John J. Audubon, a gentleman of highly respectable scientific acquirements, these introductory lines to you, under the persuasion that his acquaintance cannot fail to be one of extreme interest to you. Mr. Audubon is a native of the United States, and has spent more than twenty years in all parts of them, devoting most of his time to the study of ornithology. He carries with him a collection of over four hundred drawings, which far surpass anything of the kind I have yet seen, and afford the best evidence of his skill, and the perfection to which he has carried his researches. His object is to find a purchaser or a publisher for them, and if you can aid him in this, and introduce him either in person or by letter to men of distinction in arts and sciences, you will confer much of a favor on me. He has a crowd of letters from Mr. Clay, De Witt Clinton, and others for England, which will do much for him ; but your introduction to Mr. Roscoe and others may do more. His collection of ornithological drawings would prove a most valuable acquisition to any museum, or any moneyed patron of the arts, and, I should think, convey a far better idea of American birds than all the stuffed birds of all the museums put together.

"'Permit me likewise to recommend Mr. Audubon to your hospitable attentions ; the respectability of his life and his family connections entitle him to the good wishes of any gentleman, and you will derive much gratification from his conversation.

"'I am, dear Sir,

"'With sincere regard,

"'Most truly yours,

"'VINCENT NOLTE.

"'To RICHARD RATHBONE, ESQ.,
"'Liverpool.'"

"*June* 23. Near Cape Florida. This morning we entered the Atlantic Ocean from the Florida Straits with a fair wind. The land birds have left us. I leave America and my wife and children to visit England and Europe and publish my 'Birds of America.'

"In the Gulf of Mexico our vessel was becalmed for many days ; the tedium of which we beguiled by catching fish and watching their habits. Among the others caught we were fortunate in securing several beautiful dolphins. Dolphins move in shoals varying from four or five to twenty or more, hunting in packs in the waters as wolves pursue their prey on land. The object of their pursuit is generally the flying-fish, now and then the bonita ; and when nothing better can be had they will follow the little rudder-fish and seize it immediately under the stern of the ship. The flying-fishes, after having escaped for awhile by dint of their great velocity, on being again approached by the dolphins, emerge from the water, and spreading their broad wing-like fins, sail through the air and disperse in all directions, like a covey of timid partridges before the rapacious falcon. Some pursue a direct course, others diverge on either side, but in a short time they all drop into their natural element. While they are travelling in the air their keen and hungry pursuer, like a greyhound, follows in their wake, and performing a succession of leaps many feet in extent, rapidly gains upon the quarry, which is often seized just as it falls into the sea. Dolphins manifest a very remarkable sympathy with each other. The moment one of them is hooked or grained, as sailors technically name their manner of harpooning, those in company make up to it, and remain around until the unfortunate fish is pulled on board, when they generally move off together, seldom biting at anything thrown out to them. This, however, is the case only with the larger individuals, which keep apart from the young, in the same manner as is observed in several species of birds; for when the smaller dolphins are in large shoals they all remain under the bows of the ship, and bite in succession at any sort of line, as if determined to see what has become of their lost companions. The dolphins caught in the Gulf of Mexico during our voyage were suspected to be poisonous; and to ascertain whether this was really the case, our cook, who was an African negro, never boiled or fried one without placing beside it a dollar. If the silver was not tarnished by the time the dolphin was ready for the table, the fish was presented to the passengers with the assurance that it was perfectly good. But as not a single individual of the hundred that we caught had the property of converting silver into copper, I suspect that our African sage was no magician. One morning, that of the 22nd of June, the weather sultry, I was surprised, on getting out of my hammock, which was slung on deck, to find the water all round swarming with dolphins, which were sporting in great glee. The sailors assured me that this was a certain 'token of wind,' and, as they watched the movement of the fishes, added, 'ay, and a fair breeze

6

too.' I caught several dolphins in the course of an hour, after which scarcely any remained about the ship. Not a breath of air came to our relief all that day, nor even the next.

"The best bait for the dolphin is a long strip of shark's flesh. I think it generally prefers it to the semblance of a flying-fish, which, indeed, it does not often seize unless when the ship is under weigh, and it is made to rise to the surface. There are times, however, when hunger and the absence of their usual food will induce the dolphins to dash at any sort of bait; and I have seen some caught by means of a piece of white linen fastened to a hook. Their appetite is as keen as that of the vulture; and whenever a good opportunity occurs they gorge themselves to such a degree that they become an easy prey to their enemies, the balaconda and the bottle-nosed porpoise. One that had been brained while lazily swimming immediately under the stern of our ship was found to have its stomach completely crammed with flying-fish, all regularly disposed side by side, with their tails downwards, which suggests that the dolphin swallows its prey tail foremost. They looked, in fact, like so many salted herrings packed in a box, and were, to the number of twenty-two, each six and seven inches in length. The usual length of the dolphin caught in the Gulf of Mexico is about three feet, and I saw none that exceeded four feet two inches. The weight of one of the latter size was only eighteen pounds, for this fish is extremely narrow in proportion to its length, although rather deep in its form. When just caught, the upper fin, which reaches from the forehead to within a short distance of the tail, is of a fine dark blue. The upper part of the body in its whole length is azure, and the lower parts are of a golden hue, mottled irregularly with deep blue spots.

"One day several small birds, after alighting on the

spars, betook themselves to the deck. One of them, a female rice bunting, drew our attention more particularly, for, a few moments after her arrival, there came down, as if it were in her wake, a beautiful peregrine falcon. The plunderer hovered about for awhile, then stationed himself on the end of one of the yard-arms, and suddenly pouncing on the little gleaner of the meadows, clutched her and carried her off in exultation. I was astonished to see the falcon feeding on the finch while on the wing with the same ease as the Mississippi kite shows while devouring, high in air, a red-throated lizard, swept from one of the trees of the Louisiana woods.

"One afternoon we caught two sharks. In one of them we found ten young ones alive, and quite capable of swimming, as we proved by experiment; for on casting one of them into the sea it immediately made off, as if it had been accustomed to shift for itself. Of another that had been cut in two, the head half swam out of our sight. The rest were cut in pieces, as was the old shark, as bait for the dolphins, which, I have already said, are fond of such food. Our captain, who was much intent on amusing me, informed me that the rudder-fishes were plentiful astern, and immediately set to dressing hooks for the purpose of catching them. There was now some air above us, the sails aloft filled, the ship moved through the water, and the captain and I repaired to the cabin window. I was furnished with a fine hook, a thread line, and some small bits of bacon, as was the captain, and we dropped our bait among the myriads of delicate little fishes below. Up they came one after another, so fast in succession that, according to my journal, we caught three hundred and seventy in about two hours! What a mess! and how delicious when roasted! if ever I am again becalmed in the Gulf of Mexico, I shall not forget the rudder-fish. The little things scarcely measured three inches

in length ; they were thin and deep in form, and afforded
excellent eating.   It was curious to see them keep to the
lee of the rudder in a compact body, and so voracious
were they, that they actually leaped out of the water at
the sight of the bait.   But the very instant that the ship
became still they dispersed around her sides, and would
no longer bite.   After drifting along the Florida coast a
stiff breeze rose, and sweeping us into the Atlantic, sent
us far upon our favorable voyage.

"*July* 20, 1826.   Landed from the Delos at Liverpool,
and took lodgings at the Commercial Hotel.   Called at
the counting-house of Gordon and Forstall, and went to
deliver my letters to Mr. Rathbone, who was absent when
I called ; but he forwarded a polite note, in which he invited me to dine and meet Mr. Roscoe.

"*July* 24.   Called for Mr. Rathbone at his counting-
house, and was kindly received, and dined at his house
in Duke Street.   Was introduced to his friend Mr. Roscoe, and his son-in-law, Mr. Philemon L. Baring.   Mr.
Roscoe invited me to his country-house next day, and we
visited the Botanical Gardens.   Ransacked the city for
pastils to make a drawing for Mrs. Rathbone.

"My drawings are to be exhibited at the Liverpool
Exhibition.   Mr. Roscoe promised to introduce me to
Lord Stanley, who, he says, is rather shy.   Great anxiety
about the success of my exhibition, which has proved a
complete success.

"*Sunday, July* 30.   Went to church, and saw a picture of Christ Curing the Blind Man, and listened to the
singing of the blind musicians.

"*August* 5.   I have met Lord Stanley, and found
him a frank, agreeable man.   Tall, broad-boned, well-
formed, he reminded me of Sully the painter.   He said,
'Sir, I am glad to see you.'   He pointed out one defect
in my drawings, for which I thanked him, but he admired

them generally. He spent five hours in examining my collection, and said, 'This work is unique, and deserves the patronage of the Crown.' He invited me many times to come and see him at his town house in Grosvenor Square."

Under this date, Audubon writes to his wife : "I am cherished by the most notable people in and around Liverpool, and have obtained letters of introduction to Baron Humboldt, Sir Walter Scott, Sir Humphry Davy, Sir Thomas Lawrence, Hannah More, Miss Edgeworth, and your distinguished cousin, Robert Bakewell."

"*August* 9. By the persuasion of friends, the entrance-fee to my collection of drawings is to be charged at one shilling. Three and four pounds per day promised well for the success of this proposal. Painted a wild turkey, full size, for the Liverpool Royal Institution. Busy at work painting in my usual toilet, with bare neck and bare arms. · Dr. Traill and Mr. Rathbone, while looking on, were astonished at the speed of my work.

"At Liverpool I did the portraits of various friends desirous of obtaining specimens of my drawing, and Mr. Rathbone suggested that I ought to do a large picture, in order that the public might have an opportunity of judging of my particular talents. From various kind friends I received letters of introduction to many distinguished persons. Mr. Roscoe, in particular, favored me with an extremely kind letter to Miss Edgeworth the novelist, in which he makes reference to my pursuits and acquirements in flattering language."

Audubon has copied into his journal many of these letters, but the interest of them is not of sufficient import to warrant their reproduction.

By the exhibition of his pictures at the Royal Institution, Liverpool, he realized 100*l.* ; but he speedily removed to Manchester, and carried with him his collection of drawings for exhibition in that city. " Dr. Traill, of the Royal Institution, had ordered all my drawings to be packed up by the curator of the museum, and their transport gave me no trouble whatever.

" *September* 10. I left Liverpool and the many kind friends I had made in it. In five and a half hours the coach arrived at Manchester. I took lodgings in the King's Arms. I strolled about the city, and it seemed to me to be most miserably laid out. I was struck by the sallow looks, sad faces, ragged garments, and poverty of a large portion of the population, which seemed worse off than the negroes of Louisiana. I exhibited my pictures in a gallery at Manchester at one shilling for entrance, but the result was not satisfactory."

At Manchester Audubon made the acquaintance of two very valuable friends—Mr. Gregg and Mr. McMurray. He visited many families, and was struck with the patri-archal manner of an Englishman who called his son "my love." He enjoyed for the first time a day's shooting after the English fashion in the neighborhood of Man-chester, but does not appear to have been charmed with the sport. It was soon discovered that the exhibition of his drawings at Manchester was not going to pay; but he opened a subscription book for the publication of his work on the birds of America.

" *September* 28. Revisited Liverpool to consult about a prospectus for my book. Stayed with Mr. Rathbone, and met there Mr. John Bohn, the London bookseller, who advised me to go to Paris and consult about cost of publication, after which I ought to go to London and compare the outlays before fixing upon any plan. Mrs. Rathbone desired me to draw the wild turkey of America the size of my thumb-nail. This she had engraved on a precious stone in the form of a seal, and presented it to me.

' *October* 6. I returned to Manchester, driven in the carriage of a friend, and arrived at the hall in which my pictures were exhibited, to find that the hall-keeper had been drunk and had no returns to make. I stayed about six weeks at Manchester, but the exhibition of my pictures did not prosper. I visited Matlock, and paid five pounds for spars to take home to my wife. I pulled some flowers from the hills she had played over when a child, and passed through the village of Bakewell, called after some one of her family.

" I determined to start for Edinburgh, and paying three pounds fifteen shillings for coach-hire, started for that city.

" *October* 25. Left Manchester for Edinburgh yesterday, following the road by Carlisle into Scotland. Was struck with the bleak appearance of the country. The Scottish shepherds looked like the poor mean whites of the Slave-states. The coachmen have a mean practice of asking money from the passengers after every stage. Arrived at Edinburgh, and called with letters of introduction on Professor Jameson and Professor Duncan— on Dr. Charles and Dr. Henry at the Infirmary, and upon the celebrated anatomist Dr. Knox. Professor Jameson received me with the greatest coldness—explained there was no chance of my seeing Sir Walter Scott, who was busy with a life of Napoleon and a novel, and who lived the life of a recluse. He said his own engagements would prevent his calling for some days.

" Dr. Knox came to me in his rooms dressed in an overgown, and with bleeding hands, which he wiped. He read Dr. Traill's letter and wished me success, and promised to do all in his power for me, and appointed the next day to call upon me and introduce some scientific friends to examine my drawings. I was much struck with Edinburgh—it is a splendid old city.

" The lower class of women (fishwives) resemble the squaws of the West. Their rolling gait, inturned toes, and manner of carrying burdens on their backs, is exactly that of the Shawnee women. Their complexions are either fair, purple, or brown as a mulatto.

" The men wear long whiskers and beards, and are extremely uncouth in manners as well as in speech.

" *October* 27. Filled with sad forebodings and doubts of all progress. Miss Ewart called to see my drawings, and was delighted with them. She exclaimed, after looking, at them. ' How delighted Sir Walter Scott would be with them ! ' I presented a letter to Mr. Patrick Neil, the printer, who received me with great cordiality, invited me to his house, and promised to interest himself for me generally　Mr. Andrew Duncan gave me a note to Francis Jeffrey, the famous editor of the ' Edinburgh Review.'

" *October* 30. Called on Mr. Francis Jeffrey, who was not at home ; wrote a note for him in his library, which I found was filled with books tossed about in confusion, pamphlets, portfolios, and dirt.

" Prospects more dull and unpromising ; and I went to Mr. Patrick Neil, to express my intention of going on to London, as my pictures of the American Birds were evidently not appreciated in Edinburgh. He remonstrated kindly, spoke encouragingly, and introduced me to Mr. Lizars, the engraver of Mr. Selby's Birds.

" Mr. Lizars had the greatest admiration for Selby, but no sooner had he looked into my portfolio than he exclaimed, ' My God, I never saw any thing like these before ; ' and he afterwards said the naturalist, Sir William Jardine, ought to see them immediately.

" *November* 1. Professor Jameson has called, Mr. Lizars having, with his warmth of heart, brought the naturalist to see my collection of birds. The Professor was very kind, but his manner of speaking of my drawings leaves me to suspect that he may have been quizzing me.

"*November* 2. Breakfasted with Professor Jameson in his splendid house. The Professor's appearance is somewhat remarkable, and the oddities of his hair are worthy of notice. It seems to stand up all over his head and points in various directions, so that it looks strange and uncouth. Around a rough exterior he owns a generous heart, but which is not at first discernible. I felt my career now certain. I was spoken kindly of by the newspapers, and in the streets I heard such remarks made upon me as—'That is the French nobleman.' I spent three very delightful weeks, dining, breakfasting, and visiting many agreeable people in Edinburgh. Professor Jameson promised to introduce my work to the public in his "Natural History Magazine,' and Professor Wilson (Christopher North) offered me his services in the pages of 'Maga.'

" Professor Wilson likewise volunteered to introduce me to Sir Walter Scott, and Mr. Combe, the phrenologist. Mr. Syme, the portrait painter, requested me to sit for my portrait. A committee from the Royal Institution of Edinburgh called upon me and offered me the use of the rooms for the exhibition of my drawings, and the receipts from this source amounted to £5 per day.

"What, however,' most pleased me was the offer of Mr. Lizars to bring out a first number of my 'Birds of America,' the plates to be the size of life. I have obtained from Mr. Rathbone his name as a subscriber, and have written to him with a prospectus, and explained that I shall travel about with a specimen number until I obtain three hundred subscribers, which will assure the success of the work. Sir William Jardine, now in the midst of his extensive ornithological publication, spends many hours a day beside me examining my manner of

work, and he has invited me to make a long visit to his
residence in the country.

"*November* 28.   Saw to-day the first proof of the
first engraving of my American Birds, and was very well
pleased with its appearance.

"*November* 29.   Sir Walter Scott has promised a
friend to come and see my drawings.   Invited to dine
with the Antiquarian Society at the Waterloo Hotel.
Met the Earl of Elgin at the dinner, who was very cordial.   The dinner was sumptuous, the first course being
all Scotch dishes, a novelty to me, and consisting of mar-
row-bones, codfish-heads stuffed with oatmeal and garlick,
blackpudding, sheepsheads, &c.   Lord Elgin presided,
and after dinner, with an auctioneer's mallet brought the
company to order by rapping sharply on the table.   He
then rose and said, 'The King, four-times-four!"   All
rose and drank the monarch's health, the president saying, 'Ip! ip! ip!' followed by sixteen cheers.   Mr.
Skein, first secretary to the Society, drank my own
health, prefacing the toast with many flatteries, which
made me feel very faint and chill.   I was expected to
make a speech, but could not, and never had tried.
Being called on for a reply, I said, 'Gentlemen, my
incapacity for words to respond to your flattering notice
is hardly exceeded by that of the birds now hanging on
the walls of your institution.   I am truly obliged to you
for your favors, and can only say, God bless you all, and
may your Society prosper.'   I sat down with the perspiration running over me, and was glad to drink off a glass
of wine that Mr. Lizars kindly handed to me in my distress.   Some Scottish songs were sung; and William
Allen, the famous Scottish painter, concluded the fun by
giving a droll imitation of the buzzing of a bee about the
room, following it and striking at it with his handkerchief
as if it was flying from him."

"*November* 30. The picture representing myself dressed in a wolf-skin coat is finished, and although the likeness is not good, the picture will be hung to-morrow in the Exhibition room.

"*December* 1. Lord Elgin and another nobleman visited my exhibition to-day, and talked with me about my work and prospects. Fifteen pounds were drawn at the Exhibition to-day.

"*December* 2. Breakfasted with the wonderful David Bridges, who commenced to dust his furniture with his handkerchief. I hear that Professor Wilson has been preparing an article upon me and my ornithological labors for 'Blackwood's Magazine.' Dined with Dr. Brown, a very amiable man, and met Professor Jameson. Sir James Hall and Captain Basil Hall have called upon me to-day, the latter making inquiries in reference to some purpose to visit the United States.

"*December* 3. Nearly finished a painting of the Otter in Trap, which Mr. Lizars and Mr. Syme thought excellent. Dr. Knox has kindly promised to propose my name for membership of the Wernerian Natural History Society of Edinburgh.

December 10. My success in Edinburgh borders on the miraculous. My book is to be published in numbers containing four birds in each the size of life, in a style surpassing anything now existing, at two guineas a number. The engravings are truly beautiful; some of them have been colored, and are now on exhibition.

"*December* 12. Called on Dr. Brewster and read him an article on the Carrion Crow. After reading the paper I was introduced to Mrs. Brewster, a charming woman, whose manner put me at entire ease.

"*December* 16. Received a note from Mr. Rathbone, objecting to the large size of my book, which he suspected would be rather against its popularity. Went to the Wernerian Society to show my drawings of the Buzzard. Professor Jameson rose and pronounced quite an eulogy upon my labors, and the Society passed a vote of thanks upon them. Professor Jameson afterwards proposed me as an honorary member of the Society, which was carried by acclamation.

" Dined with Lady Hunter, mother-in-law to Captain Basil Hall, and met Lady Mary Clarke, aged eighty-two, who was acquainted with Generals Wolfe and Montgomery. I had many questions put to me upon subjects connected with America by the distinguished guests I met at the house. Captain Basil Hall has presented me with a copy of his work upon South America, accompanied by a complimentary note.

" *December* 17. Busy painting two cats fighting over a squirrel. Up at candle-light, and worked at the cats till nine o'clock.

" *December* 19. Went to breakfast with Sir William Jardine and Mr. Selby at Barry's Hotel. I was sauntering along the streets, thinking of the beautiful aspects of nature, meditating on the power of the great Creator, on the beauty and majesty of his works, and of the skill he had given man to study them, when the whole train of my thoughts was suddenly arrested by a ragged, sickly-looking beggar-boy. His face told of hunger and hardship, and I gave him a shilling and passed on. But turning again, the child was looking after me, and I beckoned to him to return. Taking him back to my lodgings, I gave him all the garments I had which were worn, added five shillings more in money, gave him my blessing, and sent him away rejoicing, and feeling myself as if God had smiled on me. I afterwards breakfasted with Sir William, and gave a lesson in drawing to him and to Mr. Selby.

" *December* 20. Breakfasted with Mr. George Combe,

the phrenologist, who examined my head and afterwards measured my skull with the accuracy and professional manner in which I measured the heads, bills, and claws of my birds. Among other talents, he said I possessed largely the faculties which would enable me to excel in painting. He noted down his observations to read at the Phrenological Society.

" Received an invitation from the Earl of Morton to visit him at his seat at some distance from Edinburgh."

December 22. From the entries in his journal under this date it appears he had written to his wife that he intended to remove to Newcastle or Glasgow. " I expect to visit the Duke of Northumberland, who has promised to subscribe for my work. I have taken to dressing again, and now dress twice a-day, and wear silk stockings and pumps. I wear my hair as long as usual. I believe it does as much for me as my paintings. One hundred subscribers for my book will pay all expenses. Some persons are terrified at the sum of one hundred and eighty guineas for a work ; but this amount is to be spread over eight years, during which time the volumes will be gradually completed. I am fêted, feasted, elected honorary member of societies, making money by my exhibition and by my paintings. It is Mr. Audubon here and Mr. Audubon there, and I can only hope that Mr. Aududon will not be made a conceited fool at last.

" *December* 23. The exhibition of my birds more crowded than ever. This day I summed up the receipts, and they amounted to eight hundred dollars. I have presented my painting of the American Turkeys to the Royal Institution for the use of their rooms. A dealer valued the picture at one hundred guineas.

" *December* 25, Christmas. Bought a brooch for Mrs. Audubon. Astonished that the Scotch have no religious ceremony on Christmas Day.

" *December* 27. Went to Dalmahoy, to the Earl of Morton's seat, eight miles from Edinburgh. The countess kindly received me, and introduced me to the earl, a small slender man, tottering on his feet and weaker than a newly-hatched partridge. He welcomed me with tears in his eyes. The countess is about forty, not handsome, but fine-looking, fair, fresh-complexioned, dark flashing eyes, superior intellect and cultivation. She was dressed in a rich crimson silk, and her mother in heavy black satin.

" My bedroom was a superb parlor with yellow furniture and yellow hangings. After completing my toilet, dinner is announced, and I enter the dining-room, where the servants in livery attend, and one in plain clothes hands about the plates in a napkin, so that his hand may not touch them. In the morning I visited the stables, and saw four splendid Abyssinian horses with tails reaching to the ground. I saw in the aviary the falcon-hawks used of old for hunting with, and which were to be brought to the house in order that I might have an opportunity of witnessing their evolutions and flight. The hawks were brought with bells and hoods and perched on gloved hands as in the days of chivalry. The countess wrote her name in my subscription-book, and offered to pay the price in advance.

" *December* 31. Dined with Captain Basil Hall, and met Francis Jeffrey and Mr. M'Culloch, the distinguished writer on political economy, a plain, simple, and amiable man. Jeffrey is a little man, with a serious face and dignified air. He looks both shrewd and cunning, and talks with so much volubility he is rather displeasing. In the course of the evening Jeffrey seemed to discover that if he was Jeffrey I was Audubon."

CHAPTER X.

Edinburgh — The Royal Society — Scott — Edinburgh People — Sydney Smith and a Sermon — Miss O'Neill the Actress — Mrs. Grant of Laggan — Prospectus of the Great Work.

EBRUARY 3. Dr. Brewster proposed that I should exhibit the five plates of my first number of the Birds of America at the Royal Society this evening. He is a great optician, and advises me to get a camera-lucida, so as to take the outline of my birds more rapidly and correctly. Such an instrument would be useful in saving time, and a great relief in hot weather, since outlining is the hardest part of the work, and more than half of the labor. I visited the Royal Society at eight o'clock, and laid my large sheets on the table : they were examined and praised. After this we were all called into the great room, and Captain Hall came and took my hand and led me to a seat immediately opposite to Sir Walter Scott, the President, where I had a perfect view of this great man, and studied nature from nature's noblest work. A long lecture followed on the introduction of the Greek language into England, after which the President rose, and all others followed his example. Sir Walter came and shook hands with me, asked how the cold weather of Edinburgh agreed with me, and so attracted the attention of many members to me, as if I had been a distinguished stranger.

"*February* 10. Visited the Exhibition at the Royal Institution. Saw the picture of the Black Cocks, which was put up there for public inspection. I know that the birds are composed and drawn as well as any birds ever have been; but what a difference exists between the drawing of one bird and the composition of a group, and harmonizing them with a landscape and sky, and well-adapted foreground! Who that has ever tried to combine these three different conceptions in a single picture, has not felt a sense of fear while engaged in his work? I looked long and carefully at the picture of a stag painted by Landseer;—the style was good, and the brush was handled with fine effect; but he fails in copying Nature, without which the best work will be a failure. A stag, three dogs, and a Highland hunter are introduced on the canvas; but the stag has his tongue out and his mouth shut! The principal dog, a greyhound, has the deer by one ear, while one of his fore-paws is around his leg, as if in the act of fondling with him. The hunter has laced the deer by one horn very prettily, and, in the attitude of a ballet-dancer, is about to throw another noose over the head of the animal. To me, and my friend Bourgeat, or Dr. Pope, such a picture is quite a farce; but it is not so in London, for there are plenty of such pictures there, and this one created a great sensation among the connoisseurs.

"Captain Hall invited me to take some of my drawings to show Lady Mansfield, who is his particular friend, and who expressed a desire to see them. Unfortunately she was not at home when we called; but her three daughters and several noblemen who were present examined them. The ladies were handsome, but seemed haughty, and wanting in that refinement of manners and condescending courtesy I had seen in the Countess of Morton; and the gentlemen evinced a like lack of good breeding. This did not disturb me, but I was troubled and pained for Captain Hall, who is so instinctively a gentleman, because I saw that he felt hurt and mortified. He requested me to leave my drawings, which cost me so many days' labor, and of which I am so jealous, and I would not add to his pain who had proved so kind a friend to me by denying him. Lunch was already on the table, but I was not asked to remain, and I was truly glad of it, and I went away almost unnoticed, and hurried to meet an engagement at the Wernerian rooms.

"When I entered the rooms of the Wernerian Society, they were full as an egg, and I was told by a friend that the large assembly had come because of a report that I was to read a paper on the habits of the rattlesnake. Professor Graham arose soon after my arrival, and said, 'Mr. President, Mr. Audubon has arrived.' But I had been too busy to finish the paper, and Mr. Lizars explained this for me. My engravings were then called for by Professor Jameson, and they were examined and highly praised. The paper on the alligator was finished soon after, and read before the Society.

"A stranger lately accosted me in the street, and suggested to me, that if I would paint an Osage Indian hunting wild turkeys, it would take with the public and increase my reputation. No doubt it would, for whatever is most strange is most taking now; but so long as my hair floats over my shoulders I shall probably attract attention enough; and if it hung to my heels it would attract more.

"*February* 11. Worked all the morning at the Royal Institution, touching up my pictures hanging there; several other artists came and worked on theirs also. It was quite amusing to hear them praising one another, and condemning the absent.

"*February* 12. Began the day by working hard on the pictures at the rooms of the Scottish Society. And to-day the Antiquarian Society held its first meeting since my election. It is customary for new members to be present at such times, and I went, and though I felt

rather sheepish, I was warmly congratulated by the mem
bers.   At one o'clock 1 visited the rooms of the Royal
Society, which were crowded, and tables were set, covered with wine and fruits and other refreshments.   The
ladies were mostly of noble families, and I saw many
there whom I knew.   But the Ladies Mansfield passed
me several times, without manifesting any recollection of
a man who, a few days before, had waited on their lady-
ships, and shown them his drawings, not for his pleasure, but their benefit.   Sir Walter Scott was present, and
came towards me and shook hands cordially, and pointing to a picture, said, ' Mr. Audubon, many such scenes
have I witnessed in my younger days.'   We talked much
of all about us, and I would gladly have asked him to
join me in a glass of wine, but my foolish habit prevented
me.   Having inquired after the health of his daughters, I
shortly left him and the room, for I was very hungry ;
and although the table was loaded with delicacies, and
the ladies were enjoying them freely, I say it to my
shame, that I had not the confidence to lay my fingers
on a single thing."

An interval of a week occurs in the journal, and it is
explained by the fact that Audubon was busily engaged
in other compositions, and writing twelve letters of introduction to persons in America for Captain Basil Hall,
and preparing an article on the habits of the wild
pigeon, which he had been requested to do, to read before the Natural History Society.   Dr. Brewster saw the
latter before it was read, and requested permission to
publish it in his journal.   "This," says Audubon, "was
killing two birds with one stone, because I had promised
to write Brewster an article.   I began that paper on
Wednesday, wrote all day, and sat up until half-past
three the next morning ; and so absorbed was my whole
soul and spirit in the work, that I felt as if I were in

the woods of America among the pigeons, and my ears were filled with the sound of their rustling wings. After sleeping a few hours, I rose and corrected it. Captain Hall called a few hours after, read the article, and begged a copy : the copy was made, and sent to him at eight o'clock that evening.

"Captain Hall expressed some doubts as to my views respecting the affection and love of pigeons, as if I made it human, and raised the possessors quite above the brutes. I presume the love of the mothers for their young is much the same as the love of woman for her offspring. There is but one kind of love ; God is love, and all his creatures derive theirs from his ; only it is modified by the different degrees of intelligence in different beings and creatures."

On February 20, he writes, in a long letter to his wife : " It is impossible yet to say how long I shall remain in England ; at least until I have spent some months in London. I am doing all I can to hasten my plans, but it will take some time to complete them. The first number of my birds will be published in March, and on the fifth of the month the ballot takes place to decide my election to the Royal Society, which, if successful, will be of great advantage to me ; and whether successful or no I shall leave Edinburgh five days after, to visit all the principal towns in the three kingdoms, to obtain subscribers for my work.

" *February* 28. A few days of idleness have completely sickened me, and given me what is called the blue-devils so severely, that I feel that the sooner I go to work and drive them off the better.

" *March* 1. Mr. Kidd, a promising young artist in landscape, only nineteen, breakfasted with me to-day, and we talked on painting a long time, and I was charmed with his talents, and thought what a difference it would have made in my life if I had begun painting in oil at his age and with his ability. It is a sad reflection that I have been compelled to hammer and stammer as if I were working in opposition to God's will, and so now am nothing but poor Audubon. I invited him to come to my rooms daily, and to eat and drink with me, and give me the pleasure of his company and the advantage of his taste in painting. I told him of my ardent desire to improve in the delightful art, and proposed to begin a new picture, in which he should assist with his advice; and proposing to begin it to-morrow, I took down my portfolio, to select a drawing to copy in oil. He had never seen my works before, and appeared astonished as his eyes ranged over the sheets. He expressed the warmest admiration, and said, ' How hopeless must be the task of my giving any instruction to one who can draw like this? I pointed out to him that nature is the great study for the artist, and assured him that the reason why my works pleased him was because they are all exact copies of the works of God, who is the great Architect and perfect Artist; and impressed on his mind this fact, that nature indifferently copied is far superior to the best idealities.

" *March* 3. For the last few days I have worked with my brushes, while it has snowed and blown as if the devil had cut the strings of the bags of Æolus, and turned all its cold blasts down upon the mists of Scotland to freeze them into snow. It is twenty years since I have seen such a storm. Dined at Mr. Ritchie's, who is a well-meaning man, and has a well-doing wife. The company was mixed, and some of the ingredients were raw; there were learned and ignorant, wise and foolish, making up the heterogeneous assembly. I enjoyed myself; but there was an actor, named Vandenhoff, who performed some theatrical pantomimes, which were disgusting to me. I never saw such pranks in good society before : he tucked one lady's fan in his boot, and broke it, and made an apology for it, and by his familiarity annoyed every one present. I felt more pain for his host than shame for himself. During the evening he made some unjust remarks about Mr. Lizars, and I rebuked him for it, telling him that he was my friend, and a good man. He left soon after, to the great relief of all.

" *March* 4. To-day the snow is so deep that the mails from all quarters are interrupted, and people are waddling through it in the streets, and giving a lively representation of a Lapland winter. Breakfasted with the Rev. Mr. Newbold, and afterwards was toted to church in a sedan chair. I had never been in one before, and I like to try everything which is going on on the face of this strange world. But so long as I have two feet and legs, I never desire to try one of these machines again; the quick up-and-down, short swinging motion, reminded me of the sensations I felt during the great earthquake in Kentucky. But I was repaid for the ride by hearing a sermon from the Rev. Sydney Smith. It was a sermon *to me.* Oh! what a soul there must be in the body of that famous man; what a mingling of energetic and sweet thoughts, what a fount of goodness there must be within him! He made me smile, and he made me think more deeply perhaps than I had ever before in my life. He interested me now by painting my foibles, and then he pained me by portraying my sins, until he made my cheeks crimson with shame, and filled my heart with penitential sorrow. And I left the church filled with veneration for God, and reverence for the wonderful man who is so noble an example of his marvellous handywork. We returned to Mr. Newbold's for lunch, and from there I walked, tumbled, and pitched home in the deep snow."

March 5. In a letter to Mrs. Audubon of this date,

he tells her of his election as a member of the Royal Society, and says : " So poor Audubon, if not rich, thou wilt be honored at least, and held in esteem among men.

" *March* 6. Finished my picture this morning, and like it better than any I have painted." [He does not say what this picture is, but it is evidently the one mentioned as begun with young Kidd.] " Mr. Ritchie, editor of the ' Scotsman,' asked for a copy of the first number of my birds, to notice it in his paper. Went to the Society of Arts, and saw there many beautiful and remarkable inventions, among them a carriage propelled by steam, which moved with great rapidity and regularity. I always enjoy my visits here more than to the literary societies. The time for leaving Edinburgh is drawing near, but I am yet undetermined whether to go first to Glasgow or Dublin, or else to Newcastle, and then to Liverpool, Oxford, Cambridge, and so on to London ; but I shall soon decide and move.

" *March* 7. Having determined to leave Edinburgh, my first course is to settle up all my business affairs, and make preparations for the future, and to this end I set about collecting the letters promised me by friends to the different places I proposed to visit. Professor Jameson and Dr. Brewster have made me promise occasionally to contribute some articles for their journals. I mentioned to Dr. Brewster the desire I had for a line from Sir Walter Scott. He told me he was to dine with him that day, and he would mention the subject to him, and he had no doubt he would kindly grant it. Passed the evening at a large party at Mr. Tytler's, where, among other agreeable ladies and gentlemen, I was introduced to Sydney Smith, the famous preacher of last Sunday. Saw his fair daughters, and heard them sweetly sing ; and he and his daughters appointed next Saturday to examine my drawings.

"*March* 8. The weather was dreadful last night, wind howling, and, what you would hardly expect, the snow six feet deep in some places. The mail-carriers from here for London were obliged to leave their horses, and go on foot with their bags. Wrote the following letter to Sir Walter Scott.

"'DEAR SIR,

"'On the eve of my departure to visit all parts of the island, and afterwards the principal cities of the Continent, I feel an ardent desire to be honored by being the bearer of a few lines from your own hand to whomever you may please to introduce me.

"'I beg this of you with the hope that my efforts to advance ornithological studies, by the publication of my collections and manuscripts, may be thought worthy of your kind attentions, and an excuse for thus intruding on your precious moments. Should you feel the least scruple, please frankly decline it, and believe me, dear sir, that I value so highly my first reception, when presented to you by my good friend Captain Basil Hall, and your subsequent civilities, that I never shall cease to be, with the highest respect and admiration,

"' Your most obedient, humble servant,

"' JOHN J. AUDUBON. '"

That same evening the following answer was received.

"' DEAR MR. AUDUBON,

"' I am sure you will find many persons better qualified than myself to give you a passport to foreign countries, since circumstances have prevented our oftener meeting, and my ignorance does not permit me to say anything on the branches of natural history of which you are so well possessed. But I can easily and truly say, that what I have had the pleasure of seeing, touching your talents and manners, corresponds with all I have heard in your favor; and that I am a sincere believer in the extent of your scientific attainments, though I have not the knowledge necessary to form an accurate judgment on the subject. I sincerely wish your travels may prove agreeable, and remain,

" ' Very much your

" ' Obedient servant,

" ' WALTER SCOTT.'

" ' Edinburgh, March 8.' "

"Spent the evening at Miss O'Neill's, the actress. Several ladies and gentlemen of musical ability were present, and after tea Miss O'Neill arose and said she would open the concert. She was beautifully dressed in plain white muslin, her fine auburn hair hanging in flowing ringlets about her neck and rose-colored scarf over her shoulders, looking as differently from what she does on the stage as can be imagined. She sang and played sweetly, her large, dark languid eyes expressing the deep emotions of her soul. She scarcely left off singing for a moment, for as soon as one thing was finished some person called for another, and she readily replied, ' Oh, yes ;' and glees, duets, and trios followed one another, filling the room with her melodies. I thought at last that she must be fatigued, and said so to her. But she replied, ' Mr. Audubon, music is like painting, it never fatigues if one is fond of it, and I am.' We had an elegant supper, and after that more music, and then more refreshments and wine; this gave new impulse to the song. Miss O'Neill played, and called on the singers to accompany her. The music travelled along the table, and sometimes leaped across it; gentlemen and ladies took turns, until, looking at my watch, I found that it was past two o'clock, when I arose, and in spite of many entreaties, shook hands with Miss O'Neill, bowed to the company, and made my exit.

" *March* 13. Breakfasted with the famous Mrs. Grant, her son and daughter the only other company. She is aged and very deaf, but very intelligent and warm-hearted. We talked of America, and she is really the first person I have met here who knows much about it. She thought it would not be for the benefit of the slaves to set them free suddenly from their masters' protection.

" Passed a most uncomfortable evening at Sir James Riddell's. The company was too high for me, for although Sir James and his lady did all that could be desired to entertain me, I did not smile nor have a happy thought, all the evening ; and had not Mrs. Hay and Mrs. Captain Hall been present, I should have been very miserable. After dinner, however, my drawings were examined and praised, and they seemed to look on me as less of a bear, and I felt relieved. My good friend Mr. Hay asked a young Russian nobleman who was present if he could not give me some letters to his country, but he was silent. I turned to Mr. Hay, and thanked him for his kind intentions in such a way as to turn the conversation, and relieve his embarrassment. The best recommendation I can have is my own talents, and the fruits of my own labors, and what others will not do for me I will try and do for myself. I was very sorry that Mr. Hay's feelings should have been hurt on my account by the young man's silence, but I soon made him at ease again. Sir James volunteered to give me letters to Sir Thomas Ackland and Sir Robert Inglis, both noblemen of distinction, and patrons of the science I cultivate. The style here far surpassed even Lord Morton's ; fine *gentlemen* waited on us at table, and two of them put my cloak about my shoulders, notwithstanding my remonstrances.

" *March* 17. Issued my ' Prospectus' this morning, for the publication of my great work.

7

" The Prospectus.

" To those who have not seen any portion of the author's collection of original drawings, it may be proper to state, that their superiority consists in the accuracy as to proportion and outline, and the variety and truth of the attitudes and positions of the figures, resulting from the peculiar means discovered and employed by the author, and his attentive examination of the objects portrayed during a long series of years. The author has not contented himself, as others have done, with single profile views, but in very many instances has grouped his figures so as to represent the originals at their natural avocations, and has placed them on branches of trees, decorated with foliage, blossoms, and fruits, or amidst plants of numerous species. Some are seen pursuing their prey through the air, searching for food amongst the leaves and herbage, sitting in their nests, or feeding their young ; whilst others, of a different nature, swim, wade, or glide in or over their allotted element.

" The insects, reptiles, and fishes that form the food of these birds have now and then been introduced into the drawings. In every instance where a difference of plumage exists between the sexes, both the male and the female have been represented ; and the extraordinary changes which some species undergo in their progress from youth to maturity have been depicted. The plants are all copied from nature, and, as many of the originals are remarkable for their beauty, their usefulness, or their rarity, the botanist cannot fail to look upon them with delight.

" The particulars of the plan of the work may be reduced to the following heads :

" I. The size of the work is double elephant folio, the paper being of the finest quality.

"II. The engravings are, in every instance, of the exact dimensions of the drawings, which, without any exception, represent the birds and other objects of their natural size.

"III. The plates are colored in the most careful manner from the original drawings.

"IV. The work appears in numbers, of which five are published annually, each number consisting of five plates.

"V. The price of each number is two guineas, payable on delivery."

Probably no other undertaking of Audubon's life illustrates the indomitable character of the man more fully than this prospectus. He was in a strange country, with no friends but those he had made within a few months, and not ready money enough in hand to bring out the first number proposed, and yet he entered confidently on this undertaking, which was to cost over a hundred thousand dollars, and with no pledge of help, but on the other hand discouragements on all sides, and from his best friends, of the hopelessness of such an undertaking.

March 19. Under this date we have an amusing entry. Audubon had been frequently importuned by his friends to cut his hair, which he had for years worn in ringlets falling to his shoulders. Hence the obituary:—

EDINBURGH.

March 19, 1827.

This day my Hair was sacrificed, and the will of GOD usurped by the wishes of Man.

As the Barber clipped my locks rapidly, it reminded me of the horrible times of the French Revolution, when the same operation was performed upon all the victims murdered by the Guillotine.

My heart sank low.

JOHN J. AUDUBON.

The margin of the sheet is painted black, about three-fourths of an inch deep all around, as if in deep mourning for the loss which he had reluctantly submitted to in order to please his friends.   He consented, sadly, because he expected soon to leave for London, and Cap-tain Hall persuaded him that it would be *better* for him to wear it according to the prevailing English fashion !

CHAPTER XI.

UITTING Edinburgh with a high heart, the indomitable naturalist began his provincial canvass, meeting, as is usual in such cases, with two kinds of treatment,—very good and very bad. He visited in succession Newcastle, Leeds, York, Shrewsbury, and Manchester, securing a few subscribers at two hundred pounds a head in each place. His diary chronicles minutely all his affairs—dining-out, tea-drinking, "receiving," —but none are very interesting. The only incident at all worth recording is a visit paid to Bewick the engraver, but as it adds nothing to our knowledge of one who was a real genius in his way, we pass on to metal more attractive,—to London, where Audubon continued his canvass, with great success among the aristocracy. From a confused heap of memoranda we take a few notes of this London visit, suppressing much, and somewhat doubtful of the relevancy even of what we select.

"*Sir Thomas Lawrence.*—My first call on this great artist and idolized portrait-painter of Great Britain, whose works are known over the whole world, was at half-past eight in the morning. I was assured he would be as hard at work at that time as I usually am. I took with me my letters and portfolio, with some original drawings. The servant said his master was in; I gave my name, and waited about five minutes, when he came down from his room. His manner and reception impressed me most favorably, and I was surprised to find him dressed as if for the whole day, in a simple but clean garb. He shook my hand, read my letters, and so gave me time to glance at the marble figures in the room and to examine his face. It did not show the marks of genius that I expected in one so eminent, but looked pale and pensive. After reading my letters he said he was pleased to meet another American introduced to him by his friend Sully, adding, that he wished much to see the drawings of a man so highly spoken of, and appointing next Thursday to call on me. He took a large card and wrote the appointment on it, and put it back in its place.

"Sir Thomas is no ornithologist, and therefore could not well judge of the correctness of the detail of my drawings, which can be appreciated fully only by those who are acquainted with the science of which I myself am yet only a student. But I found that he had a perfect idea of the rules of drawing any object whatever, as well of the forms and composition, or management of the objects offered for the inspection of his keen eyes. I thought from his face that he looked at them with astonishment and pleasure, although he did not open his lips until I had shown the last drawing, when he asked if I 'painted in oils?' On answering him in the affirmative, he invited me to examine his rooms. The room where he painted, to my utter astonishment, had a southern light: upon his easel was a canvas (kitcat), on which was a perfect drawing in black chalk, beautifully finished, of a nobleman, and on a large easel a full-sized portrait of a noble lady, represented in the open air; and on the latter he went to work. I saw that his pallet was enormous, and looked as if already prepared with the various tints wanted by some one else, and that he had an almost innumerable number of brushes and pencils of all descriptions. He now glazed one part of his picture, and then

retouched another part with fine colors, and in a deliber-
ate way which did not indicate that he was in any haste
to finish it. He next laid down his pallet, and, turning
to the chalk drawing upon the unpainted canvas, asked
me how I liked his manner of proceeding? But as no
compliment could be paid by me to such an artist, I
merely said that I thought it the very quintessence of his
art. A waiter then entered, and announced that breakfast was ready. He invited me to remain and join him
in his 'humble meal,' which I declined, while we walked
downstairs together. I remarked on the very large number of unfinished portraits I saw : to which he mildly replied, ' My dear sir, this is my only misfortune ; I cannot tell if I shall ever see the day when they will all be
finished.' Insisting on my remaining to breakfast, I
went in ; it consisted of a few boiled eggs, some dry
toast, and tea and coffee. He took the first, and I the
last : this finished, I bid him good-morning. It was ten
o'clock when I left, and as I passed out three carriages
were waiting at the door ; and had I not been a student
in ornithology I would have wished myself a Sir Thomas
Lawrence, for I thought that after all the superiority of
this wonderful man's talents I could with less powers
realize more than he by my own more constant industry.

"Sir Thomas afterwards paid me three visits ; two at
my boarding house and one at Mr. Havell's, my engraver ; and I will tell you something of each of them to
show you the kindness of his heart. It was nine in the
morning the first time he came ; he looked at some of
my drawings of quadrupeds and birds, both finished and
unfinished. He said nothing of their value, but asked
me particularly of the prices which I put on them. I
mentioned the price of several in order, and to my surprise he said he would bring me a few purchasers that
very day if I would remain at home : this I promised,

and he left me very greatly relieved. In about two hours he returned with two gentlemen, to whom he did not introduce me, but who were pleased with my work, and one purchased the 'Otter Caught in a Trap,' for which he gave me twenty pounds sterling, and the other, 'A Group of Common Rabbits,' for fifteen sovereigns. I took the pictures to the carriage which stood at the door, and they departed, leaving me more amazed than I had been by their coming.

"The second visit was much of the same nature, differing, however, chiefly in the number of persons he brought with him, which was three instead of two; each one of whom purchased a picture at seven, ten, and thirty-five pounds respectively; and as before, the party and pictures left together in a splendid carriage with liveried footmen. I longed to know their names, but as Sir Thomas was silent respecting them I imitated his reticence in restraining my curiosity, and remained in mute astonishment.

"The third call of this remarkable man was in consequence of my having painted a picture, with the intention of presenting it to the King of England, George IV. This picture was the original of the 'English Pheasants Surprised by a Spanish Dog.' I had shown it to Sir Walter Waller, who was his majesty's oculist, and he liked the picture so much, and was so pleased with my intention, as was also my friend Mr. Children, the curator of the British Museum, that they prevailed on Sir Thomas to come and see it. He came, and pushed off my roller easel, bade me hold up the picture, walked from one side of the room to the other examining it, and then coming to me tapped me on the shoulder and said, 'Mr. Audubon, that picture is too good to be given away; his majesty would accept it, but you never would be benefitted by the gift more than receiving a letter from his private secretary, saying that it had been placed in his collection. That picture is worth three hundred guineas : sell it, and do not give it away.' I thanked him, exhibited the picture, refused three hundred guineas for it soon after, kept it several years, and at last sold it for one hundred guineas to my generous friend John Heppenstall of Sheffield, England, and invested the amount in spoons and forks for my good wife.

" Without the sale of these pictures I was a bankrupt, when my work was scarcely begun, and in two days more I should have seen all my hopes of the publication blasted ; for Mr. Havell (the engraver) had already called to say that on Saturday I must pay him sixty pounds. I was then not only not worth a penny, but had actually borrowed five pounds a few days before to purchase materials for my pictures. But these pictures which Sir Thomas sold for me enabled me to pay my borrowed money, and to appear full-handed when Mr. Havell called. Thus I passed the Rubicon !

" At that time I painted all day, and sold my work during the dusky hours of evening, as I walked through the Strand and other streets where the Jews reigned ; popping in and out of Jew-shops or any others, and never refusing the offers made me for the pictures I carried fresh from the easel. Startling and surprising as this may seem, it is nevertheless true, and one of the curious events of my most extraordinary life. Let me add here, that I sold seven copies of the 'Entrapped Otter' in London, Manchester, and Liverpool, besides one copy presented to my friend Mr. Richard Rathbone. In other pictures, also, I have sold from seven to ten copies, merely by changing the course of my rambles ; and strange to say, that when in after years and better times I called on the different owners to whom I had sold the copies, I never found a single one in their hands. And

7*

I recollect that once, through inadvertence, when I called at a shop where I had sold a copy of the picture, the dealer bought the duplicate at the same price he had given for the first! What has become of all those pictures?"

About this date Sir Robert Peel returned a letter Audubon had brought to him from Lord Meadowbank, and requested him to hand it over to his successor. This Audubon interpreted as giving him to understand that he need trouble him no more. The letter was obtained with the view of gaining a presentation to the king, and Audubon was not a man to easily relinquish an idea or an object which he had once determined on. Accordingly, he says, "I made up my mind to go directly to the American minister, Mr. Gallatin, and know from him how I should proceed, and if there were really no chance of my approaching the king nearer than by passing his castle. To pay a visit of this sort in London is really no joke; but as I thought there was a possibility of it for myself, I wanted to have the opinion of one who I believed was capable of deciding the matter.

"As I reached his presence he said, laughing, 'Always at home, my dear sir, when I am not out.' I understood him perfectly, and explained the object of my visit. His intellectual face lighted up as he replied, 'What a simple man you must be to believe all that is said to you about being introduced to his majesty! It is impossible, my dear sir; the king sees nobody; he has the gout, is peevish, and spends his time playing whist at a shilling a rubber. I had to wait six weeks before I was presented to him in my position of ambassador, and then I merely saw him six or seven minutes. He stood only during the time the public functionaries from foreign countries passed him, and seated himself immediately afterwards, paying scarcely any attention to the numerous court of English noblemen and gentlemen present.' I waited a moment, and said that I thought the Duke of Northumberland would interest himself for me. Again he laughed, and assured me that my attempts there would prove ineffectual. 'Think,' continued he; 'I have called hundreds of times on like men in England, and been assured that his grace, or lordship, or ladyship, was not at home, until I have grown wiser, and stay at home myself, and merely attend to my political business, and God only knows when I will have done with that. It requires written appointments of a month or six weeks before an interview can be obtained.' I then changed the conversation to other subjects, but he kindly returned to it again, and said, ' Should the king hold a levée whilst you are here, I will take you to Court, and present you as an American scientific gentleman, but of course would not mention your work.' I remained with him a full hour; and, as I was about to leave, he asked me for all the cards I had in my case, and said he would use them well, and find me visitors if possible.

" *June* 18. The work on the first number is yet in the hands of Mr. Lizars, in Edinburgh, and this day I received a letter from him, saying that 'the colorers had all struck work, and that my work was, in consequence, at a stand.' He asked me to try to find some persons here who would engage in that part of the business, and said he would exert himself to make all right again as soon as possible. This was quite a shock to my nerves, and for nearly an hour I deliberated whether I should not go at once to Edinburgh, but an engagement at Lord Spencer's, where I expected a subscriber, decided me to remain. I reached his lordship's house about twelve o'clock, and met there Dr. Walterton and the Rt. Hon. William S. Ponsonby engaged in conversation with Lady Spencer, a fat woman, of extremely engaging and unassuming manners. She entered into conversation with me at once about the habits of the wild turkey, how to tame them, and the like; while the gentlemen examined and praised my drawings, and the two lords subscribed for my work; and I went off rejoicing, between two rows of fine waiters, who seemed to wonder who the devil I could be, that Lady Spencer should shake me by the hand, and accompany me to the door.

" From there I went to Mr. Ponton's, and met Mr. Dibdin, and twenty ladies and gentlemen, who had assembled to see my drawings. Here four more subscribers were obtained. This, I thought, was a pretty good day's work; but on returning home I found a note from Mr. Vigors, giving the name of another subscriber, and informing me of the arrival of Charles Bonaparte in the city. I walked to the lodgings of the Prince of Musignano: he was out. I left my card, and soon after my return a servant told me he was below; I was not long in getting down stairs, and soon grasped his hand; we were mutually glad to meet on this distant shore. His mustachios and bearded chin and his fine head and eye were all unchanged. He wished to see all my drawings, and for almost the only time in England I opened my portfolio with intense pleasure. He said they were worthy to be published, and I felt proud of his opinion.

" As soon as he had gone my thoughts returned to the colorers, and I started off at once to find some, but with no success; all the establishments of the kind were closed from want of employment. But happening to pass a print-shop, I inquired if the proprietor knew of any colorers, and he at once gave me the name of one, who offered to work cheaper than I was paying in Edinburgh; and I wrote instantly to Mr. Lizars to send me twenty-five copies; and so I hope all will go on well again.

After a long hunt I entered a long dark alley in search of the colorer's house, to which I had been directed. It was ten o'clock, and after mounting two stories in search of the man, I knocked, and a little door was opened. The family were surprised by the appearance of a stranger, as much as I was by what I saw. A young man was sitting by a small window drawing; a woman whom I took to be his mother was washing a few potatoes in hot water; a younger woman nursed a child, leaning on the only bed in the room; and six little children, mostly girls, shabby in appearance and sallow in complexion, showed that hunger was not a stranger there. The young man arose, offered me his seat, and asked me politely what I wanted. I told him I was looking for a colorer. He replied that he once worked at it, but had abandoned the business, because he was unable to support his large family by it, even to provide them bread and potatoes. He showed me the work he was doing: it was a caricature of Canning, hiding himself behind some Roman Catholic priests, as if listening to their talk; each one of the priests held a rope in his hand, as if ready to hang their opponents, and the whole proved that the man had a good knowledge of drawing. Just then the mother told him breakfast was ready. The poor man begged me to excuse him, saying that he had not tasted anything the day before; that the potatoes were a present, he would eat soon, and then tell me of some colorers now in the business. I sat silently and saw the food equally divided; the mother, wife, children, and father soon swallowed their share, but it was scarcely enough to appease the hunger of the moment. He gave me as he ate the names of three men, and, pained by the scene before me, I rose to go. Just then the father said to the children and wife, 'It is high time you should go to work,' and asking me at the same time to remain a few moments longer. The family went off, and I felt relieved to know that they had some employment, and asked him what it was! He replied, 'Begging, sir.' All that family, wife, and half-grown girls, turned out in the streets of London to beg. He assured me that with all their united exertions they seldom had more than one meal a day ; and that in an extremity a few days before he had been compelled to sell his best bed to pay the rent of his miserable room. Unfortunately I had but a few shillings with me, because I had been advised to carry neither watch nor money in London, and had not the gratification of doing much to relieve him. He said his caricatures brought him in but little, and that despair had prompted him more than once to drown himself, for he was only a weight on the neck of his wife and children. Oh! how sick I am of London.

" *June* 21. Received a letter from Mr. Lizars, that he must discontinue my work. Have made an engagement with Mr. Havell for coloring, which I hope will relieve my embarrassment. Have painted a great deal to-day.

" *June* 22. Am invited to dine at the Royal Society's Club, with Charles Bonaparte. Gave some lessons in drawing to the daughter of Mr. Children, Mrs. Atkins : she has fine talents, but they are not cultivated so highly as Mrs. Edward Roscoe's. This evening Charles Bonaparte came with Lord Clifton, and several other gentlemen to examine my drawings. They were all learned ornithologists, but they all said that there were birds here which they had never dreamed of, and Bonaparte offered to name them for me. I was pleased at the suggestion, and with a pencil he wrote down upwards of fifty names, and invited me to publish them at once in manuscript at the Zoological Society. We had charming discussions about birds and their habits. Oh that *our* knowledge could be arranged into a solid mass ! I am sure that then the best ornithological publication of the birds of my beloved country would be produced. I cannot tell you how it strikes me, when I am at Bonaparte's lodgings, to hear his servant call him 'Your Royal Highness.' I think it ridiculous in the extreme, and cannot imagine how good Charles can bear it; but probably he does bear it because he is Good Charles.

" *July* 2. I am so completely out of spirits, that I have several times opened my book, held the pen, and felt anxious to write; but all in vain; I am too dull, too mournful.

" I have given the copy of my first number of the Birds to Mr. Children, a proof : it is the only one in existence, for which he paid me the price of all the subscribers, i. e., two guineas, and I may say with safety that the two guineas are the only two I have had on account of that work. I have finished another picture of the Rabbits, and am glad of it; it is all my consolation. I wish I were out of London."

But it does not appear that Audubon's despondency lasted very long. He dispelled it by a sudden rush into the provinces, where he was well received by former friends. From an entry made at Leeds on September 30, it is clear that even in London the sun had begun to shine out again.

" Nearly three months since I touched one of the sheets of my dear book. And I am quite ashamed of it, for I have had several interesting incidents to record, well deserving of relation, even in my poor humble style —a style much resembling my *painting in oil*. Now, nevertheless, I will recapitulate and note down as quickly as possible the primary ones.

" 1. I removed the publication of my ornithological work from Edinburgh to London; from Mr. Lizars to Mr. Robert Havell, No. 79 Newman street; because at

Edinburgh it came on too slowly, and also because I can have it done better and cheaper in London.

" 2. The King! My dear Book! Had my work presented to his Majesty by Sir Walter Waller, Bart, K. C. H., at the request of my most excellent friend J. P. Children, of the British Museum. His Majesty was pleased to call it fine, and permitted me to publish it under his particular patronage, approbation, and protection ; and became a subscriber on usual terms, not as kings generally do, but as a gentleman. And I look on such a deed as worthy of all kings in general. The Duchess of Clarence also put down her name ; and all my friends speak as if a mountain of sovereigns had dropped in an ample purse at once—and for *me !*"

CHAPTER XII.

N September 1st, 1828, Audubon quitted London for Paris, and his diary freshens a little after the salt breeze of the Channel. Much space, however, is as usual devoted to matters quite trivial in themselves, and not likely to interest any circle beyond the little domestic one for which the pages were intended. The enjoyment of fresh scenes is youthful and honest— quite unlike the pleasure of more sophisticated persons.

On arriving in Paris, his first visit was to the Jardin des Plantes, and to the great Cuvier. We shall select in series his notes on this and other matters, suppressing, as before, all the utterly pointless matter which fills up the diary under so many a date.

"We knocked, and asked for Baron Cuvier: he was in, but we were told was too busy to be seen. However, being determined to look at the great man, we waited and knocked again, and with a degree of firmness sent up our names. The messenger returned, bowed and led us upstairs, where, in a minute, Monsieur le Baron, like an excellent good man, came to us. He had heard much of my friend Swainson, and greeted him as he deserves, and was polite and kind to me, although he had never heard of me before. I looked at him, and here follows the result. Age about sixty-five; size, corpulent, five feet and five, English measure; head large, face wrinkled and brownish; eyes, very brilliant and sparkling; nose, aquiline, large, and red; mouth, large, with good lips; teeth, few, and blunted by age, excepting one on the lower jaw, which was massive, measuring nearly three-quarters of an inch square. This was Baron Cuvier; I have described him almost as if a *new species of a man*, from the mere skin. But as he has invited us to dine with him next Saturday at six o'clock, and I expect to have an opportunity of seeing more of him, I will then describe his habits as far as I am able.

"*September* 5. After a breakfast of grapes, figs, sardines, and French coffee, friend Swainson and I proceeded to the Jardin des Plantes, by the side of the river Seine, which here, Lucy, is not so large as the Bayou Sara, where I have often watched the alligators while bathing. Walking in Paris is disagreeable in the extreme. The streets are actually paved, but with scarcely a sidewalk, and a large gutter filled with dirty black water runs through the centre of each, and the people go about without any kind of order, either along the centre, or near the houses; carriages, carts, and so forth do the same, and I have wondered that so few accidents take place. We saw a very ugly iron bridge at the entrance called Pont Neuf, where stands the splendid statue of Henry IV. We were more attracted, however, by the sight of the immense number of birds offered for sale along the quays, and saw some rare specimens. A woman took us into her house, and showed us some hundreds from Bengal and Senegal, which quite surprised us.

"Weary with walking, we took a cabriolet, that brought us for twenty-five sous, to the Jardin, and we went to our appointment with Baron Cuvier. We saw him, and he gave us a ticket to admit us to the Musée, and promised us all we wished. In the Musée, M. Valencienne was equally kind. Having in my pocket a letter of introduction to Geoffroy de St. Hilaire, we went to his house in the gardens, and with him we were particularly pleased. He offered his services with good grace, much as an English gentleman would have done. M. Geoffroy proved to us that he understood the difference of ideas existing between English and Frenchmen perfectly. He repeated the words of Cuvier, and assured us that my work had never been heard of anywhere in France. He promised to take us to the Academy of Sciences on Monday next.

" We finally reached home, dressed, and started to dine with Baron Cuvier. We arrived within a minute of the appointed time, were announced by a servant in livery, as in England, and the Baron received and presented us kindly to his only daughter, a small, well-made, good-looking lady, with black sparkling eyes, and altogether extremely amiable. As I seldom go anywhere without meeting some person I have known elsewhere, so it proved here. I found among the company which had arrived before me a Fellow of the Linnæan Society, who knew me, and who seemed to have spoken to the Baron and his daughter of my work ; and I now perceived a degree of attention from him which I had not noticed at my first interview. The Baroness came in, an old, good, motherly-looking lady, and the company, sixteen in number, being present, dinner was announced. The Baroness led the way with a gentleman, the Baron took his daughter under his arm, but made Mr. Swainson and myself go before him ; and so the company all followed. Mr. Swainson was seated next to Mademoiselle Cuvier, who, fortunately for him, speaks excellent English. I was opposite her, by the side of the Baron, and had at my right elbow the F. L. S. There was not the same show of opulence at this dinner that I have seen in the same rank in England—no, not by any means ; but we had a good dinner, served à la Française : all seemed happy,

and all went on with more simplicity than in London.
The waiter who handed the wine called out the names of
three or four different sorts, and each person had his
choice. The dinner finished (I mean the eating part),
the Baroness rose, and all followed her into the drawing room, which is the library of the Baron; and I
liked it much, for I cannot bear the drinking-matches
of wine at the English tables. We had coffee, and
the company increased rapidly; and among the new
comers were my acquaintances Captain Parry, Monsieur
Condillot, and Mr. Lesson, just returned from a voyage
round the world. Cuvier stuck to Mr. Swainson and myself, and we talked ornithology: he asked the price of
my work, and I gave him a prospectus. The company
now filled the room, and as it grew late, and we had nearly five miles to ride we left à la Française, very well satisfied with this introductory step among the savans Fran-
çais.

"*September* 8. Went to pay my respects to Baron
Cuvier and Geoffroy St. Hilaire; found only the former
at home; he invited me to the Royal Institute, and I had
just time to return home and reach it before the sitting
of the Royal Académie des Sciences. I took my portfolio, and, on entering, inquired for Cuvier, who very
politely came to me, made the porter put my book on
the table, and assigned me a seat of honor. The séance
opened, and a tedious lecture was delivered on the vision
of the mole. Mr. Swainson accompanied me. Baron
Cuvier then arose, and announced us and spoke of my
work. It was shown and admired as usual, and Cuvier
was requested to review it for the memoirs of the Academy. Cuvier asked me to leave my book. I did, and he
commended it to the particular care of the librarians,
who are to show it to any who desire to see it; he also
said he would propose to the Academy to subscribe to it,
and if so, it will be a good day's work.

"*September* 9. Went to the Jardin du Roi, where I met young Geoffroy, who took me to a man who stuffs birds for the Prince d'Essling. He told me the Prince had a copy of my work (probably Wilson's or Selby's), and said he would subscribe if I would call on him to-morrow with him. After this I walked around the boulevards, looking at the strange things I saw there, thinking of my own strange life, and how wonderful my present situation in the land of my father and ancestors. From here I went to the Louvre, and as I was about to pass the gates of the Tuileries, a sentinel stopped me, saying no one could enter there with a *fur cap.* I went to another gate, and passed without challenge, and went to the Grand Gallery. There, among the Raphaels, and Correggios, Titians, Davids, and thousands of others, I feasted my eyes and enlarged my knowledge. From there I made my way to the Institut de France, and by appointment presented my prospectus to the secretary of the library. There I met young Geoffroy, an amiable and learned young man, who examined my work, paid me every attention, and gave me a room to myself for the inspection of specimens and to write in. How very different from the public institutions in England, where, instead of being bowed to, you have to bow to every one. The porters, clerks, and secretaries had all received orders to do everything I required, and I was looked upon with the greatest respect. I have now run the gauntlet of Europe, Lucy, and may be proud of two things—that I am considered the first ornithological painter and the first practical naturalist of America !

"*September* 10. Called on the bird-stuffer of the Prince d'Essling, who proposed to take me to the Prince's town residence. We were conducted into his museum, which surpasses in magnificence, and in the number of rare specimens of birds, shells, and books, all I have yet seen. We strolled about for a while, when word was sent us, that the Prince being indisposed, we must go to him. I took my pamphlet in my hand, and entered a fine room, where he lay reclining on a sofa ; but on seeing me, he rose up, bowed, and presented me to his beautiful young wife. While untying my book, both of them asked me some questions, and looked at me with seeming curiosity ; but as soon as a print was seen, they both exclaimed, 'Ah, c'est bien beau !' and then asked me if I did not know Charles Bonaparte. And when I answered 'Yes,' they both again said, 'Ah, it is the same gentleman of whom we have heard so much, the Man of the Woods ; the drawings are all made by him,' etc. The Prince said that he regretted very much that so few persons in France were able to subscribe to such a work, and that I must not expect more than six or eight names in Paris. He named all those whom he or his lady knew, and told me it would give him pleasure to add his name to my list. I drew it out, opened it, and asked him to write it himself : this he did with a good grace, next under the Duke of Rutland. This Prince, son of the famous Marshal Massena, is thirty years of age, apparently delicate, pale, slender, and yet good-looking, entirely devoted to Natural History. His wife is a beautiful young woman of about twenty, extremely graceful and polite. They both complimented me on the purity of my French, and wished me all the success I deserved. I went back to my friend in the cabinet, well contented, and we returned to our lodgings. Not liking our rooms at our hotel, to-day I shall remove to the Hôtel de France, where I have a large, clean, and comfortable room, and pay twenty-five sous per day. But I must tell thee that in France, although a man may be a prince or duke, he is called simply monsieur, and his lady, madam, and all are as easy of access as men without a great

name : this made me quite at my ease with Prince
d'Essling.

"*September* 11. I have been travelling all over Paris
to-day, and have accomplished nothing. Called on M.
Geoffroy St. Hilaire, and he gave me some good advice
and directions respecting obtaining the King's subscription, and others.

"*September* 12. Visited, at his library, the librarian
of the king, M. Van Praet, a small and white-haired gentleman, who assured me in the politest manner imaginable that it was out of the question to subscribe for so
heavy a work. He however gave me a card to introduce
me to M. Barbier, a librarian belonging to the king's private library at the Louvre. Here I learned that the inland
postage of a single letter from Paris to London is twenty-
four sous ; there is a mail to London four times a week.
After some trouble I found the library of the king, because I followed the direction 'toujours tout droit,' until
quite out of latitude and longitude by tacking and retack-
ing ; but at last I reached the place, and entered a gate
fronting the river, and found M. Barbier absent. But
later in the day I found him ; and he, not being able to
say anything definite himself, referred me to the Baron de
Boullerie, intendant of the king's household. I wrote to
him in French, the first letter I have written in this language in twenty-five years, and I dare say a very curious
one to such a personage as he is.

"*September* 13. Took my portfolio to Geoffroy de
St. Hilaire, and then to Baron Cuvier ; the former, after
examining it, retracted his opinion respecting its size, and
expressed himself pleased with it. A Mons. Dumesnil, a
French engraver, was sent to me by Prince d'Essling, and
I learned from him that my work could be done better and
at less expense in England than in France. Copper is
dearer here than in England, and good colorers much

more scarce. I have just returned with friend Swainson from Baron Cuvier's, who gives receptions to scientific men every Saturday. My book was on the table, and Cuvier received me with especial kindness, and put me at ease. Mons. Condillot I found remarkably amiable, and the company was much the same as on last Saturday. I found much pleasure in conversation with Cuvier and M. de Condillot. The former willingly assented to sit to Mr. Parker for his portrait, and the other told me if I visited Italy I must make his house my home. My work was examined, and Cuvier pronounced it the finest in existence of the kind. As we attempted to make our escape, Cuvier noticed us, ran and took us by the hand, and wished us to return; but we had a long and dark walk before us, and on that ground excused ourselves.

"*September* 15. France is poor indeed! This day I have attended the Royal Academy of Sciences, and had my plates examined by about one hundred persons. 'Fine, very fine !' issued from many mouths ; but they said also, 'What a work! what a price! who can pay it?' I recollected that I had thirty subscribers at Manchester, and mentioned it. They stared, and seemed surprised; but acknowledged that England, the little island of England, alone was able to support poor Audubon. Some went so far as to say that, had I been here four months ago, I should not have had even the Prince d'Essling for a subscriber. Poor France, thy fine climate, rich vineyards, and the wishes of the learned avail nothing ; thou art a destitute beggar, and not the powerful friend thou wert represented to me. Now it is that I plainly see how happy, or lucky, it was in me not to have come to France first ; for if I had, my work now would not have had even a beginning. It would have perished like a flower in October ; and I should have returned to my woods, without the hope of leaving behind that eternal fame which my ambition, industry, and perseverance, long to enjoy. Not a subscriber, Lucy ; no, not one !

"I have also been again at Cuvier's to-day, to introduce Mr. Parker, to begin his portrait. You would like to hear more of Cuvier and his house. Well, we rang the bell, and a waiter came, and desired that we would wipe our feet ; we needed it, for we were very muddy. This over, we followed the man up-stairs, and in the first room we entered I saw a slight figure in black gliding out at an opposite door like a sylph. It was Miss Cuvier, not quite ready to receive company. Off she flew, like a dove before falcons. However, we followed our man, who every moment turned to us and repeated, 'This way, gentlemen.' Then we passed through eight rooms filled with beds or books, and at last reached a sort of laboratory, the sanctum sanctorum of Cuvier ; nothing there but books, the skeletons of animals, and reptiles. Our conductor bid us sit, and left us to seek for the Baron. My eyes were occupied in the interval in examining the study of this great man, and my mind in reflecting on the wonders of his knowledge. All but order was about his books, and I concluded that he read and studied, and was not fond of books because he was the owner of them, as some great men seem to be whom I have known. Our conductor returned directly, and led us to another laboratory, where we found the Baron. Great men show politeness in a particular way; they receive you without much demonstration ; a smile suffices to assure you that you are welcome, and keep about their avocations as if you were a member of the family."

"Parker was introduced while Cuvier was looking at a small lizard, through a vial of spirits that contained it. I see now his speaking eye, half closed, as if *quizzing* its qualities, and as he wrote 'ts name with a pencil on a

8

label, he bowed his body in acquiescence.   'Come and breakfast with me, Mr. Parker, on Thursday next, at ten o'clock, and I will be your man ;' and on he went quizzing more lizards.

"*September* 18.   Went with Parker to Baron Cuvier's. We met Miss Cuvier, who had made all preparations to receive us.   The Baron came in and seated himself in a comfortable arm-chair. Great men, as well as great women, have their share of vanity, and I soon discovered that the Baron thinks himself a fine-looking man.   His daughter seemed to understand this, and remarked more than once, that her father had his under lip much more swelled than usual ; and she added that the line of his nose was extremely fine.   I passed my fingers over mine, and, lo ! I thought just the same.   I see the Baron now quite as plainly as I did this morning, an old green surtout about him, a neckcloth, that would have wrapped his whole body if unfolded, loosely tied about his chin, and his silver locks looking like those of a man who loves to study books better than to visit barbers.   His fine eye glistened from under his thick eyebrows, and he smiled as he spoke to me.   Miss Cuvier is a most agreeable lady, and opening a book, she asked to read aloud to us all ; and on she went in a clear, well-accented tone, from a comic play, well calculated to amuse us for the time, and during the monotony of sitting for a portrait, which is always a great bore.   Mrs. Cuvier joined us, and I noticed her expression was one of general sadness, and she listened with a melancholy air that depressed my own spirits.   The Baron soon expressed himself fatigued, and went out, and I advised Parker to keep him as short a time as possible.   We were in one of his libraries, and he asked his daughter to show us two portraits of himself, painted some ten years ago.   They were only so so. Meanwhile the Baron named next Thursday for another sitting.

"*September* 20. This morning I had the pleasure of seeing the venerable Redouté, the flower-painter *par excellence*. After reading Lesueur's note to him, dated five years ago, he looked at me fixedly, and said, ' Well, sir, I am truly glad to become acquainted with you ;' and without further ceremony he showed me his best works. His flowers are grouped with peculiar taste, well drawn and precise in the outlines, and colored with a pure brilliancy, which resembles Nature immeasurably better than I ever saw it before. Redouté dislikes all that is not pure Nature ; he cannot bear drawings of stuffed birds or quadrupeds, and expressed a desire to see a work wherein Nature is delineated in an animated way. He said he dined every Friday at the Duke of Orleans' ; he would take my work there next week, and obtain his subscription, if not the Duchess' also. He asked for a prospectus, and invited me to return next Wednesday. I looked over hundreds of his drawings, and learned that he sold them at high prices, some as high as two hundred and fifty guineas. On my way home I met the secretary of the king's library, who told me that the Baron de la Boullerie had given orders to have my work inspected, and if approved, to subscribe for it. I have found that letters of introduction are not as useful here as in England. Cuvier, to whom I had no letter, and to whom my name was unknown before my arrival, is the only man who has yet invited me to his house. I wished to go this evening to his scientific soirée, to which he invited me, but I did not, because I have been two successive Saturdays, and I am afraid of intruding, although the rude awkwardness I formerly felt has worn nearly smooth.

"*September* 22. This was the grand day appointed by Baron Cuvier for reading his report on my work at the French Institute. The French Institute ! Shall I call it superior to the Royal Academy of London ? I cannot

better answer the interrogation, than by the reports of
the presidents of these institutions on my work.   By particular invitation of the Baron, I was at the Institute at
half-past one, and·no Baron there.   I sat opposite the
clock, and counted the minutes one after another ; but
the clock, insensible to my impatience, moved regularly,
and ticked its time just as if Audubon had never existed.
I undertook to count the numerous volumes which filled
the compartments of the library, but my eye became be·
wildered, and as it reached the distant centre of the hall,
rested on the figure of Voltaire ! Poor Voltaire ! had
he not his own share of troubles ? how was he treated?
Savants like shadows passed before me, nodded, and
proceeded to their seats, and resting their heads on their
hands, looked for more knowledge in different memoirs.
I, Lucy, began journeying to America, sailed up its rivers, across its lakes, along its coasts, and up the Mississippi, until I reached Bayou Sara, and leaping on shore,
and traversing the magnolia forests, bounded towards
thee, my dearest friend,—when the clock struck, and suddenly called me to myself in the Royal Institute, patiently waiting for the Baron.

"The number of savants increased, and my watch and
the clock told thaf the day was waning.   I took a book
and read, but it went into my mind and left no impression.   The savants increased more and more, and by-and-
by among them my quick eye discerns the Baron.   I had
been asked fifty times if I were waiting for him, and had
been advised to go to his house ; but I sat and watched
like a sentinel at his post.   I heard his voice and his
footstep, and at last saw him, warm, apparently fatigued,
and yet extremely kindly, coming towards me, with a
' My dear sir, I am sorry to know that you have waited so
long here ; I was in my cabinet; come with me.'   During
all this talk, to which I bowed, and followed him, his hand

was driving a pencil with great rapidity, and I discovered that he was actually engaged in making his report. I thought of La Fontaine's 'Fable of the Turtle and the Hare,' and of many other things; and I was surprised that so great a man, who, of course, being great, must take care of each of his actions with a thousand times more care than a common individual, to prevent falls, when surrounded, as all great men are, by envy, cowardice, malice, and all other evil spirits, should leave to the last moment the writing of a report, to every word of which the 'Forty of France' would lend a critical ear. We were now in his cabinet; my enormous book lay before him, and I shifted swiftly the different plates that he had marked for examination. His pencil kept constantly moving; he turned and returned the sheets of his pamphlet with amazing accuracy, and noted as quickly as he saw all that he saw. We were both wet with perspiration. When this was done, he invited me to call on him to-morrow at half-past ten, and went off towards the council-room.

"*September* 23. I waited in Cuvier's departmental section until past eleven, when he came in, as much in a hurry as ever, and yet as kind as ever, always the perfect gentleman. The report had been read, and the Institute, he said, had subscribed for one copy; and he told me the report would appear in next Saturday's 'Globe.' I called on M. Feuillet, principal librarian of the Institute, to inquire how I was to receive the subscription. He is a large, stout man, had on a hunting-cap, and began by assuring me that the Institute was in the habit of receiving a discount on all the works it takes. My upper lip curled, not with pleasure, but with a sneer at such a request; and I told the gentleman that I never made discounts on a work which cost me a life of much trouble and too much expense ever to be remunerated; so the matter dropped.

"*September* 24. To-day I was told that Gerard, the great Gerard, the pupil of my old master David, wished to see me and my works. I propose to visit him to-morrow.

"*Se tember* 25. I have trotted from pillar to post through this big town, from the Palais Royal to the Jardin du Luxembourg, in search of Mons. Le Médécin Bertrand, after a copy of Cuvier's Report ; such is man, all avaricious of praise by nature. Three times did I go to the ' Globe ' office, from places three miles apart, until at last, wearied and brought to bay, I gave up the chase. At last I went to the king's library, and I learned from the librarian, a perfect gentleman, that the court had inspected my work, and were delighted with it ; and he told me that kings were not generally expected to pay for works ; and I gave him to understand that I was able to keep the work if the king did not purchase.

"To-day I saw the original copy of Cuvier's report on my work. It is quite an eulogium, but not as feelingly written as Mr. Swainson's ; nevertheless, it will give the French an idea of my work, and may do good.

"The following is an extract translated from the report :—

"'The Academy of Sciences have requested me to make a verbal report on the work of Mr. Audubon, laid before it at a former session, on the "Birds of North America." It may be described in a few words as the most magnificient monument which has yet been erected to ornithology. The author, born in Louisiana, and devoted from his youth to painting, was twenty-five years ago a pupil in the school of David. Having returned to his own country, he thought he could not make a better use of his talents than by representing the most brilliant productions of that hemisphere. The accurate observation necessary for such representations as he wished to make soon rendered him a naturalist.

" ' It is in this double capacity of artist and savant that he produced the work, which has been offered to the inspection of the Academy. You have been struck by the size of the book, which is equal or superior to the largest of that kind that has ever been published, and is nearly as large as the double plates of the Description of Egypt. This extraordinary dimension has enabled him to give specimens of the eagle and vulture of their natural size, and to multiply those which are smaller in such a manner as to represent them in every attitude.

" ' He was thus able to represent on the same plates, and of the natural size, the plants which these birds most commonly frequent, and to give the fullest detail of their nests and eggs.

" ' The execution of these plates, so remarkable for their size, appears to have succeeded equally well with regard to the drawing, the engraving, and the coloring. And although it is difficult in coloring to give perspectives with as much effect as in painting, properly so called, that is no defect in a work on natural history. Naturalists prefer the real color of objects to those accidental tints which are the result of the varied reflections of light necessary to complete picturesque representations, but foreign and even injurious to scientific truth.

" ' Mr. Audubon has already prepared four hundred drawings, which contain nearly two thousand figures, and he proposes to publish them successively if he receives sufficient encouragement from lovers of science. A work conceived and executed on so vast a plan has but one fault, and doubtless in that respect my auditors have already anticipated me ; it is that its expense renders it almost inaccessible to the greater part of those to whom it would be most necessary. It certainly cannot be said that the price is exorbitant. One number of five plates costs two guineas ; each plate comes to only ten or twelve francs. As there will be published but five numbers a year, the annual expense would not be enormous. It is desirable, at least for art as well as science, that the great public libraries—and the wealthy, who love to enrich their collections with works of luxury—should be willing to secure it.

" ' Formerly the European naturalists were obliged to make known to America the riches she possessed ; but now Mitchell, Harler, and Bonaparte give back with interest to Europe what America had received. Wilson's history of the " Birds of the United States " equals in elegance our most beautiful works on ornithology. If that of Mr. Audubon should be completed, we shall be obliged to acknowledge that America, in magnificence of execution, has surpassed the old world.'

" *September* 30. Mr. Coutant, the great engraver of Paris, came to see my work to-day. When I opened the book he stared ; and as I turned over the engravings, he exclaimed often 'Oh, mon Dieu ! quel ouvrage !' Old Redouté also visited me, and brought an answer to my letter from the Duc d'Orleans. At one o'clock I went with my portfolio to the Palais Royal ; and as I do not see dukes every day, dearest, I will give you an account of my visit.

" The Palais Royal of the Duke of Orleans is actually the entrance of the Palais Royal, the public walk to which we go almost every evening, and which is guarded by many sentinels. On the right I saw a large, fat, red-coated man, through the ground window, whom I supposed to be the porter of his Royal Highness : he opened the door, and I took off my fur cap, and walked in without ceremony. I gave him my card, and requested him to send it up-stairs. He said Monseigneur was not in, but I might go into the antechamber, and I ascended one of the finest staircases my feet had ever trod. They parted at the bottom, in a rounding form of about twenty-four feet in breadth, to meet on the second-floor, on a platform, lighted by a skylight, showing the beauties of the surrounding walks, and in front of which were three doors, two of which I tried in vain to open. The third, however, gave way, and I found myself in the outer ante-chamber, with about twelve servants, who all rose up and stood until I seated myself on a soft, red, velvet-covered bench. Not a word was said to me, and I gazed on the men and place with a strange sensation of awkwardness. The walls were bare, the floor black and white squares of marble, over which a sergeant paced, wearing a broad belt. I waited some minutes, looking on this dumb show, and wondering how long it would last, when I accosted the sergeant, and told him I wished to see the duke, and that I had come here by his order. He made a profound bow, and conducted me to another room, where several gentlemen were seated writing. I told one of them my errand, and he immediately showed me into an immense and elegantly-furnished apartment, and ordered my book to be brought up. In this room I bowed to two gentlemen whom I knew belonged to the Legion of Honor, and walked about, examining the fine marble statues and pictures. A gentleman soon entered the room, and coming towards me with an agreeable smile, asked if perchance my name was Audubon. I bowed, and he replied, 'Bless me, we thought you had gone, and left your portfolio. My uncle has been waiting for you twenty minutes ; pray, sir, follow me.' We entered another room, and I saw the duke approaching me, and was introduced to him by his nephew. I do not recollect ever having seen a finer man, in form, deport-ment, and elegant manners, than this Duke of Orleans. He had my book brought in, and helped me to untie the strings and arrange the table, and began by saying that

8*

he felt a great pleasure in subscribing to the work of an American ; that he had been kindly treated in the United States, and would never forget it. When the portfolio was opened, and I held up the plate of the Baltimore oriole, with a nest swinging amongst the tender twigs of the yellow poplar, he said, 'This surpasses all I have seen, and I am not astonished now at the eulogium of M. Redouté.' He spoke partly in English and partly in French, and said much of America, of Pittsburg, the Ohio, New Orleans, the Mississippi and its steamboats; and then added, 'You are a great and noble nation, a wonderful nation!' The duke promised to write to the Emperor of Austria for me, and to the King of Sweden, and other crowned heads, and to invite them to subscribe, and requested me to send a note to-day to the Minister of the Interior. I remained talking with him and his nephew more than an hour. I asked him to give me his own signature on my list of subscribers. He smiled, took it, and wrote, in very legible letters, 'Le Duc d'Orleans.' I now thought that to remain any longer would be an intrusion, and thanking him respectfully, I bowed, shook hands, and retired. As I passed down the servants stared at me with astonishment, wondering, doubtless, what could have obtained me so long and intimate an interview with their master.

"*October* 1. Called to-day on M. Gerard, of whom France may boast without a blush. It was ten o'clock when I reached his hotel ; but as he is an Italian, born at Rome, and retains the habits of his countrymen, keeps late hours, and seldom takes his tea before one o'clock in the morning, I found him just up, and beginning his day's work. When I entered his rooms they were filled with persons of both sexes, and as soon as my name was announced, Gerard, a small, well-formed man, came towards me, took my hand, and said, 'Welcome, brother in arts!" I liked this much, and felt gratified to have broken the ice so easily, and my perspiration subsided.

"Gerard was all curiosity to see my drawings, and old Redouté, who was also present, came to me and spoke so highly of them before they were opened, that I feared Gerard would be disappointed. However, the book was opened accidentally at the plate of the parrots, and Gerard, taking it up without speaking, looked at it with an eye as critical as my own for several minutes, put it down, and took up the mocking-birds, and then offering me his hand, said, 'Mr. Audubon, you are the king of ornithological painters. We are all children in France or Europe. Who would have expected such things from the woods of America!' I received compliments on all sides, and Gerard talked of nothing but my work, and asked me to give him some prospectuses to send to Italy. He also repeated what Baron Cuvier had said in the morning, and hoped that the Minister would order a number of copies for the government. I closed the book, and sauntered around the room, admiring the superb prints, mostly taken from his own paintings. The ladies were all engaged at cards, and money did not appear to be scarce in this part of Paris. Mrs. Gerard is a small, fattish woman, to whom I made a bow, and saw but for a moment. The ladies were dressed very finely, quite in a new fashion to me, pointed corsets before, with some hanging trimmings, and very full robes of rich and differently-colored satins and other materials.

"*October* 20. Nothing to do, and fatigued with looking at Paris. Four subscriptions in seven weeks is very slow work. . . . . . The stock-pigeon, or cushat, roosts in the trees of the garden of the Tuileries in considerable numbers. They arrive about sunset, settle at first on the highest trees and driest naked branches, then gradually lower themselves to the trunks of the trees and the thickest parts of the foliage, and remain there all night. They leave at the break of day, and fly off in a northerly direction. Blackbirds also do the same, and are extremely noisy before dark ; some few rooks and magpies are seen there also. In the Jardin or walks of the Palais Royal the common sparrows are prodigiously plentiful ; very tame, fed by ladies and children, and often killed with blowguns by mischievous boys. The mountain finch passes in scattered numbers over Paris at this season, going northerly. And now, my love, wouldst thou not believe me once more in the woods, and hard at it? Alas! I wish I were. What precious time I am losing in this Europe! When shall I go home?

" *October* 26. I have not written for several days, because I have been waiting, and had no inclination. Meanwhile a note came from Baron de la Bouillerie, announcing the king's subscription for six copies; and I have appointed an agent in Paris, and am now ready to leave. I have bid adieu to Baron Cuvier and Geoffrey St. Hilaire, and have taken a seat in the rotunda for Calais and London direct. I have paid twenty francs in advance, and long for to-morrow, to be on my way to England. I shall have been absent two months, have expended forty pounds, and obtained thirteen subscribers."

CHAPTER XIII.

ONDON, Nov. 9. This is an eventful day in the history of my great work on the Birds of America. Mr. Havell has taken the drawings which are to form the eleventh number, and it will be the first number for the year 1829. I wished several numbers to be engraved as soon as possible, for reasons which, if known to thee, Lucy, would fill thy heart with joy.

"*November* 10. I am painting as much as the short days will allow; but it is so very cold to my southern constitution, that I am freezing on the side farthest from the fire. I have finished two pictures for the Duke of Orleans—one of the grouse, with which I regret to part without a copy, though I have taken the outline.

"*December* 23. After so long an absence from thee, my dear Book, it will be difficult to write up a connected record of intervening events, but I will try and recall what is worth recording. My main occupation has been painting every day. I have finished my two large pictures of the Eagle and the Lamb, and the Dog and the Pheasants, and now, as usual, can scarce bear to look at them. My amiable pupil, Miss Hudson, has kept me company, and her pencil has turned some of my drawings into pictures. I have dined out but once, with my friend J. G. Children, of the British Museum, on the Coronation Day ; and there I met several friends and scientific acquaintance. The want of exercise, and close application, have reduced my flesh very much, and I would have been off for Manchester, Liverpool, &c., but have had no complete copy of my work to take with me.

"*December* 25. Another Christmas in England! I dined at Mr. Goddard's, in the furthest opposite end of London, with a company mostly American. Sir Thomas Lawrence called to see my paintings while I was absent. Mr. Havell showed them to him, and made the following report to me :—'Looking at the picture of the Eagle and the Lamb, he said, "That is a fine picture." He examined it closely, and then turned to the Pheasants, which I call "Sauve qui peut ;" this he looked at from different points, and with his face close to the canvas, and had it rolled to different points, for more light and new views, but expressed no opinion about it. The Otter came next. He said, "The animal is very fine." He left, and promised to return in a few days.' I met him soon after, and he told me he would call and make selection of a picture to be exhibited at Somerset House, and would speak to the council about it."

By this time, as the journal shows, Audubon had resolved to visit America, and had begun to make active preparations for leaving.

"*March* 31. It is so long since I have written in my life book, that I felt quite ashamed on opening it to see that the last date was Christmas of last year. Fie, Audubon! Well, I have made up my mind to go to America, and with some labor and some trouble perfected all arrangements. I have given the agency of my work to my excellent friend Children, of the British Museum, who kindly offered to see to it during my absence. I have settled all my business as well as I could, taken my passage on board the packet-ship Columbia, Captain Joseph Delano, to sail from Portsmouth, and paid thirty pounds for my passage.

"*April* 1. I went by mail to the smoky city of Portsmouth ; have hoisted the anchor, am at sea, and *sea-sick*.

"The cry of ' land, land, land ! ' thrice repeated, roused me from my torpor, and acted like champagne to refresh my spirits. I rushed on deck, and saw in the distance a deep gray line, like a wall along the horizon, and toward which the ship was rolling and cutting her way. My heart swelled with joy, and all seemed like a pleasant dream at first ; but as soon as the reality was fairly impressed on my mind, tears of joy rolled down my cheeks. I clasped my hands, and fell on my knees, and raising my eyes to heaven—that happy land above—I offered my thanks to our God, that He had preserved and prospered me in my long absence, and once more permitted me to approach these shores so dear to me, and which hold my heart's best earthly treasures.

"*May* 5. New York. I have brought thee, my English book, all the way across the Atlantic, too sea-sick to hold any converse with thee—sea-sick all the way, until the morning when I saw my dear native land. But no matter, I have safely landed. We left England with one hundred and fifty souls, and put them all ashore at New York, except one poor black fellow, who thought proper to put an end to his existence by jumping overboard one dark night. A Mr. Benjamin Smith subscribed to my work on the passage. He had his family, eight servants, five dogs, and cloth and twine enough to fly kites the world over—an excellent and benevolent man.

"My state-room companion was a colonel from Russia, named Sir Isaac Coffin, and he did all he could to make the voyage as pleasant as possible under the circumstances. I was well received in New York by all my acquaintances, and Dr. Paxallis took me to the Collector of the Customs, who, on reading President Jackson's letters to me, gave free admission to my books and luggage. My work was exhibited here, and a report made on it to the New York Lyceum ; and I made the acquaintance of Mr. William Cooper, the friend of Charles Bonaparte, a fine, kind person.

"*May* 14. I left New York for Philadelphia, in company with Mr. Thomas Wharton, an excellent, but not remarkably intellectual man, and took board with Mrs. Bradley, in Arch Street. There I spent three days, and then removed to Camden, New Jersey, where I spent three weeks in observing the habits of the migratory warblers and other birds which arrive in vast numbers in the spring. From there I returned to Philadelphia to visit the sea-shores of New Jersey."

Here follows his elaborate account of that visit.

"GREAT EGG HARBOR.

"Having made all the necessary preparations to visit the sea-shores of New Jersey, for the purpose of making myself acquainted with their feathered inhabitants, I left early in June. The weather was pleasant, and the country seemed to smile in the prospect of bright days and gentle gales. Fishermen-gunners passed daily between Philadelphia and the various small seaports, with Jersey waggons laden with fish, fowls, and other provision, or with such articles as were required by the families of those hardy boatmen ; and I bargained with one of them to take myself and my baggage to Great Egg Harbor. One afternoon, about sunset, the vehicle halted at my lodgings, and the conductor intimated that he was anxious to proceed as quickly as possible. A trunk, a couple of guns, and such other articles as are found necessary by persons whose pursuits are similar to mine, were immediately thrust into the waggon, and were followed by their owner. The conductor whistled to his steeds, and off we went at a round pace over the loose and deep sand that in almost every part of this State forms the basis of the roads. After a while we overtook a whole caravan of similar vehicles moving in the same direction; and when we got near them our horses slackened their pace to a regular walk, the driver leaped from his seat, I followed his example, and we presently found ourselves in the midst of a group of merry waggoners, relating their adventures of the week, it being now Saturday night. One gave intimation of the number of 'sheep's-heads' he had taken to town; another spoke of the curlews which yet remained on the sands; and a third boasted of having gathered so many dozens of marsh hens' eggs. · I inquired if the fish-hawks were plentiful near Great Egg Harbor, and was answered by an elderly man, who, with a laugh, asked if I had ever seen the 'weak fish' along the coast without the bird in question. Not knowing the animal he had named, I confessed my ignorance, when the whole party burst into a loud laugh, in which, there being nothing better for it, I joined.

"About midnight the caravan reached a half-way house, where we rested a while. Several roads diverged from this spot, and the waggons separated, one only keeping us company. The night was dark and gloomy, but the sand of the road indicated our course very distinctly. Suddenly the galloping of horses struck my ear, and on looking back, we perceived that our waggon must in an instant be in imminent danger. The driver leaped off, and drew his steeds aside, barely in time to allow the runaways to pass without injuring us. Off they went at full speed, and not long after their owner came up panting, and informed us that they had suddenly taken fright

at some noise proceeding from the woods, but hoped they
would soon stop. Immediately after we heard a crash,
then for a few moments all was silent; but the neighing
of the horses presently assured us that they had broken
loose. On reaching the spot we found the waggon upset, and a few yards further on were the horses quietly
browsing by the road-side.

"The first dawn of morn in the Jerseys, in the month
of June, is worthy of a better description than I can furnish; and therefore I shall only say that the moment the
sunbeams blazed over the horizon, the loud and mellow
notes of the meadow lark saluted our ears. On each side
of the road were open woods, on the tallest trees of
which I observed at intervals the nest of a fish-hawk, far
above which the white-breasted bird slowly winged its
way as it commenced its early journey to the sea, the
odor of which filled me with delight. In half an hour
more we were in the centre of Great Egg Harbor.

"There I had the good fortune to be received into
the house of a thoroughbred fisherman-gunner, who, besides owning a comfortable cot, only a few hundred yards
from the shore, had an excellent woman for a wife, and a
little daughter as playful as a kitten, though as wild as a
sea-gull. In less than half an hour I was quite at home,
and the rest of the day was spent in devotion. Oysters,
though reckoned out of season at this period, are as good
as ever when fresh from their beds, and my first meal was
of some as large and white as any I have eaten. The
sight of them, placed before me on a clean table, with an
honest industrious family in my company, never failed to
afford more pleasure than the most sumptuous fare under
different circumstances, and our conversation being simple and harmless, gayety shone in every face. As we became better acquainted, I had to answer several questions relative to the object of my visit. The good man

rubbed his hands with joy as I spoke of shooting and fishing, and of long excursions through the swamps and marshes around. My host was then, and I hope still is, a tall, strong-boned, muscular man, of dark complexion, with eyes as keen as those of the sea eagle. He was a tough walker, laughed at difficulties, and could pull an oar with any man. As to shooting, I have often doubted whether he or Mr. Egan, the worthy pilot of Indian Isle, was best ; and rarely indeed have I seen either of them miss a shot.

" At daybreak on Monday I shouldered my double-barrelled gun, and my host carried with him a long fowling piece, a pair of oars, and a pair of oyster-tongs, while the wife and daughter brought along a seine. The boat was good, the breeze gentle, and along the inlets we sailed for parts well known to my companions. To such naturalists as are qualified to observe many different objects at the same time, Great Egg Harbor would probably afford as ample a field as any part of our coast, excepting the Florida Keys. Birds of many kinds are abundant, as are fishes and testaceous animals. The forests shelter many beautiful plants, and even on the driest sand-bar you may see insects of the most brilliant tints. Our principal object, however, was to procure certain birds known there by the name of lawyers ; and to accomplish this we entered and followed for several miles a winding inlet or bayou, which led us to the interior of a vast marsh, where, after some search, we found the birds and their nests. Our seine had been placed across the channel, and when we returned to it the tide had run out and left in it a number of fine fishes, some of which we cooked and ate on the spot. One, which I considered as a curiosity, was saved and transmitted to Baron Cuvier. Our repast ended, the seine was spread out to dry, and we again betook ourselves to the marshes, to pursue our researches until the return of the tide. Having collected enough to satisfy us, we took up our oars and returned to the shore in front of the fisherman's house, where we dragged the seine several times with success.

"In this manner I passed several weeks along those delightful and healthy shores—one day going to the woods to search the swamps in which the herons bred, passing another amid the joyous cries of the marsh hens, and on a third carrying slaughter among the white breasted sea-gulls ; by way of amusement sometimes hauling the fish called the 'sheep's-head' from an eddy along the shore ; watching the gay terns as they danced in the air, or plunged into the water to seize the tiny fry. Many a drawing I made at Egg Harbor, and many a pleasant day I spent along its shores ; and much pleasure would it give me once more to visit the good and happy family (Captain Horam's) in whose house I resided there.

"*September* 1. Having accomplished my purpose in visiting the sea-shore of New Jersey, I returned to Philadelphia, and made preparations to go to the Great Pine Swamp, in Northumberland County, Pennsylvania.

"THE GREAT PINE SWAMP.

"I left Philadelphia at four of the morning by the coach, with no other accoutrements than I knew to be absolutely necessary for the jaunt which I intended to make. These consisted of a wooden box, containing a small stock of linen, drawing-paper, my journal, colors and pencils, together with twenty-five pounds of shot, some flints, a due quantum of cash, my gun, 'Tear Jacket,' and a heart as true to nature as ever.

"Our coaches are none of the best, nor do they move with the velocity of those of some other countries. It was eight, and a dark night, when I reached Mauch Chunk, now so celebrated in the Union for its rich coal

mines, and eighty-eight miles distant from Philadelphia.
I had passed through a diversified country, part of which
was highly cultivated, while the rest was yet in a state of
nature, and consequently much more agreeable to me.
On alighting I was shown to the travellers' room, and on
asking for the landlord, saw coming towards me a fine-
looking young man, to whom I made known my wishes.
He spoke kindly, and offered to lodge and board me at a
much lower rate than travellers who go there for the very
simple pleasure of being dragged on the railway. In a
word, I was fixed in four minutes, and that most comfortably.

" No sooner had the approach of day been announced
by the cocks of the little village, than I marched out
with my gun and note-book, to judge for myself of the
wealth of the country. After traversing much ground,
and crossing many steep hills, I returned, if not wearied,
at least much disappointed at the extraordinary scarcity of
birds. So I bargained to be carried in a cart to the central parts of the Great Pine Swamp ; and although a heavy
storm was rising, ordered my conductor to proceed. The
weather had become tremendous, and we were thoroughly drenched. We wound round many a mountain, and at
last crossed the highest. But my resolution being fixed,
the boy was obliged to continue his driving. Having already travelled fifteen miles or so, we left the turnpike
and struck up a narrow and bad road, that seemed merely cut out to enable the people of the swamp to receive the
necessary supplies from the village which I had left.
Some mistakes were made, and it was almost dark when
a post directed us to the habitation of a Mr. 'edediah
Irish, to whom I had been recommended. We now
rattled down a steep declivity, edged on one side by almost perpendicular rocks, and on the other by a noisy
stream, which seemed grumbling at the approach of

strangers. The ground was so overgrown by laurels and tall pines of different kinds, that the whole presented only a mass of darkness.

"At length we got to the house, the door of which was already opened, the sight of strangers being nothing uncommon in our woods, even in the most remote parts. On entering I was presented with a chair, while my conductor was shown the way to the stable ; and on expressing a wish that I should be permitted to remain in the house for some weeks, I was gratified by receiving the sanction of the good woman to my proposal, although her husband was then from home. As I immediately fell talking about the nature of the country, and if birds were numerous in the neighborhood, Mrs. Irish, more *au fait* to household affairs than ornithology, sent for a nephew of her husband, who soon made his appearance, and in whose favor I became at once prepossessed. He conversed like an educated person, saw that I was comfortably disposed of, and finally bid me good-night, in such a tone as made me quite happy.

" The storm had rolled away before the first beams of the morning sun shone brightly on the wet foliage, displaying all its richness and beauty. My ears were greeted by the notes, always sweet and mellow, of the woodthrush, and other songsters. Before I had gone many steps the woods echoed to the report of my gun, and I picked from among the leaves a lovely bird long sought for, but till then sought for in vain. I needed no more, and standing still for a while, I was soon convinced that the Great Pine Swamp harbored many other objects interesting to me. The young man joined me, bearing his rifle, and offered to accompany me through the woods, all of which he well knew. But I was anxious to transfer to paper the form and beauty of the little bird I had in my hand ; and requesting him to break a twig of blooming laurel, we returned to the house, speaking of nothing else than the picturesque beauty of the country around.

" A few days passed, during which I became acquainted with my hostess and her sweet children, and made occasional rambles, but spent the greater portion of my time in drawing. One morning, as I stood near the window of my room, I remarked a tall and powerful man alight from his horse, loose the girth of his saddle, raise the latter with one hand, pass the bridle over the head of the animal with the other, and move towards the house, while the horse betook himself to the little brook to drink. I heard some movement in the room below, and again the same tall person walked towards the mills and stores, a few hundred yards from the house. In America, business is the first object in view at all times, and rightly it should be so. Soon after, my hostess entered my room accompanied by the fine-looking woodsman, to whom, as Mr. Jedediah Irish, I was introduced. Reader, to describe to you the qualities of that excellent man, were vain ; you should know him as I do, to estimate the value of such men in our sequestered forests. He not only made me welcome, but promised all his assistance in forwarding my views. The long walks and long talks we have had together I never can forget, nor the many beautiful birds which we pursued, shot, and admired. The juicy venison, excellent bear's flesh, and delightful trout that daily formed my food, methinks I can still enjoy. And then what pleasure I had in listening to him, as he read his favorite poems of Burns, while my pencil was occupied in smoothing and softening the drawing of the bird before me. Was not this enough to recall to my mind the early impressions that had been made upon it by the description of the golden age, which I here found realized ? The Lehigh about this place forms numerous short turns between the mountains, and affords frequent

falls, as well as, below the falls, deep pools, which render this stream a most valuable one for mills of any kind.
Not many years before this date my host was chosen by
the agent of the Lehigh Coal Company as their mill-
wright, and manager for cutting down the fine trees which
covered the mountains around.   He was young, robust,
active, industrious, and persevering.   He marched to the
spot where his abode now is, with some workmen, and
by dint of hard labor first cleared the road mentioned
above, and reached the river at the centre of a bend,
where he fixed on erecting various mills.   The pass here
is so narrow that it looks as if formed by the bursting
asunder of the mountain, both sides ascending abruptly,
so that the place where the settlement was made is in
many parts difficult of access, and the road then newly
cut was only sufficient to permit men and horses to come
to the spot where Jedediah and his men were at work. So
great in fact where the difficulties of access, that, as he
told me, pointing to a spot about 150 feet above us, they
for many months slipped from it their barrelled provisions, assisted by ropes, to their camp below.   But no
sooner was the first saw-mill erected, than the axemen began their devastation.   Trees one after another were, and
are yet constantly heard falling during the days, and in
calm nights the greedy mills told the sad tale that in a
century the noble forests around would exist no more.
Many mills were erected, many dams raised, in defiance
of the impetuous Lehigh.   One full third of the trees have
already been culled, turned into boards, and floated as
far as Philadelphia.   In such an undertaking the cutting
of the trees is not all.   They have afterwards to be hauled
to the edge of the mountains bordering the river, launched
into the stream, and led to the mills, over many shallows
and difficult places.   Whilst I was in the Great Pine
Swamp, I frequently visited one of the principal places for

the laun hing of logs. To see them tumbling from such
a height, touching here and there the rough angle of a
projecting rock, bounding from it with the elasticity of a
foot-ball, and at last falling with an awful crash into the
river, forms a sight interesting in the highest degree, but
impossible for me to describe. Shall I tell you that I
have seen masses of these logs heaped above each other
to the number of five thousand? I may so tell you, for
such I have seen. My friend Irish assured me that at
some seasons these piles consisted of a much greater number, the river becoming in these places completely
choked up. When freshets or floods take place, then is
the time chosen for forwarding to the different mills. This
is called a 'frolic.' Jedediah Irish, who is generally the
leader, proceeds to the upper leap with the men,
each provided with a strong wooden handspike and
a short-handled axe. They all take to the water,
be it summer or winter, like so many Newfoundland
spaniels. The logs are gradually detached, and aftei
a time are seen floating down the dancing stream,
here striking against a rock, and whirling many
times round, there suddenly checked in dozens by a shallow, over which they have to be forced with the handspikes. Now they arrive at the edge of a dam, and when
the party has arrived at the last, which lies just where my
friend Irish's camp was first formed, the drenched leadei
and his men, about sixty in number, make their way home,
find there a healthful repast, and spend the evening and
a portion of the night in dancing and frolicing in their
own simple manner, in the most perfect amity, seldom
troubling themselves with the idea of the labor prepared
for them on the morrow. That morrow now come, one
sounds a horn from the door of the storehouse, at the call
of which they all return to their work. The sawyers, the
millers, the rafters, and raftsmen are all immediately

9

busy. The mills all are going, and the logs, which a few months before were the supporters of broad and leafy tops, are now in the act of being split asunder. The boards are then launched into the stream, and rafts are formed of them for market.

" During the summer and autumnal months, the Lehigh, a small river of itself, soon becomes extremely shallow, and to float the rafts would prove impossible, had not art managed to provide a supply of water for this express purpose. At the breast of the lower dam is a curiously-constructed lock, which is opened at the approach of the rafts. They pass through this lock with the rapidity of lightning, propelled by the water that had been accumulated in the dam, and which is of itself generally sufficient to float them to Mauch Chunk ; after which, entering regular canals, they find no other impediments, but are conveyed to their ultimate destination. Before population had greatly advanced in this part of Pennsylvania, game of all descriptions found in that range was extremely abundant. The elk did not disdain to browse on the shoulders of the mountains near the Lehigh. Bears and the common deer must have been plentiful, as at the moment when I write, many of both kinds are seen and killed by the resident hunters. The wild turkey, the pheasant, and the grouse, are tolerably abundant ; and as to trout in the streams—ah ! reader, if you are an angler, do go there and try for yourself. For my part, I can only say that I have been made weary with pulling up from the rivulets the sparkling fish, allured by the struggles of the common grasshopper.

" A comical affair happened with some bears, which I shall relate to you, good reader. A party of my friend Irish's raftsmen, returning from Mauch Chunk one afternoon, through sundry short cuts over the mountains, at the season when huckleberries are ripe and plentiful, were suddenly apprised of the proximity of some of these animals, by their snuffing the air. No sooner was this perceived than, to the astonishment of the party, not fewer than eight bears, I was told, made their appearance. Each man being provided with his short-handled axe, faced about and willingly came to the scratch ; but the assailed soon proved the assailants, and with claw and tooth drove off the men in a twinkling. Down they all rushed from the mountain ; the noise spread quickly ; rifles were soon procured and shouldered ; but when the spot was reached, no bears were to be found ; night forced the hunters back to their homes, and a laugh concluded the affair.

"I spent six weeks in the Great Pine Forest—swamp it cannot be called—where I made many a drawing. Wishing to leave Pennsylvania, and to follow the migratory flocks of our birds to the south, I bade adieu to the excellent wife and rosy children of my friend, and to his kind nephew. Jedediah Irish, shouldered his heavy rifle, accompanied me, and trudging directly across the mountains, we arrived at Mauch Chunk in good time for dinner. At Mauch Chunk, where we both spent the night, Mr. White, the civil engineer, visited me, and looked at my drawings which I had made at the Great Pine Forest. The news he gave me of my sons, then in Kentucky, made me still more anxious to move in their direction ; and long before daybreak I shook hands with the good man of the forest, and found myself moving towards the capital of Pennsylvania, having as my sole companion a sharp frosty breeze. Left to my thoughts, I felt amazed that such a place as the Great Pine Forest should be so little known to the Philadelphians, scarcely any of whom could direct me towards it.

"Night came on as I was thinking of such things, and I was turned out of the coach, in the streets of the fair city, just as the clock struck ten. I cannot say my bones were much rested, but not a moment was to be lost. So I desired a porter to take up my little luggage, and leading him towards the nearest wharf, I found myself soon after gliding across the Delaware towards my former lodgings in the Jerseys."

CHAPTER XIV.

AFTER remaining a few days at his lodgings, Audubon started off to his wife and children, who were then residing in the south and west ; Victor at Louisville, Kentucky, and Mrs Audubon and John at Mr. Garret Johnson's, in Mississippi, about one hundred and fifty miles above New Orleans.

"I crossed the mountains to Pittsburg, in the mail-coach, with my dog and gun, and calling on my wife's relations, and one of my old partners, Mr. Thomas Pears, I proceeded down the Ohio in a steamboat to Louisville. On entering the counting-house of my relative, Mr. W. G. Bakewell, I saw my son Victor at a desk, but perhaps would not have recognized him had he not known me at once. And the pleasure I experienced on pressing him to my breast was increased when I discovered how much my dear boy had improved, as I had not seen him for five years. My son John Woodhouse I also found at Mr. Berthond's, and he had also grown and improved. After spending a few days at Louisville, I took passage on another steamer going down the Mississippi, and in a few days landed at Bayou Sara, and was soon at the house of Mr. Johnson, and came suddenly on my dear wife : we were both overcome with emotion, which found relief in tears."

The following interesting allusions to Audubon's visit, are from the pen of T. B. Thorpe, for many years a resident of the South-West. "When we first arrived in

Louisiana," he writes, "we were pleasantly surprised to find that our temporary home was within range of much of Audubon's most faithfully searched country. Almost every old resident we met could tell us something about the man; and although we heard much to satisfy us that his pursuits were altogether unappreciated, yet we never heard anything that did not reflect honor on his character as an enthusiastic disciple of nature, and a superior man, and not of one characteristic that displayed vanity. On the contrary, he was almost child-like in his habits, he was so inoffensive and unobtrusive where his pursuits were not concerned. At all events the details of his daily experiences in the swamps of the Mississippi, his patient sufferings from heat, storm and hunger, while satisfying himself of some habit of a single bird, tell of a character over which inordinate vanity could have exerted no perceptible influence.

"Audubon was of French extraction; he therefore inherited the mercurial peculiarities of his race; and when a youth, possessed of liberal resources, he was fond of display, but the grave pursuits of business and the fierce impulse he received from nature to be an ornithologist, and the many pecuniary misfortunes that befel him on the threshold of his life, sobered his judgment and prepared the way for that entire absorption of all his great powers that resulted finally in the production of his immortal works.

"In one of the first plantation houses I visited on my arrival in Louisiana, I was attracted by the covering of a rude fireboard, which upon being attentively examined, I discovered was covered over with very sketchy, but nevertheless very expressive and masterly drawings of birds, mere outlines, yet full of spirit and most suggestive. I asked my host where these things came from, and much to my surprise he informed me that the bits of paper I saw were shreds and patches left by Audubon some years previously at his house.

"Further inquiry developed the interesting fact that the great naturalist occupied a room for months together in the house I then occupied ; in fact, it was his headquarters, when he was in the vicinity, engaged in making up his collection of Southern birds. Among many illustrative incidents we learned, we recall two or three as the best proof that can be given that Audubon's was too great a mind to be marred by excessive vanity.

"My host informed me that Audubon, among other things, became interested in a little bird, not as large as the wren, that was of such peculiar gray plumage, that it so entirely harmonized with the bark of the trees it inhabited, that it was impossible to see the bird except by the most careful observation. In fact, the bird existed in numbers in localities where its existence was never suspected.

"Audubon expressed his determination to learn the history and habits of this bird, and bent all his energies with absorbing interest to the pursuit. One night he came home greatly excited, saying that he had found a pair that was evidently preparing to make a nest. The next morning he went into the woods, taking with him a telescopic microscope. This scientific instrument he erected under the tree that gave shelter to the literally invisible inhabitants he was searching for, and, making a pillow of some moss, he laid upon his back, and looking through the telescope, day after day, noted the progress of the little birds, and, after three weeks of such patient labor, felt that he had been amply rewarded for the toil and sacrifice by the results he had obtained. It was while engaged in these quiet speculations that he witnessed so many things, the record of which have prompted superficial thinkers to conclude that Audubon drew upon

his imagination, and not upon facts, for many of the wonderful adventures he relates, incidental to his ornithological descriptions.

"Sitting upon the gallery of the planter's house, I noticed some distance in front a tall magnolia tree, the upper
part of which was dead, indicating that it was of great
age. A closer examination developed the fact that the
very topmost horizontal limb had been artificially removed from the trunk, instead of falling to the ground by
the natural course of decay. I called the attention of
my host to the fact, and he informed me that it was the
result of one of Audubon's fancies. The story was as
follows :

"One evening the planter and the naturalist sat together on the gallery, watching the decline of a summer's
day, when they were surprised and delighted at the sudden appearance of a bald eagle that was circling high in
the heavens, occasionally flashing with peculiar brilliancy,
as the rays of the setting sun happened to strike the quiv-
ering plumage. The noble bird gradually descended
toward the earth, and finally settled upon the very limb
that had been cut from the tree.

"As soon as the bird alighted, Audubon got up very
deliberately, and, going into his room, brought out his
rifle and commenced very deliberately drawing a charge
of mustard-seed shot.

"'You had better hurry,' said the planter, 'that bird
seems restless already ; he won't keep his perch long.'

"'Yes he will,' said Audubon, almost drawling his
words. 'I have disturbed that eagle's nest to-day, and
he is now engaged in examining the damage, and making
his calculations about the danger of returning home ;
never fear his flying away until the day is well spent.'

"And sure enough, said the planter, Audubon understood the habits of the eagle, for there the poor bird sat,

until Audubon coolly loaded his rifle with a bullet, and then like a serpent, on his belly, he had time to noiseless-;y, and unobserved even by the keen eye of the bird of Jove, to crawl within gun-shot. I must confess I was excited. I could see the bird, standing erect, and with earnest gaze looking toward his nest, his mate and his young in the distant swamp. I had lost sight of Audubon ; he was buried among the weeds in the undergrowth of the intervening ground. Presently a sharp rifle report broke upon the air, a puff of smoke rose at the very foot of the tree, and the eagle at the same instant flapped his broad wings, made an ineffectual struggle to bear himself on the air, and then turning on his back commenced descending ingloriously to the earth. I admired Audubon's spirit, knowledge and pluck, but I must confess I felt sorry for the poor bird.

" In a few minutes Audubon appeared with the wounded, dying monarch in his possession. He called our attention to the wonderful expression of the eye, which at one time blazed as if illuminated with fire, and then glazed as if in death. As the sun finally disappeared, the eagle died.

" Audubon was now all excitement, he called up a dozen idle negroes, who had been attracted by the novelty of the event they witnessed, and ordered them to make a large fire, by the light of which, in a few hours, he stuffed and set up the bird, with a grace and naturalness that almost rivaled life.

" The next morning, on examining his work, he said it wanted one thing more to make it complete, and acting upon the idea, he took a saw and with great peril to himself and a vast amount of labor, he ascended to the top of the magnolia and sawed off the limb, the butt of which attracted your notice ; this secured, he put the eagle upon it, and thus restored the exact resemblance presented when the bird in all its native grandeur, sat perched on its eyrie the impersonation of freedom—the chosen emblem of our national glory.

"That Audubon is not always properly appreciated, is often illustrated; therefore, criticism may be expected. In the very community where Audubon lived he had, as a naturalist, no real admirers. In the early days we speak of, the people with whom he mingled were content with a semi-weekly mail, and it was the custom for some person who had a loud voice to read out to the crowd the epitome of news from some popular northern weekly paper. On one of these occasions the following item was read:

"'The Emperor Nicholas, in his recent trip from England to Russia, occupied his leisure time in looking over Audubon's great work on ornithology. The Emperor was so delighted with what he saw, that he sent the great naturalist a costly ring set with diamonds, as a mark of his appreciation of the distinguished author.'

"'What's that?' said one of the listeners, who was noted for his slovenly dress and agrarian politics; 'what's that? Read that again.'

"The request was complied with.

"'That's just my idea of these imperial Emperors; they never have anything for a poor man, but give their diamonds and gold to loafing cusses, who are too lazy to work, and so make a living shooting little chippin-birds, and then drawing their picters.'"

He remained three months with his wife, but was still actively employed. He hunted the woods for birds and animals, and brought them home alive or freshly killed, to draw from. There are several exquisite unfinished deer-heads, in his great portfolio of unfinished drawings, which were begun at that time. He drew also, at this time, the picture of the "Black Vulture Attacking

the Herd of Deer," several large hawks, and some beautiful squirrels. Having added considerably to his collection, he began again to think of returning to England,
to increase the drawings already being published there.

"Our plans," he writes, addressing his sons, "were
soon arranged. Your mother collected the moneys due
her, and on the first of January, eighteen hundred and
thirty, we started for New Orleans, taking with us the only
three servants yet belonging to us, namely, Cecilia, and
her two sons, Reuben and Lewis. We stayed a few days
at our friend Mr. Brand's, with whom we left our servants,
and on the seventh of January took passage in the splendid steamer Philadelphia for Louisville, paying sixty dollars fare. We were fourteen days getting to Louisville,
having had some trouble with the engine. I passed my
time there at Mr. Berthond's and your uncle W. Bakewell's, and amused myself hunting and stuffing birds until
the seventh of March, when we took a steamer for Cincinnati, and thence to Wheeling, and so on to Washington in the mail-coach. Congress was in session, and I
exhibited my drawings to the House of Representatives,
and received their subscription as a body. I saw the
President, Andrew Jackson, who received me with great
kindness, as he did your mother also afterwards. I became acquainted with the Hon. Edward Everett, Baron
Krudener, and other distinguished persons, and we left
for Baltimore. There my drawings were exhibited, and I
obtained three subscribers, and left for Philadelphia,
where we remained one week. I saw my friends Harlan,
Mr. McMurtrie, and Sully, and went to New York, from
whence we sailed in the packet-ship Pacific, Captain R.
Crocker, for England.

"After a passage of twenty-five days, on which nothing happened worthy of record, we had crossed the Atlantic and arrived safely in Liverpool.

" In England everything had gone well, and although my list of subscribers had not increased, it had not much diminished. During my absence I had been elected a fellow of the Royal Society of London, for which I believe I am indebted to Lord Stanley and J. S. Children, Esq., of the British Museum, and on the sixth of May I took my seat in the great hall, and paid my entrance fee of fifty pounds, though I felt myself that I had not the qualifications to entitle me to such an honor."

Soon after his arrival in England, he found that subscribers did not pay up as regularly as he expected, and money being needed to push forward the engraving of the " Birds of America," he again resorted to his pencil and brush, and painted birds and quadrupeds, for all of which he found a ready sale at satisfactory prices. Besides this he was occupied in filling up the ground-work of many of his drawings, and introducing plants and trees which had at first been given only in outline. His stay at London, however, was not long. Mrs. Audubon having joined him there after a few weeks, not liking a residence in the city, travelled with him on his journeys to obtain new subscribers.

" We visited Birmingham, Manchester, Leeds, York, Hull, Scarborough, Whitby, Newcastle, and received several subscriptions at the latter place ; and my former friends, Mr. Adamson and the Rev. Mr. Turner, were quite kind to us, as also was the family of the Earl of Ravensworth. On our way to Edinburgh we stopped a few days and were hospitably entertained at Twisel House, by Mr. Selby.

" *October* 13, 1830. We reached Edinburgh safely, and took lodgings at my old boarding-house, with Mrs. Dickie, where we were made very comfortable."

At this period Audubon began to prepare his "Ornithological Biography of the Birds of America," a work containing nearly three thousand pages, and published by Mr. Black of Edinburgh.

"I applied to Mr. James Wilson, to ask if he knew of any person who would undertake to correct my ungrammatical manuscripts, and to assist me in arranging the more scientific part of the 'Biography of the Birds.' He gave me a card with the address of Mr. W. McGillivray, spoke well of him and his talents, and away to Mr. McGillivray I went. He had long known of me as a naturalist. I made known my business, and a bargain was soon struck. He agreed to assist me, and correct my manuscripts for two guineas per sheet of sixteen pages, and I that day began to write the first volume.

"A few days after I began writing on the Biography, it was known in Edinburgh that I had arrived, and Professors Jameson, Graham, and others whom I had known, called on me ; and I found at the 'fourteenth hour,' that no less than three editions of 'Wilson's Ornithology" were about to be published, one by Jameson, one by Sir W. Jardine, and another by a Mr. Brown. Most persons would probably have been discouraged by this information, but it only had a good effect on me, because since I have been in England I have studied the character of Englishmen as carefully as I studied the birds in America. And I know full well, that in England novelty is always in demand, and that if a thing is well known it will not receive much support. Wilson has had his day, thought I to myself, and now is my time. I will write, and I will hope to be read ; and not only so, but I will push my publication with such unremitting vigor, that my book shall come before the public before Wilson's can be got out.

"Writing now became the order of the day. I sat at it as soon as I awoke in the morning, and continued the whole long day, and so full was my mind of birds and their habits, that in my sleep I continually dreamed of birds. I found Mr. McGillivray equally industrious, for although he did not rise so early in the morning as I did, he wrote much later at night (this I am told is a characteristic of all great writers); and so the manuscripts went on increasing in bulk, like the rising of a stream after abundant rains, and before three months had passed the first volume was finished. Meanwhile your mother copied it all to send to America, to secure the copyright there.

" I made an arrangement with Mr. Patrick Neill, the printer, who undertook the work, for I was from necessity my own publisher. I offered this famous book to two booksellers, neither of whom would give me a shilling for it, and it was fortunate that they would not; and most happy is the man who can, as I did, keep himself independent of that class of men called the 'gentlemen of the trade.' Poor Wilson, how happy he would have been, if he had had it in his power to bear the expenses of his own beautiful work!

"*March* 13, 1831. My book is now on the eve of being presented to the world. The printing will be completed in a few days, and I have sent copies of the sheets to Dr. Harlan and Mr. McMurtrie, at Philadelphia, and also one hundred pounds sterling to Messrs. T. Walker & Sons, to be paid to Dr. Harlan to secure the copyright, and have the book published there.

"*March* 20, 1831. Made an agreement with Mr. J. B. Kidd, a young painter whom I have known for the last four years, to copy some of my drawings in oil, and to put backgrounds to them, so as to make them appear like pictures. It was our intention to send them to the exhibition for sale, and to divide the amount between us. He painted eight, and then I proposed, if he would paint the one hundred engravings which comprise my first volume of the 'Birds of America,' I would pay him one hundred pounds.

"*April* 15. We left Edinburgh this day, and proceeded towards London by the way of Newcastle, York, Leeds, Manchester, and Liverpool. At the latter place we spent a few days, and travelled on that extraordinary road called the railway, at the rate of twenty-four miles an hour. On arriving at London I found it urgent for me to visit Paris, to collect monies due me by my agent (Pitois) there.

" Several reviews of my work have appeared ; one in ' Blackwood's Magazine' is particularly favorable. The editor, John Wilson of Edinburgh, is a clever good fellow, and I wrote to thank him. Dr. Tuke, an Irishman of lively manners, brought the editors of the 'Atlas' to see my Birds, and they have praised also. We have received letters from America of a cheering kind, and which raised my dull spirits, but in spite of all this I feel dull, rough in temper, and long for nothing so much as my dear woods. I have balanced my accounts with the 'Birds of America,' and the whole business is really wonderful ; forty thousand dollars have passed through my hands for the completion of the first volume. Who would believe that a lonely individual, who landed in England without a friend in the whole country, and with only sufficient pecuniary means to travel through it as a visitor, could have accomplished such a task as this publication? Who would believe that once in London Audubon had only one sovereign left in his pocket, and did not know of a single individual to whom he could apply to borrow another, when he was on the verge of failure in the very beginning of his undertaking ; and above all, who would believe that he extricated himself from all his difficulties, not by borrowing money, but by rising at four o'clock in the morning, working hard all day, and disposing of his works at a price which a common laborer would have thought little more than sufficient remuneration for his work? To give you an idea of my actual difficulties during the publication of my first volume, it will be sufficient to say, that in the four years required to bring that volume before the world, no less than fifty of my subscribers, representing the sum of fifty-six thousand dollars, abandoned me! And whenever a few withdrew I was forced to leave London, and go to the provinces to obtain others to supply their places, in order to enable me to raise the money to meet the expenses of engraving, coloring, paper, printing, &c.; and that with all my constant exertions, fatigues, and vexations, I find myself now having but one hundred and thirty standing names on my list.

"England is most wealthy, and among her swarms of inhabitants there are many whom I personally know, and to whom, if I were to open my heart, there would be a readiness to help me for the sake of science; but my heart revolts from asking such a favor, and I will continue to trust in that Providence which has helped me thus far."

The sixth volume of the journal abruptly ends with the above paragraph. But intimations are given in the last chapter, of Audubon's intention to return to America as soon as possible. He knew of regions which he had not explored, where he felt confident he could make large additions of new birds to his collection: and anxious to enrich his store, after making the same careful preparations as before to have his work go on during his absence, he sailed once more for his native land.

On September 3, 1831, Audubon landed in New York. After spending a few days with relatives and friends he went to Boston, and was hospitably received by his friends. There he remained but a short time, having resolved to spend the winter in East Florida.

All the most interesting incidents of what he called a rather unprofitable expedition were woven by Audubon into the striking episodes given in this and subsequent chapters.

" Soon after landing at St. Augustine, in East Florida, I formed an acquaintance with Dr. Simmons, Dr. Porcher, Judge Smith, the Misses Johnson, and many other individuals, my intercourse with whom was as agreeable as it was beneficial to me. While in this part of the peninsula I followed my usual avocations, although with little success, it being then winter. I had letters from the secretaries of the navy and treasury of the United States, to the commanding officers of vessels of war in the revenue service, directing them to afford me any assistance in their power ; and the schooner Shark having come to St. Augustine, on her way to the St. John's river, I presented my credentials to her commander, Lieutenant Piercy, who readily, and with politeness, received me and my assistants on board. We soon after set sail, with a fair breeze.

" The strict attention to duty on board even this small vessel of war afforded matter of surprise to me. Everything went on with the regularity of a chronometer : orders were given, answered to, and accomplished, before they ceased to vibrate on the ear. The neatness of the crew equalled the cleanliness of the white planks of the deck ; the sails were in perfect condition, and built as the Shark was for swift sailing, on she went bowling from wave to wave. I thought that, while thus sailing, no feeling but that of pleasure could exist in our breasts. Alas! how fleeting are our enjoyments. When we were almost at the entrance of the river the wind changed, the sky became clouded, and before many minutes had elapsed the little bark was lying to, ' like a duck,' as her commander expressed himself. It blew a hurricane : let it blow, .

reader.　At the break of day we were again at anchor within the bar of St. Augustine.　Our next attempt was successful.　Not many hours after we had crossed the bar we perceived the star-like glimmer of the light in the great lantern at the entrance into the St. John's river. This was before daylight ; and as the crossing of the sand-banks or bars which occur at the mouths of all the streams of this peninsula is difficult, and can be accomplished only when the tide is up, one of the guns was fired as a signal for the government pilot.　The good man it seemed was unwilling to leave his couch, but a second gun brought him in his canoe alongside.　The depth of the channel was barely sufficient.　My eyes, however, were not directed towards the waters, but on high, where flew some thousands of 'snowy pelicans,' which had fled affrighted from their resting grounds.　How beautifully they performed their broad gyrations, and how matchless after a while, was the marshalling of their files as they flew past us !

"On the tide we proceeded apace.　Myriads of cormorants covered the face of the waters, and over it the fish-crows innumerable were already arriving from their distant roosts.　We landed at one place to search for the birds whose charming melodies had engaged our attention, and here and there we shot some young eagles, to add to our store of fresh provision.　The river did not seem to me equal in beauty to the fair Ohio ; the shores were in many places low and swampy, to the great delight of the numberless herons that moved along in gracefulness, and the grim alligators that swam in sluggish sullenness.　In going up a bayou we caught a great number of the young of the latter, for the purpose of making experiments upon them.　After sailing a considerable way, during which our commander and officers took the soundings, as well as the angles and bearings of every nook and crook of the sinuous stream, we anchored one evening at a distance of fully one hundred miles from the mouth of the river. The weather, although it was the 12th of February, was quite warm, the thermometer on board standing at 75°, and on shore at 90°. The fog was so thick that neither of the shores could be seen, and yet the river was not a mile in breadth. The 'blind mosquitoes' covered every object, even in the cabin, and so wonderfully abundant were these tormentors, that they more than once extinguished the candles whilst I was writing my journal, which I closed in despair, crushing between the leaves more than a hundred of the little wretches. Bad as they are, however, these blind mosquitoes do not bite. As if purposely to render our situation doubly uncomfortable, there was an establishment for jerking beef on the nearer shore to the windward of our vessel, from which the breeze came laden with no sweet odors. In the morning when I arose the country was still covered with thick fogs, so that although I could plainly hear the notes of the birds on shore, not an object could I see beyond the bowsprit, and the air was as close and sultry as on the previous evening.

"Guided by the scent of 'jerkers' works,' we went on shore, where we found the vegetation already far advanced. The blossoms of the jessamine, ever pleasing, lay steeped in dew; the humming-bee was collecting her winter store from the snowy flowers of the native orange; and the little warblers frisked about the twigs of the smilax. Now, amid the tall pines of the forest, the sun's rays began to force their way, and as the dense mists dissolved in the atmosphere the bright luminary shone forth. We explored the woods around, guided by some friendly 'live oakers,' who had pitched their camp in the vicinity. After a while the Shark again displayed her sails, and as she silently glided along, we espied a Seminole Indian approaching us in his canoe. This poor dejected son of the woods, endowed with talents of the highest order, although rarely acknowledged by the proud usurpers of his native soil, has spent the night in fishing, and the morning in procuring the superb feathered game of the swampy thickets, and with both he comes to offer them for our acceptance. Alas! thou fallen one, descendant of an ancient line of free-born hunters, would that I could restore to thee thy birthright, thy natural independence, the generous feelings that were once fostered in thy brave bosom! But the irrevocable deed is done, and I can merely admire the perfect symmetry of his frame, as he dexterously throws on our deck the trout and turkeys which he has captured. He receives a recompense, and without a smile or bow, or acknowledgment of any kind, off he starts with the speed of an arrow from his own bow.

"Alligators were extremely abundant, and the heads of the fishes which they had snapped off lay floating around on the dark waters. A rifle bullet was now and then sent through the eye of one of the largest, which, with a tremendous splash of its tail, expired. One morning we saw a monstrous fellow lying on the shore. I was desirous of obtaining him, to make an accurate drawing of his head, and, accompanied by my assistant and two of the sailors, proceeded cautiously towards him. When within a few yards, one of us fired, and sent through his side an ounce ball, which tore open a hole large enough to receive a man's hand. He slowly raised his head, bent himself upwards, opened his huge jaws, swung his tail to and fro, rose on his legs, blew in a frightful manner, and fell to the earth. My assistant leaped on shore, and, contrary to my injunctions, caught hold of the animal's tail, when the alligator, awakening from its trance, with a last effort crawled slowly towards the water, and plunged heavily into it. Had he thought of once flourishing his tremendous weapon, there might have been an end of his assailant's life; but he fortunately went in peace to his grave, where we left him, as the water was too deep. The same morning, another of equal size was observed swimming directly for the bows of our vessel, attracted by the gentle rippling of the water there. One of the officers who had watched him fired, and scattered his brains through the air, when he tumbled and rolled at a fearful rate, blowing all the while most furiously. The river was bloody for yards around, but although the monster passed close by the vessel, we could not secure him, and after a while he sank to the bottom.

"Early one morning I hired a boat and two men, with a view of returning to St. Augustine by a short cut. Our baggage being placed on board, I bade adieu to the officers and crew, and off we started. About four in the afternoon we arrived at the short cut, forty miles distant from our point of departure, and where we had expected to procure a waggon, but were disappointed: so we laid our things on the bank, and leaving one of my assistants to look after them, I set out, accompanied by the other and my Newfoundland dog. We had eighteen miles to go, and as the sun was only two hours high, we struck off at a good rate. Presently we entered a pine barren. The country was as level as a floor; our path, although narrow, was well beaten, having been used by the Seminole Indians for ages; and the weather was calm, and now and then a rivulet occurred, from which we quenched our thirst, while the magnolias and other flowering plants on its banks relieved the dull uniformity of the woods. When the path separated into two branches, both seemingly leading the same way, I would follow one, while my companion took the other, and unless we met again

in a short time, one of us would go across the intervening forest. The sun went down behind a cloud, and the
south-east breeze that sprung up at this moment sounded
dolefully among the tall pines. Along the eastern horizon lay a bed of black vapor, which gradually rose, and
soon covered the heavens. The air felt hot and oppres-
sive, and we knew that a tempest was approaching.
Plato was now our guide, the white spots on his skin being the only objects we could discern amid the darkness ;
and as if aware of his utility in this respect, he kept a
short way before us on the trail. Had we imagined ourselves more than a few miles from the town, we would
have made a camp, and remained under its shelter for
the night ; but conceiving that the distance could not be
great, we resolved to trudge along. Large drops began
to fall from the murky mass overhead ; thick impenetrable darkness surrounded us, and, to my dismay, the dog
refused to proceed. Groping with my hands on the
ground, I discovered that several trails branched out at
the spot where he lay down, and when I had selected
one he went on. Vivid flashes of lightning streamed
across the heavens, the wind increased to a gale, and the
rain poured down upon us like a torrent. The water
soon rose on the level ground, so as almost to cover our
feet, and we slowly advanced, fronting the tempest.
Here and there a tall pine on fire presented a magnificent spectacle, illumining the trees around it, and surrounded with a halo of dim light, abruptly bordered with
the deep black of the night. At one time we passed
through a tangled thicket of low trees, at another crossed
a stream flushed by the heavy rains, and again proceeded over the barrens. How long we thus, half lost,
groped our way, is more than I can tell you, but at length
the tempest passed over, and suddenly the clear sky became spangled with stars. Soon after we smelt the salt

marshes, and walking directly towards them, like pointers advancing on a covey of partridges, we at last, to our great joy, descried the light of the beacon near St. Augustine. My dog began to run briskly around, and having met with ground on which he had hunted before, and taking a direct course, led us to the great causeway that crosses the marshes at the back of the town. We refreshed ourselves with the produce of the first orange-tree that we met with, and in half an hour more arrived at our hotel. Drenched with rain, steaming with perspiration, and covered to the knees with mud, you may imagine what figures we cut in the eyes of the good people whom we found snugly enjoying themselves in the sitting-room. Next morning Major Gates, who had received me with much kindness, sent a waggon with mules and two trusty soldiers for my companion and the luggage."

CHAPTER XV.

Floridian Episodes — The Live Oakers.

THE greater part of the forests of East Florida consists principally, of what in that country are called 'pine barrens.' In these districts the woods are rather thin, and the only trees that are seen in them are tall pines, of rather indifferent quality, beneath which is a growth of rank grass, here and there mixed with low bushes and sword palmettoes. The soil is of a sandy nature, mostly flat, and consequently either covered with water during the rainy season, or parched in the summer and autumn, although you meet at times with ponds of stagnant water, where the cattle—which are abundant—allay their thirst, and around which resort the various kinds of game found in these wilds. The traveller who has pursued his course for many miles over the barrens, is suddenly delighted to see in the distance the appearance of a dark 'hummock' of live oaks and other trees, seeming as if they had been planted in the wilderness. As he approaches, the air feels cooler and more salubrious, the song of numerous birds delights his ear, the herbage assumes a more luxuriant appearance, the flowers become larger and brighter, and a grateful fragrance is diffused around. These objects contribute to refresh his mind, as much as the sight of the waters of some clear spring, gliding among the undergrowth, seems already to allay his thirst. Overhead festoons of innumerable vines, jessamines, and bignonias, link each tree with those around it, their slender stems being interlaced

as if in mutual affection. No sooner in the shade of
these beautiful woods has the traveller finished his mid-
day repast, than he perceives small parties of men, lightly
accoutred, and each bearing an axe, approaching towards
his resting-place. They exchange the usual civilities, and
immediately commence their labors, for they too have just
finished their meal. I think I see them proceeding to
their work. Here two have stationed themselves on the
opposite sides of the trunk of a noble and venerable live
oak. Their keen-edged and well-tempered axes seem to
make no impression on it, so small are the chips that drop
at each blow around the mossy and wide-spreading roots.
There one is ascending the stem of another, the arms of
which in its fall, have stuck among the tangled tops of
the neighboring trees. See how cautiously he proceeds,
barefooted, and with a handkerchief around his head ;
now he has climbed to the height of about forty feet from
the ground ; he stops, and squaring himself with the trunk
on which he so boldly stands, he wields with sinewy arms
his trusty blade, the repeated blows of which,—although
the tree be as tough as it is large,—will soon sever it in
two. He has changed sides, and his back is turned to
you. The trunk now remains connected by only a thin
strip of wood. He places his feet on the part which is
lodged, and shakes it with all his might. Now swings
the huge log under his leaps, now it suddenly gives way,
and as it strikes upon the ground, its echoes are repeated
through the hummock, and every wild turkey within hearing utters his gobble of recognition. The woodcutter,
however, remains 'collected and composed,' but the next
moment he throws his axe to the ground, and assisted by
the nearest grape-vine, slides down, and reaches the earth
in an instant. Several men approach and examine the prostrate trunk. They cut at both extremities, and sound the
whole of the bark, to enable them to judge if the tree

has been attacked by white rot. If such has unfortunately been the case, there, for a century or more, this huge
log will remain, till it gradually crumbles; but if not, and
it is free of injury or 'wind shakes,' while there is no appearance of the sap having already ascended, and its
pores are altogether sound, they proceed to take its meas-
urement. Its shape ascertained, and the timber that is
fit for use laid out by the aid of models, which, like fragments of the skeleton of a ship, show the forms and sizes
required, the 'hewers' commence their labors.

"Thus, reader, perhaps every known hummock in the
Floridas is annually attacked; and so often does it happen that the white rot, or some other disease, has deteri-
orated the quality of the timber, that the woods may be
seen strewn with trunks that have been found worthless,
so that every year these valuable oaks are becoming
scarcer. The destruction of the young trees of this species, caused by the fall of the great trunks, is of course
immense; and as there are no artificial plantations of
these trees in our country, before long a good-sized live
oak will be so valuable, that its owner will exact an
enormous price for it, even while it yet stands in the
wood. In my opinion, formed on personal observation,
live-oak hummocks are not quite as plentiful as they are
represented to be; and of this I will give you one illustration.

"On the 25th of February, 1832, I happened to be
far up St. John's River, East Florida, in company with a
person employed by our government in protecting the 'live
oaks' of that section of the country, and who received a
good salary for his trouble. While we were proceeding
along one of the banks of that most singular river, my
companion pointed out some large hummocks of dark-
leaved trees on the opposite side, which he said were entirely formed of live oaks. I thought differently, and as

our controversy on the subject became a little warm, I proposed that our men should row us to the place, where we might examine the leaves and timber, and so decide the point. We soon landed, but after inspecting the woods, not a single tree of the species did we find, although there were thousands of large 'swamp oaks.' My companion acknowledged his mistake, and I continued to search for birds.

"One dark evening, as I was seated on the banks of the same river, considering what arrangements I should make for the night,—as it began to rain in torrents,—a man, who happened to see me, came up and invited me to go to his cabin, which he said was not far off. I accepted this kind offer, and followed him to his humble dwelling. There I found his wife, several children, and a number of men, who, as my host told me, were, like himself, 'live oakers.' Supper was placed on a large table, and on being desired to join the party, I willingly assented, doing my best to diminish the contents of the tin pans and dishes set before the company by the active and agreeable housewife. We then talked of the country, its climate and productions, until a late hour, when we laid ourselves down on bear-skins, and reposed till daybreak.

"I longed to accompany these hardy woodcutters to the hummock, where they were engaged in preparing live oak timber for a man-of-war. Provided with axes and guns, we left the house to the care of the wife and children, and proceeded for several miles through a pine barren, such as I have attempted to describe. One fine old turkey was shot, and when we arrived at the shanty, put up near the hummock, we found another party of woodcutters waiting our arrival before eating their breakfast, already prepared by a negro man, to whom the turkey was consigned, to be roasted for a part of that day's dinner.

Our repast was an excellent one, and vied with a Kentucky breakfast. Beef, fish, potatoes and other vegetables, were served up with coffee in tin cups, and plenty of biscuit. Every man seemed hungry and happy, and the conversation assumed the most humorous character. The sun now rose above the trees, and all excepting the cook proceeded to the hummock, on which I had been gazing with great delight, as it promised rare sport. My host, I found, was the chief of the party; and although he had an axe, he made no other use of it than for stripping here and there pieces of bark from certain trees, which he considered of doubtful soundness. He was not only well versed in his profession, but generally intelligent, and from him I received the following account, which I noted at the time.

"The men employed in cutting the live oak, after having discovered a good hummock, build shanties of small logs, to retire to at night and feed in by day. Their provisions consist of beef, pork, potatoes, biscuit, rice, flour, and fish, together with excellent whiskey. They are mostly hale, strong, and active men, from the eastern parts of the Union, and receive excellent wages, according to their different abilities. Their labors are only of a few months' duration. Such hummocks as are found near navigable streams are first chosen, and when it is absolutely necessary, this timber is hauled five or six miles to the nearest water-course, where, although it sinks, it can, with comparative ease, be shipped to its destination. The best time for cutting the 'live oak' is considered to be from the first of December to the first of March, or while the sap is completely down. When the sap is flowing the tree is 'bloom,' and more apt to be 'shaken.' The white rot, which occurs so frequently in the live oak, and is perceptible only by the best judges, consists of round spots, about an inch and a half in diameter, on the outside of the bark, through which, at that spot, a hard stick may be driven several inches, and generally follows the heart up or down the trunk of the tree. So deceiving are these spots and trees to persons unacquainted with this defect, that thousands of trees are cut and abandoned. The great number of trees of this sort strewn in the woods would tend to make a stranger believe that there is much more good oak in the country than there really is; and perhaps, in reality, not more than one fourth of the quantity usually reported is to be procured. The 'live oakers' generally revisit their distant homes in the middle and eastern states, where they spend the summer, returning to the Floridas at the approach of winter. Some, however, who have gone there with their families, remain for years in succession, although they suffer much from the climate, by which their once good constitutions are often greatly impaired. This was the case with the individual above mentioned, from whom I subsequently received much friendly assistance in my pursuits."

CHAPTER XVI.

Second Florida Episode: The Lost One.

'*LIVE OAKER*' employed on the St. John's River, in East Florida, left his cabin—situated on the banks of that stream—and, with an axe on his shoulder, proceeded towards the swamp, in which he had several times before plied his trade of felling and squaring the giant trees that afford the most valuable timber for naval architecture and other purposes. At the season which is the best for this kind of labor, heavy fogs not unfrequently cover the country, so as to render it difficult for one to see farther than thirty or forty yards in any direction. The woods, too, present so little variety, that every tree seems the mere counterpart of every other ; and the grass, when it has not been burnt, is so tall, that a man of ordinary stature cannot see over it ; whence it is necessary for him to proceed with great caution, lest he should unwittingly deviate from the ill-defined trail which he follows. To increase the difficulty, several trails often meet, in which case—unless the explorer be perfectly acquainted with the neighborhood—it would be well for him to lie down and wait until the fog should disperse. The live oaker had been jogging onwards for several hours, and became aware that he must have travelled considerably more than the distance between his cabin and the ' hummock' which he desired to reach. To his alarm, at the moment when the fog dispersed, he saw that the sun was at its meridian height, and he could not recognize a single object around him. Young, healthy, and active, he im-

agined that he had walked with more than usual speed,
and had passed the place to which he was bound. He
accordingly turned his back upon the sun, and pursued a
different route, guided by a small trail. Time passed, and
the sun headed his course ; he saw it gradually descend
in the west, but all around him continued as if enveloped
with mystery. The huge gray trees spread their giant
boughs over him, the rank grass extended on all sides,
not a living being crossed his path ; all was silent and
still, and the scene was like a dull and dreary dream of
the land of oblivion. He wandered like a forgotten ghost
that had passed into the land of spirits, without yet meeting one of his kind with whom to hold converse.

" The condition of a man lost in the woods is one of
the most perplexing that could be imagined by a person
who has not himself been in a like predicament. Every
object he sees he at first thinks he recognizes ; and while
his whole mind is bent on searching for more that may
gradually lead to his extrication, he goes on committing
greater errors the farther he proceeds. This was the case
with the live oaker. The sun was now setting with a fiery
aspect, and by degrees it sunk in its full circular form, as
if giving warning of a sultry to-morrow. Myriads of insects, delighted at its departure, now filled the air on buzzing wings. Each piping frog arose from the muddy pool
in which it had concealed itself, the squirrel retired to its
hole, the crow to its roost, and, far above, the harsh croaking voice of the heron announced that, full of anxiety, it
was wending its way to the miry interior of some distant
swamp. Now the woods began to resound to the shrill
cries of the owl and the breeze, as it swept among the
columnar stems of the forest trees, laden with heavy and
chilling dew. Alas ! no moon, with her silvery light,
shone on the dreary scene, and the *lost one*, wearied and
vexed, laid himself down on the damp ground. Prayer

is always consolatory to man in every difficulty or danger, and the woodsman fervently prayed to his Maker, wished his family a happier night than it was his lot to experience, and with a feverish anxiety waited the return of day. You may imagine the length of that cold, dull, moonless night. With the dawn of day came the usual fogs of those latitudes. The poor man started on his feet, and with a sorrowful heart pursued a course which he thought might lead him to some familiar object, although, indeed, he scarcely knew what he was doing. No longer had he the trace of a track to guide him, and yet, as the sun rose, he calculated the many hours of daylight he had before him, and the farther he went, continued to walk the faster. But vain were all his hopes : that day was spent in fruitless endeavors to regain the path that led to his home, and when night again approached, the terror that had been gradually spreading over his mind—together with the nervous debility induced by fatigue, anxiety, and hunger—rendered him almost frantic. He told me that at this moment he beat his breast, tore his hair, and, had it not been for the piety with which his parents had in early life imbued his mind, and which had become habitual, would have cursed his existence.

"Famished as he now was, he laid himself on the ground, and fed on the weeds and grass that grew around him. That night was spent in the greatest agony and terror. 'I knew my situation,' he said to me. 'I was fully aware that, unless Almighty God came to my assistance, I must perish in those uninhabited woods. I knew that I had walked more than fifty miles, although I had not met with a brook from which I could quench my thirst, or even allay the burning heat of my parched lips and bloodshot eyes.

"'I knew that if I could not meet with some stream I must die, for my axe was my only weapon ; and although

deer and bears now and then started within a few yards
or even feet of me, not one of them could I kill ; and although I was in the midst of abundance, not a mouthful
did I expect to procure, to satisfy the cravings of my
empty stomach. Sir, may God preserve you from ever
feeling as I did the whole of that day !' For several days
after no one can imagine the condition in which he was,
for when he related to me this painful adventure, he assured me he had lost all recollection of what had happened. 'God,' he continued, ' must have taken pity on
me, one day, for as I ran wildly through those dreadful
pine barrens I met with a tortoise. I gazed upon it with
delight and amazement, and although I knew that, were I
to follow it undisturbed, it would lead me to some water,
my hunger and thirst would not allow me to refrain from
satisfying both by eating its flesh and drinking its blood.
With one stroke of my axe the beast was cut in two ; in a
few moments I despatched all but the shell. Oh, sir,
how much I thanked God, whose kindness had put the
tortoise in my way ! I felt greatly renewed. I sat down
at the foot of a pine, gazed on the heavens, thought of my
poor wife and children, and again and again thanked my
God for my life, for now I felt less distracted in mind, and
more assured that before long I must recover my way,
and get back to my home.' The lost one remained and
passed the night at the foot of the same tree under which
his repast had been made. Refreshed by a sound sleep,
he started at dawn to resume his weary march. The sun
rose bright, and he followed the direction of his shadows.
Still the dreariness of the woods was the same, and he
was on the point of giving up in despair, when he observed
a raccoon lying squatted in the grass. Raising his axe,
he drove it with such violence through the helpless animal, that it expired without a struggle. What he had
done with the turtle he now did with the raccoon, the

10*

greater part of which he actually devoured at one meal. With more comfortable feelings he then resumed his wanderings,—his journey I cannot say,—for although in the possession of all his faculties, and in broad daylight, he was worse off than a lame man groping his way in the dark out of a dungeon, of which he knew not where the door stood. Days one after another passed—nay, weeks in succession. He fed now on cabbage trees, then on frogs and snakes. All that fell in his way was welcome and savory. Yet he became daily more emaciated, and at length he could scarcely crawl ; forty days had elapsed, by his own reckoning, when he at last reached the banks of the river. His clothes in tatters, his once bright axe dimmed with rust, his face begrimed with beard, his hair matted, and his feeble frame little better than a skeleton covered with parchment, there he laid himself down to die. Amid the perturbed dreams of his fevered fancy, he thought he heard the noise of oars far away on the silent river. He listened, but the sounds died away on his ear. It was indeed a dream, the last glimmer of expiring hope, and now the light of life was about to be quenched for ever. But again the sound of oars awoke him from his lethargy. He listened so eagerly that the hum of a fly could not have escaped his ear. They were indeed the measured beats of oars ; and now, joy to the forlorn soul ! the sound of human voices thrilled to his heart, and awoke the tumultuous pulses of returning hope. On his knees did the eye of God see that poor man, by the broad, still stream, that glittered in the sunbeams, and human eyes soon saw him too, for round that headland covered with tangled brushwood boldly advances the little boat, propelled by its lusty rowers. The lost one raises his feeble voice on high ; it was a loud shrill scream of joy and fear. The rowers pause, and look around. Another, but feebler scream, and they observe him. It comes—his heart flutters, his sight is dimmed, his brain reels, he gasps for breath! It comes—it has run upon the beach, and the lost one is found.

"This is no tale of fiction, but the relation of an actual occurrence, which might be embellished, no doubt, but which is better in the plain garb of truth. The notes by which I recorded it were written in the cabin of the once lost ' live oaker,' about four years after the painful incident occurred. His amiable wife and loving children were present at the recital, and never shall I forget the tears that flowed from them as they listened to it, albeit it had long been more familiar to them than a tale thrice told. It only remains for me to say that the distance between the cabin and the live oak hummock to which the woodsman was bound scarcely exceeded eight miles, while the part of the river at which he was found was thirty-eight miles from his house. Calculating his daily wanderings at ten miles, we may believe that they amounted in all to four hundred. He must therefore have rambled in a circuitous direction, which people generally do in such circumstances. Nothing but the great strength of his constitution and the merciful aid of his Maker could have supported him for so long a time."

CHAPTER XVII.

· *Third Florida Episode: Spring Garden.*

A VING heard many wonderful accounts of a certain spring near the sources of the St. John's River, in East Florida, I resolved to visit it, in order to judge for myself. On the 6th of January, 1832, I left the plantation of my friend John Bulow, accompanied by an amiable and accomplished Scotch gentleman, an engineer employed by the planters of those districts in erecting their sugar-house establishments. We were mounted on horses of the Indian breed, remarkable for their activity and strength, and were provided with guns and some provision. The weather was pleasant, but not so our way, for no sooner had we left the ' King's Road,' which had been cut by the Spanish government for a goodly distance, than we entered a thicket of scrubby oaks, succeeded by a still denser mass of low palmettoes, which extended about three miles, and among the roots of which our nags had great difficulty in making good their footing.

"After this we entered the pine barrens, so extensively distributed in this portion of Florida. The sand seemed to be all sand, and nothing but sand, and the palmettoes at times so covered the narrow Indian trail which we followed, that it required all the instinct or sagacity of ourselves and our horses to keep it. It seemed to us as if we were approaching the end of the world. The country was perfectly flat, and, so far as we could survey it, presented the same wild and scraggy aspect. My companion, who had travelled there before, assured me that at particular seasons of the year he had crossed the barrens when they were covered with water fully knee-deep, when, according to his expression, they 'looked most awful ;' and I readily believed him, as we now and then passed through muddy pools which reached the saddle-girths of our horses. Here and there large tracts covered with tall grasses, and resembling the prairies of the western wilds, opened to our view. Wherever the country happened to be sunk a little beneath the general level, it was covered with cypress-trees, whose spreading arms were hung with a profusion of Spanish moss. The soil in such cases consisted of black mud, and was densely covered with bushes, chiefly of the magnolia family. We crossed in succession the heads of three branches of Haw Creek, of which the waters spread from a quarter to half a mile in breadth, and through which we made our way with extreme difficulty. While in the middle of one, my companion told me that once, when in the very spot where he then stood, his horse chanced to place his fore-feet on the back of a large alligator, which, not well pleased at being disturbed in his repose, suddenly raised his head, opened his monstrous jaws, and snapped off a part of the lip of his affrighted pony. You may imagine the terror of the poor beast, which, however, after a few plunges, resumed its course, and succeeded in carrying its rider through in safety. As a reward for this achievement it was ever after honored with the appellation of ' Alligator.'

" We had now travelled about twenty miles, and the sun having reached the zenith, we dismounted to partake of some refreshment. From a muddy pool we contrived to obtain enough of tolerably clear water to mix with the contents of a bottle, the like of which I would strongly recommend to every traveller in these swampy regions. Our horses, too, found something to grind among the herb-

age that surrounded the little pool ; but as little time
was to be lost, we quickly remounted and resumed our
disagreeable journey, during which we had at no time
proceeded at a rate exceeding two miles and a half in the
hour. All at once, however, a wonderful change took
place ; the country became more elevated and undulating,
the timber was of a different nature, and consisted of red
and live oaks, magnolias, and several kinds of pine.
Thousands of 'mole-hills,' or the habitations of an animal here called the ' salamander,' and *Gopher's burrows*,
presented themselves to the eye, and greatly annoyed our
horses, which every now and then sank to the depth of a
foot and stumbled, at the risk of breaking their legs, and
what we considered fully as valuable—our necks. We
now saw beautiful lakes of the purest water, and passed
along a green space having a series of them on each side
of us. These sheets of water became larger and more
numerous the farther we advanced, some of them extending to a length of several miles, and having a depth of
from two to twenty feet of clear water ; but their shores
being destitute of vegetation we observed no birds near
them. Many tortoises, however, were seen basking in
the sun, and all as we approached plunged into the water.
Not a trace of man did we see during our journey, scarcely a bird, and not a single quadruped, not even a rat ;
nor can one imagine a poorer and more desolate country
than that which lies between the Halifax River, which we
had left in the morning, and the undulated grounds at
which we had now arrived.

"But at length we perceived the tracks of living beings, and soon after saw the huts of Colonel Rees' negroes.
Scarcely could ever African traveller have approached
the city of Timbuctoo with more excited curiosity than
we felt in approaching this plantation. Our Indian horses seemed to participate in our joy, and trotted at a

smart rate towards the principal building, at the door of
which we leaped from our saddles, just as the sun was
withdrawing his ruddy light. Colonel Rees was at home,
and received us with great kindness. Refreshments were
immediately placed before us, and we spent the evening
in agreeable conversation.

" The next day I walked over the plantation, examining the country around, and found the soil of good quality, it having been reclaimed from swampy ground, of a
black color, rich, and very productive. The greater part
of the cultivated land was on the borders of a lake which
communicated with others leading to St. John's River,
distant about seven miles, and navigable so far by vessels
not exceeding fifty or sixty tons. After breakfast our
amiable host showed us the way to the celebrated spring,
the sight of which afforded me pleasure sufficient to coun-
terbalance the tediousness of my journey.

" This spring presents a circular basin, having a diameter of about sixty feet, from the centre of which the
water is thrown up with great force, although it does not
rise to a height of more than a few inches above the general level. A kind of whirlpool is formed, on the edges
of which are deposited vast quantities of shells, with pieces of wood, gravel, and other substances, which have
coalesced into solid masses, having a very curious appearance. The water is quite transparent, although of a
dark color, but so impregnated with sulphur, that it emits
an odor which to me was very disagreeable, and highly
nauseous. Its surface lies fifteen or twenty feet below the
level of the woodland lakes in the neighborhood, and its
depth in the autumnal months is about seventeen feet
when the water is lowest. In all the lakes the same species of shells as are thrown up by the spring occur in
abundance ; and it seems more than probable that it is
formed of the water collected from them by infiltration,

or forms the subterranean outlet of some of them. The Lakes themselves are merely reservoirs containing the residue of the waters which fall during the rainy seasons, and contributing to supply the waters of the St. John's River, with which they communicate by similar means. This spring pours its waters into 'Rees' Lake,' through a deep and broad channel called Spring Garden Creek. This channel is said to be in some places fully sixty feet deep, but it becomes more shallow as you advance towards the entrance of the lake, at which you are surprised to find yourself on a mud flat covered only by about fifteen inches of water, under which the depositions from the spring lie to a depth of four or five feet in the form of the softest mud, while under this again is a bed of fine white sand. When this mud is stirred up by the oars of your boat or otherwise, it appears of a dark-green color, and smells strongly of sulphur. At all times it sends up numerous bubbles of air, which probably comes of sulphuretted hydrogen gas. The mouth of this curious spring is calculated to be two and a half feet square, and the velocity of its waters during the rainy season is three feet per second. This would render the discharge per hour about 499-500 gallons.

"Colonel Rees showed us the remains of another spring of the same kind, which had dried up from some natural cause.

"My companion the engineer having occupation for another day, I requested Colonel Rees to accompany me in his boat towards the river St. John, which I was desirous of seeing, as well as the curious country in its neighborhood. He readily agreed, and after an early breakfast next morning, we set out, accompanied by two servants to manage the boat. As we crossed 'Rees' Lake I observed that its north-eastern shores were bounded by a deep swamp, covered by a rich growth of tall cypresses,

while the opposite side presented large marshes and islands ornamented by pines, live oaks, and orange-trees.

"With the exception of a very narrow channel, the
creek was covered with nympheæ, and in its waters swam
numerous alligators, while ibises, gallinules, anhingas,
coots, and cormorants were pursuing their avocations on
its surface or along its margins. Over our heads the fish-
hawks were sailing, and on the broken trees around we
saw many of their nests. We followed Spring Garden
Creek for about two miles and ·a half, and passed a
mud-bar before we entered 'Dexter's Lake. The bar
was stuck full of *unios* in such profusion, that each
time the negroes thrust their hands into the mud they
took up several. According to their report these shell-
fish are quite unfit for food. In this lake the water had
changed its hue, and assumed a dark chestnut color,
although it was still transparent. The depth was uniform-
ly five feet, and the extent of the lake was about eight
miles by three. Having crossed it, we followed the creek,
and soon saw the entrance of 'Woodruff's Lake,' which
empties its still darker waters into the St. John's River.
I here shot a pair of curious ibises, which you will find
described in my fourth volume of ornithology, and landed
on a small island covered with wild orange-trees, the luxuriance and freshness of which were not less pleasing to
the sight than the perfume of their flowers was to the
smell. The group seemed to me like a rich bouquet
formed by nature to afford consolation to the weary traveller cast down by the dismal scenery of swamps, and
pools, and rank grass around him. Under the shade of
these beautiful evergreens, and amidst the golden fruits
that covered the ground, while the humming-birds fluttered over our heads, we spread our cloth on the grass,
and, with a happy and thankful heart, I refreshed myself
with the bountiful gifts of an ever-careful Providence.

Colonel Rees informed me that this charming retreat was one of the numerous *terræ incognitæ* of this region of lakes, and that it should henceforth bear the name of ' Audubon's Isle.'

" In conclusion, let me inform you that the spring has now been turned to good account by my generous host, Colonel Rees, who, aided by my amiable companion the engineer, has directed its current so as to turn a mill which suffices to grind the whole of his sugar-cane."

CHAPTER XVIII.

Fifth Florida Episode: Deer Hunting.

HE different modes of destroying deer are probably too well understood and too successfully
practised in the United States; for notwithstanding the almost incredible abundance of these beautiful animals in our forests and prairies, such havoc is
carried on amongst them, that in a few centuries they
will probably be as scarce in America as the great bus-
tard now is in Britain.

." We have three modes of hunting deer, each varying
in some slight degree in the different states and districts.
The first is termed 'still hunting,' and is by far the most
destructive. The second is called 'fire-light hunting,'
and is next in its exterminating effects. The third, which
may be looked upon as a mere amusement, is named
'driving.' Although many deer are destroyed by this
latter method, it is not by any means so pernicious as
the others. These methods I shall describe separately.

"'Still hunting' is followed as a kind of trade by
most of our frontier men. To be practised with success,
it requires great activity, an expert management of the
rifle, and a thorough knowledge of the forest, together
with an intimate acquaintance with the habits of the
deer, not only at different seasons of the year, but also
at every hour of the day, as the hunter must be aware
of the situations which the game prefers, and in which it
is most likely to be found at any particular time. I
might here present you with a full account of the habits

of our deer, were it not my intention to lay before you, at some future period, in the form of a distinct work, the observations which I have made on the various quadrupeds of our extensive territories.

"We shall suppose that we are now about to follow the *true hunter*, as the still hunter is also called, through the interior of the tangled woods, across morasses, ravines, and such places, where the game may prove more or less plentiful, even should none be found there in the first instance. We shall allow our hunter all the agility, patience, and care which his occupation requires, and will march in his rear, as if we were spies watching all his motions. His dress, you observe, consists of a leathern hunting-shirt, and a pair of trousers of the same material. His feet are well moccasined; he wears a belt round his waist; his heavy rifle is resting on his brawny shoulder; on one side hangs his ball-pouch, surmounted by the horn of an ancient buffalo, once the terror of the herd, but now containing a pound of the best gunpowder. His butcher-knife is scabbarded in the same strap; and behind is a tomahawk, the handle of which has been thrust through his girdle. He walks with so rapid a step that probably few men besides ourselves, that is, myself and my kind reader, could follow him, unless for a short distance, in their anxiety to witness his ruthless deeds. He stops, looks at the flint of his gun, its priming, and the leather cover of the lock, then glances his eye towards the sky, to judge of the course most likely to lead him to the game.

"The heavens are clear, the red glare of the sun gleams through the lower branches of the lofty trees, the dew hangs in pearly drops at the top of every leaf. Already has the emerald hue of the foliage been converted into the more glowing tints of our autumnal months. A slight frost appears on the fence rails of his little corn-field.

" As he proceeds he looks to the dead foliage under his feet, in search of the well-known traces of a buck's hoof. Now he bends toward the ground, on which something has attracted his attention. See, he alters his course, increases his speed, and will soon reach the opposite hill. Now he moves with caution, stops at almost every tree, and peeps forward, as if already within shooting distance of his game. He advances again ; but now very slowly. He has reached the declivity, upon which the sun shines in all its glowing splendor ; but mark him, he takes the gun from his shoulder, has already thrown aside the leather covering of the lock, and is wiping the edge of his flint with his tongue. Now he stands like a monumental figure, perhaps measuring the distance that lies between him and the game which he has in view. His rifle is slowly raised, the report follows, and he runs. Let us run also. Shall I speak to him, and ask him the result of his first essay? 'Pray, friend, what have you killed?' for to say, 'What have you shot at?' might imply the possibility of his having missed, and so might hurt his feelings. 'Nothing but a buck.' 'And where is it ?' 'Oh, it has taken a jump or so, but I settled it, and will soon be with it. My ball struck, and must have gone through his heart.' We arrived at the spot where the animal had laid itself down on the grass, in a thicket of grape-vines, sumachs, and spruce-bushes, where it intended to repose during the middle of the day. The place is covered with blood, the hoofs of the deer have left deep prints in the ground, as it bounded in the agonies produced by its wound ; but the blood that has gushed from its side discloses the course which it has taken. We soon reach the spot. There lies the buck, its tongue out, its eye dim, its breath exhausted ; it is dead. The hunter draws his knife, cuts the buck's throat almost asunder, and prepares to skin it. For this purpose he hangs it upon the branch of a tree. When the skin is removed, he cuts off the hams, and abandoning the rest of the carcass to the wolves and vultures, reloads his gun, flings the venison, enclosed by the skin, upon his back, secures it with a strap, and walks off in search of more game, well knowing that in the immediate neighborhood another at least is to be found.

"Had the weather been warmer, the hunter would have sought for the buck along the *shadowy* side of the hills. Had it been the spring season, he would have led us through some thick canebrake, to the margin of some remote lake, where you would have seen the deer immersed to his head in the water, to save his body from the tormenting mosquitoes. Had winter overspread the earth with a covering of snow, he would have searched the low, damp woods, where the mosses and lichens, on which at that period the deer feeds, abound, the trees being generally crusted with them for several feet from the ground. At one time he might have marked the places where the deer clears the velvet from his horns by rubbing them against the low stems of bushes, and where he frequently scrapes the earth with his fore-hoofs; at another he would have betaken himself to places where persimmon and crab-apples abound, as beneath these trees the deer frequently stops to munch their fruits. During early spring our hunter would imitate the bleating of the doe, and thus frequently obtain both her and the fawn; or, like some tribes of Indians, he would prepare a deer's head, placed on a stick, and creeping with it amongst the tall grass of the prairies, would decoy the deer within reach of his rifle. But, kind reader, you have seen enough of the 'still hunter.' Let it suffice for me to add that, by the mode pursued by him, thousands of deer are annually killed, many individuals shooting these animals merely for the skins, not caring for even the most valuable portions of the flesh, unless hunger or a near market induces them to carry off the hams.

"The mode of destroying deer by *fire-light*, or, as it is named in some parts of the country, *forest-light*, never fails to produce a very singular feeling in him who witnesses it for the first time. There is something in it which at times appears awfully grand. At other times a certain degree of fear creeps over the mind, and even affects the physical powers of him who follows the hunter through the thick undergrowth of our woods, having to leap his horse over hundreds of huge fallen trunks, at one time impeded by a straggling grape-vine crossing his path, at another squeezed between two stubborn saplings, whilst their twigs come smack in his face, as his companion has forced his way through them. Again, he every now and then runs the risk of breaking his neck by being suddenly pitched headlong on the ground, as his horse sinks into a hole covered over with moss. But I must proceed in a more regular manner, and leave you, kind reader, to judge whether such a mode of hunting would suit your taste or not.

"The hunter has returned to his camp or his house, has rested, and eaten his game. He has procured a quantity of pine-knots filled with resinous matter, and has an old frying-pan, that, for aught I know to the contrary, may have been used by his great-grandmother, in which the pine-knots are to be placed when lighted. The horses stand saddled at the door. The hunter comes forth, his rifle slung on his shoulder, and springs upon one of them, while his son or a servant mounts the other, with the frying-pan and the pine-knots. Thus accoutred, they proceed towards the interior of the forest. When they have arrived at the spot where the hunt is to begin, they strike fire with a flint and steel, and kindle the resinous wood. The person who carries the fire moves in the direction judged to be the best. The blaze illuminates the near objects, but the distant parts seem involved in deepest obscurity.

" The hunter who bears the gun keeps immediately in front, and after a while discovers before him two feeble lights, which are produced by the reflection of the pine fire from the eyes of an animal of the deer or wolf kind. The animal stands quite still. To one unacquainted with this strange mode of hunting, the glare from its eyes might bring to his imagination some lost hobgoblin that had strayed from its usual haunts. The hunter, however, nowise intimidated, approaches the object, sometimes so near as to discern its form, when, raising the rifle to his shoulder, he fires and kills it on the spot. He then dismounts, secures the skin and such portions of the flesh as he may want, in the manner already described, and continues his search through the greater part of the night, sometimes to the dawn of day, shooting from five to ten deer, should these animals be plentiful. This kind of hunting proves fatal, not to the deer alone, but also sometimes to wolves, and now and then to a horse or a cow which may have strayed far into the woods.

" Now, kind reader, prepare to mount a generous, fullblood Virginia hunter ; see that your gun is in complete order, for hark to the sound of the bugle and horn, and the mingled clamor of a pack of harriers. Your friends are waiting you under the shade of the wood, and we must together go *driving* the light-footed deer. The distance over which one has to travel is seldom felt when pleasure is anticipated as the result, so galloping we go pell-mell through the woods to some well-known place, where many a fine buck has drooped its antlers under the ball of the hunter's rifle. The servants, who are called the drivers, have already begun their search, their voices are heard exciting the hounds, and unless we put spurs to our steeds, we may be too late at our stand, and thus lose the first opportunity of shooting the fleeting game as it passes by. Hark again! The dogs are in chase, the horn sounds louder and more clearly. Hurry, hurry on! or we shall be sadly behind. Here we are at last; dismount, fasten your horse to this tree, place yourself by the side of that large yellow poplar, and mind you do not shoot me. The deer is fast approaching; I will to my own stand, and he who shoots him dead wins the prize. The deer is heard coming; it has inadvertently cracked a dead stick with its hoof, and the dogs are now so near it that it will pass in a moment. There it comes! How beautifully it bounds over the ground! What a splendid head of horns! How easy the attitudes, depending, as it seems to do, on its own swiftness for safety! All is in vain, however; a gun is fired, the animal plunges, and doubles with incomparable speed. There he goes; he passes another stand, from which a second shot, better directed than the first, brings him to the ground. The dogs, the servants, the sportsmen, are now rushing forward to the spot. The hunter who has shot it is congratulated on his skill or good luck, and the chase begins again in some other part of the woods.

" A few lines of explanation may be required to convey a clear idea of this mode of hunting. Deer are fond of following and retracing the paths which they have formerly used, and continue to do so even after they have been shot at more than once. Their tracks are discovered by persons on horseback in the woods, or a deer is observed crossing a road, a field, or a small stream. When this has been noticed twice, the deer may be shot from the places called *stands* by the sportsman, who is stationed there and waits for it, a line of stands being generally formed so as to cross the path which the game will follow. The person who ascertains the usual pass of

11

the game, or discovers the parts where the animal feeds or lies down during the day, gives intimation to his friends, who then prepare for the chase. The servants start the deer with the hounds, and, by good management, generally succeed in making it run the course that will soonest bring it to its death. But should the deer be cautious, and take another course, the hunters mounted on swift horses, gallop through the woods to intercept it, guided by the sound of the horns and the cry of the dogs, and frequently succeed in shooting it. This sport is extremely agreeable, and proves successful on almost every occasion."

CHAPTER XIX.

LEFT you abruptly, perhaps uncivilly, reader, at the dawn of day on Sandy Island, which lies just six miles from the extreme point of South Florida. I did so because I was amazed at the appearance of things around me, which, in fact, looked so different then from what they seemed at night, that it took some minutes' reflection to account for the change. When we laid ourselves down on the sand to sleep, the waters almost bathed our feet ; when we opened our eyes in the morning, they were at an immense distance. Our boat lay on her side, looking not unlike a whale reposing on a mud bank ; the birds in myriads were probing their pasture-ground. There great flocks of ibises fed apart from equally large collections of ' godwits,' and thousands of herons gracefully paced along, ever and anon thrusting their javelin bills into the body of some unfortunate fish confined in a small pool of water. Of fish-crows I could not estimate the number, but from the havoc they made among the crabs, I conjecture that these animals must have been scarce by the time of next ebb. Frigate pelicans chased the jager, which himself had just robbed a poor gull of its prize ; and all the gallinules ran with spread wings from the mud-banks to the thickets of the island, so timorous had they become when they perceived us. Surrounded as we were by so many objects that allured us, not one could we yet attain, so dangerous would it have been to venture on the mud ; and our pilot hav-

ing assured us that nothing could be lost by waiting,
spoke of our eating, and on this hint told that he would
take us to a part of the island where 'our breakfast
would be abundant, although uncooked.' Off we went,
some of the sailors carrying baskets, others large tin pans
and wooden vessels such as they use for eating their
meals in.   Entering a thicket of about an acre in extent,
we found on every bush several nests of the ibis, each
containing three large and beautiful eggs, and all hands
fell to gathering.   The birds gave way to us, and ere long
we had a heap of eggs, that promised delicious food.
Nor did we stand long in expectation; for, kindling a
fire, we soon prepared, in one way or other, enough to satisfy the cravings of our hungry maws.   Breakfast ended,
the pilot, looking at the gorgeous sunrise, said, 'Gentlemen, prepare yourselves for fun; the tide is a-coming.' '
Over these mud-flats a foot or two of water is quite sufficient to drive all the birds ashore, even the tallest heron
or flamingo; and the tide seems to flow at once over the
whole expanse.   Each of us, provided with a gun, posted
himself behind a bush, and no sooner had the water
forced the winged creatures to approach the shore, than
the work of destruction commenced.   When it at length
ceased, the collected mass of birds of different kinds
looked not unlike a small haycock.   Who could not with
a little industry have helped himself to a few of their
skins?   Why, reader, surely no one is as fond of these
things as I am.   Every one assisted in this, and even the
sailors themselves tried their hand at the work.   Our pilot, good man, told us he was no hand at such occupations, and would go after something else.   So taking
'Long Tom' and his fishing-tackle, he marched off quietly
along the shores.   About an hour afterwards we saw him
returning, when he looked quite exhausted; and on our
inquiring the cause, said, 'There is a dew-fish yonder,

and a few balacoudas, but I am not able to bring them, or
even to haul them here; please send the sailors after
them.' The fishes were accordingly brought, and as I had
never seen a 'dew-fish,' I examined it closely, and took
an outline of its form, which some days hence you may
perhaps see. It exceeded a hundred pounds in weight,
and afforded excellent eating. The balacouda is also a
good fish, but at times a dangerous one, for, according to
the pilot, on more than one occasion 'some of these gen-
try' had followed him, when waist-deep in the water in
pursuit of a more valuable prize, until in self-defence he
had to spear them, fearing that the 'gentlemen' might at
one dart cut off his legs, or some other nice bit with which
he was unwilling to part. Having filled our cask from a
fine well, long since dug in the sand of Cape Sable, either
by Seminole Indians or pirates, no matter which, we left
Sandy Isle about full tide, and proceeded homewards,
giving a call here and there at different keys, with the
view of procuring rare birds, and also their nests and
eggs. We had twenty miles to go 'as the birds fly,' but
the tortuosity of the channels rendered our course fully a
third longer. The sun was descending fast, when a black
cloud suddenly obscured the majestic orb. Our sails
swelled by a breeze that was scarcely felt by us, and the
pilot, requesting us to sit on the weather gunwale, told us
that we were 'going to get it.' One sail was hauled in
and secured, and the other was reefed, although the wind
had not increased. A low murmuring noise was heard,
and across the cloud that now rolled along in tumultuous
masses shot vivid flashes of lightning. Our experienced
guide steered directly across a flat towards the nearest
land. The sailors passed their quids from one cheek to
the other, and our pilot having covered himself with his
oil jacket, we followed his example. 'Blow, sweet breeze,'
cried he at the tiller, 'and we'll reach land before the

blast overtakes us ; for, gentlemen, it is a furious cloud
yon.' A furious cloud indeed was the one which now, like
an eagle on outstretched wings, approached so swiftly,
that one might have deemed it in haste to destroy us.
We were not more than a cable's length from the shore,
when with imperative voice the pilot calmly said to us,
'Sit quite still, gentlemen, for I should not like to lose
you overboard just now ; the boat can't upset, my word
for that, if you will but sit still ; here we have it!' Reader, persons who have never witnessed a hurricane, such
as not unfrequently desolates the sultry climates of the
south, can scarcely form an idea of their terrific grandeur.
One would think that, not content with laying waste all
on land, it must needs sweep the waters of the shallows
quite dry to quench its thirst. No respite for a moment
does it afford to the objects within the reach of its furious
current. Like the scythe of the destroying angel, it cuts
every thing by the roots, as it were, with the careless ease
of the experienced mower. Each of its revolving sweeps
collects a heap that might be likened to the full sheaf
which the husbandman flings by his side. On it goes,
with a wildness and fury that are indescribable ; and when
at last its frightful blasts have ceased, nature, weeping
and disconsolate, is left bereaved of her beautiful offspring. In instances, even a full century is required before, with all her powerful energies, she can repair her
loss. The planter has not only lost his mansion, his
crops, and his flocks, but he has to clear his lands anew,
covered and entangled as they are with the trunks and
branches of trees, that are everywhere strewn. The bark
overtaken by the storm is cast on the lee-shore, and if
any are left to witness the fatal results they are the
'wreckers' alone, who, with inward delight, gaze upon the
melancholy spectacle. Our light bark shivered like a leaf
the instant the blast reached her sides. We thought she

had gone over ; but the next instant she was on the shore, and now, in contemplation of the sublime and awful storm, I gazed around me. The waters drifted like snow ; the tough mangroves hid their tops amid their roots, and the loud roaring of the waves driven among them blended with the howl of the tempest. It was not rain that fell ; the masses of water flew in a horizontal direction, and where a part of my body was exposed, I felt as if a smart blow had been given me on it. But enough : in half an hour it was over. The pure blue sky once more embellished the heavens, and although it was now quite night, we considered our situation a good one. The crew and some of the party spent the night on board ; the pilot, myself, and one of my assistants took to the heart of the mangroves, and having found high land, we made a fire as well as we could, spread a tarpaulin, and fixing our insect-bars over us, soon forgot in sleep the horrors that had surrounded us. Next day the Marion proceeded on her cruise, and in a few more days, having anchored in another safe harbor, we visited other keys, of which I will, with your leave, give you a short account.

"The deputy collector of Indian Isle gave me the use of his pilot for a few weeks, and I was the more gratified by this, that besides knowing him to be a good man and a perfect sailor, I was now convinced that he possessed a great knowledge of the habits of birds, and could without loss of time lead me to their haunts. We were a hundred miles or so farther to the south. Gay May, like a playful babe, gambolled on the bosom of his mother nature, and every thing was replete with life and joy. The pilot had spoken to me of some birds which I was very desirous of obtaining. One morning, therefore, we went in two boats to some distant isle, where they were said to breed. Our difficulties in reaching that key might to some seem more imaginary than real, were I faithfully to

describe them. Suffice it for me to tell you that, after
hauling our boats and pushing them with our hands for
upwards of nine miles over the flats, we at last reached
the deep channel that usually surrounds each of the mangrove isles. We were much exhausted by the labor and
excessive heat, but we were now floating on deep water,
and by resting under the shade of some mangroves, we
were soon refreshed by the breeze that gently blew from
the gulf.

"The heron which I have named 'Ardea occidentalis'
was seen moving majestically in great numbers, the tide
rose and drove them away, and as they came towards us,
to alight and rest for a while on the tallest trees, we shot
as many as I wished. I also took under my charge several of their young alive. At another time we visited the
'Mule Keys;' there the prospect was in many respects
dismal enough. As I followed their shores, I saw bales
of cotton floating in all the coves, while spars of every
description lay on the beach, and far off on the reefs I
could see the last remains of a lost ship, her dismasted
hulk. Several schooners were around her; they were
'wreckers.' I turned me from the sight with a heavy
heart. Indeed, as I slowly proceeded, I dreaded to meet
the floating or cast-ashore bodies of some of the unfortunate crew. Our visit to the 'Mule Keys' was in no way
profitable, for besides meeting with but a few birds, in two
or three instances I was, while swimming in the deep
channel of a mangrove isle, much nearer a large shark
than I wish ever to be again."

CHAPTER XX.

Seventh Florida Episode: The Wreckers.

ONG before I reached the lovely islets that border the south-eastern shores of the Floridas, the accounts I had heard of ' The Wreckers ' had deeply prejudiced me against them. Often had I been informed of the cruel and cowardly methods which it was alleged they employed to allure vessels of all nations to the dreaded reefs, that they might plunder their cargoes, and rob their crews and passengers of their effects. I therefore could have little desire to meet with such men under any circumstances, much less to become liable to receive their aid ; and with the name of 'wrecker' there were associated in my mind ideas of piratical depredation, barbarous usage, and even murder. One fair afternoon, while I was standing on the polished deck of the United States revenue cutter, the Marion, a sail hove in sight, bearing in an opposite course, close-hauled to the wind. The gentle sway of her masts, as she rocked to and fro in the breeze, brought to my mind the wavings of the reeds on the fertile banks of the Mississippi. By and by the vessel, altering her course, approached us. The Marion, like a sea-bird with extended wings, swept through the waters, gently inclining to either side, while the unknown vessel leaped as it were from wave to wave, like the dolphin in eager pursuit of his prey. In a short time we were gliding side by side, and the commander of the strange schooner saluted our captain, who promptly returned the compliment. What a beautiful vessel, we all thought, how trim, how clean rigged, and how well manned. She swims like a duck, and now, with a broad

11*

sheer, off she makes for the reefs, a few miles under our
lee. There in that narrow passage, well known to her
commander, she rolls, tumbles, and dances like a giddy
thing, her copper sheathing now gleaming, and again disappearing under the waves. But the passage is made,
and now, hauling on the wind, she resumes her former
course, and gradually recedes from the view. Reader, it
was a Florida wrecker. When at the Tortugas, I paid a
visit to several vessels of this kind, in company with my
friend Robert Day, Esq. We had observed the regularity
and quickness of the men then employed at their arduous
tasks, and as we approached the largest schooner, I admired her form, so well adapted to her occupation, her
great breadth of beam, her light draught, the correctness
of her water-line, the neatness of her painted sides, the
smoothness of her well-greased masts, and the beauty of
her rigging. We were welcomed on board with all the
frankness of our native tars. Silence and order prevailed
on her decks. The commander and the second officer
led us into a spacious cabin, well lighted, and furnished
with every convenience for fifteen or more passengers.
The former brought me his collection of marine shells,
and whenever I pointed to one that I had not seen before,
offered it with so much kindness, that I found it necessary
to be careful in expressing my admiration of any particular shell. He had also many eggs of rare birds, which
were all handed over to me, with an assurance that before the month should expire a new set could easily
be procured ; for, said he, 'we have much idle time on
the reefs at this season.' Dinner was served, and we partook of their fare, which consisted of fish, fowl and other
materials. These rovers were both from down east, were
stout active men, cleanly and smart in their attire. In a
short time we were all extremely social and merry. They
thought my visit to the Tortugas in quest of birds was

rather a curious fancy, but notwithstanding, they expressed their pleasure while looking at some of my drawings, and offered their services in procuring specimens. Expeditions far and near were proposed, and on settling that one of them was to take place on the morrow, we parted friends. Early next morning several of these kind men accompanied me to a small key called Booby Island, about ten miles distant from the lighthouse. Their boats were well manned, and rowed with long and steady strokes, such as whalers and men-of-war's men are wont to draw. The captain sang, and at times, by way of frolic, ran a race with our own beautiful bark. The Booby Isle was soon reached, and our sport there was equal to any we had elsewhere. They were capital shots, had excellent guns, and knew more about boobies and noddies than nine-tenths of the best naturalists in the world.

"But what will you say when I tell you that the 'Florida wreckers' are excellent at a deer-hunt, and that at certain seasons, 'when business is slack,' they are wont to land on some extensive key, and in a few hours procure a supply of delicious venison. Some days after the same party took me on an expedition in quest of sea-shells. There we were all in the water at times to the waist, and now and then much deeper. Now they would dip like ducks, and on emerging would hold up a beautiful shell. This occupation they seemed to enjoy above all others. The duties of the Marion having been performed, intimation of our intended departure reached the wreckers. An invitation was sent me to go and see them on board their vessel, which I accepted. Their object on this occasion was to present me with some superb corals, shells, live turtles of the hawk-billed species, and a great quantity of eggs. Not a picayune would they receive in return, but putting some letters in my hands, requested me to be so good as to put them in the

mail at Charleston, adding that they were for their wives
down east. So anxious did they appear to be to do all
they could for me, that they proposed to sail before the
Marion, and meet her under weigh, to give me some
birds that were rare on the coast, and of which they
knew the haunts. Circumstances connected with the service prevented this, however, and with sincere regret, and
a good portion of friendship, I bade these excellent fellows adieu. How different, thought I, is often the knowledge of things acquired from personal observation, from
that obtained by report. I had never before seen Florida
wreckers, nor has it since been my fortune to fall in with
any; but my good friend Dr. Benjamin Strobel, having
furnished me with a graphic account of a few days he
spent with them, I shall present you with it in his own
words.

"'On the 12th day of September, while lying in harbor at Indian Key, we were joined by five wrecking vessels. Their licenses having expired, it was necessary to
go to Key West, to renew them. We determined to accompany them the next morning, and here it will not be
amiss for me to say a few words respecting these far-
famed wreckers, their captains and crews. From all that
I had heard, I expected to see a parcel of dirty, pirate-
looking vessels, officered and manned by a set of black-
whiskered fellows, who carried murder in their very looks.
I was agreeably surprised on discovering that the vessels
were fine large sloops and schooners, regular clippers,
kept in first-rate order. The captains generally were
jovial, good-humored sons of Neptune, who manifested a
disposition to be polite and hospitable, and to afford
every facility to persons passing up and down the reefs.
The crews were hearty, well-dressed, and honest-looking
men. On the 18th, at the appointed hour, we all set sail
together, that is, the five wreckers and the schooner Jane.

As our vessel was not noted for fast sailing, we accepted
an invitation to go on board of a wrecker. The fleet got
under weigh about eight o'clock in the morning, the wind
light but fair, the water smooth, and the day fine. I can
scarcely find words to express the pleasure and gratification which I this day experienced. The sea was of a
beautiful, soft, pea-green color, smooth as a sheet of glass,
and as transparent, its surface agitated only by our vessels as they parted its bosom, or by the pelican in pursuit
of his prey, which, rising for a considerable distance in the
air, would suddenly plunge down with distended mandi-
bles, and secure his food. The vessels of our little fleet,
with every sail set that could catch a breeze, and the
white foam curling round the prows glided silently along,
like islands of flitting shadows on an immovable sea of
light. Several fathoms below the surface of the water,
and under us, we saw great quantities of fish diving and
sporting amongst the sea-grass, sponges, sea-feathers, and
corals, with which the bottom was covered. On our
right hand the Florida Keys, as we made them in the distance, looked like specks upon the water, but as we
neared them, rose to view as if by enchantment, clad in
the richest livery of spring, each variety of color and hue
rendered soft and delicate by a clear sky and brilliant sun
overhead. All was like a fairy scene ; my heart leaped
up in delighted admiration, and I could not but exclaim,
in the language of Scott,

> Those seas behold,
> Round thrice an hundred islands rolled.

The trade-winds played around us with balmy and refreshing sweetness ; and to give life and animation to the
scene, we had a contest for the mastery between all the
vessels of the fleet, while a deep interest was excited in
this or that vessel, as she shot ahead or fell astern.

About three o'clock of the afternoon we arrived off the
Bay of Honda. The wind being light, and no prospect
of reaching Key West that night, it was agreed we should
make a harbor here. We entered a beautiful basin, and
came to anchor about four o'clock. Boats were launched, and several hunting parties formed. We landed, and
were soon on the scent, some going in search of shells,
others of birds. An Indian who had been picked up
somewhere along the coast by some wrecker, and who
was employed as a hunter, was sent on shore in search
of venison. Previous to his leaving the vessel a rifle was
loaded with a single ball, and put into his hands. After
an absence of several hours he returned with two deer,
which he had killed at a single shot. He watched until
they were both in range of his gun, side by side, when
he fired and brought them down. All hands having returned, and the fruits of our excursion being collected,
we had wherewithal to make an abundant supper. Most
of the game was sent on board of the larger vessel, where
we proposed supping. Our vessels were all lying within
hail of each other, and as soon as the moon arose, boats
were seen passing from one to the other, and all were
busily and happily engaged in exchanging civilities.
One would never have supposed that these men were
professional rivals, so apparent was the good feeling that
prevailed amongst them. About nine o'clock we started
for supper. A number of persons had already collected,
and as soon as we arrived on board the vessel, a German
sailor, who played remarkably well on the violin, was
summoned to the quarter-deck, when all hands with a
good will cheerily danced to lively airs until supper was
ready. The table was laid in the cabin, and groaned under its load of venison, wild ducks, pigeons, curlews and
fish. Toasting and singing succeeded the supper, and
among other curious matters introduced, the following

song was sung by the German fiddler, who accompanied his voice with his instrument. He was said to be the author of the song. I say nothing of the poetry, but merely give it as it came on my ear. It is certainly very characteristic.

THE WRECKERS' SONG.

Come all ye good people one and all,
  Come listen to my song ;
A few remarks I have to make,
  Which won't be very long.
'Tis of our vessel, stout and goot,
As ever yet was built of woot ;
Along the reef where the breakers roar,
De wreckers on de Florida shore.

Key Tavernier's our rendezvous,
  At anchor there we lie ;
And see the vessels in the Gulf
  Carelessly passing by.
When night comes on we dance and sing,
Whilst the current some vessel is floating in ;
When daylight comes, a ship's on shore,
Among de rocks where de breakers roar.

When daylight dawns we're under weigh,
  And every sail is set ;
And if the wind it should prove light,
  Why then our sails we wet.
To gain her first each eager strives,
To save de cargo and de pepole's lives ;
Amongst de rocks, where de breakers roar,
De wreckers on the Florida shore.

When we get 'longside, we find she's bilged,
  We know vell vat to do ;
Save de cargo dat we can,
  De sails and rigging too.
Den down to Key West we soon vill go,

When quickly our salvage we shall know;
When every ting it is fairly sold,
Our money down to us it is told.

Den one week's cruise we'll have on shore,
　Before we do sail again;
And drink success to the sailor lads
　Dat are ploughing of de main.
And when you are passing by this way,
On Florida Reef should you chance to stray, .
Why, we will come to you on the shore,
Amongst de rocks where de breakers roar.

" 'Great emphasis was laid upon particular words by
the singer, who had a broad German accent. Between
the verses he played a symphony, remarking, "Gentle-
mens, I makes dat myself." The chorus was trolled by
twenty or thirty voices, which in the stillness of the night
produced no unpleasant effect.' "

CHAPTER XXI.

Eighth Florida Episode: The Turtlers of Florida.

THE Tortugas are a group of islands lying about eighty miles from Key West, and the last of those that seem to defend the peninsula of the Floridas. They consist of five or six extremely low uninhabitable banks, formed of shelly sand, and are resorted to principally by that class of men called wreckers and turtlers. Between these islands are deep channels, which, although extremely intricate, are well known to those adventurers, as well as to the commanders of the revenue cutters whose duties call them to that dangerous coast. The great coral reef or wall lies about eight miles from these inhospitable isles, in the direction of the Gulf, and on it many an ignorant or careless navigator has suffered shipwreck. The whole ground around them is densely covered with corals, sea-fans, and other productions of the deep, amid which crawl innumerable testaceous animals; while shoals of curious and beautiful fishes fill the limpid waters above them. Turtles of different species resort to these banks, to deposit their eggs in the burning sand, and clouds of sea-fowl arrive every spring for the same purpose. These are followed by persons called 'eggers,' who, when their cargoes are completed, sail to distant markets to exchange their ill-gotten ware for a portion of that gold on the acquisition of which all men seem bent.

" The Marion having occasion to visit the Tortugas, I gladly embraced the opportunity of seeing those cele-

brated islets. A few hours before sunset the joyful cry
of 'land' announced our approach to them, but as the
breeze was fresh, and the pilot was well acquainted with
all the windings of the channels, we held on, and dropped
anchor before twilight. If you have never seen the sun
setting in those latitudes, I would recommend you to
make a voyage for that purpose, for I much doubt if, in
any other portion of the world, the departure of the orb
of day is accompanied with such gorgeous appearances.
Look at the great red disc, increased to triple its ordinary dimensions. Now it has partially sunk beneath the
distant line of waters, and with its still remaining half ir-
radiates the whole heavens with a flood of light, purpling
the far-off clouds that hover over the western horizon.
A blaze of refulgent glory streams through the portals of
the west, and the masses of vapor assume the semblance
of mountains of molten gold. But the sun has now disappeared, and from the east slowly advances the gray
curtain which night draws over the world. The night-
hawk is flapping his noiseless wings in the gentle sea-
breeze ; the terns, safely landed, have settled on their
nests ; the frigate pelicans are seen wending their way
to distant mangroves ; and the brown gannet, in search
of a resting-place, has perched on the yard of the vessel.
Slowly advancing landward, their heads alone above the
water, are observed the heavily-laden turtles, anxious to
deposit their eggs in the well-known sands. On the surface of the gently rippling stream I dimly see their broad
forms as they toil along, while at intervals may be heard
their hurried breathings, indicative of suspicion and fear.
The moon with her silvery light now illumines the scene,
and the turtle having landed, slowly and laboriously
drags her heavy body over the sand, her 'flappers' being better adapted for motion in water than on the shore.
Up the slope however she works her way, and see how in-

dustriously she removes the sand beneath her, casting it out on either side. Layer after layer she deposits her eggs, arranging them in the most careful manner, and with her hind paddles brings the sand over them. The business is accomplished, the spot is covered over, and with a joyful heart the turtle swiftly retires toward the shore and launches into the deep.

" But the Tortugas are not the only breeding-places of the turtle : these animals, on the contrary, frequent many other keys as well as various parts of the coast of the mainland. There are four different species, which are known by the names of the green turtle, the hawk-billed turtle, the logger-head turtle, and the trunk turtle. The first is considered the best as an article of food, in which capacity it is well known to most epicures. It approaches the shores, and enters the bays, inlets, and rivers, early in the month of April, after having spent the winters in the deep waters. It deposits its eggs in convenient places, at two different times, in May, and once again in June. The first deposit is the largest, and the last the least, the total quantity being at an average about two hundred and forty. The hawk-billed turtle, whose shell is so valuable as an article of commerce, being used for various purposes in the arts, is the next with respect to the quality of its flesh. It resorts to the outer keys only, where it deposits its eggs in two sets, first in July and again in August, although it *crawls* the beaches much earlier in the season, as if to look for a safe place. The average number of its eggs is about three hundred. The logger-head visits the Tortugas in April, and lays·from that period until late in June three sets of eggs, each set averaging a hundred and seventy. The trunk turtle, which is sometimes of an enormous size, and which has a pouch like a pelican, reaches the shores latest. The shell and fish are so soft that one may push the finger into them almost as into a lump of butter. This species is therefore considered as the least valuable, and indeed is seldom eaten, unless by the Indians, who, ever alert when the turtle season commences, first carry off the eggs which it lays in the season, and afterwards catch the turtles themselves. The average number of eggs which it lays at two sets may be three hundred and fifty.

"The logger-head and the trunk turtles are the least cautious in choosing the places in which to deposit their eggs, whereas the two other species select the wildest and most secluded spots. The green turtle resorts either to the shores of the Main, between Cape Sable and Cape Florida, or enters Indian, Halifax, and other large rivers or inlets, from which it makes its retreat as, speedily as possible, and betakes itself to the open sea. Great numbers, however, are killed by the turtlers and Indians, as well as by various species of carnivorous animals, as cougars, lynxes, bears, and wolves. The hawk-bill, which is still more wary, and is always the most difficult to surprise, keeps to the sea-islands. All the species employ nearly the same method in depositing their eggs in the sand, and as I have several times observed them in the act, I am enabled to present you with a circumstantial account of them.

"On first nearing the shores, and mostly on fine calm moonlight nights, the turtle raises her head above the water, being still distant thirty or forty yards from the beach, looks around her, and attentively examines the objects on the shore. Should she observe nothing likely on the shore to disturb her intended operations, she emits a loud hissing sound, by which such of her enemies as are unaccustomed to it are startled, and so are apt to remove to another place, although unseen by her. Should she hear any noise, or perceive indications of danger, she instantly sinks and goes off to a considerable distance;

but should every thing be quiet, she advances slowly towards the beach, crawls over it, her head raised to the
full stretch of her neck, and when she has reached a
place fitted for her purpose she gazes all round in silence.
Finding 'all well,' she proceeds to form a hole in the sand,
which she effects by removing it from under her body
with her hind flappers, scooping it out with so much dex-
terity that the sides seldom if ever fall in. The sand is
raised alternately with each flapper, as with a large ladle,
until it has accumulated behind her, when supporting herself with her head and fore part on the ground fronting
her body, she, with a spring from each flapper, sends the
sand around her, scattering it to the distance of several
feet. In this manner the hole is dug to the depth of
eighteen inches, or sometimes more than two feet. This
labor I have seen performed in the short period of nine
minutes. The eggs are then dropped one by one, and
disposed in regular layers to the number of a hundred
and fifty, or sometimes two hundred. The whole time
spent in this part of the operation may be about twenty
minutes. She now scrapes the loose sand back over the
eggs, and so levels them and smooths the surface, that
few persons on seeing the spot could imagine any thing
had been done to it. This accomplished to her mind,
she retreats to the water with all possible despatch, leaving the hatching of the eggs to the heat of the sand.
When a turtle, a logger-head for example, is in the act of
dropping her egg, she will not move, although one should
go up to her, or even seat himself on her back, for it
seems that at this moment she finds it necessary to proceed at all events, and is unable to intermit her labor.
The moment it is finished, however, off she starts, nor
would it then be possible for one, unless he were as strong
as Hercules, to turn her over and secure her. To upset
a turtle on the shore one is obliged to fall on his knees,

and placing his shoulder behind her fore-arm, gradually raise her up by pushing with great force, and then with a jerk throw her over. Sometimes it requires the united strength of several men to accomplish this, and if the turtle should be of very great size, as often happens on that coast, even handspikes are employed. Some turtlers are so daring as to swim up to them while lying asleep on the surface of the water, and turn them over in their own element, when, however, a boat must be at hand to enable them to secure their prize. Few turtles can bite beyond the reach of their fore-legs, and few, when they are once turned over, can, without assistance, regain their natural position. But notwithstanding this, their flappers are generally secured by ropes, so as to render their escape impossible. Persons who search for turtle-eggs are provided with a light stiff cane or gun-rod, with which they go along the shores, probing the sand near the tracks of the animal, which, however, cannot always be seen on account of the winds and heavy rains that often obliterate them. The nests are discovered not only by men but also by beasts of prey, and the eggs are collected o· destroyed on the spot in great numbers.

"On certain parts of the shore hundreds of turtles are known to deposit their eggs within the space of a mile. They form a new hole each time they lay, and the second is generally dug near the first, as if the animal were quite unconscious of what had befallen it. It will readily be understood that the numerous eggs seen in a turtle on cutting it up could not be all laid the same season. The whole number deposited by an individual in one summer may amount to four hundred; whereas if the animal be caught on or near her nest, as I have witnessed, the remaining eggs, all small, without shells, and as it were threaded like so many beads, exceed three thousand. In an instance where I found that number, the turtle weighed nearly four hundred pounds.

" The young, soon after being hatched, and when yet scarcely larger than a dollar, scratch their way through their sandy covering, and immediately betake themselves to the water. The food of the green turtle consists chiefly of marine plants, more especially the grass-wrack (*Zostera marina*), which they cut near the roots, to procure the most tender and succulent parts. Their feeding-grounds, as I have elsewhere said, are easily discovered by floating masses of these plants on the flats or along the shores to which they resort. The hawk-billed species feeds on seaweeds, crabs, and various kinds of shell-fish and fishes ; the logger-head mostly on the fish of conch-shells, of large size, which they are enabled, by means of their powerful beak, to crush to pieces with apparently as much ease as a man cracks a walnut. One which was brought on board the Marion, and placed near the fluke of one of her anchors, made a deep indentation in that hammered piece of iron that quite surprised me. The trunk-turtle feeds on mollusca, fish, crustacea, sea-urchins, and various marine plants. All the species move through the water with surprising speed; but the green and hawk-billed in particular remind you by their celerity, and the ease of their motions, of the progress of a bird in the air. It is therefore no easy matter to strike one with a spear, and yet this is often done by an accomplished turtler. While at Key West and other islands on the coast, where I made the observations here presented to you, I chanced to have need to purchase some turtles to feed my friends on board the Lady of the Green Mantle—not my friends, her gallant officers, or the brave tars who formed her crew, for all of them had already been satiated with turtle soup; but my friends the herons, of which I had a goodly number in coops, intending to carry them to John Bachman of Charleston, and other persons for whom I felt a sincere regard. So I went to a ' crawl,' accompanied by Dr. Benjamin Strobel, to inquire about prices, when to my surprise I found the smaller the turtles, ' above ten pounds' weight,' the dearer they were, and that I could have purchased one of the logger-head kind, that weighed more than seven hundred pounds, for little more money than another of only thirty pounds.

" While I gazed on the turtle I thought of the soups the contents of its shell would have furnished for a lord-mayor's dinner, of the numerous eggs which its swollen body contained, and of the curious carriage which might be made of its shell—a car in which Venus herself might sail over the Caribbean Sea, provided her tender doves lent their aid in drawing the divinity, and provided no shark or hurricane came to upset it. The turtler assured me that, although the great monster was in fact better meat than any other of a less size, there was no disposing of it, unless indeed it had been in his power to have sent it to some very distant market. I would willingly have purchased it, but I knew that if killed the flesh could not keep much longer than a day, and on that account I bought eight or ten small ones, which ' my friends' really relished exceedingly, and which served to support them for a long time. Turtles such as I have spoken of are caught in various ways on the coasts of the Floridas, or in estuaries or rivers. Some turtlers are in the habit of setting great nets across the entrance of streams, so as to answer the purpose either at the flow or at the ebb of the waters. These nets are formed of very large meshes, into which the turtles partially get entangled. Others harpoon them in the usual manner ; but in my estimation, no method is equal to that employed by Mr. Egan, the pilot, of Indian Isle.

" That extraordinary turtler had an iron instrument which he called a 'peg,' and which at each end had a point, not unlike what nailmakers call a *brad*, it being four-cornered, but flattish, and of a shape somewhat resembling the beak of an ivory-billed woodpecker, together with a neck and shoulder. Between the two shoulders of this instrument a fine tough line, fifty or more fathoms in length, was fastened by one end, being passed through a hole in the centre of the peg, and the line itself was carefully coiled up and placed in a convenient part of the canoe. One extremity of this peg enters a sheath of iron that loosely attaches it to a long wooden spear, until a turtle has been pierced through the shell by the other extremity. He of the canoe paddles away as silently as possible whenever he espies a turtle basking on the water, until he gets within a distance of ten or twelve yards, when he throws the spear so as to hit the animal about the place which an entomologist would choose, were it a large insect, for pinning to a piece of cork. As soon as the turtle is struck, the wooden handle separates from the peg, in consequence of the looseness of its attachment. The smart of the wound urges on the animal as if distracted, and it appears that the longer the peg remains in its shell, the more firmly fastened it is, so great a pressure is exercised upon it by the shell of the turtle, which being suffered to run like a whale, soon becomes fatigued, and is secured by hauling in the line with great care. In this manner, as the pilot informed me, eight hundred green turtles were caught by one man in twelve months.

"Each turtle has its 'crawl,' which is a square wooden building or pen, formed of logs, which are so far separated as to allow the tide to pass freely through, and stand erect in the mud. The turtles are placed in this enclosure, fed and kept there till sold. There is, however, a circumstance relating to their habits which I cannot omit, although I have it not from my own ocular evidence, but from report. When I was in Florida several of the turtlers assured me, that any turtle taken from the depos-

12

iting ground, and carried on the deck of a vessel several hundred miles, would, if then let loose, certainly be met with at the same spot, either immediately after, or in the following breeding season. Should this prove true, and it certainly may, how much will be enhanced the belief of the student in the uniformity and solidity of nature's arrangements, when he finds that the turtle, like a migratory bird, returns to the same locality, with perhaps a delight similar to that experienced by the traveller who, after visiting different countries, once more returns to the bosom of his cherished family."

CHAPTER XXII.

Ninth Florida Episode: Death of a Pirate.

IN the calm of a fine moonlight night, as I was admiring the beauty of the clear heavens, and the broad glare of light that glanced from the trembling surface of the waters around, the officer on watch came up and entered into conversation with me. He had been a turtler in other years, and a great hunter to boot, and although of humble birth and pretensions, energy and talent, aided by education, had raised him to a higher station. Such a man could not fail to be an agreeable companion, and we talked on various subjects, principally, you may be sure, birds and other natural productions. He told me he once had a disagreeable adventure when looking for game, in a certain cove on the shores of the Gulf of Mexico ; and on my expressing a desire to hear it, he willingly related to me the following particulars, which I give you, not perhaps precisely in his own words, but as nearly as I can remember.

"Towards evening, one quiet summer day, I chanced to be paddling along a sandy shore, which I thought well fitted for my repose, being covered with tall grass, and as the sun was not many degrees above the horizon, I felt anxious to pitch my mosquito bar or net, and spend the night in this wilderness. The bellowing notes of thousands of bull-frogs in a neighboring swamp might lull me to rest, and I looked upon the flocks of black-birds that were assembling as sure companions in this secluded retreat.

"I proceeded up a little stream to insure the safety of my canoe from any sudden storm, when, as I gladly advanced, a beautiful yawl came unexpectedly in view. Surprised at such a sight in a part of the country then scarcely known, I felt a sudden check in the circulation of my blood. My paddle dropped from my hands, and fearfully indeed as I picked it up, did I look towards the unknown boat. On reaching it, I saw its sides marked with stains of blood, and looking with anxiety over the gunwale, I perceived to my horror two human bodies covered with gore. Pirates or hostile Indians I was persuaded had perpetrated the foul deed, and my alarm naturally increased; my heart fluttered, stopped and heaved with unusual tremors, and I looked towards the setting sun in consternation and despair. How long my reveries lasted, I cannot tell; I can only recollect that I was roused from them by the distant groans of one apparently in mortal agony. I felt as if refreshed by the cold perspiration that oozed from every pore, and I reflected that though alone, I was well armed, and might hope for the protection of the Almighty.

"Humanity whispered to me that, if not surprised and disabled, I might render assistance to some sufferer, or even be the means of saving a useful life. Buoyed up by this thought, I urged my canoe on shore, and seizing it by the bow, pulled it at one spring high among the grass.

"The groans of the unfortunate person fell heavy on my ear, as I cocked and reprimed my gun, and I felt determined to shoot the first that should rise from the grass. As I cautiously proceeded, a hand was raised over the weeds, and waved in the air in the most supplicating manner. I levelled my gun about a foot below it; when the next moment, the head and breast of a man covered with blood were convulsively raised, and a faint hoarse voice asked me for mercy and help! a death-like silence followed his fall to the ground. I surveyed every object around with eyes intent, and ears impressible by the slightest sound, for my situation that moment I thought as critical as any I had ever been in. The croakings of the frogs, and the last blackbirds alighting on their roosts, were the only sounds or sights; and I now proceeded towards the object of my mingled alarm and commiseration.

"Alas! the poor being who lay prostrate at my feet, was so weakened by loss of blood, that I had nothing to fear from him. My first impulse was to run back to the water, and having done so, I returned with my cap filled to the brim. I felt at his heart, washed his face and breast, and rubbed his temples with the contents of a phial, which I kept about me as an antidote for the bites of snakes. His features, seamed by the ravages of time, looked frightful and disgusting. But he had been a powerful man, as the breadth of his breast plainly showed. He groaned in the most appalling manner, as his breath struggled through the mass of blood that seemed to fill his throat. His dress plainly disclosed his occupation— a large pistol he had thrust into his bosom, a naked cutlass lay near him on the ground, and a silk handkerchief was bound over his projecting brows, and over a pair of loose trousers he wore a fisherman's boots. He was, in short, a Pirate!

"My exertions were not in vain, for, as I continued to bathe his temples, he revived, his pulse resumed some strength, and I began to hope that he might perhaps survive the deep wounds which he had received. Darkness, deep darkness, now enveloped us. I spoke of making a fire. 'Oh! for mercy's sake,' he exclaimed, 'don't.' Knowing, however, that under existing circumstances it was expedient for me to do so, I left him, went to his boat, and brought the rudder, the benches and the oars, which with my hatchet I soon splintered. I then struck a light, and presently stood in the glare of a blazing fire. The Pirate seemed struggling between terror and gratitude for my assistance; he desired me several times in half English and Spanish to put out the flames, but after I had given him a draught of strong spirits, he at length became more composed. I tried to staunch the blood that flowed from the deep gashes in his shoulders and his side. I expressed my regret that I had no food about me, but when I spoke of eating, he sullenly waved his head.

"My situation was one of the most extraordinary that I have ever been placed in. I naturally turned my talk towards religious subjects; but, alas! the dying man hardly believed in the existence of a God. 'Friend,' said he, 'for friend you seem to be, I never studied the ways of Him of whom you talk. I am an outlaw, perhaps you will say a wretch—I have been for many years a Pirate. The instructions of my parents were of no avail to me, for I have always believed that I was born to be a most cruel man. I now lie here, about to die in the weeds, because I long ago refused to listen to their many admonitions. Do not shudder, when I tell you these now useless hands murdered the mother whom they had embraced. I feel that I have deserved the pangs of the wretched death that hovers over me; and I am thankful that one of my kind will alone witness my last gaspings.' A fond but feeble hope that I might save his life, and perhaps assist in procuring his pardon,—'it is all in vain, friend—I have no objection to die—I am glad that the villains who wounded me were not my conquerors—I want no pardon from any one— give me some water, and let me die alone.'

"With the hope that I might learn from his conversation something that might lead to the capture of his guilty associates, I returned from the creek with another

cap full of water, nearly the whole of which I managed
to introduce into his parched mouth, and begged him, for
the sake of his future peace, to disclose his history to me.
'It is impossible,' said he, 'there will not be time, the
beatings of my heart tell me so ; long before day, these
sinewy limbs will be motionless ; nay, there will hardly be
a drop of blood in my body, and that blood will only
serve to make the grass grow. My wounds are mortal,
and I must and will die without what you call confession.'
The moon rose in the east. The majesty of her placid
beauty impressed me with reverence. I pointed towards
her, and asked the Pirate if he could not recognize God's
features there. 'Friend, I see what you are driving at,'
was his answer, 'you, like the rest of our enemies, feel
the desire of murdering us all—well—be it so—to die is
after all nothing more than a jest ; and were it not for the
pain, no one, in my opinion, need care a jot about it.
But as you really have befriended me, I will tell you all
that is proper.'

"Hoping his mind might take a useful turn, I again
bathed his temples and washed his lips with spirits. His
sunk eyes seemed to dart fire at mine, a heavy and deep
sigh swelled his chest and struggled through his blood-
choked throat, and he asked me to raise him a little. I
did so, when he addressed me somewhat as follows, for,
as I have told you, his speech was a mixture of Spanish,
French and English, forming a jargon the like of which
I had never heard before, and which I am utterly unable.
to imitate. However, I shall give you the substance of
his declaration.

"'First tell me how many bodies you found in the
boat, and what sort of dresses they had on.' I mentioned their number and described their apparel. 'That's
right,' said he, 'they are the bodies of the scoundrels who
followed me in that infernal Yankee Barge. Bold rascals

they were, for when they found the water too shallow for
their craft, they took to it and waded after me. All my
companions had been shot, and to lighten my own boat
I flung them overboard; but as I lost time in this,
the two ruffians caught hold of my gunwale, and struck
on my head and body in such a manner, that after I had
disabled and killed them both in the boat, I was scarcely
able to move. The other villains carried off our schooner and one of our boats, and perhaps, ere now, have hung
all my companions whom they did not kill at the time.
I have commanded my beautiful vessel many years, captured many ships, and sent many rascals to the devil. I
always hated the Yankees, and only regret that I have
not killed more of them. I sailed from Mantanzas. I
have often been in concert with others. I have money
without counting, but it is buried where it will never be
found, and it would be useless to tell you of it.' His
throat filled with blood, his voice failed, the cold hand of
death was laid on his brow; feebly and horribly he mut-
tered, 'I am dying, man, farewell.'

"Alas! it is painful to see death in any shape; in
this it was horrible, for there was no hope. The rattling
of his throat announced the moment of dissolution, and
already did the body fall on my arms with a weight that
was insupportable. I laid him on the ground. A mass
of dark blood poured from his mouth; then came a
frightful groan, the last breathing of that foul spirit; and
what now lay at my feet in the wild desert was a mangled
mass of clay.

"The remainder of the night was passed in no envi-
able mood; but my feelings cannot be described. At
dawn I dug a hole with the paddle of my canoe, rolled
the body into it and covered it. On reaching the boat, I
found several buzzards feeding on the bodies, which I in
vain attempted to drag to the shore. I therefore covered

them with mud and weeds, and launching my canoe, paddled from the cove, with a secret joy for my escape,
overshaded with the gloom of mingled dread and
horror. '

CHAPTER XXIII.

In America : Episode in New Brunswick.

IN the beginning of August, Audubon, accompanied by his wife and two sons, went on a journey to the State of Maine, to examine the birds in the most unfrequented parts ; and the following episodes contain the naturalist's own summary of that visit. They travelled in a private conveyance through Maine, going towards the British provinces, and the country was explored at leisure as they travelled.

JOURNEY IN NEW BRUNSWICK.

"The morning after that we had spent with Sir Archibald Campbell and his delightful family, saw us proceeding along the shores of St. John's River in the British province of New Brunswick. As we passed the government house our hearts bade its generous inmates adieu ; and as we left Frederickton behind, the recollection of the many acts of kindness which we had received from its inhabitants came powerfully on our minds. Slowly advancing over the surface of the translucent stream, we still fancied our ears saluted by the melodies of the unrivalled band of the 43d Regiment. In short, with the remembrance of the kindness experienced, the feeling of expectations gratified, the hope of adding to our knowledge, and the possession of health and vigor, we were luxuriating in happiness. The Favorite, the bark in which we were, contained not only my family, but nearly a score and a half of individuals of all descriptions ; so that the crowded state of her cabin soon began to prove rather disagreeable. The boat itself was a mere *scow*, commanded by a person of rather uncouth aspect and rude manners. Two sorry nags he had fastened to the end of a long tow-line, on the nearer of which rode a negro youth less than half clad, with a long switch in one hand and the joined bridles in the other, striving with all his might to urge them on at the rate of something more than two miles an hour. How fortunate it is for one to possess a little knowledge of a true traveller! Following the advice of a good, and somewhat aged one, we had provided ourselves with a large basket, which was not altogether empty when we reached the end of our agreeable excursion. Here and there the shores of the river were beautiful ; the space between it and the undulating hills that bounded the prospect being highly cultivated, while now and then its abrupt and rocky banks assumed a most picturesque appearance. Although it was late in September, the mowers were still engaged in cutting the grass, and the gardens of the farmers showed patches of green peas. The apples were yet green, and the vegetation in general reminded us that we were in a northern latitude. Gradually and slowly we proceeded, until in the afternoon we landed to exchange our jaded horses. We saw a house on an eminence, with groups of people assembled around it, but no dinner could be obtained, because, as the landlord told us, an *election* was going on. So we had recourse to the basket, and on the green sward we refreshed ourselves with its contents. This done, we returned to the scow, and resumed our stations. As is usual in such cases, in every part of the world that I have visited, our second set of horses was worse than the first. However, on we went ; but to tell you how often the tow-line gave way would not be more amusing to you than it was annoying to us. Once our commander was in con-

sequence plunged into the stream, but after some exertion
he succeeded in gaining his gallant bark, when he con-
soled himself by giving utterance to a volley of blasphe
mies, which it would ill become me to repeat, as it would
be disagreeable to you to hear. We slept somewhere
that night; it does not suit my views to tell you where.
Before day returned to smile on the Favorite, we proceeded. Soon we came to some rapids, when every one,
glad to assist her, leaped on shore, and tugged *à la cordelle.*
Some miles further we passed a curious cataract, formed
by the waters of the Pokioke.

"There Sambo led his steeds up the sides of a high
bank, when, lo! the whole party came tumbling down
like so many hogsheads of tobacco rolled from a storehouse to the banks of the Ohio. He at the steering oar,
'Hoped the black rascal had broken his neck,' and congratulated himself in the same breath for the safety of his
horses, which presently got on their feet. Sambo, however, alert as an Indian chief, leaped on the naked back
of one, and, showing his teeth, laughed at his master's
curses. Shortly after this, we found our boat very snugly secured on the top of a rock, midway in the stream,
just opposite the mouth of Eel River. Next day at noon
—none injured, but all chop-fallen—we were landed at
Woodstock Village, yet in its infancy. After dining
there, we procured a cart and an excellent driver, and
proceeded along an execrable road towards Houlton, in
Maine, glad enough, after all our mishaps, at finding ourselves in our own country. But before I bid farewell to
the beautiful river of St. John, I must tell you that its
navigation seldom exceeds eight months each year, the
passage during the rest being performed on the ice, of
which we were told that last season there was an unusual
quantity; so much indeed as to accumulate, by being
jammed at particular spots, to the height of nearly fifty

feet above the ordinary level of the river, and that when it broke loose in the spring the crash was awful. All the low grounds along the river were suddenly flooded, and even the elevated plain on which Frederickton stands was covered to the depth of four feet. Fortunately, however, as on the greater streams of the Western and Southern districts, such an occurrence seldom takes place.

"Major Clarke, commander of the United States garrison, received us with remarkable kindness. The next day was spent in a long, though fruitless, ornithological excursion; for although we were accompanied by officers and men from the garrison, not a bird did any of our party procure that was of any use to us. We remained a few days, however; after which, hiring a cart, two horses, and a driver, we proceeded in the direction of Bangor. Houlton is a neat village, consisting of some fifty houses. The fort is well situated, and commands a fine view of Mars Hill, which is about thirteen miles distant. A custom-house has been erected here, the place being on the boundary line of the United States and the British provinces. The road, which was cut by the soldiers of this garrison, from Bangor to Houlton, through the forests, is at this moment a fine turnpike of great breadth, almost straight in its whole length, and perhaps the best now in the Union. It was incomplete, however, for some miles, so that our travelling over that portion was slow and disagreeable. The rain, which fell in torrents, reduced the newly-raised earth to a complete bed of mud; and at one time our horses became so completely mired that, had we not been extricated by two oxen, we must have spent the night near the spot. Jogging along at a very slow pace, we were overtaken by a gay waggoner, who had excellent horses, two of which a little 'siller' induced him to join to ours, and we were taken to a tavern at the 'cross roads,' where we spent the night in comfort.

While supper was preparing, I made inquiry respecting
birds, quadrupeds, and fishes, and was pleased to hear
that all of these animals abounded in the neighborhood.
Deer, bears, trouts, and grouse, were quite plentiful, as
was the great gray owl. When we resumed our journey
next morning Nature displayed all her loveliness, and
autumn, with her mellow tints, her glowing fruits, and
her rich fields of corn, smiled in placid beauty. Many
of the fields had not yet been reaped ; the fruits of the
forests and orchards hung clustering around us ; and as
we came in view of the Penobscot River, our hearts
thrilled with joy. Its broad transparent waters here
spread out their unruffled surface, there danced along the
rapids, while canoes filled with Indians swiftly glided in
every direction, raising before them the timorous water-
fowl, that had already flocked in from the north. Mountains which you well know are indispensable in a beautiful landscape, reared their majestic crests in the distance.
The Canada jay leaped gayly from branch to twig ; the
kingfisher, as if vexed at being suddenly surprised, rattled loudly as it swiftly flew off ; and the fish-hawk and
eagle spread their broad wings over the waters. All
around was beautiful, and we gazed on the scene with delight as, seated on a verdant bank, we refreshed our
frames from our replenished stores. A few rare birds
were procured here, and the rest of the road being level
and firm, we trotted on at a good pace for several hours,
the Penobscot keeping company with us. Now we came
to a deep creek, of which the bridge was undergoing repairs, and the people saw our vehicle approach with much
surprise. They, however, assisted us with pleasure, by
placing a few logs across, along which our horses, one
after the other, were carefully led, and the cart afterwards
carried. These good fellows were so averse to our rec-
ompensing them for their labor that, after some alterca-

tion, we were obliged absolutely to force what we deemed
a suitable reward upon them. Next day we continued
our journey along the Penobscot, the country changing
its aspect at every mile ; and when we first descried Old
Town, that village of saw-mills looked like an island covered with manufactories. The people are noted for their
industry and perseverance ; any one possessing a mill, and
attending to his saws and the floating of the timber into
his dams, is sure to obtain a competency in a few years.

" Speculations in land covered with pine, lying to the
north of this place, are carried on to a great extent, and
to discover a good tract of such ground many a miller of
Old Town undertakes long journeys. Reader, with your
leave, I will here introduce one of them.

" Good luck brought us into acquaintance with Mr.
Gillies, whom we happened to meet in the course of our
travels, as he was returning from an exploring tour.
About the first of August he formed a party of sixteen
persons, each carrying a knapsack and an axe. Their
provisions consisted of two hundred and fifty pounds of
pilot bread, one hundred and fifty pounds of salted pork,
four pounds of tea, two large loaves of sugar, and some
salt. They embarked in light canoes, twelve miles north
of Bangor, and followed the Penobscot as far as Wassa-
taquoik River, a branch leading to the north-west, until
they reached the Sebois Lakes, the principal of which lie
in a line, with short portages between them. Still proceeding north-west, they navigated these lakes, and then
turning west, carried their canoes to the great lake
' Baamchenunsgamook ;' thence north to ' Wallaghasque-
gamook ' Lake ; then along a small stream to the upper
' Umsaskis ' Pond, when they reached the Alleguash
River, which leads into the St. John's, in about latitude
47° 3'. Many portions of that country had not been visited before even by the Indians, who assured Mr. Gillies

of this fact. They continued their travels down the St.
John's to the grand falls, where they met with a portage
of half a mile, and, having reached Medux-mekcag
Creek, a little above Woodstock, the party walked to
Houlton, having travelled twelve hundred miles, and described almost an oval over the country by the time they
returned to Old Town on the Penobscot. While anx-
iously looking for 'lumber lands,' they ascended the emi-
nences around, then climbed the tallest trees, and, by
means of a great telescope, inspected the pine woods in
the distance. And such excellent judges are these persons of the value of the timber which they thus observe,
when it is situated at a convenient distance from water,
that they never afterwards forget the different spots at all
worthy of their attention. They had observed only a few
birds and quadrupeds, the latter principally porcupines.
The borders of the lakes and rivers afforded them fruits
of various sorts, and abundance of cranberries, while the
uplands yielded plenty of wild white onions and a species
of black plum. Some of the party continued their journey in canoes down the St. John's, ascended Eel River,
and the lake of the same name to Mattawamkeag River,
due south-west of the St. John's, and, after a few portages, fell into the Penobscot. I had made arrangements
to accompany Mr. Gillies on a journey of this kind, when
I judged it would be more interesting, as well as useful
to me, to visit the distant country of Labrador.

"The road which we followed from Old Town to
Bangor was literally covered with Penobscot Indians returning from market. On reaching the latter beautiful
town, we found very comfortable lodgings in an excellent
hotel, and next day proceeded by the mail to Boston."

The following chapter gives some further knowledge
of what Audubon saw during his journey through the interior of Maine.

CHAPTER XXIV.

Episodes in Maine: The Maine Lumbermen.

THE men who are employed in cutting down the trees, and conveying the logs to the saw-mills or the places for shipping, are, in the State of Maine, called 'lumberers.' Their labors may be said to begin before winter has commenced, and, while the ground is yet uncovered by any great depth of snow, they leave their homes to proceed to the interior of the pine forests, which in that part of the country are truly magnificent, and betake themselves to certain places already well known to them. Their provisions, axes, saws, and other necessary articles, together with the provender for their cattle, are conveyed by oxen on heavy sleds. Almost at the commencement of their march they are obliged to enter the woods ; and they have frequently to cut a way for themselves for considerable spaces, as the ground is often covered with the decaying trunks of immense trees, which have fallen either from age or in consequence of accidental burnings. These trunks, and the undergrowth which lies entangled in their tops, render many places almost impassable even to men on foot. Over miry ponds they are sometimes forced to form causeways, this being, under all the circumstances, the easiest mode of reaching the opposite side. Then, reader, is the time for witnessing the exertions of their fine large cattle. No rods do their drivers use to pain their flanks ; no oaths or imprecations are ever heard to fall from the lips of these most industrious and temperate

men ; for in them, as indeed in most of the inhabitants of
our Eastern States, education and habit have tempered
the passions and reduced the moral constitution to a
state of harmony—nay, the sobriety that exists in many
of the villages of Maine I have often considered as carried to excess, for on asking for brandy, rum, or whiskey,
not a drop could I obtain ; and it is probable there was
an equal lack of spirituous liquors of every other kind.
Now and then I saw some good old wines, but they were
always drunk in careful moderation. But to return to
the management of the oxen. Why, reader, the lumberers speak to them as if they were rational beings : few
words seem to suffice, and their whole strength is applied
to the labor, as if in gratitude to those who treat them
with so much gentleness and humanity.

" While present, on more than one occasion, at what
Americans 'call ploughing matches,' which they have annually in many of the States, I have been highly gratified,
and in particular at one—of which I still have a strong
recollection,—and which took place a few miles from the
fair and hospitable city of Boston. There I saw fifty or
more ploughs drawn by as many pairs of oxen, which performed their work with so much accuracy and regularity,
without the infliction of whip or rod, but merely guided
by the verbal mandates of the ploughmen, that I was perfectly astonished.

" After surmounting all obstacles, the lumberers, with the
stock they have provided, arrive at the spot which they
have had in view, and immediately commence building a
camp. The trees around soon fall under the blows of
their axes, and, before many days have elapsed, a low
habitation is reared and fitted within for the accommodation of their cattle, while their provender is secured on a
kind of loft, covered with broad shingles or boards. Then
their own cabin is put up ; rough bedsteads, manufactured

on the spot, are fixed in the corners; a chimney, composed of a frame of sticks plastered with mud, leads away the smoke; the skins of bears or deer, with some blankets, form their bedding; and around the walls are hung their changes of homespun clothing, guns, and various necessaries of life. Many prefer spending the night on the sweet-scented hay and corn blades of their cattle, which are laid on the ground. All arranged within, the lumberers set around their camp their 'dead falls,' large 'steel traps,' and 'spring guns,' in suitable places to procure some of the bears that ever prowl around such establishments. Now the heavy clouds of November, driven by the northern blast, pour down the snow in feathery flakes. The winter has fairly set in, and seldom do the sun's gladdening rays fall on the woodcutter's hut. In warm flannels his body is enveloped, the skin of a racoon covers his head and brow, his moose-skin leggings reach the girdle that secures them round his waist, while on broad moccasins, or snow-shoes, he stands from the earliest dawn till night hacking away at the majestic pines that for a century past have embellished the forest. The fall of these valuable trees no longer resounds on the ground; and as they tumble here and there, nothing is heard but the rustling and crackling of their branches, their heavy trunks sinking into the deep snow. Thousands of large pines thus cut down every winter afford room for the younger trees, which spring up profusely to supply the wants of man. Weeks and weeks have elapsed, the earth's pure white covering has become thickly and firmly crusted by the increasing intensity of the cold, the fallen trees have all been sawn into measured logs, and the long repose of the oxen has fitted them for hauling them to the nearest frozen stream. The ice gradually becomes covered with the accumulating mass of timber, and their task completed, the lumberers wait impatiently for the breaking up of winter. At this period they pass the time in hunting the moose, the deer and the bear, for the benefit of their wives and children ; and as these men are most excellent woodsmen, great havoc is made among the game ; many skins, sables, martins and muskrats, they have procured during the intervals of their labor, or under night. The snows are now giving way as the rains descend in torrents, and the lumberers collect their utensils, harness their cattle, and prepare for their return. This they accomplish in safety. From being lumberers, they become millers, and with pleasure each applies the grating file to his saws. Many logs have already reached the dams on the swollen waters of the rushing streams, and the task commences, which is carried on through the summer, of cutting them up into boards. The great heat of the dog-days has parched the ground ; every creek has become a shallow, except here and there where, in a deep hole, the salmon and the trout have found a retreat : the sharp slimy angles of multitudes of rocks project, as if to afford resting-places to the wood-ducks and herons that breed on the borders of these streams. Thousands of 'saw-logs' remain in every pool, beneath and above each rapid or fall. The miller's dam has been emptied of its timber, and he must now resort to some expedient to procure a fresh supply. It was my good fortune to witness the method employed for the purpose of collecting the logs that had not reached their destination, and I had the more pleasure that it was seen in company with my little family. I wish, for your sake, reader, that I could describe in an adequate manner the scene which I viewed ; but although not so well qualified as I could wish, rely upon it that the desire which I feel to gratify you will induce me to use all my endeavors to give you an *idea* of it. It was the month of September.

"At the upper extremity of Dennisville, which is itself a pretty village, are the saw-mills and ponds of the hospitable Judge Lincoln and other persons. The creek that conveys the logs to these ponds, and which bears the name of the village, is interrupted in its course by many rapids and narrow embanked gorges. One of the latter is situated about half a mile above the mill-dam, and is so rocky and rugged in the bottom and sides as to preclude the possibility of the trees passing along it at low water, while, as I conceived, it would have given no slight labor to an army of woodsmen or millers to move the thousands of large logs that had accumulated in it. They lay piled in confused heaps to a great height along an extent of several hundred yards, and were in some places so close as to have formed a kind of dam. Above the gorge there is a large natural reservoir, in which the headwaters of the creek settle, while only a small portion of these ripple through the gorge below, during the latter weeks of summer and in early autumn, when their streams are at the lowest. At the neck of this basin the lumberers raised a temporary barrier with the refuse of their sawn logs. The boards were planted nearly upright, and supported at their tops by a strong tree extended from side to side of the creek, which might there be about forty feet in breadth. It was prevented from giving way under the pressure of the rising waters by having strong abutments of wood laid against its centre, while the ends of these abutments were secured by wedges, which could be knocked off when necessary. The temporary dam was now finished. Little or no water escaped through the barrier, and that in the creek above it rose in the course of three weeks to its top, which was about ten feet high, forming a sheet that extended upwards fully a mile from the dam. My family were invited early one morning to go and witness the extraordinary effect which would e produced by the breaking down of the barrier, and we all

accompanied the lumberers to the place. Two of the
men, on reaching it, threw off their jackets, tied hand-
kerchiefs round their heads, and fastened to their bodies
a long rope, the end of which was held by three or four
others, who stood ready to drag their companions ashore,
in case of danger or accident. The two operators, each
bearing an axe, walked along the abutments, and, at a
given signal, knocked out the wedges. A second blow
from each sent off the abutments themselves, and the men,
leaping with extreme dexerity from one cross-log to another, sprung to the shore with almost the quickness of
thought. Scarcely had they effected their escape from
the frightful peril that threatened them, when the mass of
waters burst forth with a horrible uproar. All eyes were
bent towards the huge heaps of logs in the gorge below.
The tumultuous burst of the waters instantly swept away
every object that opposed their progress, and rushed in
foaming waves among the timber that everywhere blocked
up the passage. Presently a slow heavy motion was perceived in the mass of logs ; one might have imagined that
some mighty monster lay convulsively writhing beneath
them, struggling, with a fearful energy, to extricate himself from the crushing weight. As the waters rose this
movement increased ; the mass of timber extended in all
directions, appearing to become more and more entangled each moment ; the logs bounced against each
other, thrusting aside, submerging or raising into the air,
those with which they came in contact. It seemed as if
they were waging a war of destruction, such as the
ancient authors describe the efforts of the Titans, the
foaming of whose wrath might, to the eye of the painter,
have been represented by the angry curlings of the waters, while the tremulous and rapid motions of the logs,
which at times reared themselves almost perpendicularly,
might by the poet have been taken for the shakings of

the confounded and discomfited giants. Now the rushing element filled up the gorge to the brim. The logs,
once under way, rolled, reared, tossed, and tumbled amid
the foam, as they were carried along. Many of the smaller trees broke across ; from others, great splinters were
sent up, and all were in some degree seamed and scarred.
Then, in tumultuous majesty, swept along the mangled
wreck : the current being now increased to such a pitch,
that the logs, as they were dashed against the rocky
shores, resounded like the report of distant artillery, or
the rumblings of the thunder. Onward it rolls, the emblem of wreck and ruin, destruction and chaotic strife.
It seemed to me as if I witnessed the rout of a rash
army, surprised, overwhelmed, and overthrown : the roar
of the cannon, the groans of the dying, and the shouts of
the avengers, were thundering through my brain ; and
amid the frightful confusion of the scene there came over
my spirit a melancholy feeling, which had not entirely
vanished at the end of many days. In a few hours almost all the timber that had lain heaped in the rocky
gorge was floating in the great pond of the millers, and
as we walked homewards we talked of the *force of the
waters.*"

CHAPTER XXV.

Visit to the Bay of Fundy.

HILE visiting Eastport, Audubon made a trip to the Bay of Fundy and some of its neighboring islands, in search of the birds which resort there; and the following episode is his own graphic account of that journey :—

" THE BAY OF FUNDY.

" It was in the month of May that I sailed in the United States revenue cutter the Swiftsure, engaged in a cruise in the Bay of Fundy. Our sails were quickly unfurled, and spread out to the breeze.

" The vessel seemed to fly over the liquid element, as the sun rose in full splendor, while the clouds that floated here and there formed, with their glowing hues, a rich contrast with the pure azure of the heavens above us. We approached apace the island of Grand Menan, of which the stupendous cliffs gradually emerged from the deep, with the majestic boldness of her noblest native chief. Soon our bark passed beneath its craggy head, covered with trees which, on account of the height, seemed scarcely larger than shrubs. The prudent raven spread her pinions, launched from the cliff, and flew away before us; the golden eagle, soaring aloft, moved majestically along in wide circles; the guillemots sat on their eggs upon the shelvy precipices, or, plunging into the water, dived and rose again at a great distance; the broad-breasted eider-duck covered her eggs among the grassy tufts; on a

naked rock the seal lazily basked, its sleek sides glisten-
ing in the sunshine ; while shoals of porpoises were
swiftly gliding through the waters around us, showing by
their gambols that, although doomed to the deep, their
life was not devoid of pleasure. Far away stood the bold
shores of Nova Scotia, gradually fading in the distance,
of which the gray tints beautifully relieved the wing-like
sails of many a fishing-bark. Cape after cape, forming
eddies and counter-currents far too terrific to be described by a landsman, we passed in succession, until we
reached a deep cove near the shores of White-head Isl-
and, which is divided from Grand Menan by a narrow
strait, where we anchored secure from every blast that
could blow. In a short time we found ourselves under
the roof of Captain Frankland, the sole owner of the isle,
of which the surface contains about fifteen hundred acres.
He received us all with politeness, and gave us permission
to seek out its treasures, which we immediately set about
doing, for I was anxious to study the habits of certain
gulls that breed there in great numbers. As Captain
Coolidge, our worthy commander, had assured me, we
found them on their nests on almost every tree of a wood
that covered several acres. What a treat, reader, was it
to find birds of this kind lodged on fir-trees, and sitting
comfortably on their eggs !

"Their loud cackling notes led us to their place of
resort, and ere long we had satisfactorily observed their
habits, and collected as many of themselves and their
eggs as we considered sufficient. In our walks we noticed a rat, the only quadruped found in the island, and
observed abundance of gooseberries, currants, rasps,
strawberries, and huckleberries. Seating ourselves on the
summit of the rocks, in view of the vast Atlantic, we
spread out our stores and refreshed ourselves with our
simple fare. Now we followed the objects of our pursuit

13

through the tangled woods, now carefully picked our steps over the spongy grounds. The air was filled with the melodious concerts of birds, and all Nature seemed to smile in quiet enjoyment. We wandered about until the setting sun warned us to depart, when, returning to the house of the proprietor, we sat down to an excellent repast, and amused ourselves with relating anecdotes and forming arrangements for the morrow. Our captain complimented us on our success when we reached the Swiftsure, and in due time we betook ourselves to our hammocks. The next morning, a strange sail appearing in the distance, preparations were instantly made to pay her commander a visit. The signal-staff of 'Whitehead Island' displayed the British flag, while Captain Frankland and his men stood on the shore, and as we gave our sails to the wind, three hearty cheers filled the air, and were instantly responded to by us. The vessel was soon approached, but all was found right with her, and, squaring our yards, onward we sped, cheerily bounding over the gay billows, until our captain set us ashore at Eastport. At another time my party was received on board the revenue cutter's tender, the Fancy, a charming name for so beautiful a craft. We set sail towards evening. The cackling of the 'old wives,' that covered the bay, filled me with delight, and thousands of gulls and cormorants seemed as if anxious to pilot us into ' Head Harbor Bay,' where we anchored for the night. Leaping on the rugged shore, we made our way to the lighthouse, where we found Mr. Snelling, a good and honest Englishman, from Devonshire. His family consisted of three wild-looking lasses, beautiful, like the most finished productions of Nature. In his lighthouse, snugly ensconced, he spent his days in peaceful forgetfulness of the world, subsisting principally on the fish of the bay. When day broke, how delightful it was to see fair Nature open her

graceful eyelids, and present herself arrayed in all that
was richest and purest before her Creator! Ah! reader,
how indelibly are such moments engraved upon my soul!
with what ardor have I at such times gazed around me,
full of the desire of being enabled to comprehend all that
I saw! How often have I longed to converse with the
feathered inhabitants of the forest, all of which seemed
then intent on offering up their thanks to the object of my
own adoration! But the wish could not be gratified,
although I now feel satisfied that I have enjoyed as much
of the wonders and beauties of Nature as it was proper
for me to enjoy. The delightful trills of the winter wren
rolled through the underwood, the red squirrel smacked
time with his chops, the loud notes of the robin sounded
clearly from the tops of the trees, the rosy grosbeak nip-
ped the tender blossoms of the maples, and high overhead the loons passed in pairs, rapidly wending their way
toward far-distant shores. Would that I could have followed in their wake! The hour of our departure had
come, and, as we sailed up the bay, our pilot, who had
been fishing for cod, was taken on board. A few of his
fish were roasted on a plank before the embers, and formed the principal part of our breakfast. The breeze was
light, and it was not until afternoon that we arrived at
Point Lepreaux Harbor, where every one, making choice
of his course, went in search of curiosities or provender.
Now, reader, the little harbor in which, if you wish it, we
shall suppose we still are, is renowned for a circumstance
which I feel much inclined to endeavor to explain to you.
Several species of ducks, that in myriads cover the waters
of the Bay of Fundy, are at times destroyed in this particular spot in a very singular manner. When July has
come, all the water birds that are no longer capable of
reproducing remain, like so many forlorn bachelors and
old maids, to renew their plumage along the shores. At

the period when these poor birds are unfit for flight, troops
of Indians make their appearance in light bark canoes,
paddled by their squaws and papooses. They form their
flotilla into an extended curve, and drive the birds before
them ; not in silence, but with simultaneous horrific yells,
at the same time beating the surface of the water with
their long poles and paddles. Terrified by the noise, the
birds swim a long way before them, endeavoring to escape
with all their might. The tide is high, every cove is filled, and into the one where we now are thousands of ducks
are seen entering. The Indians have ceased to shout,
and the canoes advance side by side. Time passes on,
the tide swiftly recedes as it rose, and there are the birds
left on the beach. See with what pleasure each wild in-
habitant of the forest seizes his stick, the squaws and
younglings following with similar weapons! Look at
them rushing on their prey, falling on the disabled birds,
and smashing them with their cudgels, until all are destroyed! In this manner upwards of five hundred wild
fowls have often been procured in a few hours. Three
pleasant days were spent about Point Lepreaux, when
the Fancy spread her wings to the breeze. In one harbor we fished for shells, with a capital dredge, and in
another searched along the shore for eggs. The Passama-
quoddy chief is seen gliding swiftly over the deep in his
fragile bark. He has observed a porpoise breathing.
Watch him, for now he is close upon the unsuspecting
dolphin. He rises erect ; aims his musket : smoke rises
curling from the pan, and rushes from the iron tube, when
soon after the report reaches the ear : meantime, the
porpoise has suddenly turned back downwards; it is
dead. The body weighs a hundred pounds or more, but
this, to the tough-fibred son of the woods, is nothing ; he
reaches it with his muscular arms, and, at a single jerk—
while with his legs he dexterously steadies the canoe—

he throws it lengthwise at his feet. Amidst the highest
waves of the Bay of Fundy, these feats are performed by
the Indians during the whole of the season, when the
porpoises resort thither.

"You have often, no doubt, heard of the extraordinary tides of this bay; so had I, but, like others, I was loth
to believe that the reports were strictly true. So I went
to the pretty town of Windsor, in Nova Scotia, to judge
for myself.

"But let us leave the Fancy for awhile, and fancy ourselves at Windsor. Late one day in August, my companions and I were seated on the grassy elevated bank
of the river, about eighty feet or so above its bed, which
was almost dry, and extended for nine miles below like a
sandy wilderness. Many vessels lay on the high banks,
taking in their cargo of gypsum. We thought the appearance very singular, but we were too late to watch the
tide that evening. Next morning we resumed our station, and soon perceived the water flowing toward us, and
rising with a rapidity of which we had previously seen no
example. We planted along the steep declivity of the
bank a number of sticks, each three feet long, the base
of one being placed on a level with the top of that below
it, and when about half flow the tide reached their tops,
one after another, rising three feet in ten minutes, or
eighteen in the hour, and at high water the surface was
sixty-five feet above the bed of the river. On looking
for the vessels which we had seen the previous evening,
we were told that most of them had gone with the night
tide. But now we are again on board the Fancy; Mr.
Claredge stands near the pilot, who sits next to the man
at the helm. On we move swiftly, for the breeze has
freshened; many islands we pass in succession; the wind
increases to a gale. With reefed sails we dash along,
and now rapidly pass a heavily-laden sloop, gallantly run-

ning across our course with undiminished sail, when suddenly we see her upset. Staves and spars are floating around, and presently we observe three men scrambling up her sides, and seating themselves on the keel, where they make signals of distress to us. By this time we have run to a great distance ; but Claredge, cool and prudent, as every seaman ought to be, has already issued his orders to the helmsman and crew, and, now near the wind, we gradually approach the sufferers. A line is thrown to them, and next moment we are alongside the vessel. A fisher's boat, too, has noticed the disaster, and with long strokes of her oars, advances, now rising on the curling wave, and now sinking out of sight. By our mutual efforts the men are brought on board, and the sloop is slowly towed into a safe harbor. In an hour after my party was safely landed at Eastport, where, on looking over the waters, and observing the dense masses of vapors that veiled the shore, we congratulated our‑selves at having escaped from the *Bay of Fundy*."

CHAPTER XXVI.

FROM Frederickton Audubon returned in a private conveyance to Houlton, thence along the United States military road to Bangor, and thence by public stages to Boston, where he arrived early in October. Finding that it would improve his great work on the " Birds " to remain another year in America, and visit parts of the country yet unexplored by him, Audubon determined to send his eldest son Victor to England, to superintend the engraving, and to look after his general interests there. Victor Audubon accordingly sailed from New York for Liverpool, toward the end of October, while his father remained in Boston during that and the following winter, actively engaged in making drawings of new birds which he had discovered, and also in redrawing and greatly improving some of his older drawings. He also made frequent excursions into the surrounding country. "Here," says the Journal, "I was witness to the melancholy death of the great Spurzheim, and was myself suddenly attacked by a short but severe illness, which greatly alarmed my family ; but thanks to Providence and my medical friends, Parkman, Shattuck, and Warren, I was soon enabled to proceed with my labor—a sedentary life and too close application being the cause assigned for my indisposition. I resolved to set out again in quest of fresh materials for my pencil and pen. My wishes directing me to Labrador, I returned eastward with my youngest son, and had the pleasure of being joined by four young gentlemen, all fond of natural history, and willing to encounter the difficulties and privations of the voyage—George Shattuck, Thomas Lincoln, William Ingalls, and Joseph Coolidge."

The schooner Ripley was chartered at Boston for fifteen hundred dollars for the trip to Labrador. The journal containing the narrative begins at Eastport.

" *June* 4, 1833. The day has been fine, and I dined with Captain Childs, commanding the United States troops here. We had a pleasant dinner, but I am impatient to be under weigh for Labrador. The vessel is being prepared for our reception and departure; and we have concluded to ship two extra sailors, and a boy, to be a sort of major-domo, to clean our guns, hunt for nests and birds, and assist in skinning them, &c. While rambling in the woods this morning I discovered a crow's nest with five young ones in it, and as I climbed the tree the parents came to the rescue of their children, crying loudly and with such perseverance, that in fifteen minutes more than fifty pairs of these birds had joined in their vociferations, although I saw only a single pair when I began to climb the tree.

" *June* 6. We sailed from Eastport about one o'clock P. M., and the whole male population seemed to have turned out to witness our departure, just as if no schooner of the size of the Ripley had ever gone from this mighty port to Labrador; our numerous friends came with the throng, and we all shook hands as if we were never to meet again; and as we pushed off with a trifling accident or so, the batteries of the garrison and the cannon of the revenue cutter in the stream saluted us with stout, loud, and oft-repeated reports. Captain Coolidge accompanied us, and was, indeed, our pilot, until we passed Lubec. The wind was light and ahead, and yet with the assistance of the tide we drifted twenty-five miles down to Little River during the night.

" *June* 7. This morning found us riding at anchor near some ugly-looking rocks, the sight of which caused our captain to try to get out of their way, and the whole morning was spent in trying to get into Little River, but the men were unable to tow us in. We landed for a few minutes and shot a hermit thrush, but the wind sprang up, and we returned to the vessel and tried to put out to sea ; we were for a time in danger of drifting upon the rocks, but the wind increased, and we made our way out to sea. Suddenly, however, the fog came drifting in, and was so thick that we could hardly see the bowsprit, and the night was spent in direful apprehension of some impending evil ; although, about twelve, squalls of wind decided in our favor, and when day dawned the wind was blowing fresh from the north, and we were driving on the waters, all sea-sick, and crossing that worst of all dreadful bays, the Bay of Fundy.

" *June* 8. We sailed between Seal and Mud Islands. In the latter the procellaria (a species of gull) breed abundantly ; their nests are dug in the sand to the depth of two feet or more, and the whole island is covered with them, looking like rat holes. They lay three white eggs."

The next two days recorded in the Journal describe the winds and sights, and birds which were seen as the voyagers scudded from Cape Sable to the Gut of Canseau, so named by the early French voyagers, because they found vast quantities of wild geese there. The wind was fair, and the captain of the Ripley wished to continue his course to Labrador. But Audubon, anxious to explore every part of the coast along which they were sailing, persuaded the captain to come to anchor in a harbor in the Gut of Canseau, of the same name.

13*

Here he found twenty sail of Labrador fishermen at anchor, and obtained the information which enabled him to write the following episode.

" Although I had seen, as I thought, abundance of fish along the coasts of the Floridas, the numbers which I found in Labrador quite astonished me. Should your surprise while reading the following statements be as great as mine was while observing the facts related, you will conclude, as I have often done, that Nature's means for providing small animals for the use of large ones, *vice versâ*, are as ample as is the grandeur of that world which she has so curiously constructed. The coast of Labrador is visited by European as well as American fishermen, all of whom are, I believe, entitled to claim portions of fishing ground, assigned to each nation by mutual understanding. For the present, however, I shall confine my observations to those who chiefly engage in this department of our commerce. Eastport in Maine sends out every year a goodly fleet of schooners and ' pick-axes' to Labrador, to procure cod, mackerel, halibut, and sometimes herring, the latter being caught in the intermediate space. The vessels from that port, and others in Maine and Massachusetts, sail as soon as the warmth of spring has freed the gulf of ice, that is from the beginning of May to that of June.

" A vessel of one hundred tons or so is provided with a crew of twelve men, who are equally expert as sailors and fishers, and for every couple of these hardy tars a Hampton boat is provided, which is lashed on the deck or hung in stays. Their provision is simple, but of good quality, and it is very seldom any spirits are allowed ; beef, pork, and biscuit, with water, being all they take with them. The men are supplied with warm clothing, waterproof oil jackets and trousers, large boots, broad-brimmed hats with a round crown, and stout mittens, with a few shirts. The owner or captain furnishes them with lines, hooks, and nets, and also provides the bait best adapted to insure success. The hold of the vessel is filled with casks of various dimensions, some containing salt, and others for the oil that may be procured. The bait generally used at the beginning of the season consists of mussels, salted for the purpose ; but as soon as the capelings reach the coast, they are substituted to save expense ; and, in many instances, the flesh of gannets and other sea-fowl is employed. The wages of fishermen vary from sixteen to thirty dollars per month, according to the qualifications of the individual. The labor of these men is excessively hard, for, except on Sunday, their allowance of rest in the twenty-four hours seldom exceeds three. The cook is the only person who fares better in this respect, but he must also assist in curing the fish. He has breakfast, consisting of coffee, bread, and meat, ready for the captain and the whole crew, by three o'clock every morning except Sunday. Each person carries with him his dinner ready cooked, which is commonly eaten on the fishing-ground. Thus, at three in the morning, the crew are prepared for their day's labor, and ready to betake themselves to their boats, each of which has two oars and lug-sails. They all depart at once, and either by rowing or sailing, reach the banks to which the fishes are known to resort. The little squadron drop their anchors at short distances from each other, in a depth of from ten to twenty feet, and the business is immediately commenced. Each man has two lines, and each stands in one end of the boat, the middle of which is boarded off to hold the fish. The baited lines have been dropped into the water, one on each side of the boat ; their leads have touched the bottom ; a fish has taken the hook, and after giving the line a slight jerk, the fisherman hauls up his prize with a continued pull, throws the fish athwart a small round bar of iron placed near his back, which forces open the mouth, while the weight of the body, however small the fish may be, tears out the hook. The bait is still good, and over the side the line again goes, to catch another fish, while that on the left is now drawn up, and the same course pursued. In this manner, a fisher busily plying at each end, the operation is continued, until the boat is so laden that her gunwale is brought within a few inches of the surface, when they return to the vessel in harbor, seldom distant more than eight miles from the banks. During the greater part of the day the fishermen have kept up a constant conversation, of which the topics are the pleasures of finding a good supply of cod, their domestic affairs, the political prospects of the nation, and other matters similarly connected. Now the repartee of one elicits a laugh from the other ; this passes from man to man, and the whole flotilla enjoy the joke. The men of one boat strive to outdo those of the others in hauling up the greatest quantity of fish in a given time, and this forms another source of merriment. The boats are generally filled about the same time, and all return together. Arrived at the vessel, each man employs a pole armed with a bent iron, resembling the prong of a hay-fork, with which he pierces the fish and throws it with a jerk on deck, counting the number thus discharged with a loud voice. Each cargo is thus safely deposited, and the boats instantly return to the fishing ground, when, after anchoring, the men eat their dinner and begin anew. There, good reader, with your leave, I will let them pursue their avocations for awhile, as I am anxious that you should witness what is doing on board the vessel. The captain, four men, and the cook have, in the course of the morning, erected long tables fore and aft of the main hatchway. They have taken to the shore most of the salt barrels, and have placed in a row their large empty casks to receive the livers. The hold of the vessel is quite clear, except a corner, where is a large heap of salt. And now the men, having dined precisely at twelve, are ready with their large knives. One begins with breaking off the head of the fish, a slight pull of the hand and a gash with the knife effecting this in a moment. He slits up the belly, with one hand pushes it aside to his neighbor, then throws overboard the head and begins to doctor another; the next man tears out the entrails, separates the liver, which he throws into a cask, and casts the rest overboard. A third person dexterously passes his knife beneath the vertebræ of the fish, separates them from the flesh, heaves the latter through the hatchway, and the former into the water. Now, if you will peep into the hold, you will see the last stage of the process, the salting and packing. Six experienced men generally manage to head, gut, bone, salt, and pack all the fish caught in the morning, by the return of the boats with fresh cargoes, when all hands set to work and clear the deck of the fish. Thus their labors continue until twelve o'clock, when they wash their faces and hands, put on clean clothes, hang their fishing apparel on the shrouds, and, betaking themselves to the forecastle, are soon in a sound sleep.

"At three next morning comes the captain from his berth, rubbing his eyes, and in a loud voice calling, 'All hands, ho!' Stiffened in limb, and but half awake, the crew quickly appear on deck. Their fingers and hands are so cramped and swollen by pulling the lines that it is difficult for them even to straighten a thumb; but this matters little at present, for the cook, who had a good nap yesterday, has risen an hour before them, and prepared their coffee and eatables. Breakfast despatched, they exchange their clean clothes for the fishing apparel, and leap into their boats, which had been washed the previous night, and again the flotilla bounds to the fishing ground. As there may be not less than 100 schooners or pick-axes in the harbor, 300 boats resort to the banks each day; and as each boat may procure 2,000 cod per diem, when Saturday night comes, about 600,000 fishes have been brought to the harbor. This having caused some scarcity on the fishing grounds, and Sunday being somewhat of an idle day, the captain collects the salt ashore, and sets sail for some other convenient harbor, which he expects to reach before sunset. If the weather be favorable the men get a good deal of rest during the voyage, and on Monday things go on as before. I must not omit to tell you, reader, that while proceeding from one harbor to another the vessel has passed near a rock which is the breeding place of myriads of puffins. She has laid to for an hour or so, while part of the crew have landed and collected a store of eggs, excellent as a substitute for cream, and not less so when hard boiled as food for the fishing grounds. I may as well inform you also how these adventurous fellows distinguish the fresh eggs from the others. They fill up some large tubs with water, throw in a quantity of eggs, and allow them to remain a minute or so, when those which come to the surface are tossed overboard, and even those that manifest any upward tendency share the same treatment. All that remain at bottom, you may depend upon it, good reader, are perfectly sound, and not less palatable than any that you have ever eaten, or that your best guinea-fowl has just dropped in your barnyard ; but let us return to the cod-fish. The fish already procured and salted is taken ashore at the new harbor by part of the crew, whom the captain has marked as the worst hands at fishing. There on the bare rocks, or elevated scaffolds of considerable extent, the salted cods are laid side by side to dry in the sun. They are turned

several times a day, and in the intervals the men bear a
hand on board at clearing and stowing away the daily
produce of the fishing banks. Towards evening they return to the drying grounds, and put up the fish in piles
resembling so many haystacks, disposing those towards
the top in such a manner that the rain cannot injure
them, and placing a heavy stone on the summit to prevent their being thrown down, should it blow hard during the night. You see, reader, that the life of a Labrador fisherman is not one of idleness. The capelings
have approached the shores, and in myriads enter every
basin and stream to deposit their spawn, for now July
is come, the cods follow them as the bloodhound follows
his prey, and their compact masses literally line the
shores. The fishermen now adopt another method.
They have brought with them long and deep seines, one
end of which is, by means of a line, fastened to the shore,
while the other is in the usual manner drawn out in a
broad sweep, to inclose as great a space as possible, and
hauled on shore by means of a capstan. Some of the
men in boats support the corked part of the net, and
beat the water to frighten the fishes within towards the
land ; while others, armed with poles, enter the water,
hook the fishes, and fling them on the beach, the net being gradually drawn closer as the number of fishes diminish. What do you think, reader, as to the number of
cods secured in this manner at a single haul ?—twenty or
thirty thousand. You may form some notion of the matter when I tell you that the young gentlemen of my party,
while going along the shores, caught cod-fish alive with
their hands, and trouts of weight with a piece of twine
and a mackerel hook hung to their gun rods ; and that
if two of them walked knee-deep along the rocks, holding
a handkerchief by the corners, they swept it full of
capelings : should you not trust me in this, I refer you

to the fishermen themselves, or recommend you to go to
Labrador, where you will give credit to the testimony of
your eyes. The seining of the cod-fish is not, I believe,
quite lawful, for a great proportion of the codlings which
are dragged ashore at last are so small as to be considered useless, and, instead of being returned to the
water as they ought to be, are left on the shore, where
they are ultimately eaten by bears, wolves, and ravens.
The fishes taken along the coast or fishing stations only
a few miles off are of small dimensions, and I believe I
am correct in saying that few of them weigh more than
two pounds when perfectly cured, or exceed six when
taken out of the water. The fish are liable to several
diseases, and at times are annoyed by parasitic animals,
which in a short time render them lean and unfit for use.
Some individuals, from laziness or other causes, fish with
naked hooks, and thus frequently wound the cod without
securing them, in consequence of which the shoals are
driven away, to the detriment of the other fishers. Some
carry their cargoes to other ports before drying them,
while others dispose of them to agents from distant
shores. Some have only a pick-axe of fifty tons, while
others are owners of seven or eight vessels of equal or
larger burden ; but whatever be their means, should the
season prove favorable, they are generally well repaid
for their labor. I have known instances of men who on
their first voyage ranked as ' boys,' and in ten years after
were in independent circumstances, although they still
continued to resort to the fishing. ' For,' said they to
me, ' how could we be content to spend our time in idleness at home ? ' I know a person of this class who has
carried on the trade for many years, and who has quite a
little fleet of schooners, one of which, the largest and
most beautifully built, has a cabin as neat and comfortable as any that I have ever seen in a vessel of the same

size. This vessel took fish on board only when perfectly cured, or acted as pilot to the rest, and now and then would return home with an ample supply of halibut, or a cargo of prime mackerel. On another occasion I will offer some remarks on the improvements which I think might be made in the cod fisheries of the coast of Labrador."

CHAPTER XXVII.

" *June* 11. From the entrance to the Gut of Canseau, where the Ripley lay at anchor, Audubon had the first view of the South-eastern coast of Nova Scotia, which he describes as ' dreary, rocky, poor and inhospitable look-ing.' It snowed the next day, yet when the party went ashore, they found not only trees in bloom, but the ground plants were in flower, and some tolerably good-looking grass ; and they saw also robins, and sparrows, and finches, and their nests with young ones. But no custom-house officer appeared, nor any individual who could give them any valuable information. They found lobsters very abundant, and caught forty in a very short time ; but to their surprise they did not see a single bird.

" *June* 12. To day there has been cold, rain and hail, but the frogs are piping in the pools. By-and-by the weather became beautiful, and the wind fair, and we were soon under way, following in the wake of the whole fleet, which had been anchored in the harbor of Canseau, and gliding across the great bay under full press of sail. The land locked us in, the water was smooth, the sky serene, and the thermometer at 46°, and the sunshine on deck was very agreeable. After sailing twenty-one miles we entered the real Gut of Canseau, passing one after another every vessel of the fleet with which we had sailed.

" The land on each side now rose in the form of an am-phitheatre, and on the Nova Scotia side to a considerable height; dwellings appeared here and there, but the country is too poor for comfort: the timber is small, and the land too stony; a small patch of ploughed land planted, or ready for potatoes, was all the cultivation we saw. Near one house we saw a few apple trees, which were not yet in bloom. The general appearance of this passage reminded me of some parts of the Hudson River, and, accompanied as we were by thirty sail of vessels, the time passed agreeably. Vegetation appeared as forward as at Eastport: saw a few chimney swallows, and heard a few blue jays. As we passed Cape Porcupine, a high rounding hill, we saw some Indians in birch-bark canoes, and clearing Cape George we were soon in the gulf of St. Lawrence. From this place, on the 20th of May last year, the sea was a sheet of ice as far as the eye could reach with the aid of a good spy-glass.

"We ran down the west coast of Cape Breton Island, and the country looked well in the distance; large undulating hills were covered with many hamlets, and patches of cultivated land were seen. It being calm when we neared Jestico Island, about three miles from Cape Breton, I left the vessel and landed on it. It was covered with well-grown grass, and filled with strawberry vines in full bloom. The sun shone brightly, the weather was pleasant, and we found many northern birds breeding there; the wild gooseberries were plentiful, about the size of a pea, and a black currant also. The wind arose, and we hurried back to the vessel; on the way my son John and some of the sailors nearly killed a seal with their oars.

"*June* 13. This morning at four o'clock we came in sight of the Magdalene Islands, distant about twenty miles. The morning was dull, and by breakfast-time a thick fog obscured the horizon, and we lost sight of the islands; the wind rose sluggishly and dead ahead, and several ships and brigs loaded with timber from the Miramichie came near us beating their way to the Atlantic. At nine o'clock we dropped anchor, being partly land-locked between Breton Island and the Highlands, and within a quarter of a mile of an Island, which formed a part of the group. The pilot, who is well acquainted here, informed me that the islands are all connected by dry sand-bars, and with no channel between them except the one we are in, called Entree Bay, which is formed by Entree Island and a long sand-spit connecting it with the mainland. The island is forty-eight miles long, and three in breadth; the formation is a red rough sandy soil, and the north-west side is constantly wearing away by the action of the sea. Guillemots were seated upright along the projecting shelvings in regular order, resembling so many sentinels on the look-out; many gannets also were seen on the extreme points of the island. On one of the islands were many houses, and a small church, and on the highest land a large cross, indicating the religion of the inhabitants. Several small vessels lay in the harbor called Pleasant Bay, but the weather is so cold we cannot visit them until to-morrow.

" *June* 14, 1833. Magdalene Islands, Gulf of St. Lawrence. It is one week since we left Eastport, and we breakfasted with the thermometer at 44° in our cabin, and on deck it feels like mid-winter. We landed on the island next to us so chilled that we could scarcely use our hands; two large bluffs frowned on each side of us, the resort of many sea-birds, and some noble ravens which we saw. Following a narrow path we soon came upon one of God's best finished jewels, a woman. She saw us first, for women are always keenest in sight and perception, in patience and fortitude and love, in faith and sorrow, and, as I believe, in everything else which adorns our race. She was hurrying towards her cottage, with a child in her arms having no covering but a little shirt.

The mother was dressed in coarse French homespun, with a close white cotton nightcap on her head, and the mildest-looking woman I had seen in many a day. At a venture I addressed her in French, and it answered well, for she replied in an unintelligible jargon, about one-third of which I understood, which enabled me to make out that she was the wife of a fisherman who lived there.

"We walked on through the woods toward the church. Who would have expected to find a church on such an island, among such impoverished people? Yet here it was, a Roman Catholic church. And here we came suddenly on a handsome, youthful, vigorous, black-haired and black-bearded fellow, covered with a long garment as black as a raven, and having a heart as light as a young lark's. He was wending his way to the church, at the sound of a bell, which measured twelve inches by nine in diameter, of about thirty pounds weight, which could nevertheless be heard for a quarter of a mile. It was the festival among the Roman Catholics of La Petite Fête de Dieu. The chapel was lighted with candles, and all the old women on the island had trudged from their distant dwellings, staff in hand, backs bent with age, and eyes dimmed by time. They crossed their breasts and knelt before the tawdry images in the church, with so much simplicity and apparent sincerity of heart, that I could not help exclaiming to myself, 'Well, this is religion after all.'

"The priest, named Brunet, was from Quebec, and these islands belong to Lower Canada, but are under the jurisdiction of the Bishop of Halifax. He is a shrewd-looking fellow, and, if I do not mistake his character, with a good deal of the devil in him. He told us there were no reptiles on the island; but we found by our own observations that he was mistaken, as he was also in the representations he made respecting the quadrupeds. This priest, who I hope is a good and worthy man, told us that the land is very poor and destitute of game, and that the seal-fisheries were less profitable last year than common ; that there are about one hundred and sixty families on a dozen islands, and that cod, mackerel, and herring-fishing were the employments of the inhabitants. One or two vessels come from Quebec yearly to collect the produce (of the sea). The priest said he led the life of a recluse here, but if we would accompany him to his boarding-house he would give us a glass of good French wine.

"On our rambles we found the temperature on land quite agreeable, and in sheltered situations the sun was warm and pleasant. The grass looked well, and strawberry blossoms were plenty. The woods, such as they were, were filled with warblers : the robin, thrush, finch, bunting, &c. The fox-tailed sparrow and siskin breed here, the hermit and tawny thrush crossed our path, the black-capped warbler gambolled over the pools, and even the wrens were everywhere. Of water-birds the great terns were abundant, and the piping plovers breed here. We also collected several species of land-snails, and some specimens of gypsum. We crossed the bay in the afternoon, and found a man who had some fox-skins for sale : he asked five pounds apiece for the black fox, and one dollar and fifty cents for the red skins. The woods here are small, scrubby evergreens, almost impenetrable and swampy beneath. Thermometer this evening 44°.

"*June* 15. Day dawned with the weather dull, but the wind fair, and we pulled up anchor and left the Magdalene Islands for Labrador, the ultimatum of our present desires. About ten o'clock we saw on the distant horizon a speck, which I was told was the Rock ; the wind now freshened, and I could soon see it plainly from the deck, the top apparently covered with snow. Our pilot said that the snow, which seemed two or three feet thick, was the white gannets which resort there. I rubbed my eyes, and took my spy-glass, and instantly the strange picture stood before me. They were indeed birds, and such a mass of birds, and of such a size as I never saw before. The whole of my party were astonished, and all agreed that it was worth a voyage across the Bay of Fundy and the Gulf of St. Lawrence to see such a sight. The nearer we approached, the greater was our surprise at the enormous number of these birds, all calmly seated on their eggs, and their heads turned to the windward towards us. The air for a hundred yards above, and for a long distance around, was filled with gannets on the wing, which from our position made the air look as if it was filled with falling snowflakes, and caused a thick, foggy-like atmosphere all around the rock. The wind was too high to allow us to land, but we were so anxious to do so that some of the party made the attempt. The vessel was brought to, and a small whale-boat launched, and young Lincoln and John pushed off with clubs and guns; the wind increased and rain set in, but they gained the lee of the rock, but after an hour's absence returned without landing. The air was filled with birds, but they did not perceptibly diminish the numbers on the rock. As the vessel drifted nearer the rock, we could see that the birds sat so close as almost to touch one another in regular lines, looking like so many mole-hills. The discharge of a gun had no effect on those which were not touched by the shot, for the noise of the birds stunned all those out of reach of the gun. But where the shot took effect the birds scrambled and flew off in such multitudes and such confusion that, whilst eight or ten were falling in the water dead or wounded, others shook down their eggs, which fell into the sea by hundreds in all directions. The sea became rougher, and the boat was compelled to return, bringing some birds and some eggs, but without the party being able to climb the rock.

"The top of the main rock is a quarter of a mile wide from north to south, and a little narrower from east to west; its elevation above the sea is between three and four hundred feet. The sea dashes around it with great violence: except in long calms it is extremely difficult to land on it, and much more difficult to climb to its platform. The whole surface was perfectly covered with nests, about two feet apart, in rows as regular as a potato field. The fishermen kill these birds and use their flesh for bait for cod-fish. The crews of several vessels unite, and, armed with clubs, as they reach the top of the rock the birds rise with a noise like thunder, and attempt to fly in such hurried confusion as to knock each other down, often piling one on another in a bank of many feet thickness. The men beat and kill them until they have obtained a supply, or wearied themselves. Six men in this way have killed five or six hundred in one hour. The birds are skinned and cut into junks, and the bait keeps good for a fortnight. Forty sail of fishermen annually supply themselves with bait from this rock in this way. By the twentieth of May the birds lay their eggs, and hatch about the twentieth of June.

" *June* 17. The wind is blowing a gale, and nearly all my party is deadly sick. Thermometer 43°, and raining nearly all day. We laid to all night, and in the morning were in sight of Anticosti Island, distant about twenty miles. It soon became thick, and we lost sight of it.

" *June* 18. The weather is calm, beautiful, and much warmer. We caught many cod-fish, which contained crabs of a curious structure. At six P. M. the wind sprung up fair, and we made all sail for Labrador.

" *June* 19. I was on deck at three o'clock A. M., and although the sun was not above the horizon it was quite light. The sea was literally covered with foolish guillemots playing in the very spray under our bow, plunging as if in fun under it, and rising like spirits close under our rudder. The wind was fair, and the land in sight from aloft, and I now look forward to our landing on Labrador as at hand, and my thoughts are filled with expectation of the new knowledge of birds and animals which I hope to acquire there. The Ripley sails well, but now she fairly skipped over the water. The cry of land soon made my heart bound with joy ; and as we approached it we saw what looked like many sails of vessels, but we soon found that they were snow-banks, and the air along the shore was filled with millions of velvet ducks and other aquatic birds, flying in long files a few yards above the water.

" We saw one vessel at anchor, and the country looked well from the distance ; and as we neared the shore the thermometer rose from 44° to 60°, yet the appearance of the snow-drifts was forbidding. The shores appeared to be margined with a broad and handsome sand-beach, and we saw imaginary bears, wolves and other animals scampering away on the rugged shore. About thirty boats were fishing, and we saw them throwing the fish on deck by thousands.

" We soon reached the mouth of the Natasquan River, where the Hudson Bay Company have a fishing establishment, and where no American vessel is allowed to come. The shore was filled with bark-covered huts, and some vessels were anchored within the sand-point which forms one side of the entrance to the river. We sailed on four miles further to the American harbor, and came to anchor in a beautiful bay, wholly secure from any winds.

" And now we are positively at Labrador, lat. 50°, and farther north than I ever was before on this continent. But what a country ! When we landed and reached the summit we sank nearly up to our knees in mosses of dif-

14

ferent sorts, producing such a sensation as I never felt
before. These mosses in the distance look like hard
rocks, but under the feet they feel like a velvet cushion.
We rambled about and searched in vain for a foot of square
earth; a poor, rugged, and miserable country; the trees
are wiry and scraggy dwarfs; and when the land is not
rocky it is boggy to a man's waist. All the islands about
the harbor were of the same character, and we saw but
few land birds, one pigeon, a few hawks, and smaller
birds. The wild geese, eider-ducks, loons, and many
other birds breed here.

" *June* 19. The boats went off to neighboring islands
in search of birds and eggs, and I remained all day on
board drawing. Eggers from Halifax had robbed nearly
all the eggs.

"The cider-ducks build their nests under the scraggy
boughs of the fir-trees, which here grow only a few inches
above the ground. The nests are scraped a few inches
deep in the rotten moss which makes the soil, and the
boughs have to be raised to find the nests. The eggs are
deposited in down, and covered with down, and keep
warm a long time in absence of the duck. They commonly lay six eggs.

" *June* 20. The vessel rolls at her anchorage, and I
have drawn as well as I could. Our party has gone up
the Natasquan in search of adventures and birds. It
seems strange to me that in this wonderfully wild country
all the wild birds should be so shy.

" *June* 21. To-day I went four miles to the falls of
the little Natasquan River. The river is small, its water
dark and irony, and its shores impenetrable woods, except here and there a small interval overgrown with a
wiry grass, unfit for cattle, and of no use if it were, for
there are no cattle here. We saw several nets in the
river for catching salmon; they are stretched across the

river, and the fish entangle their fins in trying to pass them, and cannot get away. We visited the huts of the Canadian fishermen of the Hudson Bay Company. They are clothed and fed, and receive eight dollars a year besides, for their services. They have a cow, an ox, and one acre of potatoes planted. They report seven feet of snow in winter, and that only one-third as many salmon are taken now as ten years ago; one hundred barrels now is regarded as a fair season. This river is twelve miles long, has three rapids, is broad, swift, and shallow, and discharges a quantity of fine gravelly sand.

"*June* 22. Drew all day. Thermometer 60° at twelve. We are so far north that we have scarcely any darkness at night. Our party visited some large ponds on a neighboring island; but they had neither fish, shells, nor grass about them; the shore a reddish sand: saw only a few toads, and those pale-looking and poor. The country a barren rock as far as the eye could reach, and mosses of several species were a foot in depth. So sonorous is the song of the fox-colored sparrow, that I heard it to-day while drawing in the cabin, from the distance of a quarter of a mile. The mosquitoes and black gnats are bad on shore.

"*June* 23. We heard to-day that a party of four men from Halifax, last spring, took in two months four hundred thousand eggs, which they sold in Halifax at twenty five cents a dozen. Last year upwards of twenty sail of vessels were engaged in this business; and by this one may form some idea of the number of birds annually destroyed in this way, to say nothing of the millions of others disposed of by the numerous fleet of fishermen which yearly come to these regions, and lend their hand to swell the devastation. The eggers destroy all the eggs that are sat upon, to force the birds to lay fresh eggs, and by robbing them regularly compel them to lay until nature is exhausted, and so but few young ones are raised. These wonderful nurseries must be finally destroyed, and in less than half a century, unless some kind government interposes to put a stop to all this shameful destruction The wind blows here from the south-east, and it brings rain continually."

The following episode epitomizes what Audubon saw or learned about the men engaged in hunting eggs on those wild and desolate islands.

CHAPTER XXVIII.

Labrador Episodes : The Eggers of Labrador.

THE distinctive appellation of 'eggers' is given to certain persons who follow principally or exclusively the avocation of procuring eggs of wild birds, with the view of disposing of them at some distant port. Their great object is to plunder every nest, whenever they can find it, no matter where, and at whatever risk. They are the pest of the feathered tribes, and their brutal propensity to destroy the poor creatures after they have robbed them is abundantly gratified whenever an opportunity presents itself. Much had been said to me respecting these destructive pirates before I visited the coast of Labrador, but I could not entirely credit all their cruelties until I had actually witnessed their proceedings, which were such as to inspire no small degree of horror. But you shall judge for yourself.

"See yon shallop shyly sailing along; she sneaks like a thief, wishing, as it were, to shun the very light of heaven. Under the lee of every rocky isle some one at the tiller steers her course.

"Were his trade an honest one he would not think of hiding his back behind the terrific rocks that seem to have been placed there as a resort to the myriads of birds that annually visit this desolate region of the earth for the purpose of rearing their young at a distance from all disturbers of their peace. How unlike the open, bold, the honest mariner, whose face needs no mask, who scorns to skulk under any circumstances! The vessel herself is a shabby thing; her sails are patched with stolen pieces of better canvas, the owners of which have

probably been stranded on some inhospitable coast, and
have been plundered, perhaps murdered, by the wretches
before us. Look at her again. Her sides are neither
painted nor even pitched; no, they are daubed over,
plastered and patched with stripes of seal-skins, laid
along the seams. Her deck has never been washed or
sanded, her hold, for she has no cabin, though at present
empty, sends forth an odor pestilential as that of a char-
nel-house. The crew, eight in number, lie sleeping at
the foot of their tottering mast, regardless of the repairs
needed in every part of her rigging. But see! she scuds
along, and, as I suspect her crew to be bent on the commission of some evil deed, let us follow her to the first
harbor. There rides the filthy thing! The afternoon is
half over. Her crew have thrown their boat overboard;
they enter and seat themselves, one with a rusty gun.
One of them sculls the skiff towards an island, for a century past the breeding-place of myriads of guillemots,
which are now to be laid under contribution. At the approach of the vile thieves, clouds of birds rise from the
rock and fill the air around, wheeling and screaming
over their enemies; yet thousands remain in an erect
posture, each covering its single egg, the hope of both
parents. The reports of several muskets loaded with
heavy shot are now heard, while several dead and wounded birds fall heavily on the rock or into the water. Instantly all the sitting birds rise and fly off affrighted to
their companions above, and hover in dismay over their
assassins, who walk forward exultingly, and with their
shouts mingling oaths and execrations. Look at them!
See how they crush the chick within its shell! how they
trample on every egg in their way with their huge and
clumsy boots! Onwards they go, and when they leave
the isle not an egg that they can find is left entire. The
dead birds they collect and carry to their boat. Now

they have regained their filthy shallop, they strip the
birds by a single jerk of their feathery apparel, while the
flesh is yet warm, and throw them on some coals, where
in a short time they are broiled : the rum is produced
when the guillemots are fit for eating, and after stuffing
themselves with this oily fare, and enjoying the pleasures of beastly intoxication, over they tumble on the
deck of their crazed craft, where they pass the short
hours of night in turbid slumber. The sun now rises
above the snow-clad summit of the eastern mount ;
'sweet is the breath of morn,' even in this desolate land.
The gay bunting erects his white crest, and gives utterance to the joy he feels in the presence of his brooding
mate ; the willow grouse on the rock crows his challenge
aloud ; each floweret, chilled by the night air, expands
its pure petals ; the gentle breeze shakes from the blades
of grass the heavy dewdrops. On the Guillemot Isle the
birds have again settled, and now renew their loves.
Startled by the light of day, one of the eggers springs on
his feet, and rouses his companions, who stare around
them for awhile, endeavoring to recollect their senses.
Mark them, as with clumsy fingers they clear their
drowsy eyes ; slowly they rise on their feet. See how
the lubbers stretch out their arms and yawn ; you shrink
back, for verily 'that throat might frighten a shark.' But
the master, soon recollecting that so many eggs are
worth a dollar or a crown, casts his eye towards the rock,
marks the day in his memory, and gives orders to depart.
The light breeze enables them to reach another harbor,
a few miles distant ; one which, like the last, lies con
cealed from the ocean by some other rocky isle. Arrived there, they react the scene of yesterday, crushing
every egg they can find. For a week each night is passed in drunkenness and brawls, until, having reached the
last breeding place on the coast, they return, touch at

every isle in succession, shoot as many birds as they need, collect the fresh eggs, and lay in a cargo. At every step each ruffian picks up an egg, so beautiful that any man with a feeling heart would pause to consider the motive which could induce him to carry it off. But nothing of this sort occurs to the egger, who gathers and gathers until he has swept the rock bare. The dollars alone chink in his sordid mind, and he assiduously plies the trade which no man would ply who had the talents and industry to procure subsistence by honorable means. With a bark nearly filled with fresh eggs they proceed to the principal rock, that on which they first landed. But what is their surprise when they find others there helping themselves as industriously as they can! In boiling rage they charge their guns, and ply their oars. Landing on the rock, they run up to the eggers, who, like themselves, are desperadoes. The first question is a discharge of musketry; the answer another: now, man to man, they fight like tigers. One is carried to his craft with a fractured skull, another limps with a shot in his leg, and a third feels how many of his teeth have been driven through the hole in his cheek. At last, however, the quarrel is settled, the booty is to be equally divided; and now see them all drinking together. Oaths and curses and filthy jokes are all that you hear; but see! stuffed with food, and reeling with drink, down they drop, one by one; groans and execrations from the wounded mingle with the snorings of the heavy sleepers. There let the brutes lie! Again it is dawn, but no one stirs. The sun is high; one by one they open their heavy eyes, stretch their limbs, yawn and raise themselves from the deck. But see a goodly company. A hundred honest fishermen, who for months past have fed on salt meat, have felt a desire to procure some eggs. Gallantly their boats advance, impelled by the regular pull of their long oars.

Each buoyant bark displays the flag of its nation. No weapon do they bring, nor anything that can be used as such, save their oars and fists. Cleanly clad in Sunday attire, they arrive at the desired spot, and at once prepare to ascend the rock. The eggers, now numbering a dozen, all armed with guns and bludgeons, bid defiance to the fishermen. A few angry words pass between the parties. One of the eggers, still under the influence of drink, pulls his trigger, and an unfortunate sailor is seen to reel in agony. Three loud cheers fill the air. All at once rush on the malefactors : a horrid fight ensues, the result of which is that every egger is left on the rock beaten and bruised. Too frequently the fishermen man their boats, row to the shallops, and break every egg in the hold. The eggers of Labrador not only rob the birds in this cruel manner, but also the fishermen, whenever they can find an opportunity ; and the quarrels they excite are numberless. While we were on the coast none of our party ever ventured on any of the islands, which these wretches call their own, without being well provided with means of defence. On one occasion when I was present we found two eggers at their work of destruction. I spoke to them respecting my visit, and offered them premiums for rare birds and some of their eggs ; but although they made fair promises, not one of the gang ever came near the Ripley. These people gather all the eider-down they can find, yet, so inconsiderate are they, that they kill every bird that comes in their way. The puffins and some other birds they massacre in vast numbers for the sake of their feathers. The eggs of gulls, guillemots, and ducks are searched for with care also. So constant and persevering are their depredations, that these species, which, according to the accounts of the few settlers I saw in the country, were exceedingly abundant twenty years ago, have abandoned their ancient

14*

breeding-places, and removed much farther north, in search of peaceful security. Scarcely, in fact, could I procure a young guillemot before the eggers had left the coast, nor was it until late in July that I succeeded, after the birds had laid three or four eggs each instead of one, and when nature having been exhausted, and the season nearly spent, thousands of these birds left the country without having accomplished the purpose for which they had visited it. This war of extermination cannot last many years more. The eggers themselves will be the first to repent the entire disappearance of the myriads of birds that made the coast of Labrador their summer residence, and unless they follow the persecuted tribes to the northward they must renounce their trade."

CHAPTER XXIX.

JUNE 23. We met here two large boats loaded with Mountaineer Indians, about twenty, old and young, male and female. The boats had small canoes lashed to their sides, like whale boats, for seal fishing. The men were stout and good-looking, and spoke tolerable French; their skins were redder and clearer than any other Indians I have ever seen. The women also appeared cleaner than usual, their hair was braided, and dangled over their shoulders, like so many short ropes. They were all dressed in European cos- tumes except their feet, on which coarse moccasins made of seal skin supplied the place of shoes.

" On leaving the harbor this morning, we saw a black man-of-war-like looking vessel entering it, bearing the English flag; it proved to be the Quebec cutter. I wrote a note to the commander, sent him my card, and requested an interview. He proved to be Captain Bay- field of the Royal Navy, the vessel was the Gulnare, and he replied that he would receive me in two hours. After dinner, taking some credentials in my pocket, I went aboard of the Gulnare, was politely received, and intro- duced to the surgeon, who seemed a man of ability, and is a student of botany and conchology. Thus the lovers of nature meet everywhere, but surely I did not expect to

meet a naturalist on the Labrador station. The first
lieutenant is a student of ornithology, and is making collections. I showed a letter from the Duke of Sussex to
the captain, and after a pleasant hour, and a promise
from him to do anything in his power to aid us, I returned to our vessel.

"*June* 24. It was our intention to leave this harbor
to-day for one fifty miles east, but the wind is ahead, and
I have drawn all day. Shattuck and I took a walk over
the dreary hills towards evening, and we found several
flowers in bloom, among which was a small species of
the Kulnua Glauca. We visited the camp of the Mountaineer Indians about half a mile from us, and found
them skinning seals, and preparing their flesh for use.
We saw a robe the size of a good blanket made of seal
skin, and tanned so soft and beautiful with the hair on,
that it was as pleasant to the touch as a fine kid glove.
They refused to sell it. The chief of this party is well
informed, talks French so as to be understood, is a fine-
looking fellow, about forty years old, and has a good-
looking wife and baby. His brother also is married, and
has several sons between fourteen and twenty. The
whole group consists of about twenty persons. They
came and saluted us soon after we landed, and to my astonishment offered us a glass of rum. The women were
all seated outside of their tents, unpacking bundles of
clothing and provisions. We entered one tent, and seated ourselves before a blazing fire, the smoke of which
escaped through the top of the apartment. To the many
questions I put to the chief and his brother, the following
is the substance of his answers.

"The country from this place to the nearest settlement of the Hudson Bay Company is as barren and
rocky as this about us. Very large lakes of water abound
two hundred miles inland from the sea : these lakes con-

tain carp, trout, white fish, and many mussels unfit to eat ; the latter are described as black outside and purple within, and are no doubt ' unios.' Not a bush is to be met with ; and the Indians who now and then cross that region carry their tent-poles with them, and also their canoes, and burn moss for fuel. So tedious is the travelling said to be, that not more than ten miles a day can be accomplished, and when the journey is made in two months, it is considered a good one. Wolves and black bears abound, but no deer nor caraboos are seen, and not a bird of any kind except wild geese and brants about the lakes, where they breed. When the journey is undertaken in winter, they go on snow shoes, without canoes. Fur animals are scarce, but a few beavers and otters, martins and sables, are caught, and some foxes and lynxes, while their numbers yearly diminish. Thus the Fur Company may be called the exterminating medium of these wild and almost uninhabitable regions, which cupidity or the love of money alone would induce man to venture into. Where can I now go and find nature undisturbed ?

" *June* 25. Drawing all day until five o'clock, when I went to dine on board the Gulnare ; quite a bore to shave and dress in Labrador. The company consisted of the captain, doctor, and three other officers ; we had a good sea dinner, cod and mutton, good wine and some excellent snuff, of which I took a pinch or two. Conversation turned on Botany, politics, and the Established Church of England, and ranged away to hatching eggs by steam. I saw the maps the officers are making of the coast, and was struck with the great accuracy of the shape of our perfect harbor. I returned to our vessel at ten in the evening ; the weather is warm, and the mosquitoes abundant and hungry.

" *June* 26. We have now been waiting five days for

a fair wind to take us eastward in our explorations. The waters of all the streams we have seen are of a rusty color, probably derived from the decomposing mosses which form the soil on the rocks. The rivers seem to be the drain from swamps fed by rain and melting snow; the soil in the low grounds is of quite a peaty nature. The freshets take down sand and gravel from the decomposed rocks, and form bars at the mouths of all the rivers. Below the mouth of each stream is the best fishing ground for cod fish. They accumulate there to feed on the fry which run into the rivers to deposit their spawn, and which they follow again to sea, when they return to strike out into deep water.

"It is quite remarkable how shy the agents of the Fur Company here are of strangers. They refused to sell me a salmon: and one of them told me he would be discharged if it were known he had done so. They evade all questions respecting the interior of the country, and indeed tell the most absurd things, to shock you, and cut short inquiries   This is probably to prevent strangers from settling here, or interfering with their monopoly. "

Much of the journal of these dates in Labrador is taken up with an account of the birds, and nests, and eggs found here, and matters relating to ornithology. But as these notes were used by Mr. Audubon in compiling his " Biographies of the Birds," we have omitted them here, and used only that part of the records which have a more general interest.

" *June* 27. The morning dawned above rain and fogs, which so enveloped us below that we could scarcely discern the shore, distant only a hundred yards. Drawing all day.

" *June* 28. The weather shocking, rainy, foggy, dark, and cold. Began drawing a new finch I discovered, and outlined another. At twelve the wind suddenly changed, and caused such a swell and rolling of the vessel, that I had to give up my drawing. After dinner the wind hauled to the south-west, and all was bustle, heaving up anchor, loosing sails, and getting ready for sea. We were soon under weight and went out of the harbor in good style ; but the sea was high, and we were glad to go to our beds.

" *June* 29. At three o'clock this morning we were about fifteen miles from land, and fifty from American Harbor. The thermometer was 54°, and the wind light and favorable ; at ten the breeze freshened, but our pilot did not know the land, and the captain had to find a harbor for himself. We passed near an island covered with foolish guillemots, and came to for the purpose of landing on it, which we did through a great surf; there we found two eggers searching the rocks for eggs. They told us they visited all the islands in the vicinity, and obtained fresh eggs every day. They had eight hundred dozen, and expected to increase them to two thousand dozen before they returned to Halifax. The quantities of broken eggs on this and all the islands where eggs are obtained, causes a stench which is scarcely endurable. From this island we went to another about a mile distant, and caught many birds and collected many eggs.

" *June* 30. I have drawn three birds to-day since eight o'clock. Thermometer 50°.

" *July* 1. The thermometer 48°, and the weather so cold that it has been painful for me to draw, but I worked all day.

" *July* 2. A beautiful day for Labrador. Went ashore and killed nothing, but was pleased with what I saw. The country is so grandly wild and desolate, that I am charmed by its wonderful dreariness. Its mossy gray-clad rocks, heaped and thrown together in huge masses,

hanging on smaller ones, as if about to roll down from
their insecure resting-places into the sea below them.
Bays without end, sprinkled with thousands of rocky
inlets of all sizes, shapes, and appearances, and wild
birds everywhere, was the scene presented before me.
Besides this there was a peculiar cast of the uncertain
sky, butterflies flitting over snow-banks, and probing un-
folding dwarf flowerets of many hues pushing out their
tender stems through the thick beds of moss which everywhere covers the granite rock. Then there is the morass,
wherein you plunge up to your knees, or the walking over
the stubborn, dwarfish shrubbery, whereby one treads
down the forests of Labrador ; and the unexpected bunting or sylvia which perchance, and indeed as if by chance
alone, you now and then see flying before you, or hear
singing from the ground creeping plant. The beautiful
fresh-water lakes, deposited on the rugged crests of greatly elevated islands, wherein the red and black divers
swim as proudly as swans do in other latitudes ; and
wherein the fish appear to have been cast as strayed beings from the surplus food of the sea. All, all is wonderfully wild and grand, ay, terrific. And yet how beautiful
it is now, when your eye sees the wild bee, moving from
one flower to another in search of food, which doubtless
is as sweet to her as the essence of the orange and magnolia is to her more favored sister in Louisiana. The
little ring-plover rearing its delicate and tender young ;
the eider duck swimming man-of-war-like amid her floating brood, like the guard-ship of a most valuable convoy ;
the white-crowned bunting's sonorous note reaching your
ears ever and anon ; the crowds of sea-birds in search of
places wherein to repose or to feed. I say how beautiful
all this, in this wonderful rocky desert at this season, the
beginning of July, compared with the horrid blasts of
winter which here predominate by the will of God ; when

every rock is hidden beneath snow so deep, that every step the traveller takes, he is in danger of falling in his grave ; while avalanches threaten him from above, and if he lifts his eyes to the horizon, he sees nothing but dark clouds filled with frost and snow, and inspiring him with a feeling of despair.

" *July* 3. We have had a stiff easterly wind all day, rainy, and the water so rough we could not go ashore, for plants to draw, until late in the afternoon. The view of the sea from the highest rocks was grand, the small islands were covered with the foam and surf thrown up by the agitated ocean. Thank God that we are not tossing on its billows.

" *July* 4. Two parties went out to-day to get birds and plants, and I remained on board all day drawing. Captain Bayfield sent us a quarter of mutton for our fourth of July dinner, and I dare say it is a rarity on this coast of Labrador, even on this day.

" *July* 5. Thermometer 50°. I drew from four o'clock this morning until three this afternoon, and then went on an expedition for a few miles to a large rough island, which I traversed until I was weary, for walking on this spongy moss of Labrador is a task no one can imagine without trying it ; at every step the foot sinks in a deep moss cushion, which closes over it, and requires considerable exertion to draw it up. When the moss is over a marshy tract, then you sink a couple of feet deep every step you take, and to reach a bare rock is delightful, and quite a relief. This afternoon the country looked more terrifyingly wild than ever, the dark clouds throwing their shadows on the stupendous masses of rugged rocks, presented one of the wildest pictures of nature that the eye can find to look on anywhere.

" *July* 6. Thermometer 48°. At noon my fingers were so cold that I could no longer hold my pencil to draw, and I was compelled to go on shore for exercise. The fact is I am growing old too fast, alas ! I feel it, and yet work I will, and may God grant me life to see the last plate of my mammoth work finished.

" *July* 7. Drawing all day ; finished the female grouse and five young ones, and preparing the male bird.

" *July* 8. Rainy, dirty weather, wind east, thermometer 48°. Began drawing at half-past three a.m, but my condition very disagreeable in such weather. The fog collects and falls in large drops from the rigging on my table, and now and then I am obliged to close the skylight, and work almost in darkness. Notwithstanding, I have finished my plate of the cock ptarmigan.

" *July* 9. The wind east, wet, disagreeable, and foggy. This is the most wonderful climate in the world ; the thermometer 52°, mosquitoes in profusion, plants blooming by millions, and at every step you tread on flowers such as would be looked on in more temperate climates with pleasure. I only wish I could describe plants as well as I can the habits of birds. I have drawn all day on the loon, a most difficult bird to imitate.

" *July* 10. Thermometer 54°. Could I describe one of those dismal gales which blow ever and anon over this dismal country, it would probably be interesting to any one unacquainted with the inclemency of this climate. Nowhere else are the north-east blasts, which sweep over Labrador, felt as they are here. But I cannot describe them. All I can say is, that while we are safe in a landlocked harbor, their effects on our vessel are so strong, that they will not allow me to draw, and sometimes send some of us to our beds. And what the force of these horrid blasts outside of the harbor at sea is I can hardly imagine ; but it seems as if it would be impossible for any vessel to ride safely before them, and that they will rend these rocky islands asunder. The rain is driven in sheets, and falls with difficulty upon its destination of sea or land. Nay, I cannot call it rain, as it is such a thick cloud of water, that all objects at a distance are lost sight of at intervals of three or four minutes, and the waters around us come up and beat about in our rock-bound harbor, as a newly caught and caged bird beats against the wire walls of his prison cage.

" *July* 11. The gale or hurricane of yesterday subsided about midnight, and at sunrise this morning the sky was clear and the horizon fiery red. It was my intention to have gone one hundred miles further north, but our captain says I must be content here.

" On rambling over the numerous bays and inlets, which are scattered by thousands along this coast, as pebbles are on a common sand beach, one sees immense beds of round stones (boulders ?) of all sizes, and some of large dimensions, rolled side by side, and piled up in heaps, as if cast there by some great revolution of nature. I have seen many such places, and always look on them with astonishment, because they seem to have been vomited up by the sea, and cast hundreds of yards inland, by its powerful retchings ; and this gives some idea of what a hurricane at Labrador can do.

" *July* 12. Thermometer 48°, and it is raining hard, and blowing another gale from the east, and the vessel rocks so much that I am unable to finish my drawing.

" *July* 13. Rose this morning at half-past three, and found the wind north-east, and but little of it. The weather is cloudy and dull, as it is always here after a storm. I was anxious to stay on board, and finish the drawing of a grouse I had promised to Dr. Kelly of the Gulnare. But at seven the wind changed, and we prepared to leave our fine harbor. We beat out to sea, and made our course for the harbor of Little Macatine, distant forty-three miles. By noon the wind died away, but the sea rolled, and we were all sea-sick, and glad to go to our berths.

" *July* 14. Awoke this morning to find a cold northeast wind blowing, and ourselves twenty miles from our destination, a heavy sea beating against the vessel's bows, as she is slowly beating tack after tack against the wind. We are in despair of reaching our destination to-day. Towards evening however the wind favored us, and as we approached the island, it proved the highest land we have seen, and looked rugged and horrid.

"When we came within a mile and a half of the shore we took a small boat, and pushed off for the land. As we came near it, the rocks appeared stupendously high and rough, and frowned down on our little boat, as we moved along and doubled the little cape which made one side of the entrance of Macatine's Harbor, but it looked so small to me, that I doubted if it were the place ; and the shores were horribly wild, fearfully high and rough, and nothing but the croaking of a pair of ravens was heard mingling with the dismal sound of the surge which dashed on the rocky ledges, and sent the foaming water into the air.

" By the time we reached the shore the wind began to freshen, the Ripley's sails now swelled, and she cut her way through the water, and rounded the point of land which formed part of the harbor, and shot ahead towards the place where we were standing. Our harbor represents the bottom of a large bowl, in the centre of which our vessel is anchored, surrounded by rocks full a thousand feet high, and the wildest looking place I was ever in. We went aboard, ate a hasty supper, and all scampered ashore again, and climbed the nearest hills. But John, Shattuck, and myself went up the harbor, and ascended to the top of a mountain (for I cannot call it a hill), and there we saw the crest of the island beneath our feet, all rocks, barren, bare rocks, wild as the wildest Apennines. The moss was only a few inches deep, and the soil beneath it so moist, that whenever the declivities were much inclined, the whole slipped from under us like an avalanche, and down we would slide for feet, and sometimes yards. The labor of climbing was excessive, and at the bottom of each ravine the scrub bushes intercepted us for twenty or thirty paces, and we scrambled over them with great effort and fatigue. On our return we made one slide of forty or fifty feet, and brought up in a little valley or pit filled with moss and mire.

" *July* 15. We rose and breakfasted at three o'clock, every one being eager to go ashore and explore this wild country. But the wind was east, and the prospects of fine weather not good. But two boats' crews of young men rowed off in different directions, while I renewed my drawing. By ten the rain poured, and the boats returned.

" *July* 16. Another day of dirty weather, and obliged to remain on board nearly all the day. Thermometer 52°, mosquitoes plenty. This evening the fog is so thick, that we cannot see the summit of the rocks around us.

" *July* 17. Mosquitoes so annoyed me last night that I did not close my eyes. I tried the deck of the vessel, and although the fog was as thick as fine rain, the air was filled with these insects, and I went below and fought them until daylight, when I had a roaring fire made and got rid of them. I have been drawing part of the day, and besides several birds, I have outlined one of the mountainous hills near our vessel, as a back-ground to my willow grouse.

" *July* 18. After breakfast, all hands except the cook left the Ripley, in three boats, to visit the main shore, about five miles off. The fog was thick, but the wind promised fair weather, and soon fulfilled its promise. Directly after landing our party found a large extent of marsh land, the first we have seen in this country; the soil was wet, our feet sank in it, and walking was tiresome. We also crossed a large savannah of many miles in extent. Its mosses were so wet and spongy, that I never in my life before experienced so much difficulty in travelling. In many places the soil appeared to wave and bend under us like old ice in the spring of the year, and we expected at each step to break through the surface, and sink into the mire below. In the middle of this quagmire we met with a fine small grove of good-sized white birch trees, and a few pines full forty feet high, quite a novelty in this locality.

"From the top of a high rock I obtained a good view of the most extensive and dreary wilderness I ever beheld. It chilled the heart to gaze on these barrens of Labrador. Indeed I now dread every change of harbor, so horridly rugged and dangerous is the whole coast and country to the eye, and to the experienced man either of the sea or the land. . Mosquitoes, many species of horse-flies, small bees, and black gnats fill the air. The frogs croaked, and yet the thermometer was not above 55°. This is one of the real wonders of this extraordinary country. The parties in the boats, hunting all day, brought back but nineteen birds, and we all concluded that no one man could provide food for himself here from the land alone.

" *July* 19. Cold, wet, blowing, and too much motion of the vessel for drawing. In the evening it cleared up a little, and I went ashore, and visited the hut of a seal-fisher. We climbed over one rocky precipice and fissure after another, holding on to the moss with both hands and feet, for about a mile, when we came to the deserted hut of a Labrador seal-catcher. It looked snug outside, and we walked in; it was floored with short slabs, all very well greased with seal oil. A fire-oven without a pipe, a salt-box hung to a wooden peg, a three-legged stool for a table, and wooden box for a bedstead, were all its furniture. An old flour-barrel, containing some hundreds of seine floats, and an old seal seine, comprised the assets of goods and chattels. Three small windows, with four panes of glass each, were still in pretty good order, and so was the low door, which swung on wooden hinges, for which I will be bound the maker had asked for no patent. The cabin was made of hewn logs, brought from the mainland, about twelve feet square, and well put together. It was roofed with birch bark and spruce, well thatched with moss a foot thick; every chink was crammed with moss, and every aperture rendered air-tight with oakum. But it was deserted and abandoned. The seals are all caught, and the sailors have nothing to do now-a-days. We found a pile of good hard wood close to the cabin, and this we hope to appropriate to-morrow. I found out that the place had been inhabited by two Canadians, by the chalk marks on the walls, and their almanac on one of the logs ran thus : L 24, M 25, M 26, I 27, V 28, S 29, D 30, giving the first letter of the day of the week. On returning to the vessel, I stopped several times to look on the raging waves rolling in upon the precipitous rocks below us, and thought how dreadful it would be for any one to be wrecked on this inhospitable shore. The surges of surf which rolled in on the rocks were forty or fifty feet high where they dashed on the precipices beneath us, and any vessel cast ashore there must have been immediately dashed to pieces.

"*July* 20. The country of Labrador deserves credit for one fine day. This has been, until evening, calm, warm, and really such a day as one might expect in the Middle States about the middle of May. I drew until ten o'clock, and then made a trip to the island next to us, and shot several birds. We passed several small bays, where we found vast quantities of stones thrown up by the sea, and some of them of enormous size. I now think that these stones are brought from the sea on the thick drift ice, or icebergs, which come down from the arctic regions, and are driven in here and broken by the jagged rocks; they are stranded, and melt, and leave these enormous pebbles in layers from ten to one hundred feet deep.

"*July* 21. I write now from a harbor which has no name, for we have mistaken it for the one we were looking for, which lies two miles east of this. But it matters little, for the coast of Labrador is all alike, comfortless, cold, and foggy. We left the Little Macatine this morning at five o'clock, with a stiff south-west breeze, and by ten dropped anchor where we now are. As we doubled the cape of the island called Great Macatine, we had the pleasure of meeting the officers of the Gulnare, in two boats, engaged in surveying the coast. We made an excursion into the island, but found nothing of interest.

"In the evening we visited the officers of the Gulnare, encamped in tents on shore, living in great comfort; the tea-things were yet on the iron bedstead which served as a table, the trunks formed their seats, and the clothes-bags their cushions and pillows. Their tent was made of tarred cloth, which admitted neither wind nor rain. It was a comfortable camp, and we were pleased to find ourselves on the coast of Labrador in company with intelligent officers of the royal navy of England, gentlemen of education and refined manners; it was indeed a treat, a precious one. We talked of the wild country around us, and of the enormous destruction of everything which is going on here, except of the rocks; of the aborigines, who are melting away before the encroachments of a stronger race, as the wild animals are disappearing before

them. Some one said, it is rum which is destroying the
poor Indians. I replied, I think not, they are disappearing here from insufficiency of food and physical comforts,
and the loss of all hope, as he loses sight of all that was
abundant before the white man came, intruded on his
land, and his herds of wild animals, and deprived him of
the furs with which he clothed himself. Nature herself
is perishing. Labrador must shortly be depopulated, not
only of her aboriginal men, but of every thing and animal which has life, and attracts the cupidity of men.
When her fish, and game, and birds are gone, she will be
left alone like an old worn-out field."

" *July* 22. This morning Captain Bayfield and his
officers came alongside to bid us good-bye, to pursue their
labors further westward. After breakfast we manned
three boats, and went to explore a small harbor about
one mile east of our anchorage. There we found a whal-
ing schooner, fifty-five tons burthen, from Cape Gaspe.
We found the men employed in boiling blubber in a large
iron vessel like a sugar-boiler. The blubber lay in heaps
on the shore, in junks of six or eight pounds each, looking filthy enough. The captain or owner of the vessel
appeared to be a good sensible man of his class, and cut
off for me some strips of the whale's skin from under the
throat, with large and curious barnacles attached to the
skin. They had struck four whales, and three had sunk,
and were lost to them. This, the men said, was a very
rare occurrence. We found, also, at this place, a French
Canadian seal-catcher, from whom I gathered the following information.

" This portion of Labrador is free to any one to settle
on, and he and another person had erected a cabin, and
had nets and traps to catch seals and foxes, and guns to
shoot bears and wolves. They take their quarry to Quebec, receiving fifty cents a gallon for seal oil, and from

15

three to five guineas for black and silver fox skins, and others in proportion. In the months of November and December, and indeed until spring, they kill seals in large numbers ; seventeen men belonging to their party killed twenty-five hundred seals once in three days. This great feat was done with short sticks, and each seal was killed with a single blow on the snout, whilst lying on the edges of the floating or field ice. The seals are carried home on sledges drawn by Esquimaux dogs, which are so well trained that, on reaching home, they push the seals from the sledges with their noses, and return to the killers with regular despatch. (Th's, reader, is hearsay !) At other times the seals are driven into nets, one after another, until the poor animals become so hampered and confined, that they are easily and quickly dispatched with guns. The captain showed me a spot, within a few yards of his log cabin, where last winter he caught six fine large silver-gray foxes. Bears and caraboos abound during winter, and also wolves, hares and porcupines. The wolves are of a dun color, very ferocious and daring ; a pack of thirty followed a man to his cabin, and they have several times killed his dogs at his own door. I was surprised at this, because his dogs were as large as any wolves I have ever seen. These dogs are extremely tractable, so much so that, when geared into a sledge, the leader immediately starts at the word of command for any given course, and the whole pack gallop off at the rate of seven or eight miles an hour. The Esquimaux dogs howl like wolves, and are not at all like our common dogs. They were extremely gentle, and came to us, and jumped on and caressed us as if we were old acquaintances. They do not take to the water, and are fit only for draught and the chase of caraboos ; and they are the only dogs which can at all near the caraboo while running.

"As soon as winter storms and thick ice close the

harbors and the intermediate spaces between the mainland and the sea islands, the caraboos are seen moving on
the ice in great herds, first to the islands, where the snow
is most likely to be drifted, because there in in the shallows—from which the snow has blown away—he easily
scrapes down to the mosses, which at this season are the
only food they can find. As the severity of winter increases, these animals follow the coast northwest, and
gradually reach a comparatively milder climate. But
notwithstanding all this, on their return in the spring,
which is as regular as the migration of the birds, they are
so poor and emaciated, that the men take pity on them,
and will not kill them. Merciful beings, these white
men ! They spare life when the flesh is off from their
bones, and there is no market for their bones at hand.

' The otter is tolerably abundant here. These are
chiefly trapped at the foot of the waterfalls, to which they
resort, being the latest to freeze and the earliest to thaw
in spring. A few martins and sables are caught, but every
year reduces their number. This Frenchman receives
his supplies from Quebec, where he sends his furs and
oil. The present time he calls ' the idle season,' and he
loiters about his cabin, lies in the sunshine like a seal,
eats, drinks, and sleeps his life away, careless of the busy
world, and of all that is going on there. His partner has
gone to Quebec, and his dogs are his on'y companions
until he returns ; and the dogs, perhaps, are the better
animal of the two. He has selected a delightful site for
his castle, under the protection of an island, and on the
south side, where I found the atmosphere quite warm,
and the vegetation actually rank, for I saw plants with
leaves twelve inches broad, and grasses three feet high.

" This afternoon the wind has been blowing a tremendous gale, and our anchors have dragged with sixty
fathoms of chain out. Yet one of the whaler's boats

came with six men to pay us a visit. They wished to see some of my drawings, and I gratified them ; and in return they promised to show me a whale before it was cut up, should they catch one before we leave this place for Bras d'Or.

" *July* 23. We visited to-day the seal establishment of a Scotchman, named Robertson, about six miles east of our anchorage. He received us politely, addressed me by name, and told me he had received information of my visit to this country through the English and Canadian newspapers. This man has resided here twenty years, and married a Labrador lady, the daughter of a Monsieur Chevalier of Bras d'Or ; has a family of six children, and a good-looking wife. He has a comfortable house, and a little garden, in which he raises a few turnips, potatoes, and other vegetables. He appeared to be lord of all these parts, and quite contented with his lot. He told me that his profits last year amounted to three thousand dollars. He does not trade with the Indians, of whom we saw about twenty of the Mountaineer tribe, and he has white men-servants. His seal-oil tubs were full, and he was then engaged in loading a schooner bound to Quebec. He complained of the American fishermen, and said they often acted as badly as pirates towards the Indians, the white settlers, and the eggers, all of whom have more than once retaliated, when bloody combats have followed. He assured me that he had seen a fisherman's crew kill thousands of guillemots in a day, pluck off their feathers, and throw their bodies into the sea.

" Mr. Robertson also told me that, during mild winters, his little harbor is covered with thousands of white gulls, and that they all leave on the appproach of spring. The travelling here is altogether over the ice, which is covered with snow, and in sledges drawn by Esquimaux dogs, of which this man keeps a famous pack. He often

goes to Bras d'Or, seventy-five miles distant, with his wife
and children on one sledge, drawn by ten dogs. Scarcely
any travelling is done on land, the country is so precipitous and broken. Fifteen miles north of here he says
there is a lake, represented by the Indians as four hundred miles long and one hundred broad, and that this
sea-like lake is at times as rough as the ocean in a storm.
It abounds with fish, and some water-birds resort there,
and breed by millions along its margin. We have had a
fine day, but Mr. R. says that the summer has been un-
usually tempestuous. The caraboo flies drove our hunters on board to-day, and they looked as bloody as if they
had actually had a gouging fight with some rough Kentuckians. Here we found on this wonderful wild coast
some newspapers from the United States, and received
the latest intelligence from Boston to be had at Labrador."

"*July* 24 and 25 were engaged in hunting birds and
drawing, and contain much valuable information on
ornithology, which is given in the " Birds of America."

" *July* 26. We left our anchorage, and sailed with a
fair wind to visit the Chevalier's settlement, called Bonne
Espérance, forty-seven miles distant. When we had gone
two-thirds of the distance the wind failed us ; calms were
followed by severe squalls, and a tremendous sea rolled,
which threatened to shake our masts out. At eight
o'clock, however, we came abreast of the settlement, but
as our pilot knew nothing of the harbor, the captain
thought it prudent to stand off, and proceed on to Bras
d'Or. The coast here, like all that we have seen before,
was dotted with rocky islands of all sizes and forms, and
against which the raging waves dashed in a frightful manner, making us shudder at the thought of the fate of the
wretched mariners who might be thrown on them.

" *July* 27. At daylight this morning we found ourselves at the mouth of Bras d'Or Harbor, where we are now snugly moored. We hoisted our colors, and Captain Billings, of American Harbor, came to us in his Hampton boat, and piloted us in. This Bras d'Or is the grand rendezvous of almost all the fishermen, that resort to this coast for cod-fish ; and we found here a flotilla of one hundred and fifty sails, principally fore-and-aft schooners, and mostly from Halifax and the eastern parts of the United States.

"There was a life and bustle in the harbor which surprised us, after so many weeks of wilderness and loneliness along the rocky coast. Boats were moving to and fro over the whole bay, going after fish, and returning loaded to the gunwale ; some with seines, others with caplings, for bait, and a hundred or more anchored out about a mile from us, hauling the poor cod-fish by thousands, and hundreds of men engaged in cleaning and salting them, and enlivening their work with Billingsgate slang, and stories, and songs.

"As soon as breakfast was over we went ashore, and called on Mr. Jones, the owner of the seal-fishing establishment here, a rough, brown-looking Nova-Scotia man, who received us well, and gave us considerable information respecting the birds which visit his neighborhood. This man has forty Esquimaux dogs, and he entertained us with an account of his travels with them in winter. They are harnessed with a leather collar, belly and back bands, through the upper part of which the line of sealskin passes which is attached to the sledge, and it serves the double purpose of a rein and trace to draw with. An odd number of dogs is used for the gang employed in drawing the sledge, the number varying according to the distance to be travelled or the load to be carried. Each dog is estimated to carry two hundred pounds, and to travel with that load at the rate of five or six miles an hour. The leader, which is always a well-broken dog, is placed ahead of the pack, with a draft line of from six to ten fathoms in length, and the rest with successively shorter ones, until they come to within eight feet of the sledge. They are not coupled, however, as they are usually represented in engravings, but are attached each loose from all others, so that when they are in motion, travelling, they appear like a flock of partridges all flying loosely, and yet all the same course. They always travel in a gallop, no matter what the state of the country may be. Going down hill is most difficult and danger-ous, and at times it is necessary for the rider to guide the sledge with his feet, as boys steer their sleds sliding down hills, and sometimes it is done by long poles stuck into the snow. When the sledge is heavily laden, and the descent steep, the dogs are often taken off, and the vehicle made to slide down the precipice by the man alone, who lies flat on the sledge, and guides it with his toes from behind, as he descends head-foremost. The dogs are so well acquainted with the courses and places in the neighborhood, that they never fail to take their master and his sledge to the house where he wishes them to go, even should a severe snow-storm come on while they are on the journey ; and it is always safer for the rider at such times to trust to the instincts of the dogs, than to attempt to guide them by his own judgment. Cases have occurred where men have done this, and paid the penalty by freezing to death in a desolate wilderness. In such cases the faithful dogs, if left to themselves, make directly for their home.

"When two travellers meet on a journey, it is neces-sary for both parties to come circuitously and slowly to-wards each other, and give the separate packs the oppor-tunity of observing that their masters are acquainted, or otherwise a fight might ensue between the dogs. Mr.

Jones lost a son, fourteen years of age, a few years ago in the snow, in consequence of a servant imprudently turning the dogs from their course, thinking they were wrong. The dogs obeyed the command, and took them towards Hudson's Bay. When the weather cleared the servant found his mistake ; but, alas ! it was too late for the tender boy, and he froze to death in the servant's arms.

" We saw also to-day the carcasses of fifteen hundred seals stripped of their skins, piled up in a heap, and the dogs feeding on them. The stench filled the air for half a mile around. They tell us the dogs feed on this filthy flesh until the next seal season, tearing it piecemeal when frozen in winter.

" Mr. Jones's house was being painted white, his oil-tubs were full, and the whole establishment was perfumed with odors which were not agreeable to my olfactory nerves. The snow is to be seen in large patches on every hill around us, while the borders of the water-courses are fringed with grasses and weeds as rank as any to be found in the Middle States in like situations. I saw a small brook with fine trout, but what pleased me more was to find the nest of the shore-lark ; it was embedded in moss, so exactly the color of the bird, that when the mother sat on it, it was impossible to distinguish her. We see Newfoundland in the distance, looking like high mountains, whose summits are far above the clouds at present. Two weeks since the harbor where we now are was an ice-field, and not a vessel could approach it ; since then the ice has sunk, and none is to be seen far or near.

" *July* 28. A tremendous gale has blown all day, and I have been drawing. The captain and the rest of our company went off in the storm to visit Blanc Sablons, four miles distant. The fishermen have corrupted the

French name into the English of " Nancy Belong." To-wards evening the storm abated, and although it is now almost calm, the sea runs high, and the Ripley rolls in a way which makes our suppers rest unquietly in our stomachs. We have tried in vain to get some Esquimaux mocassins and robes ; and we also asked to hire one of them, to act as a guide for thirty or forty miles into the interior. The chief said his son might go, a boy of twenty-three, but he would have to ask his mother, as she was always fearing some accident to her darling. This darling son looked more like a brute than a Christian man, and was so daring, that he would not venture on our journey.

" We proceeded over the table-lands towards some ponds, and I found three young shore-larks just out of the nest, and not yet able to fly. They hopped about pretty briskly over the moss, uttering a soft *peep*, to which the parent birds responded at every call. They were about a week old, and I am glad that I shall now have it in my power to make a figure of these birds in sum-mer, winter, and young plumage. We also found the breeding-place of the Fuligula Histrionica, in the corner of a small pond in some low bushes. The parent bird was so shy, that we could not obtain her. In another pond we found the nest also of the velvet duck, called here white-winged coot (Fuligula Fusca) ; it was placed on the moss, among the grass, close to the edge of the water, and contained feathers, but no down, as others do. The female had six young, five of which were secured. They were about one week old, and I could readily dis-tinguish the male birds from the females, the former all exhibiting the white spot under the eye. They were black and hairy (not downy) all over except under the chin, where a patch of white showed itself. They swam swiftly and beautifully, and when we drove them into a

narrow place, for the purpose of getting them on land
and catching them alive, they turned about face and dived
most beautifully, and made their way towards the middle of the pond, where four were shot at one discharge.
Another went on shore and squatted in the grass, where
Lincoln caught it ; but I begged for its life, and we left
it to the care of its mother and of the Maker! The
mother showed all imaginable anxiety, and called to her
young all the while she remained in the pond, with a
short squeaking note by no means unpleasant.

"*July* 29. Bras d'Or. Another horrid stormy day;
the fishermen complain, although five or six left the harbor for further east ; and I wish them joy, but for my
part I wish I was further westward. Our party of young
men went off this morning early to a place called Port
Eau, eighteen miles distant, to try to buy some Esquimaux mocassins and dresses. They will not come back
till to-morrow, and I was glad when the boat returned,
as I was sure they were on terra firma. I feel quite lone-
some on account of their absence, for when all are on
board we have lively times, with music, and stories, and
jokes, and journalizing. But I have amused myself drawing three young shore-larks, the first ever portrayed by
man.

"These birds are just now beginning to congregate,
by associating their families together; even those of
which the young are scarcely able to fly fifty yards are
urging the latter to follow the flock ; so much for short
seasons here. In one month all these birds must leave
this coast or begin to suffer. The young of many birds
are now fledged, and scamper over the rocks about us,
amid the stinking drying cod-fish, with all the sprightli-
ness of youth. The young ravens are out, and fly in
flocks with their parents also ; and the young of almost
all the land birds are full fledged. The ducks alone

seem to me to be backward in their growth, but being more hardy, they can stand the rigidity of the climate until the month of October, when the deep snows drive them off, ready or not, for their toilsome journey.

"The water of our harbor is actually covered with oil, and the bottom fairly covered with the offal of codfish, so that I feel as if smelling and breathing an air impregnated with the essence of cod-fish.

"*July* 30. The morning was beautiful when I arose, but such a thing as a beautiful morning in this mournful country amounts almost to an unnatural phenomenon. The captain and myself visited Mr. Jones this afternoon. We found his wife a good motherly woman, who talked well, and gave us some milk ; she also promised us some fresh butter, and asked to see my drawings of the birds of this vicinity.

"At Port Eau our young men saw an iceberg of immense size. At that place there is a large fishing establishment, having a store connected with it, belonging to fishermen who come yearly from the Island of Jersey. It is again blowing a young hurricane.

"*July* 31. Another horrid hurricane, accompanied by heavy rain, and the vessel rolling so that I cannot go on with my drawing.

"*August* 1. The weather has quite changed, the wind blows from the south-west; it is dry, and I have used the time in drawing. At noon we were visited by an iceberg, which was driven by the easterly wind and storm of yesterday to within three miles of us, and grounded at the entrance of the bay. It looks like a large man-of-war, dressed in light greenish muslin instead of canvas ; and when the sun shines on it it glitters most brilliantly.

"When these transient monuments of the sea happen to tumble or roll over, the fall is tremendous, and the sound produced resembles that of loud distant thunder.

These icebergs are common here all summer, being wafted from the lower end of the straits with every heavy easterly wind or gale. And as the winds generally prevail from the south and south-west, the coast of Newfoundland is more free from them than Labrador; and the navigation along the straits is generally performed along the coast of Newfoundland. My time and our days now weigh heavily on our hands; nothing to be seen, nothing to be shot, therefore nothing to be drawn. I have now determined on a last thorough ransack of the mountain tops, and plains, and ponds, and if no success follows, to raise anchor and sail towards the United States once more; and blessed will the day be when I land on those dear shores where all I long for in this world exists and lives, I hope.

"*August* 2. Thermometer 58° at noon. Thank God it has rained all day. I say thank God, though rain is no rarity, because it is the duty of every man to be thankful for whatever happens by the will of the Omnipotent Creator; yet it was not so agreeable to any of my party as a fine day would have been. We had an arrival of a handsome schooner, called the Wizard, from Boston to-day, but she brought neither papers nor letters; but we learned that all our great cities have a healthy season, and we thanked God for this. The retrograde movement of many land and water birds has already commenced, especially of the lesser species.

"*August* 3. The Wizard broke her moorings and ran into us last night, causing much alarm but no injury. The iceberg of which I have spoken has been broken into a thousand pieces by the late gale, and now lies stranded along the coast. One such monster deposits hundreds of tons of rocks, and gravel, and boulders, and so explains the phenomena which I have before mentioned as observable along the coast.

"*August* 4. It is wonderful how quickly every living thing in this region, whether animal or vegetable, attains its growth. In six weeks I have seen the eggs laid, the birds hatched, and their first moult half gone through; their association into flocks begun, and preparations for leaving the country.

"That the Creator should have ordered that millions of diminutive, tender creatures, should cross spaces of country, in all appearance a thousand times more congenial for all their purposes, to reach this poor, desolate, and deserted land, to people it, as it were, for a time, and to cause it to be enlivened with the songs of the sweetest of the feathered musicians, for only two months at most, and then, by the same extraordinary instinct, should cause them all to suddenly abandon the country, is as wonderful as it is beautiful and grand.

"Six weeks ago this whole country was one sheet of ice; the land was covered with snow, the air was filled with frost, and subject to incessant storms, and the whole country a mere mass of apparently useless matter. Now the grass is abundant, and of rich growth, the flowers are met with at every step, insects fill the air, and the fruits are ripe. The sun shines, and its influence is as remarkable as it is beautiful; the snow-banks appear as if about to melt, and here and there there is something of a summerish look. But in thirty days all is over; the dark northern clouds will come down on the mountains; the rivulets and pools, and the bays themselves, will begin to freeze; weeks of snow-storms will follow, and change the whole covering of these shores and country, and Nature will assume not only a sleeping state, but one of desolation and death. Wonderful! wonderful! But it requires an abler pen than mine to paint the picture of this all-wonderful country.

"*August* 5. This has been a fine day! We have had

no new hurricane, and I have finished the drawings of several new birds. It appears that northern birds come to maturity sooner than southern ones; this is reversing the rule in the human species. The migration of birds is much more wonderful than that of fishes, because the latter commonly go feeling their way along the shores, from one clime to another, and return to the very same river, creek, or even hole, to deposit their spawn, as the birds do to their former nest or building-ground as long as they live. But the latter do not feel their way, but launching high in the air, go at once, and correctly, too, across immense tracts of country, seemingly indifferent to them, but at once stopping, and making their abode in special parts heretofore their own, by previous knowledge of the advantages and comforts which they have enjoyed, and which they know await them there.

"*August* 10. I now sit down to post up my poor book, while a furious gale is blowing without. I have neglected to make daily records for some days, because I have been so constantly drawing, that when night came, I was too weary to wield my pen. Indeed, all my physical powers have been taxed to weariness by this little work of drawing; my neck and shoulders, and most of all my fingers, have ached from the fatigue; and I have suffered more from this kind of exertion than from walking sixty-five miles in a day, which I once did.

" To-day I have added one more new species to the ' Birds of America,' the Labrador falcon ; and may we live to see its beautiful figure multiplied by Havell's graver."

The journal gives a list of the names of one hundred and seventy-three skins of birds, which were obtained on the coast of Labrador by Audubon and his party on this expedition. The episode given in the following chapter seems to summarize Audubon's observations of the inhabitants of Labrador.

CHAPTER XXX.

Labrador Episodes: The Squatters of Labrador.

GO where you will, if a shilling can there be procured, you may expect to meet with individuals in search of it. In the course of last summer I met with several persons as well as families whom I could not compare to anything else than what in America we understand by the appellation of squatters. The methods they employed to accumulate property form the subject of the observations which I now lay before you. Our schooner lay at anchor in a beautiful basin on the coast of Labrador, surrounded by uncouth granite rocks, partially covered with stunted vegetation. While searching for birds and other objects I chanced one morning to direct my eyes towards the pinnacle of a small island, separated from the mainland by a very narrow channel, and presently commenced inspecting it with my telescope. There I saw a man on his knees, with clasped hands, and face inclined heavenwards. Before him was a small monument of unhewn stones supporting a wooden cross. In a word, reader, the person whom I thus unexpectedly discovered was engaged in prayer. Such an incident in that desolate land was affecting, for there one seldom finds traces of human beings, and the aid of the Almighty, although necessary everywhere, seems there peculiarly required to enable them to procure the means of subsistence. My curiosity having been raised, I betook myself to my boat, landed on the rock, and scrambled to the

place, where I found the man still on his knees. When
his devotions were concluded he bowed to me and addressed me in very indifferent French. I asked why he
had chosen so dreary a spot for his prayers. ' Because,
answered he, ' the sea lies before me, and from it I receive my spring and summer sustenance. When winter
approaches I pray fronting the mountains on the main,
as at that period the caraboos come towards the shore
and I kill them, feed on their flesh, and form my bedding
of their skins.' I thought the answer reasonable, and, as
I longed to know more of him, followed him to his hut.
It was low and very small, formed of stones plastered
with mud to a considerable thickness. The roof was
composed of a sort of thatching made of weeds and
moss. A large Dutch stove filled nearly one half of the
place; a small port-hole, then stuffed with old rags, serv·
ed at times instead of a window; the bed was a pile of
deer-skins; a bowl, a jug, and an iron pot were placed
on a rude shelf; three old and rusty muskets, their locks
fastened by thongs, stood in a corner; and his buck-shot,
powder, and flints were tied up in bags of skin. Eight
Esquimaux dogs yelled and leaped about us. The strong
smell that emanated from them, together with the smoke
and filth of the apartment, rendered my stay in it very
disagreeable. Being a native of France, the good man
showed much politeness, and invited me to take some refreshment, when, without waiting for my assent, he took
up his bowl and went off I knew not whither. No sooner
had he and his strange dogs disappeared, than I went out
also to breathe the pure air and gaze on the wild and majestic scenery around. I was struck with the extraordinary luxuriance of the plants and grasses that had sprung
up on the scanty soil in the little valley which the squatter
had chosen for his home. Their stalks and broad blades
reached my waist. June had come, and the flies, mos-

quitoes, and other insects filled the air, and were as troublesome to me as if I had been in a Florida swamp. The squatter returned, but he was 'chopfallen;' nay, I thought his visage had assumed a cadaverous hue. Tears ran down his cheeks, and he told me that his barrel of rum had been stolen by the 'eggers' or some fishermen. He said that he had been in the habit of hiding it in the bushes to prevent its being carried away by those merciless thieves, who must have watched him in some of his *frequent* walks to the spot. 'Now,' said he, 'I can expect none till next spring, and God knows what will become of me in the winter.' Pierre Jean Baptiste Michaux, ' had resided in that part of the world for upwards of ten years ; he had run away from the fishing-smack that had brought him from his fair native land, and expected to become rich some day by the sale of his furs, skins, and eider-ducks' down, seal-skins, and other articles which he collected yearly, and sold to the traders who regularly visited his dreary abode. He was of moderate stature, firmly framed, and as active as a wild cat.' He told me that, excepting the loss of his rum, he had never experienced any other cause of sorrow, and that he felt as 'happy as a lord.' Before parting with this fortunate mortal, I inquired how his dogs managed to find sufficient food. 'Why, sir, during spring and summer they ramble along the shores, where they meet with abundance of dead fish, and in winter they eat the flesh of the seals which I kill late in the autumn, when these animals return from the north. As to myself, everything eatable is good, and when hard pushed, I assure you I can relish the fare of my dogs just as much as they do themselves.' Proceeding along the rugged indentations of the bay with my companions, I reached the settlement of another person, who, like the first, had come to Labrador with the view of making his fortune. We found him after many diffi-

culties; but as our boats turned a long point jutting out
into the bay we were pleased to see several small schooners at anchor and one lying near a sort of wharf. Several neat-looking houses enlivened the view, and on landing
we were kindly greeted with a polite welcome from a man
who proved to be the owner of the establishment. For
the rude simplicity of him of the rum-cask we found here
the manners and dress of a man of the world. A handsome fur cap covered his dark brow, his clothes were similar to our own, and his demeanor was that of a gentleman. On my giving him my name he shook me heartily
by the hand, and on introducing each of my companions
to him he addressed me as follows: 'My dear sir, I have
been expecting you these three weeks, having read in *the
papers* your intention to visit Labrador, and some fishermen told me of your arrival at Little Natashquan. Gentlemen, walk in.' Having followed him to his neat and
comfortable mansion, he introduced me to his wife and
children. Of the latter there were six, all robust and
rosy. The lady, although a native of the country, was of
French extraction, handsome, and sufficiently accomplished to make an excellent companion to a gentleman. A
smart girl brought us a luncheon, consisting of bread,
cheese, and good port wine, to which, having rowed fourteen or fifteen miles that morning, we helped ourselves in
a manner that seemed satisfactory to all parties. Our
host gave us newspapers from different parts of the
world, and showed us his small but choice collection of
books. He inquired after the health of the amiable
Captain Bayfield of the Royal Navy, and the officers under him, and hoped they would give him a call. Having
refreshed ourselves, we walked out with him, when he
pointed to a very small garden where a few vegetables
sprouted out anxious to see the sun. Gazing on the desolate country around, I asked him how *he* had thus se-

cluded himself from *the world*. For *it* he had no relish,
and although he had received a liberal education and had
mixed with society, he never intended to return to it.
'The country round,' said he, 'is all my own much farther
than you can see. No fees, no lawyers, no taxes are *here*.
I do pretty much as I choose. My means are ample
through my own industry. These vessels come here for
seal-skins, seal oil, and salmon, and give me in return all
the necessaries, and, indeed, comforts of the life I love to
follow; and what else could *the world* afford me?' I
spoke of the education of his children. 'My wife and I
teach them all that is *useful* for them to know, and is not
that enough? My girls will marry their countrymen, my
sons the daughters of my *neighbors*, and I hope all of
them will live and die in the country.' I said no more,
but by way of compensation for the trouble I had given
him, purchased from his eldest child a beautiful fox-skin.
Few birds, he said, came round in summer, but in winter
thousands of ptarmigans were killed, as well as great
numbers of gulls. He had a great dislike to all fishermen and eggers, and I really believe was always glad to
see the departure of even the hardy navigators who annually visited him for the sake of his salmon, his seal-
skins, and oil. He had more than forty Esquimaux dogs;
and as I was caressing one of them he said, 'Tell my
brother-in-law at *Bras-d'Or* that we are all well here, and
that after visiting my wife's father I will give him a call.

"Now, reader, his wife's father resided at the distance
of seventy miles down the coast, and like himself was a
recluse. He of *Bras-d'Or* was at double that distance;
but when the snows of winter have thickly covered the
country, the whole family in sledges drawn by dogs travel
with ease and pay their visits or leave their cards. This
good gentleman had already resided there more than
twenty years. Should he ever read this article, I desire

him to believe that I shall always be grateful to him and
his wife for their hospitable welcome. When our schooner, the Ripley, arrived at *Bras-d'Or*, I paid a visit to
Mr. ——, the brother-in-law, who lived in a house im-
ported from Quebec, which fronted the strait of *Belle Isle*,
and overlooked a small island, over which the eye reached the coast of Newfoundland whenever it was the wind's
pleasure to drive away the fogs that usually lay over both
coasts. The gentleman and his wife, we were told, were
both out on a walk, but would return in a very short time,
which they in fact did, when we followed them into the
house, which was yet unfinished. The usual immense
Dutch stove formed the principal feature of the interior.
The lady had once visited the metropolis of Canada, and
seemed desirous of acting the part of a 'blue stocking.'
Understanding that I knew something of the fine arts,
she pointed to several of the vile prints hung on the bare
walls, which she said were elegant Italian pictures, and
continued her encomiums upon them, assuring me that
she had purchased them from an Italian who had come
there with a trunk full of them. She had paid a shilling
sterling for each, frame included. I could give no answer
to the good lady on this subject, but I felt glad to find
that she possessed a feeling heart. One of her children
had caught a *siskin*, and was tormenting the poor bird,
when she rose from her seat, took the little flutterer from
the boy, kissed it, and gently launched it into the air.
This made me quite forget the tattle about the fine arts.
Some excellent milk was poured out for us in clean
glasses. It was a pleasing sight, for not a cow had we
yet seen in the country. The lady turned the conversation on music, and asked if I played on any instrument.
I answered that I did, but very indifferently. Her forte, she
said, was music, of which she was indeed immoderately
fond. Her instrument had been sent to Europe to be re-

paired, but would return that season, when the whole of
her children would again perform many beautiful airs, for
in fact anybody could use it with ease, as when she or the
children felt fatigued the servant played on it for them.
Rather surprised at the extraordinary powers of this family of musicians, I asked what sort of an instrument it
was, when she described it as follows : ‘Gentlemen, my
instrument is large, longer than broad, and stands on four
legs like a table ; at one end is a crooked handle, by
turning which round either fast or slow I do assure you
we make excellent music.’ The lips of my young friends
and companions instantly curled, but a glance from me as
instantly recomposed their features. Telling the fair one
it must be a hand-organ she used, she laughingly said,
‘Oh, that is it, it is a hand-organ, but I had forgotten the
name, and for the life of me could not recollect it.’ The
husband had gone out to work, and was in the harbor
caulking an old schooner. He dined with me on board
the Ripley, and proved to be an excellent fellow. Like
his brother-in-law, he had seen much of the world, having
sailed nearly round it ; and although no scholar, like him,
too, he was disgusted with it. He held his land on the
same footing as his neighbors, caught seals without number, lived comfortably and happily, visited his father-in-
law and the scholar by the aid of his dogs, of which he
kept a great pack, bartered or sold his commodities as his
relations did, and cared about nothing else in the world.
Whenever the weather was fair he walked with his dame
over the snow-covered rocks of the neighborhood, and
during winter killed ptarmigans and caraboos, while his
eldest son attended to the traps and skinned the animals
caught by them. He had the only horse that was to be
found in that part of the country, as well as several cows ;
but, above all, he was kind to every one, and every one
spoke well of him. The only disagreeable thing about

the plantation or settlement was a heap of fifteen hundred carcasses of skinned seals, which at the time when
we visited the place, in the month of August, notwithstanding the coolness of the atmosphere, sent forth a
stench that, according to the idea of some naturalists,
might have sufficed to attract all the vultures in the United States.   During our stay at *Bras-d'Or* the kind-heart-
ed and good Mrs. —— daily sent us fresh milk and
butter, for which we were denied the pleasure of making
any return."

CHAPTER XXXI.

AUGUST 11. At sea, Gulf of St. Lawrence. We are now fully fifty miles from the coast of Labrador. Fresh water was taken on board, and all preparations were made last evening, and this morning we bid adieu to the friends we had made at Labrador.

" Seldom in my life have I left a country with as little regret as this ; next in order would come East Florida, after my excursion up the St. John's River. As we sailed away I saw probably for the last time the high and rugged hills, partly immersed in large banks of fog, that usually hang over them.

" Now we are sailing before the wind in full sight of the south-west coast of Newfoundland, the mountains of which are high, spotted with drifted snow-banks, and cut horizontally with floating strata of fogs extending along the land as far as the eye can reach. The sea is quite smooth, or else I have become a better sailor by this rough voyage. Although the weather is cloudy, it is such as promises in this region a fair night. Our young men are playing the violin and flute, and I am scribbling in my book.

" It is worth telling that during the two months we have spent on the coast of Labrador, moving from one harbor to another, or from behind one rocky island to another, only three nights have been passed at sea. Twenty-three drawings have been commenced or finished, and now I am anxious to know if what remains of the voyage will prove as fruitful ; and only hope our Creator will permit us all to reach our friends in safety and find them well and happy.

"*August* 13. Harbor of St. George's Bay, Newfoundland. By my dates you will see how long we were running, as the sailors call it, from Labrador to this place, where we anchored at five this evening. Our voyage here was all in sight of, and indeed along the north-west side of Newfoundland ; the shores presenting the highest lands we have yet seen. In some places the views were highly picturesque and agreeable to the eye, although the appearance of vegetation was but little better than at Labrador. The wind was fair for two-thirds of the distance, and drew gradually ahead and made us uncomfortable.

"This morning we entered the mouth of St. George's Bay, which is about forty miles wide and fifty miles deep, and a more beautiful and ample basin cannot be found ; there is not a single obstruction within it. The northeast shores are high and rocky, but the southern are sandy, low, and flattish. It took us until five o'clock to ascend it, when we came to anchor in sight of a small village, the only one we have seen in two months ; and we are in a harbor with a clay bottom, and where fifty line-of-battle ships could snugly and safely ride.

"The village is built on an elongated point of sand or sea wall, under which we now are, and is perfectly secure from all winds except the north-east. The country on ascending the bay became gradually more woody and less rough in shape. The temperature changed quite suddenly this afternoon, and the weather was so mild that we found it agreeable lolling on deck, and it felt warm even to a southron like myself. Twenty-two degrees difference in temperature in two days is a very considerable change.

"We found here several sail of vessels engaged in the fisheries, and an old hulk from Hull in England, called Charles Tennison, which was wrecked near here four years ago, on her way from Quebec to Hull. As we sailed up the bay two men boarded us from a small boat and assisted us as pilots. They had a half barrel of fine salmon, which I bought from them for ten dollars. As soon as we dropped anchor our young men went ashore to buy fresh provisions, but they returned with nothing but two bottles of milk, though the village contains two hundred inhabitants. Mackerel, and sharks of the man-eating kind, are said to be abundant here. Some signs of cultivation are to be seen across the harbor, and many huts of Michmaes Indians adorn the shores. We learn that the winters are not nearly as severe here as at Quebec, yet not far off I could see dots of snow of last year's crop. Some persons say birds are plenty, others say there are none hereabouts.

"The ice did not break up, so that this bay was not navigable until the 17th of May, and I feel confident that no one can enter the harbors of Labrador before the 10th or middle of June.

"*August* 14. All ashore in search of birds, plants, and the usual et ceteras belonging to our vocations, but all had to return soon on account of a storm of wind and rain, showing that Newfoundland is cousin to Labrador in this respect. We found the country quite rich however in comparison with the latter place ; all the vegetable productions are larger and more abundant. We saw a flock of house sparrows, all gay and singing, and on their passage to the south-west."

16

Audubon names about twenty different species of birds which he saw here; hares and caraboos are among the animals, and among the wild plants he found two species of roses.

"The women flew before us as if we were wild beasts, and one who had a pail of water, at sight of us, dropped it, and ran to hide herself; another who was looking for a cow, on seeing us coming, ran into the woods, and afterwards crossed a stream waist deep to get home to her hut without passing us. We are told that no laws are administered here, and to my surprise not a sign of a church exists. The people are all fishermen and live poorly; in one enclosure I saw a few pretty good-looking cabbages. We can buy only milk and herrings, the latter ten cents a dozen; we were asked eight dollars for a tolerable calf, but chickens were too scarce to be obtained. Two clearings across the bay are the only signs of cultivated land. Not a horse has yet made its way into the country, and not even a true Newfoundland dog, nothing but curs of a mixed breed.

"Some of the buildings looked like miserable hovels, others more like habitable houses. Not a blacksmith's shop here, and yet one would probably do well. The customs of the people are partly Canadian and partly English. The women all wear cotton caps covering their ears. The passage to and from our vessel to the shore was the roughest I ever made in an open boat, and we were completely soaked by the waves which dashed over us.

"*August* 15. We have had a beautiful day. This morning some Indians came alongside of our vessel with half a reindeer, a caraboo, and a hare of a species I had never seen before. We gave them twenty-one pounds of pork for forty-four pounds of venison, thirty-three pounds of bread for the caraboo, and a quarter of a dollar for the hare. The Indians showed much cleverness in striking the bargain. I spent part of the day drawing, and then visited the wigwams of the Indians across the bay. We found them, as I expected, all lying down pell-mell in their wigwams, and a strong mixture of blood was perceptible in their skins, shape, and deportment: some were almost white, and sorry I am to say, that the nearer they were to our nobler race the filthier and the lazier they were. The women and children were particularly disgusting in this respect. Some of the women were making baskets, and others came in from collecting a fruit called here the baked apple (*Rubus chamænrous*), and when burnt a little it tastes exactly like a roasted apple. The children were catching lobsters and eels, of which there are a great many in the bay, as there are in all the bays of the island, whilst at Labrador this shell-fish is very rare. The young Indians found them by wading to their knees in eel grass.

"We bargained with two of the hunters to go with our young men into the interior to hunt for caraboos, hares, and partridges, which they agreed to do for a dollar a day. The Indians cook lobsters by roasting them in a pile of brushwood, and eat them without any salt or other condiment. The caraboos are at this date in 'velvet,' their skins are now light grey, and the flesh poor but tender. The average weight of this animal, when in good condition, is four hundred pounds. In the early part of March they leave the hilly grounds, where no moss or any other food can be obtained, and resort to the shores of the sea to feed on kelp and other sea grasses cut up by the ice and cast up by the waves along the shore. Groups of several hundreds may be seen at one time thus feeding: their flesh here is not much esteemed; it tastes like indifferent, poor, but very tender venison.

"*August* 17. We should now be ploughing the deep had the wind been fair, but it has been ahead, and we

remain here *in statu quo.* The truth is, we have determined not to leave this harbor without a fair prospect of a
good run, and then we shall trust to Providence after that.
I have added a curious species of alder to my drawing of
the white-winged cross-bill, and finished it. We received
a visit from Mr., Mrs., and Miss Forest; they brought us
some salad and fresh butter, and in return we gave them
a glass of wine and some raisins. The old lady and gentleman talked well; he complained of the poverty of the
country and the disadvantages *he* experienced from the
privileges granted to the French on this coast. They
told me they were relatives of Lord Plunket, and that
they were well acquainted with our friend Edward Harris
and his family. I gave them my card, and showed them
the Duke of Sussex's letter, which they borrowed and
took home to copy. I had also a visit from an old Frenchman who has resided on this famous island for fifty years.
He assured me that no red Indians are now to be found ;
the last he had heard of were seen twenty-two years ago.
It is said that these natives give no quarter to anybody,
but, after killing their foes, cut off their heads and leave
their bodies to the wild beasts of the country.

"Several flocks of golden-winged plovers passed over
the bay this forenoon, and two lestris pomerania came in
this evening. The ravens abound here, but no crows
have yet been seen; the great tern are passing south by
thousands, and a small flock of Canada geese were also
seen. The young of the golden-crested wren were shot.
A muscipcapa was killed, which is probably new. I
bought seven Newfoundland dogs for seventeen dollars :
two bitches, four pups, and a dog two years old. With
these I shall be able to fulfill promises made to friends to
bring them dogs.

"On the 18th of August at daylight the wind promised to be fair, and although it was rather cloudy we broke

our anchorage, and at five o'clock were under weigh. We
coasted along Newfoundland until evening, when the wind
rose to a tempest from the south-west, and our vessel was
laid to at dark, and we danced and kicked over the waves
the whole of that night and the next day. The next day
the storm abated, but the wind was still so adverse that
we could not make the Gannet Rock or any part of Newfoundland, and towards the latter we steered, for none of
us could bear the idea of returning to Labrador. During
the night the weather moderated, and the next day we
laid our course for the Straits of Canseau ; but suddenly
the wind failed, and during the calm it was agreed that
we would try and reach Pictou in Nova Scotia, and travel by land. We are now beating about towards that port,
and hope to reach it early to-morrow morning. The
captain will then sail for Eastport, and we, making our
way by land, will probably reach there as soon as he.
The great desire we all have to see Pictou, Halifax, and
the country between there and Eastport is our induce-
ment."

"*August* 22. After attempting to beat our vessel into
the harbor of Pictou, but without succeeding, we concluded that myself and party should be put on shore, and the
Ripley should sail back to the Straits of Canseau, the
wind and tide being favorable. We drank a parting glass
to our wives and friends, and our excellent little captain
took us to the shore, whilst the vessel stood up to the
wind, with all sails set, waiting for the captain.

"We happened to land on an island called Ruy's Isl-
and, where, fortunately for us, we met some men making hay. Two of them agreed to carry our trunks and
two of our party to Pictou for two dollars. Our effects
were put in a boat in a trice, and we shook hands heartily with the captain, towards whom we all now feel much
real attachment, and after mutual adieus, and good

wishes for the completion of our respective journeys, we parted, giving each other three most hearty cheers.

"We were now, thank God, positively on the main shore of our native land ; and after four days' confinement in our births, and sea-sickness, and the sea and vessel, and all their smells and discomforts, we were so refreshed, that the thought of walking nine miles seemed nothing more than figuring through a single quadrille. The air felt uncommonly warm, and the country, compared with those we had so lately left, appeared perfectly beautiful, and we inhaled the fragrance of the new mown grass, as if nothing sweeter ever existed. Even the music of crickets was delightful to my ears, for no such insect is to be found either at Labrador or Newfoundland. The voice of a blue jay sounded melody to me, and the sight of a humming-bird quite filled my mind with delight.

"We were conveyed to the main, only a very short distance, Ingalls and Coolidge remaining in the boat ; and the rest took the road, along which we moved as lightly as, if boys just released from school. The road was good, or seemed to be so ; the woods were tall timber, and the air, which circulated freely, was all perfume ; and every plant we saw brought to mind some portion of the United States, and we all felt quite happy. Now and then as we crossed a hill, and cast our eyes back on the sea, we saw our beautiful vessel sailing freely before the wind, and as she diminished towards the horizon, she at last appeared like a white speck, or an eagle floating in the air, and we wished our captain a most safe voyage to Quoddy.

"We reached the shore opposite Pictou in two and a half hours, and lay down on the grass to await the arrival of the boat, and gazed on the scenery around us. A number of American vessels lay in the harbor loading with coal. The village located at the bottom of a fine bay on the north-west side looked well, although small. Three churches appeared above the rest of the buildings, all of wood, and several vessels were building on the stocks.

"The whole country seemed to be in a high state of cultivation, and looked well. The population is about two thousand. Our boat came, and we crossed the bay, and we put up at the Royal Oak, the best hotel in the place, where we obtained an excellent supper. The very treading of a carpeted floor was comfortable. In the evening we called on Professor McCullough, who received us kindly, gave us a glass of wine, and showed us his collection of well-preserved birds and other things, and invited us to breakfast to-morrow at eight o'clock, when we are further to inspect his curiosities. The professor's mansion is a quarter of a mile from the town, and looks much like a small English villa.

"*August* 23. We had an excellent Scotch breakfast at the professor's this morning, and his family, consisting of wife, four sons and daughters, and a wife's sister, were all present. The more I saw and talked with the professor, the more I was pleased with him. I showed him a few of my Labrador drawings, after which we marched in a body to the university, and again examined his fine collection. I found there half a dozen specimens of birds, which I longed for, and said so, and he offered them to me with so much apparent good will, that I took them and thanked him. He then asked me to look around and see if there were any other objects I would like to have. He offered me all his fresh-water shells, and such minerals as we might choose, and I took a few specimens of iron and copper. He asked me what I thought of his collection, and I gave him my answer in writing, adding F.R.S. to my name, and telling him that I wished it might prove useful to him. I am much surprised that his valuable collection has not been purchased by the Governor of the province, to whom he offered it for five hundred pounds. I think it worth a thousand pounds.

"On our return to the hotel we were met by Mr. Blanchard, the deputy consul for the United States, an agreeable man, who offered frankly to do anything in his power to make our visit fruitful and pleasant. 'Time up,' and the coach almost ready, our bill was paid, our birds packed, and I walked ahead about a mile out of the town, with Mr. Blanchard, who spoke much of England, and was acquainted with Mr. Adamson, and some other friends whom I knew at Newcastle-on-Tyne.

"The coach came up, I shook hands with Mr. Blanchard, jumped in, and away we went for Truro, distant forty miles. The rain began to fall, and the wind to blow from the east, a good wind for the Ripley, and on we rolled on as good a road as any in England, were it only a little broader. We now passed through a fine tract of country, well wooded, well cultivated, and a wonderful relief to our fatigued eyes, which had so long been seeing only desolate regions, snow, and tempestuous storms.

"By four in the afternoon we were hungry, and stopped at a house to dine, and it now rained faster than before. Two ladies, and the husband of one of them as I supposed, had arrived before us, in an open cart or Jersey waggon; and I, with all the gallantry belonging to my nature, offered to exchange vehicles with them, which they readily accepted, but without expressing any thanks in return. After dinner Shattuck, Ingalls, and myself jumped into the open thing; I was seated by the side of my so-so Irish dame, and our horse moved off at a very good speed.

"Our exchange soon proved an excellent one, for the weather cleared up, and we saw the country much better than we could have done in the coach, where there were so many passengers that we should have been squeezed together closely. Directly Professor McCullough came

up with us, and told us he would see us to-morrow at
Truro. Towards sunset we arrived in sight of this pretty, loosely-built village, near the head-waters of the Bay
of Fundy. The view filled me with delight, and the
pleasure was deepened by the consciousness that my
course was homeward, and I was but a few days from the
dearest being to me on earth.

"We reached the tavern, which the hotel where we
stopped was called, but as it could accommodate only
three of us, we crossed the street to another house, where
we ordered a substantial supper. Professor McCullough
came in, and introduced us to several members of the
Assembly of this province.

"We tried in vain to get a conveyance to take us to
Halifax, distant sixty-four miles, in the morning, to avoid
riding all night in the mail-coach, but could not succeed.
Mr. McCullough then took me to the residence of Samuel G. Archibald, Esq., Speaker of the Assembly, who received me most affably, and introduced me to his lady
and handsome young daughter; the former wore a cap
fashionable four years ago at home (England). I showed
them a few drawings, and received a letter from the
Speaker to the Chief Justice at Halifax, and bid them all
good night; and am now waiting the mail to resume my
journey. Meanwhile let me say a few words on this little village. It is situated in the centre of a most beautiful valley of great extent, and under complete cultivation;
looking westerly a broad sheet of water is seen, forming
the head of the famous Bay of Fundy, and several brooks
run through the valley emptying into it. The buildings,
although principally of wood, are good-looking, and as
cleanly as any of our pretty New England villages, well
painted, and green blinds. The general appearance of
the people quite took me by surprise, being extremely
genteel. The coach is at the door, the corner of my

16*

trunk is gasping to swallow this book, and I must put it in and be off.

"*August* 24. Wind east, and hauling to the north-east—all good for the Ripley. We are at Halifax, Nova Scotia, and this is the way we got here:—Last night at eleven we seated ourselves in the coach ; the moon shone bright, and the night was beautiful ; but we could only partially observe the country until the day dawned. But we found out that the road was hilly and the horses lazy, and after riding twenty miles we stopped to change horses and warm ourselves. Shortly the cry came, 'Coach ready, gentlemen.' In we jumped, and on we rode for a mile and a half, when the linch-pin broke, and we came to a stand-still. Ingalls took charge of the horses, and responded to the hoot of the owls, which sounded out from the woods, and the rest of the party, excepting Coolidge and myself, slept soundly, while we were enduring that disagreeable experience of travellers —detention—which is most disagreeable in this latitude, and especially at night. Looking up the road, the vacillating glimmer of the candle, intended to assist the driver in finding the linch-pin, was all that could be distinguished, and we began to feel what is called 'wolfish.' The man returned, but found no pin—it could not be found, and another quarter of an hour was spent in fumbling round with ropes to tie our vehicle together. At length the day dawned beautifully, and I ran ahead of the coach for a mile or so to warm myself; and when the coach came up I got up with the driver to try to obtain some information respecting the country, which was becoming poorer and poorer the further we travelled. Hunger again now began to press us, and we were told that it was twenty-five miles from the lost linch-pin to the breakfast-house. I persuaded the driver to stop at a wayside tavern, and inquire the prospects for getting some chickens or boiled eggs ; but the proprietor said it was impossible for him to furnish a breakfast for six persons of our appearance.

"We passed on, and soon came to the track of a good-sized bear in the road, and after a wearisome ride reached the breakfast ground, at a house situated on the margin of a lake called Grand Lake, which abounds with fine fish, and soles in the season. This lake forms part of the channel which was intended to be cut for connecting the Atlantic Ocean and the Bay of Fundy with the Gulf of St. Lawrence at Bay Verte. Ninety thousand pounds have been expended on the enterprise, and the canal is not finished, and probably never will be ; for the government will not assist, and private efforts seem to have exhausted themselves. This point is seventeen miles from Halifax, and must afford a pleasant residence for summer.

"The road from that tavern to Halifax is level and good, though rather narrow, and a very fine drive for private carriages. We saw the flag of the garrison at Halifax, two miles before we reached the place, when we suddenly turned short, and brought up at a gate fronting a wharf, at which lay a small steam-ferry boat. The gate was shut, and the mail was detained nearly an hour waiting for it to be opened. Why did not Mrs. Trollope visit Halifax? The number of negro men and women, beggarly-looking blacks, would have furnished materials for her descriptive pen.

"We crossed the harbor, in which we saw a sixty-four gun flag-ship riding at anchor. The coach drove up to the house of Mr. Paul, the best hotel, where we with difficulty obtained one room with four beds for six persons. With a population of eighteen thousand souls, and two thousand more of soldiers, Halifax has not one good hotel, and only two very indifferent private boarding-houses, where the attendance is miserable, and the table by no means good. We are, however, settled.

"We have walked about the town; but every one of us has sore feet in consequence of walking on hard ground, after having roamed for two months on the soft, deep mosses of Labrador. The card of an Italian was sent to our rooms, telling us that he had fine baths of all sorts, and we went off to his rooms and found only one tin tub, and a hole underground, into which the sea-water filters, about the size of a hogshead. I plunged into this hole with Ingalls and Shattuck, then rubbed ourselves dry with curious towels, and paid six cents each for the accommodation. We then walked to the garrison, listened to the music, returned to the hotel, and have written this, and now send in my card to the aide-de-camp of the Governor of Newfoundland, who resides in this house.

"*August* 25. To-day I walked to the wharves, and was surprised to find them every one gated and locked, and sentinels standing guard everywhere. In the afternoon there was a military funeral; it was a grand sight, the soldiers walked far apart, guns inverted, to the sound of the finest anthem, and wonderfully well executed by an excellent band.

"There are no signs of style here; only two ordinary barouches came to church to-day (the Episcopal), where the bishop said the prayers and preached. All the churches receive a certain number of soldiers dressed in uniform. The natives of the province are called 'Blue Noses,' and to-morrow we intend to see all we can of them.

"*August* 26. To-day I delivered letters which I brought to Bishop Inglis and the Chief Justice, but did not find them at home. To-morrow we hope to leave here for Windsor, distant forty-five miles.

"*August* 27. At nine o'clock we entered the coach, or

rather five of us entered it, as it would hold no more, and one was obliged to take an outside seat in the rain. The road from Halifax to Windsor is macadamized and good, winding through undulating hills and valleys ; our horses were good, and although we had but one pair at a time, we travelled six and a half miles an hour. For more than nine miles our course was along the borders of the Bay of Halifax ; the view was pleasant, and here and there we noticed tolerably gook-looking summer-houses. Near the head of this bay, said the driver, an English fleet pursued a squadron of seven French ships, and forced them to haul down their colors ; but the French commander, or admiral, sunk all his vessels, preferring to do this to surrendering them to the British. The water was so deep at this place that the tops of the masts of the vessels went deep out of sight, and have been seen only once since then, which was more than twenty years ago.

" We passed the abandoned lodge of Prince Edward, who spent about one million of pounds on this building and the grounds, but the whole is now a ruin ; thirty years have passed since it was in its splendor. On leaving the waters of the bay, we followed those of the Salmon River, a small rivulet of swift water, which abounds with salmon, trout, elwines, &c. The whole country is poor, very poor, yet under tolerable cultivation all the way. We passed the seat of Mr. Jeffries, the President of the Assembly, now Acting Governor ; his house is good-looking, large, and the grounds around it are in fine order. It is situated between two handsome fresh-water lakes ; indeed the whole country through which we travelled is interspersed with lakes, all of them abounding in trout and eels.

" We passed the college and common school, both looking well, and built of fine freestone ; a church and several other fine buildings line the road, on which the president and rector reside. We crossed the head of the St. Croix River, which rolls its waters impetuously into the Bay of Fundy. Here the lands were all dyked, and the crops looked very well, and from that river to Windsor the country improved rapidly.

"Windsor is a small and rather neat village, on the east side of the River Windsor, and is supported by the vast banks of plaster of Paris around it. This valuable article is shipped in British vessels to Eastport and elsewhere in large quantities.

"Our coach stopped at the door of the best private boarding-house, for nowhere in this province have we heard of hotels. The house was full, and we went to another, where, after waiting two hours, we obtained an indifferent supper. The view from this village was as novel to me as the coast of Labrador. The bed of the river, which is here about one mile wide, was quite bare as far as the eye could reach, say for ten miles, scarcely any water to be seen, and yet the place where we stood was sixty-five feet above the bed, which plainly showed that at high tide this wonderful basin must be filled to the brim. Opposite us, and indeed the whole country, is dyked in ; and vessels left dry at the great elevation, fastened to the wharves, had a singular appearance. We are told that now and then some vessels have slid sideways from the top of the bank down to the level of the gravelly bed of the river. The shores are covered for a hundred yards with a reddish mud. This looks more like the result of a great freshet than of a tide, and I long to see the waters of the sea advancing at the rate of four knots an hour to fill this basin, a sight I hope to see to-morrow."

August 28. Here follows the description of the extraordinary rise and fall of the waters, and they are evidently the notes from which Audubon wrote his episode of the Bay of Fundy. The day was passed in rambling in search of birds in this vicinity. The record for the day concludes: "We intended to have paid our respects to Mr. Halliburton, author of the 'Description of Nova Scotia,' and other works, but we learned that he was in Boston, where I heartily wished myself.

"*Eastport, Maine, August* 31, 1833. We arrived here yesterday afternoon in the steamer Maid of the Mist, all well. We left Windsor a quarter before twelve, and reached St. John's, New Brunswick, at two o'clock at night; passed Cape Blow-me-Down, Cape Split, and Cape D'Or; the passengers were few, and we were comfortable. We traversed the streets of St. John's by moonlight, and in the morning I had the pleasure to meet my friend Edward Harris, and to receive letters from home; and I am now preparing to leave for Boston as soon as possible."

The account of the voyage concludes with this sentence:

"We reached New York on the morning of the 7th of September, and, thank God, found all well. I paid the balance of the Ripley's charter (eight hundred and sixty-two dollars), and a balance of four hundred and thirty dollars to Dr. Parkman, which he advanced to Dr. Shattuck for me. And I was not very well pleased that nearly the whole burden of the Labrador voyage was put on my shoulders, or rather taken out of my poor purse; but I was silent, and no one knew my thoughts on that subject."

CHAPTER XXXII.

EPTEMBER 7, 1833. After Audubon's return from Labrador he remained three weeks in New York, and then made all his preparations for a journey to Florida. He forwarded to his son Victor, in England, thirteen drawings of land birds, which he had prepared to complete the second volume of the great work; and he left seventeen drawings of sea birds to be forwarded in October, for the commencement of his third volume. As an evidence of the value Audubon set on these drawings, we may note that he insured both parcels for two thousand dollars each.

September 25. Mr. and Mrs. Audubon left New York for Philadelphia on their way to Florida, leaving their son John to sail from New York by water, "with all our articles of war," for Charleston, where they proposed to meet. The journal says: "The weather was delightful, and we reached Philadelphia at three o'clock, and took lodgings with Mrs. Newlin, No. 112 Walnut Street. Here I called on some of my former friends and was kindly received. I visited several public places in the city, but no one stopped me to subscribe for my book."

The following letter from Dr. McKenney of Philadelphia is inserted here as a capital specimen of a racy let-

ter, and as evincing, moreover, how Audubon was estimated by his friends :

"PHILADELPHIA, *September* 30, 1833.

"MY DEAR GOVERNOR,

"I do not know when I have done a more acceptable
service to my feelings, nor when I have been just in a situation to afford as much gratification to yours, as in presenting to your notice, and private and official friendship,
the bearer, Mr. Audubon. It were superfluous to tell you
who he is ; the whole world knows him and respects him,
and no man in it has the heart to cherish or the head to
appreciate him, and such a man, beyond the capacity of
yourself.

"Mr. Audubon makes no more of tracking it in all
directions over this, and I may add other countries, than
a shot star does in crossing the heavens. He goes after
winged things, but sometimes needs the aid of—at least
a few feathers, to assist him the better to fly. He means
to coast it again round Florida—make a track through
Arkansas—go up the Missouri—pass on to the Rocky
Mountains, and thence to the Pacific. He will require
some of your official aid. I took an unmerited liberty
with your name and readiness of purpose, and told him
you were the *very man ;* and I need not say how happy
I shall be to learn that you have endorsed my promise
and ratified it. God bless you.

"In haste,
"THOS. L. MCKENNEY.

"To the Hon. LEWIS CASS, Secretary of War,
            Washington City."

"*Richmond, Virginia, October (no date).* Travelling
through the *breeding-places of* OUR *species* is far from being
as interesting to me as it is to inspect the breeding-places

of the feathery tribes of our country. Yet as it is the lot of every man like me to know something of both, to keep up the clue of my life, I must say something of the cities through which I pass, and of the events which transpire as I go along.

"At Philadelphia I of course received no subscriptions ; nay, I was arrested there for debt,* and was on the point of being taken to prison, had I not met with William Norris, Esq., who kindly offered to be my bail. This event brings to my mind so many disagreeable thoughts connected with my former business transactions, in which I was *always* the *single* loser, that I will only add I made all necessary arrangements to have it paid.

"We left Philadelphia for Baltimore, where I obtained four new subscribers, and received many civilities, and especially from Mr. Theodore Anderson, the collector of the customs. He is fond of birds, and that made me fond of *him*.

"From Baltimore we went to Washington, for the purpose of obtaining permission for myself to accompany an expedition to the Rocky Mountains under the patronage of the Government. Generals McComb, Jesup, Colonel Abert, and other influential persons received me as usual with marked kindness. I called on Governor Cass, Secretary of War, and met with a reception that nearly disheartened me. He said in an indifferent and cold manner that any request of that sort must be made in writing to the Department ; and it recalled to my mind how poor Wilson was treated by the famous Jefferson when he made a similar application to that great diplomatist. I had forgotten to take with me the flattering letter of introduction I had received from Dr. McKenney, and I inquired if he would allow me to send the let-

* One of his old partnership debts.

ter: he said, 'Certainly, sir,' and I bowed and retired, determined never to trouble him or the War Department again.

"I was revolving in my mind how I might get to the Rocky Mountains without the assistance of the Secretary of War, when I suddenly met with a friendly face, no less than Washington Irving's. I mentioned my errand to him and the answer I had received, and he thought I was mistaken. I might have been: but those eyes of mine have discovered more truth in men's eyes than their mouths were willing to acknowledge. However, I listened to good Irving with patience and calmness, and he promised to see the Secretary of War; and he also at once accompanied me to Mr. Taney, the Secretary of the Treasury, who received me well, and at once kindly gave me a letter, granting me the privilege of the revenue cutters along the coast south of Delaware Bay."

Mr. Audubon returned to Baltimore, took the bay steamer for Norfolk, went aboard the Potomac, which was there ready to sail for Richmond, where he arrived at the above date. There he called on Governor Floyd, who promised to try to induce the State of Virginia to subscribe for his "Birds of America."

"*October* 16. We left Richmond this morning in a stage well crammed with Italian musicians and southern merchants, arrived at Petersburg at a late hour, dined, and were again crammed in a car drawn by a locomotive, which dragged us twelve miles an hour, and sent out sparks of fire enough to keep us constantly busy in extinguishing them on our clothes. At Blakely we were again crammed into a stage, and dragged about two miles an hour. We crossed the Roanoke River by torchlight in a flat boat, passed through Halifax, Raleigh, Fayetteville, and Columbia, where we spent the night. Here I met Dr. Gibbs, at whose house we passed the evening, and who assisted me greatly ; at his house I met President Thomas Cooper, who assured me he had seen a rattlesnake climb a five-rail fence on his land. I received from the treasury of the State four hundred and twenty dollars on account of its subscription for one copy of the ' Birds of America.' "

Dreading the railway, he hired a carriage for forty dollars to proceed to Charleston, where he arrived in four days, and found his son John, and was kindly received, with his wife, by the Rev. John Bachman.

Charleston, S. C., *October* 24, 1833. Our time at Charleston has been altogether pleasant. The hospitality of our friends cannot be described, and now that we are likely to be connected by family ties I shall say no more on this head." John and Victor Audubon were subsequently married to daughters of this gentleman.

"My time was well employed ; I hunted for new birds or searched for more knowledge of old. I drew ; I wrote many long pages. I obtained a few new subscribers, and made some collections on account of my work.

" My proposed voyage to Florida, which was arranged for the 3d of November, was abandoned on account of the removal of my good friend Captain Robert Day from his former station to New York, and I did not like to launch on the Florida reefs in the care of a young officer unknown to me ; and besides this, my son Victor wrote me from England desiring my return. So we began to prepare gradually for a retrograde movement toward the north, and on the 1st of March we left our friends and Charleston to return to New York. We travelled through North and South Carolina, and reached Norfolk, Va., on the 6th ; went up the bay to Washington, thence to Baltimore, and took lodgings at Theodore Anderson's in Fayette Street.

" At Baltimore we saw all our friends and obtained

three new subscribers, and lost one, a banker." Here
Audubon remained about a month ; went to Philadelphia
to collect money, which he found rather difficult; and
passed on to New York.

April 16, 1834. After remaining two weeks in
New York, Audubon, his wife, and son John, sailed
on the above date for Liverpool, "in the superb pack-
et, the North America, commanded by that excellent
gentleman, Mr. Dixey of Philadelphia. Our company
was good ; our passage was good ; the first land we
saw was Holyhead, and in nineteen days after leaving
America we were put ashore in Old England." Audubon
saw his friends in Liverpool, who had lost none of their
former cordiality and kindness ; and after a few days he
left with his family, by the way of Birmingham, for London.

"*May* 12. We reached London to-day and found our
son Victor quite well, and were all happy. My work
and business were going on prosperously." After remaining several weeks in London, and seeing to matters relating to his publication there, Audubon and his
son Victor went to deliver letters of introduction which
they had brought. Among those letters was one from one
of the firm of the distinguished American banking-house
Prime, Ward, and King, to the famous London banker, Rothschild. "The letter was addressed to Baron
Rothschild, the man who, notwithstanding his original
poverty, is now so well known through his immense wealth,
which he uses as banker, jobber, and lender of money.
We found no difficulty in ascertaining the place of business of the great usurer. Business in London is thoroughly matter of fact ; no external pomp indicated the
counting-house of the baron ; there was nothing to dis-
tinguish it from those of men of less enormous capital;
and we walked into his private office without any hin-

drance, and introduced ourselves without any introducer.

"The Baron was not present, but we were told by a good-loking young gentleman that he would come in in a few minutes ; and so he did. Soon a corpulent man appeared, hitching up his trousers, and a face red with the exertion of walking, and without noticing any one present, dropped his fat body into a comfortable chair, as if caring for no one else in this wide world but himself. While the Baron sat, we stood, with our hats held respectfully in our hands. I stepped forward, and with a bow tendered him my credentials. ' Pray, sir,' said the man of golden consequence, ' is this a letter of business, or is it a mere letter of introduction ? ' This I could not well answer, for I had not read the contents of it ,and I was forced to answer rather awkwardly that I could not tell. The banker then opened the letter, read it with the manner of one who was looking only at the temporal side of things, and after reading it said, ' This is only a letter of introduction, and I expect from its contents that you are the publisher of some book or other and need my subscription.'

"Had a man the size of a mountain spoken to me in that arrogant style in America, I should have indignantly resented it ; but where I then was it seemed best to swallow and digest it as well as I could. So in reply to the offensive arrogance of this banker, I said I should be *honored* by his subscription to the ' Birds of America.' ' Sir,' he said, ' I never sign my name to any subscription list, but you may send in your work and I will pay for a copy of it. Gentlemen, I am busy, I wish you goodmorning.' We were busy men, too, and so bowing respectfully, we retired, pretty well satisfied with the small slice of his opulence which our labor was likely to obtain.

" A few days afterwards I sent the first volume of my work half bound, and all the numbers besides, then published. On seeing them we were told that he ordered the bearer to take them to his house, which was done directly. Number after number was sent and delivered to the Baron, and after eight or ten months my son made out his account and sent it by Mr. Havell, my engraver, to his banking-house. The Baron looked at it with amazement, and cried out, 'What, a hundred pounds for birds! Why, sir, I will give you five pounds, and not a farthing more!' Representations were made to him of the magnificence and expense of the work, and how pleased his Baroness and wealthy children would be to have a copy; but the great financier was unrelenting. The copy of the work was actually sent back to Mr. Havell's shop, and as I found that instituting legal proceedings against him would cost more than it would come to, I kept the work, and afterwards sold it to a man with less money but a nobler heart. What a distance there is between two such men as the Baron Rothschild of London and the merchant of Savannah!"

Audubon remained in London looking after his work and interests there until the fall of 1834, when he went with his family to Edinburgh, where he hired a house and spent a year and a half.

There is no journal describing the incidents of that residence in Edinburgh; and it is probable that Audubon did not keep a daily record there at all. The journal was written chiefly with the design to keep his wife and children informed of all his doings when he was absent from them, and they were with him during this period, and so there was no necessity for it; and secondly, he was daily so busily occupied with other writing that he had no time to devote to that, or even his favorite work of drawing and painting. Some idea of the amount of his labor at that period may be inferred from the fact, that the introduction to volume second of his "American Ornitholog-

ical Biography," which contains five hundred and eighty-
five pages of closely-printed matter, is dated December
1st, 1834; and that in just one year from that date, the
third volume, containing six hundred and thirty-eight
pages, was printed and published.

In the summer of 1836 he removed his family to
London, and having settled them in Wimpole-street, Cav-
endish Square, he again made his preparations to return
to America, and make the excursion into some of the
southern States, which he had been contemplating for a
long time, for the purpose of increasing the new varieties
of birds for his great work.

July 30, 1836, the journal begins, saying that Mr.
Audubon left London that day with his son John for
Portsmouth, where he arrived the next day, and took pas-
sage on board the packet-ship Gladiator, for New York.

"*August* 1. Somewhat before the setting of the sun
we went on board, ate and drank, and laid ourselves down
in those floating catacombs, vulgarly called berths. When
the Gladiator left St. Katharine's Dock she had on our
account two hundred and sixty live birds, three dogs received as a present from our noble friend, the Earl of
Derby, and a brace of tailless cats from our friend George
Thackery, D. D., provost of King's College. They had
been on board several days, and seemed not to have received much care, and some of the birds had died. But
the dogs and some of the birds were alive, and crossed
the Atlantic safely.

August 2. About five this afternoon the anchor was
apeak, several new persons were hoisted on deck, our
sails were spread to the breeze, and the Gladiator
smoothly glided on her course. The passengers were a
fair average as to agreeability, and among them was Wal-
lack the actor, who amused us with some admirable puns.
The voyage was prosperous, and the time passed pleas-

antly, until we approached the banks of Newfoundland, when we began to fear and dream of icebergs and disasters; but none came, and the Gladiator kept her course steadily onward, when, just five weeks after leaving England, in the afternoon, the highlands of Neversink were discovered, about fifteen miles distant. The welcome news of our approach to the Hook thrilled my heart with ecstacy.

"The evening was dark, and no pilot in sight; and rockets were thrown up from the ship to attract one. This soon brought one alongside, and an American tar leaped on board. Oh! my Lucy, thou knowest me, but I cried like a child, and when our anchor was dropped, and rested on the ground of America, thy poor husband laid himself down on his knees, and there thanked God for His preservation of myself and our dear son.

"All was now bustle and mutual congratulations; our commander was praised for his skill by some, and others praised his whiskey punch, which the waiters handed about, and the night was nearly spent in revelry; but John and myself retired at two o'clock.

"It rained hard and blew all night, but I slept comfortably, and awoke the next morning at four o'clock as happy as any man could be three thousand miles from the dearest friend he had on earth. As a gleam of daylight appeared, my eyes searched through the hazy atmosphere to catch a glimpse of the land, and gradually Staten Island opened on my view; then the boat of the custom-house officer appeared, and soon he boarded us, arranged the sailors and passengers on deck, and called their names. Then followed breakfast, and soon another boat with a yellow flag flying landed the health officer, and there being no sickness on board, myself and John returned to Staten Island in the doctor's boat, and were taken by the steamer Hercules to the city, where we were welcomed by relatives and friends."

17

CHAPTER XXXIII.

SEPTEMBER 13. Audubon remained in New York until this date, obtained two subscribers and the promise of two more, visited the markets and found a few specimens of new birds, and left for Philadelphia; paid three dollars for his fare on the steamer Swan, and fifty cents for his dinner; "but," the journal adds, "we were too thick to thrive. I could get only a piece of bread and butter, snatched from the table at a favorable moment.

"I found the country through which we passed greatly improved, dotted with new buildings, and the Delaware River seemed to me handsomer than ever. I reached Philadelphia at six o'clock P. M., and found Dr. Harlan waiting for me on the wharf, and he took me in his carriage to his hospitable house, where I was happy in the presence of his amiable wife and interesting son.

"*September* 24. Went to the market with Dr. Harlan at five o'clock this morning; certainly this market is the finest one in America. The flesh, fish, fruit and vegetables, and fowls, are abundant, and about fifty per cent. less than in New York; where, in fact, much of the produce of Pennsylvania and New Jersey is taken now-a-days for sale—even game! I bought two soras (cedar birds) for forty cents, that in New York would have brought eighty cents. After breakfast went to the Academy of Natural Sciences, met Dr. Pickering, and had a great treat in looking over and handling the rare collection made by Nuttall and Townsend in their excursion on and over the Rocky Mountains. It belongs to the Academy, which assisted the travellers with funds to prosecute their journey ; it contains about forty new species of birds, and its value cannot be described."

Audubon spent only a day or two in Philadelphia, saw his old friends there, was present at one of the meetings of the Academy, obtained a few new birds, and returned to New York. Mr. Edward Harris, his old friend, called to see him ; and when he was told of the new species of birds obtained by Townsend, "offered to give me five hundred dollars towards purchasing them. Is not this a noble generosity to show for the love of science? "

" *Boston, September* 20, 1836. I came here from New York, *viâ* the steamer Massachusetts and the Providence Railroad, for seven dollars, which included supper and breakfast. There were three hundred passengers, and among them several persons known to me. A thick fog compelled the steamer to anchor at midnight; in the morning our sail up the bay to Providence was like a fairy dream. Nature looked so beautiful and grand, and so congenial to my feelings, that I wanted nothing but thy dear self here, Lucy, to complete my happiness. The locomotive pulled us from Providence to Boston at the rate of fifteen miles an hour ; we arrived at four P. M. ; a cart took my trunk, and sitting myself by the side of the owner, we drove to the house of my friend Dr. George C. Shattuck. The family soon gathered for tea, and I was now happy, and after talking for a while I retired to rest in the same room and bed where John and I slept after our return from Labrador."

Audubon spent several days in Boston, visiting the

public institutions and his friends, among whom he mentions Mr. Everett, Dr. Bowditch, Dr. Gould, and Mr. David, "where I found Maria D——, now Mrs. Motley, as handsome as ever, and her husband not far short of seven feet high."

"*September* 20. Went to the market and bought a fine pigeon hawk which is now found in Massachusetts, for two cents. Visited Roxbury with Thomas Brewer, a young man of much ornithological taste, to see his collection of skins and eggs: found his mother and family very kind and obliging, and received from him seven eggs of such species as I have not. Returned and visited David Eckley, the great salmon fisher : promised to breakfast with him to-morrow.

"*September* 21. Went to market and bought a female blue teal for ten cents. Called on Dr. Storer, and heard that our learned friend Thomas Nuttall had just returned from California. I sent Mr. Brewer after him, and waited with impatience for a sight of the great traveller, whom we admired so much when we were in this fine city. In he came, Lucy, the very same Thomas Nuttall, and in a few minutes we discussed a considerable portion of his travels, adventures, and happy return to this land of happiness. He promised to obtain me duplicates of all the species he had brought for the Academy at Philadelphia, and to breakfast with us to-morrow, and we parted as we have before, friends, bent on the promotion of the science we study.

"*September* 22. This has been a day of days with me ; Nuttall breakfasted with us, and related much of his journey on the Pacific, and presented me with five new species of birds obtained by himself, and which are named after him. One of Dr. Shattuck's students drove me in the doctor's gig to call on Governor Everett, who received me as kindly as ever ; and then to the house of Presi-

dent Tinnay of Harvard University, where I saw his family ; and then to Judge Story's. Then crossing the country, we drove to Col. J. H. Perkins', and on the way I
bought a fine male white-headed eagle for five dollars.
On my return I learned that at a meeting of the Nationa'
History Society yesterday a resolution was passed to
subscribe for my work.

"Dr. Bowditch advised me to go to Salem, and with
his usual anxiety to promote the welfare of every one,
gave me letters to Messrs. Peabody and Cleveland of that
place, requesting them to interest themselves to get the
Athenæum to subscribe for my work.

"*Salem, Mass., September* 23, 1836. Rose early this
morning, and made preparations to go to Salem ; and at
seven o'clock I was in the stage, rolling out of Boston towards this beautiful and quiet village. The road might
be called semi-aquatic, as it passes over bridges and embankments through salt marshes of great extent, bounded
by wooded hills towards the sea, and distant ones inland.
We stopped a few moments at Shoemaker Town (Lynn),
where I paid one dollar for my fare, and reached this
place afterwards at half-past ten.

"I was put down at the Lafayette Hotel, and soon
made my way to Mr. Cleveland's office ; he received me
kindly, and invited me to dine with him at one o'clock.
I took some back numbers of my 'Birds of America' to
Miss Burley, and found her as good, amiable, and generous as ever ; and she at once interested herself to make
the object of my visit successful. Called on Dr. Pierson,
to whom I had a letter, and met a most congenial spirit,
a man of talents and agreeable manners. The Doctor
went with me to see several persons likely to be interested
in my work ; and I then called alone on a Miss Sitsby, a
beautiful 'blue,' seven or eight seasons beyond her teens,
and very wealthy. Blues do not knit socks, or put on

buttons when needed ; they may do for the parlor, but not for the kitchen. Although she has the eyes of a gazelle, and capital teeth, I soon discovered that she would be no help to me : when I mentioned subscription, it seemed to fall on her ears, not as the cadence of the wood thrush or mocking-bird does in mine, but as a shower-bath in cold January. Ornithology seemed to be a thing for which she had no taste ; she said, however, 'I will suggest your wish to my father, sir, and give you an answer to-morrow morning.' She showed me some valuable pictures, especially one by that king of Spanish painters, Murillo, representing himself, and gun, and dog ; the Spanish dress and *tout ensemble* brought to my mind my imaginations respecting Gil Blas. At last I bowed, she curtsied, and so the interview ended.

" *September* 23. 'Chemin faisant.' I met the curator of the Natural History Society of Salem, and gladly accepted his invitation to examine the young collection of that new-born institution, and there I had the good fortune to find one egg of the American bittern.

" It was now nearly one o'clock, and going to the office of Mr. Cleveland, I found him waiting to conduct me to his house. We soon entered it and his dining-room, where I saw three lovely daughters and a manly-looking youth, their brother. The dinner was excellent, and served simply ; but as our future bread and butter depend on my exertions, I excused myself as soon as convenient, and went to Dr. Pierson, who accompanied me to call on some gentlemen who would be likely to take an interest in my work."

Audubon returned on September 24th to Boston, and remained there one week, visiting his friends and looking for subscribers to his Birds.

" *September* 27. The citizens are all excitement ; guns are firing, flags flying, and troops parading, and John

Quincy Adams is delivering a eulogy on the late President Madison. The mayor of Boston did me the honor to invite me to join in the procession, but I am no politician, and declined.

"I dined with Dr. B. C. Green, President of the Natural History Society, with President Quincy, Isaac P. Davis, and Mr. Nuttall. In the evening Dr. Shattuck finished the subscription list of the society, by presenting me to his lady, who subscribed for one-tenth, and the Dr. then put down his son George's name for one-twentieth, making in his own family one-fourth of the whole, or two hundred and twenty dollars, for which he gave me his cheque. Without the assistance of this generous man, it is more than probable that the society never would have had a copy of the 'Birds of America.'

"*September* 29. Mr. Isaac P. Davis called to invite me to spend the evening at his house, and to meet Daniel Webster. I met him at the Historical Society, where I saw the last epaulets worn by our glorious Washington, many of his MS. letters, and the coat Benjamin Franklin wore at the French and English courts.

"Mr. Davis has some fine pictures, which I enjoyed looking at, and after a while Daniel Webster came, and we welcomed each other as friends indeed, and after the usual compliments on such occasions we had much conversation respecting my publication. He told me he thought it likely a copyright of our great work might be secured to you and our children. We took tea, talked of ornithology and ornithologists; he promised to send me some specimens of birds, and finished by subscribing to my work. I feel proud, Lucy, to have that great man's name on our list, and pray God to grant him a long life and a happy one. Mr. Webster gave me the following note :—

"' I take this mode of commending Mr. Audubon to

any friends of mine he may meet in his journey to the west. I have not only great respect for Mr. Audubon's scientific pursuits, but entertain for him personally much esteem and hearty good wishes.

" ' Daniel Webster.' "

After obtaining a few more subscribers, and delivering some numbers of his birds to former ones, Audubon bid adieu to his friends in Boston, and returned to New York.

" *October* 10. Had a pleasant call from Washington Irving, and promise of valuable letters to Van Buren and others in Washington. After dinner went to Mr. Cooper's, the naturalist, who at first with some reluctance showed me his birds. We talked of ornithology, and he gave me five pairs of sylvia, and promised to see me to-morrow.

" *October* 11. At nine o'clock Mr. Cooper came to see me, and examined the third volume of our work. He remained two hours, conversing on our favorite study, and I was pleased to find him more generously inclined to forward my views after he had seen the new species given me by Nuttall. I went to his house with him, and he gave me several rare and valuable specimens, and promised me a list of the birds found by himself and Ward in the State of New York.

" *October* 13. Called on Inman the painter; saw the sketch intended for thee, but found it not at all like thy dear self. He says he makes twelve thousand dollars a year by his work. Dined at Samuel Swartwout's, a grand dinner, with Mr. Fox, the British minister, Mr. Buckhead, secretary of legation, Thomas Moore, the poet, Judge Parish, and sundry others. Mrs. S. and her daughter were present; all went off in good style, and I greatly enjoyed myself. Several of the party invited me to visit them at their residences, and General Stewart of Baltimore invited me to make his house my home when I visited there.

"*October* 15. We have packed our trunks and sent them on board the steamer, and leave this evening for Philadelphia. The weather has been perfectly serene and beautiful, and the Bay of New York never looked more magnificent and grand to me. We soon glided across its smooth surface and entered the narrow and sinuous Raritan ; and as I saw flocks of ducks winging their way southward, I felt happy in the thought that I should ere long follow them to their winter abode. We soon reached the railroad, and crossed to the Delaware, and before six o'clock reached the house of my good friend Dr. Harlan."

Here Audubon saw many of his old friends, visited the public works and institutions, and obtained a few new species of birds. After speaking of the great changes in that city, the journal says : "Passed poor Alexander Wilson's school-house, and heaved a sigh. Alas, poor Wilson ! would that I could once more speak to thee, and listen to thy voice. When I was a youth, the woods stood unmolested here, looking wild and fresh as if just from the Creator's hands ; but now hundreds of streets cross them, and thousands of houses and millions of diverse improvements occupy their places: Barton's Garden is the only place which is unchanged. I walked in the same silent mood I enjoyed on the same spot when first I visited the present owner of it, the descendant of William Barton, the generous friend of Wilson."

On November 8th, Audubon arrived in Washington. Among many other letters of introduction given to people in Washington, and transcribed carefully in the journal, are the two following from Washington Irving.

MY DEAR SIR,

This letter will be handed to you by our distinguished naturalist, Mr. J. J. Audubon. To one so purely devoted as yourself to anything liberal and enlightened, I know I need say nothing in recommendation of Audubon and his works; he himself will best inform you of his views in visiting Washington, and I am sure you will do anything in your power to promote them.

He has heretofore received facilities on the part of the government, in prosecuting his researches along our coast, by giving him conveyance in our revenue cutters and other public vessels. I trust similar civilities will be extended to him, and that he will receive all aid and countenance in his excursions by land.

The splendid works of Mr. Audubon, on the sale of which he depends for the remuneration of a life of labor, and for provision for his family, necessarily, from the magnificence of its execution, is put beyond the means of most individuals. It must depend therefore on public institutions for its chief sale. As it is a national work, and highly creditable to the nation, it appears to me that it is particularly deserving of national patronage. Why cannot the departments of Washington furnish themselves with copies, to be deposited in their libraries or archives? Think of these suggestions, and, if you approve of them, act accordingly.

> With the highest esteem and regard,
>
> I am, dear sir, Yours very truly,
>
> WASHINGTON IRVING.

BENJAMIN F. BUTLER, Esq.,
Attorney-General of the United States, Washington, D. C.

TARRYTOWN, *October*, 19, 1836.

MY DEAR SIR,

I take pleasure in introducing to you our distinguished and most meritorious countryman, J. J. Audubon, whose splendid work on American ornithology must of course be well known to you. That work, while it reflects such great credit on our country, and contributes so largely to 'the advancement of one of the most delightful departments of science, is likely, from the extreme expense attendant upon it, to repay but poorly the indefatigable labor of a lifetime. The high price necessarily put on the copies of Mr. Audubon's magnificent work places it beyond the means of the generality of private individuals. It is entitled therefore to the especial countenance of our libraries and various other public institutions. It appears to me, that the different departments in Washington ought each to have a copy deposited in their libraries or archives. Should you be of the same opinion you might be of great advantage in promoting such a measure."

Reference is then made to the assistance rendered to Audubon by the revenue cutters and public vessels, and the letter continues :—

" I trust similar facilities will still be extended to him ; in fact, as his undertakings are of a decidedly national character, and conducive of great national benefit, the most liberal encouragement in every respect ought to be shown to him on the part of our government.

I am, my dear Sir,

• Your attached Friend,

WASHINGTON IRVING."

" The Honorable Martin Van Buren."

" *November* 8. Called on Colonel Abert, who received me with his wonted civility, promised to assist me in all my desires, and walked with me to the President's, to present my letters. There we found Colonel Donaldson and Mr. Earle, both nephews, I believe, of General Jackson, and in a moment I was in the presence of this famed man, and had shaken his hand. He read Mr. Swartwout's letter twice, with apparent care, and having finished, said, ' Mr. Audubon, I will do all in my power to serve you, but the Seminole war will, I fear, prevent you from having a cutter; however, as we shall have a committee at twelve o'clock, we will consider this, and give you an answer to-morrow.' The general looked well, he was smoking his pipe, and gave his letters to Colonel Donaldson, who read them attentively, and as I left the room he followed us, and we talked to him respecting the subscription of the different departments. I like this man and his manners; and I gave him the letters of the Duke of Sussex and the Governor of the Hudson Bay Company to read, and went to see Colonel Earle, who is engaged in painting General Jackson's portrait.

"Colonel Abert then took me to Mr. Woodbury, Secretary of the Treasury, who received me very politely, and after reading my letters to him, promised me the use of the cutter. The subscription was also broached to him, but nothing decisive was said; and so we passed over to Mr. Butler's office, who is a young man. He read Washington Irving's letter, laid it down, and began a long talk about his talents, and after a while came round to my business; saying, that the government allows so little money to the departments, that he did not think it probable that their subscription could be obtained without a law to that effect from Congress. This opinion was anything but gratifying; but he made many courteous promises to bring the matter before the next Congress, and I bid him adieu, hoping for the best.

"Called on Mr. John S. Mechan, librarian to Congress, and found him among his books. After some agreeable conversation respecting his work and my own, he asked me to dine with him to-day, and to-morrow to visit the curious chimney-sweep possessing curious knowl-

edge of the Sora Rail, a water bird vulgarly supposed to
bury itself in the mud and lie torpid all winter. Accompanied by John, I took tea at Colonel Abert's, and then
walked to Mr. Woodbury's, to spend the evening. There
the Colonel handed me an order for the use of the cutter,
and informed me that the Treasury Department had subscribed for one copy of our work. Mr. Woodbury also
offered us a passage to Charleston in the cutter, Campbell, about to sail for that station. The vessel is only
fifty-five tons ; and although Columbus crossed the Atlantic in search of a new world in a barque yet more frail,
and although thy husband would go to the world's end
after new birds on land, he would not like to go from Baltimore on such a vessel carrying three guns and twenty-
one men. I am now hoping soon to see again the breeding grounds of the wood ibis, and the roseate spoonbill.

"*November* 9. To-day Colonel Abert called with me
on Secretary Dickinson, of the navy. He received us
frankly, talked of the great naval and scientific expedition
round the world now proposed to be fitted out by the
government. To my surprise and delight his views co-
incided exactly with mine. He said he was opposed to
frigates and large ships, and to great numbers of extra
sailors on such an enterprise, when only peaceful objects
were. intended. We differed, however, respecting the
number of the scientific corps : he was for a few, and I
for duplicates *at least;* because in case of death or illness
some of the departments of science would suffer if only
one person were sent. He asked me respecting the fit-
ness of certain persons whose names had been mentioned
for the voyage. But I gave evasive answers, not wishing
to speak of individuals who are both unfit and inimical to
me to this very day. Most sincerely do I hope that this,
our first great national expedition, may succeed, not only
for the sake of science, but also for the honor of our be-

loved country. I strongly recommended George Lehman, my former assistant, as he is in every respect one of the best general draftsmen I know. I also recommended the son of Dr. McMurtrie (how strange, you will say), and young Reynolds, of Boston, as an entomologist.

"The secretary paid me some compliments, and told me the moment the expedition had been mentioned he had thought of me, and Nuttall, and Pickering—a glorious trio! I wish to God that I were young once more; how delighted I would be to go in such company, learned men and dear friends. He also took us to his house, to see the work published by the French government, of the voyages of L'Athalie, and presented by that government to our own. It is a magnificent production, quite French, and quite perfect. I next took John to the White House, which is the vulgar name for the President's residence. Mr. Earle introduced us, and John saw for the first time that extraordinary man, General Andrew Jackson. He was very kind, and as soon as he heard that we intended departing to-morrow evening for Charleston, invited us to dine with him *en famille.* At the named hour we went to the White House, and were taken into a room, where the President soon joined us. I sat close to him; we spoke of olden times, and touched slightly on politics, and I found him very averse to the cause of the Texans. We talked also of the great naval expedition, European affairs, &c. Dinner being announced, we went to the table with his two nephews, Colonel Donaldson being in the truest sense of the word a gentleman. The dinner was what might be called plain and substantial in England; I dined from a fine young turkey, shot within twenty miles of Washington. The general drank no wine, but his health was drunk by us more than once; and he ate very moderately, his last dish consisting of bread and milk. As soon as dinner was over we returned to the first room, where was a picture, ay, a picture of our great Washington, painted by Stewart, when in the prime of his age and art. This picture, Lucy, was found during the war with England by Mrs. Madison, who had it cut out of the frame, rolled up, and removed to the country, as Mr. Earle told me. It is the only picture in the whole house —so much for precious republican economy. Coffee was handed, and soon after John and I left, bidding adieu to a man who has done much good and much evil to our country."

CHAPTER XXXIV.

Excursion South—Starts in Cutter for Galveston Bay, Texas—Bara-
taria Bay—Great Hunting Excursion with a Squatter—Notes in
Texas—Wretched Population—Buffalo Bayou—Texan Capitol
and Houses of Congress—Reaches New Orleans—Charleston—In
England Again—Literary Labors—Back to America.

CHARLESTON, S. C., November 17, 1836. We
arrived here last evening, after an irksome and fa-
tiguing journey, and seemingly very slowly performed, in my anxiety to reach a resting place, where
friendship and love would combine to render our time
happy, and the prosecution of our labor pleasant. We were
hungry, thirsty, and dusty as ever two men could be ; but
we found our dear friends all well, tears of joy ran from
their eyes, and we embraced the whole of them as if born
from one mother. John Bachman was absent from home,
but returned at nine from his presidential chair at the
Philosophical Society."

Audubon passed the winter of 1836 and 1837 in
Charleston, with his friend Dr. Bachman, making occa-
sional excursions into the country, to the neighboring sea
islands, and also to Savannah and Florida. But the
Seminole war then raging, he was unable to penetrate
much into the interior. This winter he began the studies
in Natural History, which led to the publication of the
Quadrupeds of North America, in connection with Dr.
Bachman. Early in the spring, he appears to have left
Charleston, in the revenue cutter Campbell, Captain
Coste, for explorations in the Gulf of Mexico. The journals are lost which describe the interval between the 17th
of January and the 1st of April, under which latter date

we read that Audubon, his son John, and Mr. Edward
Harris, came down from New Orleans, in the cutter, to
the S. W. pass, provisioned for two months, and bound
westwardly from the mouth of the Mississippi to Galveston Bay, in Texas, with the intention of exploring the
harbors, keys, and bayous along the coast, and to examine
the habits of the birds of this region, and to search for
new species, to furnish materials for the completion of the
fourth volume of the "Birds of America."

"*April* 3. We were joined this day by Captain W. B.
G. Taylor, of the Revenue service, with the schooner
Crusader, twelve tons burden, two guns, and four men
completely equipped for our expedition, with a supply of
seines, cast-nets, and other fishing-tackle."

The same day they entered Barataria Bay, and began
operations, and found a variety of birds which are described in the journal. The next day the party landed,
and made excursions in different directions, in pursuit of
birds and eggs. Among the spoils of game taken this
day, were two white pelicans, of which there was an
abundance.

The next three weeks were spent in visiting the
islands and bayous, and penetrating some of the rivers
which pour into the latter that occur along the coast between the Mississippi river and Galveston. The parties
landed at various points, and found many new species of
birds, and other interesting objects of Natural History.
In the course of one of these rambles, Audubon made
the acquaintance of a squatter, a great hunter, and with
whom he went on an excursion, which is thus described :—

"I entered the squatter's cabin, and immediately
opened a conversation with him respecting the situation
of the swamp and its natural productions. He told me
he thought it the very place I ought to visit, spoke of the

game which it contained, and pointed to some bear and deer skins, adding, that the individuals to which they had belonged formed but a small portion of the number of those animals which he had shot within it. My heart swelled with delight; and on asking if he would accompany me through the great swamp, and allow me to become an inmate of his humble but hospitable mansion, I was gratified to find that he cordially assented to all my proposals, so I immediately unstrapped my drawing materials, laid up my gun, and sat down to partake of the homely but wholesome fare intended for the supper of the squatter, his wife, and his two sons. The quietness of the evening seemed in perfect accordance with the gentle demeanour of the family. The wife and children, I more than once thought, seemed to look upon me as a strange sort of person, going about, as I told them I was, in search of birds and plants; and were I here to relate the many questions which they put to me, in return for those which I addressed to them, the catalogue would occupy several pages. The husband, a native of Connecticut, had heard of the existence of such men as myself, both in our own country and abroad, and seemed greatly pleased to have me under his roof. Supper over, I asked my kind host what had induced him to remove to this wild and solitary spot. 'The people are growing too numerous now to thrive in New England,' was his answer. I thought of the state of some parts of Europe, and calculating the denseness of their population, compared with that of New England, exclaimed to myself, how much more difficult must it be for men to thrive in those populous countries! The conversation then changed, and the squatter, his sons and myself spoke of hunting and fishing, until at length tired, we laid ourselves down on pallets of bear-skins. and reposed in peace on the floor of the only apartment of which the hut consisted. Day dawned, and the squatter's call to his hogs, which, being almost in a wild state, were suffered to seek the greater portion of their food in the woods, awakened me. Being ready dressed, I was not long in joining him. The hogs and their young came grunting at the well-known call of their owner, who threw them a few ears of corn, and counted them, but told me that for some weeks their number had been greatly diminished by the ravages committed upon them by a large panther, by which name the cougar is designated in America, and that the ravenous animal did not content himself with the flesh of his pigs, but now and then carried off one of his calves, notwithstanding the many attempts he had made to shoot it. The 'painter,' as he sometimes called it, had on several occasions robbed him of a dead deer; and to these exploits, the squatter added several remarkable feats of audacity which it had performed, to give me an idea of the formidable character of the beast. Delighted by his description, I offered to assist him in destroying the enemy; at which he was highly pleased, but assured me that unless some of his neighbors should join us with their dogs and his own, the attempt would prove fruitless. Soon after, mounting a horse, he went off to his neighbors, several of whom lived at a distance of some miles, and appointed a day of meeting. The hunters accordingly made their appearance one fine morning at the door of the cabin, just as the sun was emerging from beneath the horizon. They were five in number, and fully equipped for the chase, being mounted on horses, which in some parts of Europe might appear sorry nags, but which in strength, speed, and bottom, are better fitted for pursuing a cougar or a bear through woods and morasses than any in their country. A pack of large ugly curs was already engaged in making acquaintance with those of the squatter. He and myself mounted his two

best horses, whilst his sons were bestriding others of inferior quality. Few words were uttered by the party
until we had reached the edge of the swamp, where it
was agreed that all should disperse, and seek for the
fresh track of the 'painter,' it being previously settled
that the discoverer should blow his horn, and remain on
the spot until the rest should join him. In less than an
hour the sound of the horn was clearly heard, and sticking close to the squatter, off we went through the thick
woods, guided only by the now-and-then repeated call of
the distant huntsman. We soon reached the spot, and in
a short time the rest of the party came up. The best
dog was sent forward to track the cougar, and in a few
moments the whole pack was observed diligently trailing
and bearing in their course for the interior of the swamp.
The rifles were immediately put in trim, and the party
followed the dogs at separate distances, but in sight of
each other, determined to shoot at no other game than
the panther.

"The dogs soon began to mouth, and suddenly
quickened their pace. My companions concluded that
the beast was on the ground, and putting our horses to a
gentle gallop, we followed the curs, guided by their
voices. The noise of the dogs increased, when all of a
sudden their mode of barking became altered, and the
squatter urging me to push on, told me that the beast
was *treed*, by which he meant, that it had got upon some
low branch of a large tree to rest for a few moments, and
that should we not succeed in shooting him when thus
situated, we might expect a long chase of it. As we approached the spot, we all by degrees united into a body,
but on seeing the dogs at the foot of a large tree, separated again, and galloped off to surround it. Each hunter now moved with caution, holding his gun ready, and
allowing the bridle to dangle on the neck of his horse, as

it advanced slowly towards the dogs. A shot from one of the party was heard, on which the cougar was seen to leap to the ground, and bound off with such velocity as to show that he was very unwilling to stand our fire longer. The dogs set off in pursuit with great eagerness, and a deafening cry. The hunter who had fired came up and said that his ball had hit the monster, and had probably broken one of his forelegs, near the shoulder, the only place at which he could aim. A slight trail of blood was discovered on the ground, but the curs proceeded at such a rate that we merely noticed this, and put spurs to our horses, which galloped on towards the centre of the swamp. One bayou was crossed, then another still larger and more muddy, but the dogs were brushing forward, and as the horses began to pant at a furious rate, we judged it expedient to leave them, and advance on foot. These determined hunters knew that the cougar, being wounded, would shortly ascend another tree, where in all probability he would remain for a considerable time, and that it would be easy to follow the track of the dogs. We dismounted, took off the saddles and bridles, set the bells attached to the horses' necks at liberty to jingle, hoppled the animals, and left them to shift for themselves. Now, kind reader, follow the group marching through the swamp, crossing muddy pools, and making the best of their way over fallen trees, and amongst the tangled rushes that now and then covered acres of ground. If you are a hunter yourself all this will appear nothing to you ; but if crowded assemblies of 'beauty and fashion,' or the quiet enjoyment of your 'pleasure grounds' delight you, I must mend my pen before I attempt to give you an idea of the pleasure felt on such an expedition. After marching for a couple of hours, we again heard the dogs : each of us pressed forward, elated at the thought of terminating the career of the cougar. Some of the dogs were heard whining, although the greater number barked vehemently. We felt assured that the cougar was treed, and that he would rest for some time to recover from his fatigue. As we came up to the dogs, we discovered the ferocious animal lying across a large branch, close to the trunk of a cotton-wood tree. His broad breast lay towards us ; his eyes were at one time bent on us and again on the dogs beneath and around him ; one of his fore-legs hung loosely by his side, and he lay crouched, with his ears lowered close to his head, as if he thought he might remain undiscovered. Three balls were fired at him at a given signal, on which he sprang a few feet from the branch, and tumbled headlong to the ground, attacked on all sides by the enraged curs. The infuriated cougar fought with desperate valour ; but the squatter advancing in front of the party, and, almost in the midst of the dogs, shot him immediately behind and beneath the left shoulder. The cougar writhed for a moment in agony, and in another lay dead. The sun was now sinking in the west. Two of the hunters separated from the rest to procure venison, whilst the squatter's sons were ordered to make the best of their way home, to be ready to feed the hogs in the morning. The rest of the party agreed to camp on the spot. The cougar was despoiled of his skin, and the carcass left to the hungry dogs. Whilst engaged in preparing our camp, we heard the report of a gun, and soon after one of our hunters returned with a small deer. A fire was lighted, and each hunter displayed his 'pone' of bread, along with a flask of whisky. The deer was skinned in a trice, and slices placed on sticks before the fire. These materials afforded us an excellent meal ; and as the night grew darker, stories and songs went round, until my companions, fatigued, laid themselves down, close under the smoke of the fire, and soon fell asleep. I walked for

some minutes round the camp to contemplate the beauties
of that Nature, from which I have certainly derived my
greatest pleasure. I thought of the occurrences of the
day ; and glancing my eye around, remarked the singular
effects produced by the phosphorescent qualities of the
large decayed trunks, which lay in all directions around
me. How easy, I thought, would it be for the confused
and agitated mind of a person bewildered in a swamp
like this to imagine in each of these luminous masses
some wondrous and fearful being, the very sight of which
might make the hair stand erect on his head! The
thought of being myself placed in such a predicament
burst upon my mind ; and I hastened to join my companions, beside whom I laid me down and slept, assured
that no enemy would approach us without first rousing
the dogs, which were growling in fierce dispute over the
remains of the cougar. At daybreak we left our camp,
the squatter bearing on his shoulders the skin of the late
destroyer of his stock, and retraced our steps until we
found our horses, which had not strayed far from the
place where we left them. These we soon saddled ; and
jogging along in a direct course, guided by the sun, con-
gratulating each other on the destruction of so formidable
a neighbour as the panther had been, we soon arrived at
my host's cabin. The five neighbours partook of such
refreshments as the house could afford, and, dispersing,
returned to their homes, leaving me to follow my favorite
pursuits.

"*April* 24. Arrived in Galveston Bay this afternoon,
having had a fine run from Atchafalaya Bay. We were
soon boarded by officers from the Texan vessels in the
harbor, who informed us that two days before the U. S.
sloop of war Natchez fell in with the Mexican squadron
off the harbor of Velasco, captured the brig Urea, and
ran two other vessels ashore ; another report says they

sunk another ship, and went in pursuit of the squadron. These vessels were taken as pirates—the fleet having sailed from Vera Cruz without being provisioned, had been plundering American vessels on the coast. There is also a rumor that the Texan schooner Independence has been captured by a Mexican cruiser. The American schooner Flash was driven ashore a few days since by a Mexican cruiser, and now lies on the beach at the lower end of the island.

"*April* 25. A heavy gale blew all night, and this morning the thermometer in the cabin is 63°, and thousands of birds, arrested by the storm in their migration northward, are seen hovering around our vessels, and hiding in the grass, and some struggling in the water, completely exhausted.

"We had a visit this morning from the Secretary of the Texan navy, Mr. C. Rhodes Fisher, who breakfasted with us. He appeared to be a well-informed man, and talked a great deal about the infant republic, and then left us for the seat of government at Houston, seventy miles distant, on the steamer Yellow Stone, accompanied by Captains Casto and Taylor, taking the Crusader in tow.

"*April* 26. Went ashore at Galveston. The only objects we saw of interest were the Mexican prisoners; they are used as slaves; made to carry wood and water, and cut grass for the horses, and such work; it is said that some are made to draw the plow. They all appear to be of delicate frame and constitution, but are not dejected in appearance.

"*April* 27. We were off at an early hour for the island, two miles distant; we waded nearly all the distance, so very shallow and filled with sandbanks is this famous Bay. The men made a large fire to keep off the mosquitoes, which were annoying enough for even me. Besides many interesting birds, we found a new species of rattlesnake, with a double row of fangs on each side of its jaws.

"*April* 28. We went on a deer hunt on Galveston Island, where these animals are abundant; we saw about twenty-five, and killed four.

"*April* 29. John took a view of the rough village of Galveston, with the Lucida. We found much company on board on our return to the vessel, among whom was a contractor for beef for the army; he was from Connecticut, and has a family residing near the famous battle-ground of San Jacinto. He promised me some skulls of Mexicans, and some plants, for he is bumped with botanical bumps somewhere.

"*Galveston Bay, May* 1, 1837. I was much fatigued this morning, and the muscles of my legs were swelled until they were purple, so that I could not go on shore. The musk-rat is the only small quadruped found here, and the common house-rat has not yet reached this part of the world.

"*May* 2. Went ashore on Galveston Island, and landed on a point where the Texan garrison is quartered. We passed through the troops, and observed the miserable condition of the whole concern; huts made of grass, and a few sticks or sods cut into square pieces composed the buildings of the poor Mexican prisoners, which, half clad, and half naked, strolled about in a state of apparent inactivity. We passed two sentinels under arms, very unlike soldiers in appearance. The whole population seemed both indolent and reckless. We saw a few fowls, one pig, and a dog, which appeared to be all the domestic animals in the encampment. We saw only three women, who were Mexican prisoners. The soldiers' huts are placed in irregular rows, and at unequal distances; a dirty blanket or coarse rag hangs over the entrance in place of a door. No windows were seen, except in one or two cabins occupied by Texan officers and soldiers. A dozen or more long guns lay about on the sand, and one of about the same calibre was mounted. There was a look-out house fronting and commanding the entrance to the harbor, and at the point where the three channels meet there were four guns mounted of smaller calibre. We readily observed that not much nicety prevailed among the Mexican prisoners, and we learned that their habits were as filthy as their persons. We also found a few beautiful flowers, and among them one which Harris and I at once nicknamed the Texan daisy ; and we gathered a number of their seeds, hoping to make them flourish elsewhere. On the top of one of the huts we saw a badly-stuffed skin of a grey or black wolf, of the same species as I have seen on the Missouri. When we were returning to the vessel we discovered a large sword-fish grounded on one of the sandbanks, and after a sharp contest killed her with our guns. In what we took to be a continuation of the stomach of this fish, we found four young ones, and in another part resembling the stomach six more were packed, all of them alive and wriggling about as soon as they were thrown on the sand. It would be a fact worth solving to know if these fish carry their young like viviparous reptiles. The young were about thirty inches in length, and minute sharp teeth were already formed.

" *May* 8. To-day we hoisted anchor, bound to Houston : after grounding a few times, we reached Red Fish Bar, distant twelve miles, where we found several American schooners and one brig. It blew hard all night, and we were uncomfortable.

" *May* 9. We left Red Fish Bar with the Crusader and the gig, and with a fair wind proceeded rapidly, and soon came up to the new-born town of New Washington, owned mostly by Mr. Swartwout the collector of customs of New York. We passed several plantations ; and the general appearance of the country was more pleasing than otherwise. About noon we entered Buffalo Bayou, at the mouth of the San Jacinto River, and opposite the famous battle-ground of the same name. Proceeding smoothly up the bayou, we saw abundance of game, and at the distance of some twenty miles stopped at the house of a Mr. Batterson. This bayou is usually sluggish, deep, and bordered on both sides with a strip of woods not exceeding a mile in depth. The banks have a gentle slope, and the soil on its shores is good ; but the prairies in the rear are cold and generally wet, bored by innumerable cray-fish, destitute of clover, but covered with coarse grass and weeds, with a sight here and there of a grove of timber, rising from a bed of cold, wet clay.

It rained and lightened, and we passed the night at Mr. Batterson's. The tenth it rained again, but we pushed on to Houston, and arrived there wet and hungry. The rain had swollen the water in the bayou, and increased the current so that we were eight hours rowing twelve miles.

"*May* 15. We landed at Houston, the capital of Texas, drenched to the skin, and were kindly received on board the steamer Yellow Stone, Captain West, who gave us his state-room to change our clothes, and furnished us refreshments and dinner.

"'The Buffalo Bayou had risen about six feet, and the neighboring prairies were partly covered with water : there was a wild and desolate look cast on the surrounding scenery. We had already passed two little girls encamped on the bank of the bayou, under the cover of a few clap-boards, cooking a scanty meal ; shanties, cargoes of hogsheads, barrels, &c., were spread about the landing ; and Indians drunk and hallooing were stumbling about in the mud in every direction. These poor beings had come here to enter into a treaty proposed by the whites ; many of them were young and well looking, and with far less decorations than I have seen before on such occasions. The chief of the tribe is an old and corpulent man.

" We walked towards the President's house, accompanied by the secretary of the navy, and as soon as we rose above the bank, we saw before us a level of far-extending prairie, destitute of timber, and rather poor soil. Houses half finished, and most of them without roofs, tents, and a liberty pole, with the capitol, were all exhibited to our view at once. We approached the President's mansion, however, wading through water above our ankles. This abode of President Houston is a small loghouse, consisting of two rooms, and a passage through, after the Southern fashion. The moment we stepped over the threshold, on the right hand of the passage we found ourselves ushered into what in other countries would be called the ante-chamber ; the ground floor however was muddy and filthy, a large fire was burning, a small table covered with paper and writing materials, was in the centre, camp-beds, trunks, and different materials, were strewed around the room. We were at once presented to several members of the cabinet, some of whom bore the stamp of men of intellectual ability, simple though bold, in their general appearance. Here we were presented to Mr. Crawford, an agent of the British Minister to Mexico, who has come here on some secret mission.

" The President was engaged in the opposite room on national business, and we could not see him for some time. Meanwhile we amused ourselves by walking to the capitol, which was yet without a roof, and the floors, benches, and tables of both houses of Congress were as well saturated with water as our clothes had been in the morning. Being invited by one of the great men of the

place to enter a booth to take a drink of grog with him,
we did so ; but I was rather surprised that he offered his
name, instead of the cash to the bar-keeper.

"We first caught sight of President Houston as he
walked from one of the grog-shops, where he had been to
prevent the sale of ardent spirits. He was on his way to
his house, and wore a large gray coarse hat ; and the
bulk of his figure reminded me of the appearance of General Hopkins of Virginia, for like him he is upwards of
six feet high, and strong in proportion. But I observed
a scowl in the expression of his eyes, that was forbidding
and disagreeable. We reached his abode before him, but
he soon came, and we were presented to his excellency.
He was dressed in a fancy velvet coat, and trowsers
trimmed with broad gold lace ; around his neck was tied
a cravat somewhat in the style of seventy-six. He received us kindly, was desirous of retaining us for awhile,
and offered us every facility within his power. He at
once removed us from the ante-room to his private cham-
ber, which by the way was not much cleaner than the
former. We were severally introduced by him to the
different members of his cabinet and staff, and at once
asked to drink grog with him, which we did, wishing success to his new republic. Our talk was short ; but the
impression which was made on my mind at the time by
himself, his officers, and his place of abode, can never be
forgotten.

"We returned to our boat through a melee of Indians
and blackguards of all sorts. In giving a last glance back
we once more noticed a number of horses rambling about
the grounds, or tied beneath the few trees that have been
spared by the axe. We also saw a liberty pole, erected
on the anniversary of the battle of San Jacinto, on the
twenty-first of last April, and were informed that a brave
tar, who rigged the Texan flag on that occasion, had been

personally rewarded by President Houston, with a town
lot, a doubloon, and the privilege of keeping a ferry
across the Buffalo Bayou at the town, where the bayou
forks diverge in opposite directions.

" *May* 16. Departed for New Washington, where we
received kind attentions from Col. James Morgan ; crossed San Jacinto Bay to the Campbell, and the next day
dropped down to Galveston.

" *May* 18. Left the bar of Galveston, having on board
Mr. Crawford, British Consul at Tampico, and a Mr. Allen of New Orleans.

" *May* 24. Arrived at the S. W. Pass, and proceeded
to the Balize, and thence to New Orleans, where we arrived in three days.

" *New Orleans, May* 28. Breakfast with Ex-Governor
Roman and his delightful family, with Mr. Edward Harris."

Audubon suffered greatly during this expedition to
Texas, and lost twelve pounds in weight. He found New
Orleans nearly deserted, and dull, and the weather op-
pressively hot and disagreeable.

" *May* 31. We bid adieu to our New Orleans friends,
leaving in their care for shipment our collections, clothing, and dog Dash for Mr. W. Bakewell. Harris went up
the river, and we crossed to Mobile in the steamer Swan,
paying fare twelve dollars each, and making the trip of
one hundred and fifty miles in twenty-one hours. If New
Orleans appeared prostrated, Mobile, seemed quite dead.
We left in the afternoon for Stockton, Alabama, forty-five
miles distant, where we were placed in a cart, and tumbled and tossed for one hundred and sixty-five miles to
Montgomery ; fare twenty-three dollars each, miserable
road and rascally fare. At Montgomery we took the
mail coach, and were much relieved ; fare to Columbus
twenty-six dollars each. Our travelling companions were

without interest, the weather was suffocating, and the
roads dirty and very rough ; we made but three miles an
hour for the whole journey, walking up the hills, and galloping down them to Augusta, and paying a fare of thirteen dollars and fifty cents each, and thence by rail to
Charleston for six dollars and seventy-five cents each,
distance one hundred and thirty-six miles, and making
eight and a half days from New Orleans."

After remaining a short time in Charleston, Audubon
returned to New York, and in the latter part of the summer sailed for Liverpool. After landing there and greeting his friends, he went to London, taking the new
drawings he had made to Mr. Havell, and then, after
spending a few days with his family, departed for Edinburgh. There he went diligently to work in preparing
the fourth volume of his "Ornithological Biography" for
the press. The work held him until the Fall of 1838, and
was published in November of that year. His family
now joined him in Edinburgh, and the winter was devoted to finishing the drawings for the completion of his
great volume on the "Birds of America," and also to preparing his fifth volume of the "Ornithological Biography,"
which was published in Edinburgh in May, 1839.

In the Fall of 1839 he returned to America with his
family, and settled in New York city, there to spend the
remainder of his days. But he did not intend to be idle,
but immediately began preparing his last great ornithological work, which is a copy of his original English publication, with the figures reduced and lithographed, in
seven octavo volumes. The first volume was published
within a little more than a year after his return, two more
volumes appeared in 1842, another in 1843, while he was
absent on his expedition to the Yellow-stone River, and
the last one after his return.

Besides all this labor, he devoted occasional spare

hours to improving and increasing the drawings of the quadrupeds of North America, which he had begun some years before in connection with the Rev. John Bachman of South Carolina.

The early pages of the journal show that Audubon had been anxious to visit the great interior valley of the Mississippi and the Rocky Mountains ever since he began to devote his time exclusively to ornithological research ; and twenty years before his return to America, he had traced out the course he wished to go. During all those years of unremitting toil, the desire and hope of seeing the Great Plains and the Rocky Mountains never deserted him. But after he had resolved to complete and publish his work on the Quadrupeds of America, he felt that it would be impossible for him to do it satisfactorily until he had seen with his own eyes the buffaloes of the plains, and other animals of those regions whose habits had never been described.

Much of his earthly work was done ; the infirmities of age were stealing upon him ; and the Journal often alludes to the fact that his physical powers were not equal to his mental longings. He seems to have determined therefore to make an effort to accomplish the long-cherished desire of his heart, to look on the magnificent scenery of the prairies and mountains of the West, and to gather the materials for his Quadrupeds, which he knew would probably be his last work on earth. So as soon as he had settled his family at Minnie's land, where he invested all the money he had made by his publications up to that date, he prepared at once for his last great journey, the grandest of all his journeys, to the Western Wilderness.

CHAPTER XXXV.

Excursion to the Great Western Prairies—Up the Missouri—River Pictures—Indians—The Mandans—The "Medicine Lodge"—Ricaree Indians—Fort Union—Arrival at Yellow Stone River—Buffalo Hunt—Small-Pox among the Indians—Return to New York.

MARCH 11, 1843. Left New York this morning with my son Victor, on an expedition to the Yellow-stone River, and regions adjacent and unknown, undertaken for the sake of our work on the ' Quadrupeds of North America,' and arrived in Philadelphia late in the evening.

"As we landed, a tall, robust-looking man, tapped me on the shoulder, whom I discovered in the dim darkness to be my friend, Jedediah Irish, of the Great Pine Swamp. I also met my friend, Edward Harris, who, besides John G. Bell, Isaac Sprague, and Lewis Squires, were to accompany me on this long campaign. The next morning we left for Baltimore, and Victor returned home to Minnie's Land."

There are four folio volumes of MS. containing a detailed account of that whole journey, which lasted about eight months. But as most of the journals were inwoven into the three volumes on the "Quadrupeds of North America," which were published in the years 1846, 1851, and 1854, we give but an outline of the journey, and the gleanings of such incidents as were not used in those volumes.

Audubon and his party crossed the Alleghany Moun-
18*

tains to Wheeling, went from there to Cincinnati and St Louis by steamers, where they arrived on the 28th of March. From thence they ascended the Missouri River to Jefferson City, the capital of the State, about one hundred and seventy miles from St. Louis. There they saw nothing worthy of note except the State House and Penitentiary.

The town was a poor-looking place, and the neighboring country poor and broken; but the public buildings commanded a fine view up and down the river. "Yesterday," says the Journal, "we passed many long lines of elevated banks, ornamented by stupendous rocks of limestone, having many curious holes, into which we saw vultures and eagles enter towards evening.

"As we ascended the river the strength of the current increased, and in some places we stemmed it with difficulty; and near Willow Islands it ran so rapidly, that we found ourselves going down stream, and were compelled to make fast to the shore.

"*March* 30. As we sail along the shores, I notice young willows and cotton-trees half submerged by the freshet, waving to and fro, as if trembling at the rage of the rushing water, and in fear of being destroyed by it; and it really seemed as if the mighty current was going to overwhelm in its rage all that the Creator had lavished on its luxuriant shore. The banks are falling in and taking thousands of trees, and the current is bearing them away from the places where they have stood and grown for ages. It is an awful exemplification of the course of Nature, where all is conflict between life and death.

"*March* 31. As we sail up the river, squatters and planters are seen abandoning their dwellings, which the water is overflowing, and making towards the highlands, that are from one to four miles inland. We passed two houses filled with women and children, entirely surrounded by water; the whole place was under water, and all around was a picture of utter desolation. The men had gone to seek assistance, and I was grieved that our captain did not offer to render them any; the banks kept on falling in, and precipitating majestic trees into the devouring current.

"*May* 2. We are now three hundred and eighty miles from St. Louis, and are landing freight and traders for Santa Fé.

"*May* 3. We reached Fort Leavenworth this morning. The garrison here is on a fine elevation, commanding a good view of the river above and below for a considerable distance. Leaving here, we entered the real Indian country on the west side of the river; for the State of Missouri, by the purchase of the Platte River country, continues for two hundred and fifty miles farther; and here only are any settlements of white inhabitants.

"*May* 5. After grounding on sand-bars, and contending against head-winds and currents, we reached the Black Snake Hills settlement, which is a delightful site for a populous city that will be here some fifty years hence. The hills are two hundred feet above the level of the river, and slope down gently on the opposite side to the beautiful prairies, that extend over thousands of acres of the richest land imaginable. Here the general aspect of the river greatly changes; it becomes more crooked, and filled with naked sand-bars, from which the wind whirls the sand in every direction. We passed through a narrow and swift chute, which, in the time of high water, must be extremely difficult to ascend.

"*May* 6. We fastened our boat to the edge of a beautiful prairie, to land freight and passengers. Here eighty Indians came to visit us, some on foot and some on horseback, generally riding double, on skins and Spanish saddles; some squaws rode, and rode well. We landed some Indians here, who came as passengers with us, and I noticed that when they joined their relatives and friends, they neither shook hands nor exchanged any congratulations. I saw no emotion, nothing to corroborate Mr. Catlin's views of savage life.

"When the boat started, all these Indians followed us along the shore, running on foot, and galloping on horseback to keep up with us. When we approached the next landing, I saw some of these poor creatures perched on the neighboring banks, while others crowded down to our landing-place. They belonged to the Iowa and Fox Indians : the two tribes number about twelve thousand, and their country extends for seventy miles up the river.

"*May* 8. To-day we passed the boundary of Missouri, and the country consists of prairies extending back to the inland hills.

"*May* 9. This evening we arrived at the famous settlement of Belle Vue, where the Indian agent, or customhouse officer, as he might better be called, resides. Here a large pack of rascally-looking, dirty, and half-starved Indians awaited our arrival ; and here we paid for five cords of wood, with five tin cups of sugar, and three cups of coffee, all worth twenty-five cents at St. Louis. And we saw here the first plowed ground we had seen since leaving the settlements near St. Louis.

"*May* 10. Arrived at Fort Croghan, named after an old friend of that name, with whom I hunted raccoons on his father's plantation in Kentucky, thirty-five years before. His father and mine were well acquainted, and fought together with the great General Washington and Lafayette, in the Revolutionary War against 'Merry England.' The parade-ground here had been four feet under water in the late freshet.

"*May* 11. The officers of this post last July were nearly destitute of provisions, and they sent off twenty dragoons and twenty Indians on a buffalo hunt; and within eighty miles of the fort, they killed fifty-one buffaloes, one hundred and four deer, and ten elks.

"We were told that the Pottowatomie Indians were formerly a warlike people, but recently their enemies, the Sioux, have frequently killed them, when they met them on hunting excursions, and that they have become quite cowardly, which is a great change in their character.

"We cast off our lines from the shore at twelve o'clock, and by sunset reached the Council Bluffs, where the river-bed is utterly changed, though that called the Old Missouri is now visible. These Bluffs rise from a truly beautiful bank about forty feet above the river, and slope down into as beautiful a prairie to the hills in the rear, which render the scenery very fine and very remarkable.

"*May* 12. We have arrived at the most crooked part of the river yet seen, the shores on both sides are lower, the hills are more distant, and the intervening plains are more or less covered with water. We passed the Blackbird Hills, where a famous Indian chief of this name was buried, and his horse buried alive with him at his request.

"*May* 13. To-day we passed some beautiful bluffs, composed of a fine white sandstone, of a soft texture, but beautiful to the eye, and covered with cedars. We saw also many fine prairies; and the bottom lands appeared to be of an extremely rich soil. Indians hailed us along the shore, but no notice was taken of them: they followed us to the next landing, and boarded us; but our captain hates them, and they go away without a chew of tobacco, and I pity the poor creatures with all my heart.

"This evening we came to the Burial-ground Bluff; so called by the ever-memorable expedition of Lewis and Clark, because here they buried Sergeant Floyd, as they were on the way to the Pacific Ocean across the Rocky Mountains. The prairies are now more frequent and more elevated ; and we have seen more evergreens to-day than in the two preceding weeks.

"We have entered the mouth of the Big Sioux River, which is a clear stream, abounding with fish : on one of its branches is found the famous red clay of which the Indians make their calumets. We saw on the banks of the river several Indian canoe frames, formed of bent sticks made into a circle, the edges fastened together by a long pole or stick, with another one in the bottom, holding the frame like the inner keel of a boat. Outside of this frame the Indians stretch a buffalo-skin with the hair on, and it is said to make a safe boat to convey two or three persons, even when the current is rapid. Here, as well as on the shores of the Mississippi and Missouri, the land along the river banks is higher than further inland ; tangled brushwood and tall reeds grow along the margins, while the prairies abound with mud and muddy water. Willows are plenty, and the general aspect of the country is pleasing.

"*May* 16. Came to an Indian log-cabin, which had a fence enclosure around it. Passed several dead buffaloes floating down the stream. A few hundred miles above here the river is confined between high steep bluffs, many of them nearly perpendicular, and impossible for the buffalo to climb : when they have leaped or fallen down these, they try to ascend them or swim to the opposite shore, which is equally difficult ; but unable to ascend them, they fall back time and again until they are exhausted ; and at last, getting into the current, are borne away and drowned : hundreds thus perish every year, and their swollen and putrid bodies have been seen floating as low down as St. Louis. The Indians along shore watch for these carcasses, and no matter how putrid they are, if the 'hump' is fat, they drag them ashore and cut it out for food."

Many pages of the Journal describe the daily incidents of the next few weeks, in which the party were slowly pushing their way up the river, and making occasional excursions from the boat in pursuit of the objects of their journey. The country was inundated in many places, and from the tops of the neighboring hills it is represented as about equally divided between land and water ; on the eastern side of the river the flat prairies had become great lakes. And they noticed that the floating ice had cut the trees on the banks of the river as high as the shoulder of a man. Barges from above passed them, bringing down the spoils of the hunters, and one from St. Pierre had ten thousand buffalo-robes on board. The men reported that the country above was filled with buffaloes, and the shores of the river were covered with the dead bodies of old and young ones.

As they ascended they found the river more shallow in some parts, and again opening into broad places like great lagoons. They passed Vermillion River, a small stream running out of muddy banks filled with willows. At a landing near there, a man told them that a hunter had recently killed an Indian chief near the foot of the Rocky Mountains, and that it would be dangerous for white men to visit that region.

They also found on the river's bank the plant called the white apple, much used by the Indians for food, which they dry, pound, and make into mash. It is more of a potato than apple, for it grows six inches under ground, is about the size of a hen's egg, covered with a dark-brown woody hard skin the sixteenth of an inch thick : the fruit is easily drawn from the skin, and is of a whitish color. It has no flowers, the roots were woody, leaves ovate and attached in fives. When dry, the apple is hard as wood, and has to be pounded for use.

The country grew poorer the farther they ascended

the river ; and the bluffs showed traces of iron, sulphur, and magnesia.

"*May* 28. We now see buffaloes every day: they are extremely poor, but they are sporting among themselves, beating and tearing up the earth. They have roads to the river, along which they go and come for water.

"To-day some Indians hailed us from the shore, and when the captain refused to stop for them, they began firing at us with rifles: several of the balls hit our vessel, and one passed through the pantaloons of a Scotch passenger. These rascals belong to a party of the Santeo tribe, which range across the country from the Missouri to the Mississippi River.

"*May* 29. This morning a party of Indians came on board the boat at a landing-place, and it was some hours before we could get rid of these beggars by trade. Both banks of the river were covered with buffaloes, as far as the eye could see ; and although many of them were near the water, they did not move until we were close upon them, and those at the distance of half a mile kept on quietly grazing. We saw several buffaloes and one large gray wolf swimming across the river only a short distance ahead of us.

"'The prairies appear better now, and the grass looks green, and the poor buffaloes, of which we have seen more than two thousand this morning, will soon grow fat.

"*May* 30. We reached Fort George this morning, which is called 'The Station of the Opposition Line.' We saw some Indians, and a few lodges on the edge of the prairie, and sundry bales of buffalo-robes were taken aboard. Major Hamilton is acting Indian Agent during the absence of Major Crisp. We are a long way beyond the reach of civil law, and they settle disputes here with sword and pistol. The major pointed to an island where

Mr. ——, a New Yorker belonging to the opposition line, killed two white men recently, and shot two others, who were miserable miscreants.

"We are yet thirty miles below St. Pierre, and do not expect to reach it until to-morrow. Indians were seen along both sides of the river: many trade at this post and at St. Pierre; at the latter I am told there are five hundred lodges. The Indian dogs resemble the wolves so much that I should readily mistake the one for the other were I to meet them in the woods.

"Soon after leaving Fort George, we sounded and found only three and a half feet of water, and the captain gave orders to 'tie up,' and we started on a walk for St. Pierre. On reaching the camp, we found it a strongly-built low log-cabin, in which was a Mr. Cutting, who had met my son Victor in Cuba. Yesterday, while he was on a buffalo-hunt, a cow hooked his horse, and threw him about twenty feet, and injured his ankle. This he thought remarkable, as the cow had not been wounded. He showed me a petrified head of a wolf, which I discovered to be not a wolf's but a beaver's. There were fifteen lodges here, and a great number of squaws and half-breed children; and these are accounted for by the fact that every clerk and agent has his Indian wife as she is called.

June 1. The party had arrived at St. Pierre, and from thence the Omega, in which they had made their trip, was expected to return to St. Louis. The Journal continues: "I am somewhat surprised that Sprague asked me to allow him to return in the Omega. I told him he was at liberty to do so of course if he desired it, though it will cause me double the labor I expected to have. Had I known this before leaving New York, I could have had any number of young artists, who would have been glad to have accompanied and remained with me to the end of the expedition.

" *June* 2. We have left St Pierre and are going on up the river, deeper and deeper in the wilderness. We passed the Cheyenne River, which is quite a large stream."

Audubon hired a hunter named Alexis Bouibarde at St. Pierre to accompany him to the Yellow-stone River, and thus describes him : ' He is a first-rate hunter, powerfully built, is a half-breed, and wears his hair loose about his head and shoulders, as I formerly did. . . .'

" I am now astonished at the poverty of the bluffs we pass : there are no more of the beautiful limestone formations which we saw below, but they all appear to be poor and crumbling clay, dry and hard now, but soft and sticky whenever it rains. The cedars in the ravines, which below were fine and thrifty, are generally dead or dying, probably owing to their long inundation. To-day we have made sixty miles ; the country is much poorer than any we have passed below, and the sand-bars are much more intricate.

" *June* 4. The country we have seen to-day is a little better than what we saw yesterday. We passed the old Riccaree village, where General Ashley was beaten by the Indians, and lost eighteen of his men, with the very weapons and ammunition he had sold the Indians, against the remonstrances of his friends and the interpreter. It is said that it proved fortunate for him, for he turned his course in another direction, where he purchased one hundred packs of beaver-skins for a mere song.

" Passed the Square Hills, so called because they are more level and less rounded than the majority of the hills. From the boat the country looks as if we were getting above the line of vegetation ; the flowers are scarce, and the oaks have hardly any leaves on them. We are now sixteen miles below the Mandan village, and hope to reach there to-morrow.

" *June* 7. We are now at Fort Clark and the Mandan
village ; a salute was fired from the Fort in honor of our
arrival, and we answered it. The Fort is situated on a
high bank, quite a hill ; here the Mandans have their
mud huts, which are not very picturesque, and a few enclosed fields, where they grow corn, pumpkins, and
beans. We saw more Indians here than at any other
place since we left St. Louis ; they have about one hundred huts, and they resemble the potato winter-houses
in our Southern and Eastern States. As we approached
the shore, every article that could be taken conveniently
was removed from the deck and put under lock and key,
and all the cabin-doors were closed. The captain told
me that last year, when he was here, the Indians stole
his cap, shot-pouch, hone, and such like things. These people appeared very miserable ; as we approached the landing they stood shivering in the rain, wrapped in buffalo-
robes and red blankets ; some of them were curiously be-
smeared with mud. They came on board, and several
shook me by the hand, but their hands had a clammi-
ness that was quite repulsive ; their legs were naked, feet
covered with mud ; and they stared at me with apparent
curiosity because of my long beard, which also attracted
the Indians at St. Pierre. It is estimated that there are
three thousand men, women, and children, who cram
themselves into these miserable houses in winter ; they
are said to be the *ne plus ultra* of thieves, and most of the
women are destitute of virtue.

" At the request of the interpreter, one of the Indians
took me into the village to see the Medicine lodge. I
followed my guide through mud and mire to a large hut,
built like all the rest, but measuring twenty-three yards
in diameter, with a large square opening in the centre of
the roof six feet long by four feet in width. We entered
this curiosity-shop by pushing aside an elk-skin stretched

on four sticks. Among the medicines I saw a number of calabooses, eight or ten skulls of otters, two large buffalo-skulls with the horns on, some sticks, and other magical implements, with the use of which no one but a great Medicine is acquainted. There lay crouched on the floor a lousy Indian, wrapped in a dirty blanket, with nothing but his head sticking out : the guide spoke to him, but he made no reply. At the foot of one of the props that support this large house lay a parcel, which I took for a bundle of buffalo-robes, but directly it moved, and the emaciated body of a poor blind Indian crept out of it ; he was shrivelled, and the guide made signs that he was about to die. We shook hands with him, and he pressed mine, as if glad of the sympathy of even a stranger ; he had a pipe and tobacco-box, and soon lay down again. As we left this abode of mysteries, I told the guide I was anxious to see the inside of one of their common dwellings, and he led us through the mud to his own lodge, which had an entrance like the other. All the lodges have a sort of portico that leads to the door, and on the top of most of them I observed skulls of buffaloes. This lodge contained the wife and children of the guide and another man, whom I took for his son-in-law ; all these, except the man, were in the outer lodge, squatting on the ground, and the children skulked out of the way as we approached. Nearly equi-distant from each other were a kind of berths, raised two feet above the ground, made of leather, and with square apertures for the sleepers. The man of whom I have spoken was lying down in one of these. I walked up to him, and after disturbing his seemingly happy slumbers, shook his hand, and he made signs for me to sit down. I did so, and he arose, and squatted himself near us ; and taking a large spoon made of a buffalo's horn, handed it to a young girl, who brought a large wooden bowl filled with pemmican mixed with corn and some other stuff; I ate a mouthful of it, and found it quite palatable. Both lodges were alike dirty with water and mud; but I am told that in dry times they are kept more cleanly. A round shallow hole was in the centre, and a chain hung from above near the fire, and on this they hang their meat and cook. On leaving I gave our guide a small piece of tobacco, and he seemed well pleased, but followed us on board the boat : and as he passed my room, and saw my specimens of stuffed animals and birds, manifested some curiosity to see them.

"The general appearance of the fort is poor, and the country around is overgrown with the weed called ' family quarter.' And I saw nothing here corresponding to the poetical descriptions of writers who make their clay-banks enchanted castles, and this wretched savage life a thing to be desired, even by the most happy civilized men. These Indians are mostly Ricarees ; they are tall, lank, and redder than most others that I have seen, but they are all miserable-looking and dirty. They occupy the village where the powerful tribe of Mandans once lived, but which were swept away by the dreadful scourge of the small-pox ; only twelve or fifteen families survive, and they removed three miles up the river.

" *June* 8. To-day we have had a famous Indian council on board our boat. It consisted of thirty-four Indians of the first class ; they squatted on their rumps on both sides of our long cabin, and received refreshments of coffee and ship-bread, and I assisted in doing this duty ; and a box of tobacco was then opened and placed on the table ; the captain then made a speech to them, and one Indian interpreted it to the others. They frequently expressed their approbation by grunting, and were evidently much pleased. Two Indians came in, dressed in blue uniforms, with epaulettes on their shoulders, and feathers in their caps, and with ornamented mocassins and leggings : these were the braves of the tribe, and they did not grunt or shake hands with any of us.

" As soon as the tobacco was distributed, the whole company rose simultaneously, and we shook hands with each one, and gladly bid them good riddance. The two braves waited until all the others were on shore, and then retired majestically as they had entered, not shaking hands even with the captain, who had entertained them and made the speech. This is a ceremony which takes place yearly as the Company's boat goes up. Each Indian carried away about two pounds of tobacco. Two of the Indians who distributed the tobacco, and were of the highest rank, were nearly naked, and one by my side had only a clout and one legging on. They are now all gone but one, who goes with us to the Yellow-stone River.

"This morning the thermometer stood at 37°. We have passed the village of the poor Mandans, and of the Grosventres, to-day: the latter is cut off from the river by an enormous sand-bar, now covered with willows. We saw a few Indian corn-fields ; the plants were sickly-looking, and about two inches high. The prairies are very extensive, stretching away to the hills, and there are deep ravines in them filled with water sufficiently saline to be used by the Indians for seasoning their food.

" *June* 13. *Fort Union.* Thermometer 53°, 72°, 68°. We arrived here to-day, and have made the shortest trip from St. Louis on record, just forty-eight days. We have landed our effects, and established ourselves in a log-house, with one room and one window, intending to spend three weeks here before launching into the wilderness.

" There has been no ardent spirits sold here for two years, and the result is, the Indians are more peaceable than formerly. On the plains we saw the mounds where many Indians had been buried who died here of the small-pox. There were apparently several bodies in each mound, and a buffalo's skull was put over each one : this relic has some superstitious value in the estimation of these poor ignorant creatures.

"Our boat has been thronged with these dirty savages ever since we fastened her to the landing, and it is with difficulty we can keep them from our rooms. All around the village the filth is beyond description, and the sights daily seen will not bear recording ; they have dispelled all the romance of Indian life I ever had, and I am satisfied that all the poetry about Indians is contained in books ; there certainly is none in their wild life in the woods. The captain of our vessel told me that on his first trip here in a steamer, the Indians called her a great ' Medicine,' supposed that he fed her with whisky, and asked, how much he gave her at a time. To which he replied, ' a whole barrel.' "

It appears that the Omega did not, as originally intended, return from St. Pierre, but kept on to the Yellowstone River. There Audubon bade the captain adieu, with much regret, and wrote him a complimentary letter, which all the passengers signed.

"*June* 14. To-day, Mr. Chouteau, and Mr. Murray, a Scotchman, arrived from the Crow Indian nation. They told me the snow was yet three feet deep, and quite abundant near the mountains. I learned to-day, that the Prince of Canino, with his secretary and bird-stuffer, occupied the rooms I now have, for two months."

The interval between this and the 20th of June was employed in various excursions and exciting hunts after the buffalo.

June 20. A stormy day prevents out-door excursions, and Audubon employs it in recording in his Journal an account of the ravages of the small-pox among the Indians, which he received from an eye-witness. The Mandans and Ricarees suffered most, though many Sioux and Blackfoot Indians perished with them.

" Early in the spring of 1837 the steamer Assiniboine arrived at Fort Clark, with several cases of small-pox on board.   There an Indian stole a blanket belonging to a watchman on the boat, who was then at the point of death, and took it away to sow the seeds of this disease among his tribe, which caused his own death and the death of thousands of his nation. When it was known that he had taken it, a benevolent person on the boat went to one of the chiefs, told him the fatal consequences which would follow, and offered to give a new blanket and a reward besides if he would have it returned ; but suspicion, fear, or shame prevented the man from giving it up, and the pestilence broke out and began to spread among the Mandans at first, to which nation the thief belonged.

" Most of the Indians were distant eighty miles at that time killing buffaloes and preparing their winter food ; and the whites sent an express begging them not to re- turn to their villages, and telling them what would be the fatal consequences. The Indians sent back word that their corn was suffering to be worked, and that they would return and face the danger, which they thought was fab- ulous. Word was again sent them that certain destruc- tion would attend their return ; but it was all in vain, come back they would, and come back they did, and the plague began in its most malignant form, their habits and im- proper food making them a ready prey, and a few hours sometimes terminating the loathsome disease by death.

" The Mandans were enraged because at first it was confined to them, and they supposed the whites had caused it, and saved themselves and the Ricarees from the pestilence ; and they threatened the lives of all the former, supposing they had a medicine to prevent it, which they would not give them. But by-and-by Rica rees and whites died also; the disease increased in malignity—hundreds died daily, and their bodies were thrown beneath the bluffs, and created an intolerable stench, which added to its fatality. Men shot each other when they found they were attacked : one man killed his wife and children, and then loaded his gun and placing the muzzle in his mouth, touched the trigger with his toe and blew out his own brains. One young chief made his friends dig a grave for him, and putting on his war-robes, he tottered out to it, singing his death-song, and jumping in, cut his body nearly in two with a knife, and was buried there ; and others committed suicide after they were attacked, rather than die of the loathsome disease. The annals of pestilence do not furnish another such example of horrors, or where the mortality was so great in proportion to the population : of the once powerful tribe of Mandans only twenty-seven persons remained, and one hundred and fifty thousand persons perished, and the details are too horrible to relate. Added to this, the few whites were alarmed lest the Indians should massacre them as the cause of the evil. One influential chief attempted to instigate the Indians to kill all the whites, but he was himself seized and died before his plans were matured ; but in his last moments he confessed his wickedness, and expressed sorrow for it, and begged that his body might be laid before the gate of the fort until it was buried, with the superstitious belief that if this were done the white man would always think of him and forgive his meditated crime."

The Journal is taken up until the end of July with narratives of almost daily excursions in various directions in search of all kinds of game. Many anecdotes are related of the Indians, their mode of life, habits, and peculiarities, most of which have been described by other writers, and hardly merit repeating here. Audubon found this region so rich in novelties of the kinds he had come in pursuit of, that he was anxious that some of the young men of his party should remain through the winter. "My regrets that I cannot remain myself are beyond description, and I now sadly regret that I promised you all that I would return home this Fall.

"*August* 3. We observed yesterday for the first time that the atmosphere wore the hazy appearance of the Indian summer. The nights and mornings are cool, and summer clothes are beginning to be uncomfortable."

This seems to have caused Audubon to begin to think seriously of turning his course homeward. The exposure and hardships he had encountered in this long journey, and on his hunting excursions, had made an impression on his health.

He began to find that his age was telling on his energy, and that he could not endure hardships as formerly.

The Journal continues for ten days more, then abruptly ends, from which we conclude that the writer began to make preparations to return home. He reached New York early in October, 1843.

CHAPTER XXXVI.

HEN Audubon returned from his expedition to the Western Prairies, he was between sixty and seventy years old, yet he began at once to work with his usual energy and diligence. In a little more than two years appeared the first volume of the "Quadrupeds of North America;" and this was almost his last work. The second volume was prepared mostly by his sons Victor and John, and was published the year their father died.

The interval of about three years which passed between the time of Audubon's return from the West and the period when his mind began to fail, was a short and sweet twilight to his adventurous career. His habits were simple. Rising almost with the sun, he proceeded to the woods to view his feathered favorites till the hour at which the family usually breakfasted, except when he had drawing to do, when he sat closely to his work. After breakfast he drew till noon and then took a long walk. At nine in the evening he generally retired.

He was now an old man, and the fire which had burned so steadily in his heart was going out gradually. Yet there are but few things in his life more interesting and beautiful than the tranquil happiness he enjoyed in the bosom of his family, with his two sons and their children

under the same roof, in the short interval between his return from his last earthly expedition, and the time when
his sight and mind began to grow dim, until mental
gloaming settled on him, before the night of death came.
He was very fond of his grandchildren, and used often to
take them on his knees and sing to them amusing French
songs that he had learned in France when he was a boy.

His loss of sight was quite peculiar in its character.
His glasses enabled him to see objects and to read, long
after his eye was unable to find a focus on the canvas.
The first day he found that he could not adjust his glasses so as to enable him to work at the accustomed distance from the object before him, he drooped.   Silent,
patient sorrow filled his broken heart.   From that time
his wife never left him ; she read to him, walked with him,
and toward the last she fed him.   Bread and milk were
his breakfast and supper, and at noon he ate a little fish
or game, never having eaten animal food if he could
avoid it.

He took great pleasure in listening to reading and to
the singing of one of his daughters-in-law, who had an
exceedingly sweet and well cultivated voice.   He found
much amusement too in walking through his grounds.
His home, on the banks of the Hudson, was just such
a spot as a lover of Nature would choose for his closing
days.   It was a piece of land extending from where the
Tenth Avenne now is, to the river ; it contained twenty-
four acres, about half of which was high level ground, the
other half a gradual slope to the river.   There was no
Hudson River Railroad then, and the waves dashed
upon the sandy beach near the house.   From a little pro-
jection called The Point, there was a beautiful and extensive view down the river ; the view towards the north was
obstructed by Fort Washington.   On the hill were corn-
fields and a peach orchard, and two or three little cot-

tages where the men lived who worked on the place. In the valley were the dwelling-house, a large barn and stable, and a little cottage where the coachman lived with his wife and family. A beautiful little stream ran through the grounds, widening out in one place into a pond, at the lower end of which was a waterfall five or six feet high and very broad; the water fell into another pond, and below that the brook divided into two parts, forming a little island. Just before the brook reached the river, it was crossed by a picturesque bridge which was quite an ornament to the scene. This estate he named Minnie's Land, Minnie, the Scotch word for mother, being the name by which he generally addressed his wife, and to her he left the whole of it at his death.

About half of this beautiful place forms what is now called "Audubon Park," so named by some of the gentlemen, friends of the Audubon family, who resided there after the naturalist's death; but no one would recognize the spot; where formerly there was but one dwelling-house, there are now about forty. The portion called Audubon Park contains above a dozen houses, and though it is still very beautiful, there is of course a total change in the arrangement of the grounds, and the very house Mr. Audubon lived in, is so metamorphosed that he would scarcely recognize it for the one that once was his.

Rufus W. Griswold, who visited Audubon in 1846, gives us the following picture of his home: "The house was simple and unpretending in its architecture, and beautifully embowered amid elms and oaks. Several graceful fawns, and a noble elk, were stalking in the shade of the trees, apparently unconscious of the presence of a few dogs, and not caring for the numerous turkeys, geese, and other domestic animals that gabbled and screamed around them. Nor did my own approach startle the wild, beautiful creatures, that seemed as docile as any of their tame companions.

"'Is the master at home?'" I asked of a pretty maidservant, who answered my tap at the door; and who, after informing me that he was, led me into a room on the left side of the broad hall. It was not, however, a parlor, or an ordinary reception-room that I entered, but evidently a room for work. In one corner stood a painter's easel, with a half finished sketch of a beaver on the paper; in the other lay the skin of an American panther. The antlers of elks hung upon the walls; stuffed birds of every description of gay plumage ornamented the mantel-piece; and exquisite drawings of field-mice, orioles, and woodpeckers, were scattered promiscuously in other parts of the room, across one end of which a long rude table was stretched to hold artist materials, scraps of drawing-paper, and immense folio volumes, filled with delicious paintings of birds taken in their native haunts.

"'This,' said I to myself, 'is the studio of the naturalist,' but hardly had the thought escaped me, when the master himself made his appearance. He was a tall, thin man, with a high arched and serene forehead, and a bright penetrating gray eye; his white locks fell in clusters upon his shoulders, but were the only signs of age, for his form was erect, and his step as light as that of a deer. The expression of his face was sharp, but noble and commanding, and there was something in it, partly derived from the aquiline nose and partly from the shutting of the mouth, which made you think of the imperial eagle.

"His greeting, as he entered, was at once frank and cordial, and showed you the sincere, true man. 'How kind it is,' he said, with a slight French accent, and in a pensive tone, 'to come to see me; and how wise, too, to leave that crazy city!' He then shook me warmly by the hand. 'Do you know,' he continued, 'how I wonder that men can consent to swelter and fret their lives away amid those hot bricks and pestilent vapors, when the woods and fields are all so near? It would kill me soon to be confined in such a prison-house; and when I am forced to make an occasional visit there, it fills me with loathing and sadness. Ah! how often when I have been abroad on the mountains has my heart risen in grateful praise to God that it was not my destiny to waste and pine among those noisome congregations of the city.'"

Another visitor to the naturalist's happy home has left the following admirable description of the sunset of Audubon's life: "In my interview with the naturalist, there were several things that stamped themselves indelibly upon my mind. The wonderful simplicity of the man was perhaps the most remarkable. His enthusiasm for facts made him unconscious of himself. To make him happy, you had only to give him a new fact in natural history, or introduce him to a rare bird. His self-forgetfulness was very impressive. I felt that I had found a man who asked homage for God and Nature, and not for himself.

"The unconscious greatness of the man seemed only equalled by his child-like tenderness. The sweet unity between his wife and himself, as they turned over the original drawings of his birds, and recalled the circumstances of the drawings, some of which had been made when she was with him; her quickness of perception, and their mutual enthusiasm regarding these works of his heart and hand, and the tenderness with which they unconsciously treated each other, all was impressed upon my memory. Ever since, I have been convinced that Audubon owed more to his wife than the world knew, or ever would know. That she was always a reliance, often a help, and ever a sympathising sister-soul to her noble husband, was fully apparent to me. I was deeply im--

pressed with the wonderful character of those original drawings.

"Their exquisite beauty and life-likeness, and the feeling of life they gave me, I have preserved in my memory; and the contrast between these impressions and those of the published works of Audubon is very marked. The great work recalls the feelings I then had, but by no means creates such emotions. The difference is as great as the difference between the living Audubon and his admirable picture by Cruikshank. I looked from him to his picture in that interview. It was the naturalist, and yet it was not. There was a venerable maturity in the original that had been gained since the features and the the spirit of the young and ardent enthusiast had been imprisoned by the artist. The picture expressed decidedly less than the living man who stood before me. It had more of youth and beauty and the prophecy of greatness, and less of the calm satisfaction of achievement; the sense of riches gained, not for himself, but for the world, and less of all that makes a man venerable.

"I could sympathize with the manhood that looked out of the picture—I could find a certain equality between myself and the man whom Cruikshank had painted. I could have followed him like his dog, and carried his gun and blanket like a younger brother; but before the man Audubon, who turned over the drawings, and related anecdotes of one and another, I could have knelt in devotion and thankfulness. He had done his work. He was a hero, created and approved by what he had accomplished, and I bowed my spirit before him and asked no endorsement of my hero-worship of Carlyle or the Catholic Church.

"When I left, I said to him, 'I have seen Audubon, and I am very thankful.'

" 'You have seen a poor old man,' said he, clasping my hand in his—and he was then only seventy years of age. He had measured life by what he had done, and he seemed to himself to be old.

" It is hard to confine one's self to dates and times when contemplating such a man as Audubon. He belongs to all time. He was born, but he can never die."

A few years before Audubon's death he exhibited in New York his wonderful collection of drawings, consisting of several thousands of animals and birds, all of which the naturalist had studied in their native homes, all drawn of the size of life by his own hand, and all represented with their natural foliage around them. A portion of this collection was exhibited in Edinburgh, and as Prof. Wilson has said of the same pictures, the spectator immediately imagined himself in the forest. The birds were all there,—" all were of the size of life, from the wren and the humming-bird to the wild turkey and the bird of Washington. But what signified the mere size? The colors were all of life too, bright as when borne in beaming beauty through the woods. There too were their attitudes and postures, infinite as they are assumed by the restless creatures, in motion or rest, in their glee and their gambols, their loves and their wars, singing, or caressing, or brooding, or preying, or tearing one another to pieces. The trees on which they sat or sported all true to nature, in bole, branch, spray, and leaf, the flowery shrubs and the ground flowers, the weeds and the very grass, all American—as were the atmosphere and the skies. It was a wild and poetical vision of the heart of the New World, inhabited as yet almost wholly by the lovely or noble creatures that " own not man's dominion." It was, indeed, a rich and magnificent sight, such as we would not for a diadem have lost."

" Surrounded " wrote Audubon in 1846, "by all the

members of my dear family, enjoying the affection of numerous friends, who have never abandoned me, and possessing a sufficient share of all that contributes to make life agreeable, I lift my grateful eyes towards the Supreme Being and feel that I am happy."

After 1848 the naturalist's mind entirely failed him; and during the last years of his life his eye lost its brightness, and he had to be led to his daily walks by the hand of a servant. This continued until the Monday before his death. In the words of William Wilson:

> "Waning life and weary,
>   Fainting heart and limb,
> Darkening road and dreary,
>   Flashing eye grown dim;
> All betokening night-fall near,
> Day is done and rest is dear."

On Monday morning he declined to eat his breakfast, and was unable to take his usual morning walk. Mrs. Audubon had him put to bed, and he lay without apparent suffering, but refusing to receive any nourishment, until five o'clock on Thursday morning, January 27th, 1851, when a deep pallor overspread his countenance. The other members of his family were immediately sent for to his bedside. Then, though he did not speak, his eyes, which had been so long nearly quenched, rekindled into their former lustre and beauty; his spirit seemed to be conscious that it was approaching the spirit-land. One of the sons said, "Minnie, father's eyes have now their natural expression;" and the departing man reached out his arms, took his wife's and children's hands between his own, and passed peacefully away.

Four days later the friends and neighbors, together with numerous men of letters and *savants* from New York, who were not deterred by the stormy day from attending Audubon's unostentatious funeral, accompanied the family from the residence to the resting place he had chosen for himself in Trinity Church cemetery, adjoining his own estate, and saw his remains laid tenderly away by those who loved him best, in the family vault, where his sons have since been placed by his side.

FINIS.